DM.

THE RETURNS

THE RETURNS

THE
RETURNS

A NOVEL

PHILIP
SALOM

transit lounge

MELBOURNE, AUSTRALIA
www.transitlounge.com.au

Copyright © 2019 Philip Salom
First published 2019
Transit Lounge Publishing

Cover design: Josh Durham/Design by Committee
Author photograph: Tanja Rankin Photography
Typeset in Adobe Caslon Pro by Cannon Typesetting

Printed in Australia by McPherson's Printing Group

A pre-publication-entry is available from the
National Library of Australia
ISBN: 978-1-925760-26-2

Part One

Part One

THE WOMAN OUTSIDE Trevor's bookshop window hesitates when she sees him approaching from across the street. Cars are driving past. There are dead flies against the glass. She seems to fade, dizzy perhaps from low salt, or blood pressure, and tilts forward with both hands against the glass. Her eyes are shut. Trevor is not a man of action, but he is deft enough to rush across the pavement and reach to stop her falling. She is conscious enough to mumble something as she tries to straighten up.

Then she looks at him. She is big-eyed and wide-cheeked, whereas he is merely big. He looks like the guy holding the ballerina: she has the intense expression and body of a ballerina. For some strange reason her hair is purple.

'Sorry,' she says, sounding clearer now, but looking away. 'Bit of a worry, that. Whatever that was.'

He sees her teeth are large and white and even. He waits, door key in his other hand.

'Yes, whatever it was,' he says. 'Are you OK?'

He realises this sounds pretty stupid. Clearly she's not.

'Come into the shop and sit down,' he adds. 'I'm sorry if I'm sounding like a daytime soapie. I can make you an invigorating herb tea, I have several varieties. In place of the traditional swig of brandy.'

'Think I'd prefer the brandy.'

'Well, I can stretch to a brandy if you'd like one.'

'No, I don't drink it.'

'Ah, right.'

'My diet ...'

'You're on a *diet*?'

Her arm had felt slim, even skinny, like one of those worrying anorexics. Trevor is not the most tolerant of people. Nor is he slim, life has come to his waistline. His obvious bulk makes her lack of it seem more extreme. *Starving and fainting, the next thing you know she'll be down under the shelf between fad diets and Dickens' waifs.*

'No, I'm not on a bloody "diet",' she says. 'I just have to be careful not to ...'

The impulse to explain her eating habits is oddly strong. But the man has helped her and shouldn't be caught in his own shop on the logic of her dietary compulsions, the food you should and the food you shouldn't. Well, she shouldn't.

Tea, then, he decides, and opens the shop. When the bell above the door tinkles he looks up and frowns.

He indicates the chair near the books on the display shelf and when he sees she can walk steadily enough and sit without leaning he moves into a back room to make the tea, leaving her to look around the shop without any necessity of speaking. A CD begins playing and she isn't sure if it's bookshop opera or her addled head.

'Cheese,' he says, 'is a pretty safe bet. In diets, I mean. Just as long as you don't drive your cholesterol up like those zealous vegetarians who eat cheese like fast food. With their hearts so pure but their arteries as full of fat-bergs as a London sewer ...'

'*Cheese?*'

'You don't approve of cheese? Ah, you're a vegan.'

Now that she is easing back into regular breathing she thinks she is inside the cliché of 'fainted away and rescued by a strange gentleman'. Very strange in this case. She is surrounded by books, shelf after shelf of words, left to right and unread, until one book is carried out in a paper bag. And a man isn't a stranger if he has a public shop, if you follow the logic. Even though he sounds clipped and as deep as a character in a Russian movie, he talks as if he knows her.

'And I am not a bloody vegan, either,' she says, looking around her. 'I'm a book person. Ah, you have a blue wall.'

'I mean it's my job,' she adds, more loudly now he's in the adjoining room. 'I'm a book editor. I sometimes inspect your window display. Interesting design.'

The thump of a fridge door covers something he is saying until he steps back into the shop.

'Yes, I know.'

'What do you mean, you know?'

'Inspected my book window,' he says. 'People forget themselves when they stare at displays, like the diamond rings and bracelets in the jewellery shop next door. I have noticed it: people are dazed by jewellery. But when they inspect books they frown, or look questioning. Though, as far as I can see, more people walk past noting their reflection-selfie than look at the books.'

'You've seen me stop here and frown?'

'Can't vouch for frowning but you came into the shop. You looked around the F's anyway ... Elena Ferrante? A lot of women are reading her. Pity she was outed, though. I enjoyed not knowing who she was. Anonymity.'

He is doing the full bass-baritone.

'In my experience,' says Elizabeth, 'readers get a significant thrill from knowing about their favourite authors.'

It is annoying – a stranger having the jump on you like this. Anyone having the jump on you like this. She hasn't forgotten that she came inside once, looked through the fiction shelves without purchasing anything, just made a mental note to return and then, as with most mental notes, didn't.

She stands and stares at him. She is quite tall. But she wavers. He wonders if he should reach out to reassure her, even hold her arm. Instead, he sees her face shut.

'Don't need the tea,' she says, pulling back. 'Really, I am feeling better. I have things to do … I'll come back this afternoon.'

She moves to the door and escapes. While the door is open he hears the accelerating sounds as cars appear over the crest and speed downhill from the lights. Then, more slowly, a tram, with several very slow faces staring out.

He is still holding the steaming mug.

She looks like the English actress Sally Hawkins, star of the Oscar-winning movie, a fable of sorts. But Trevor is no actor and the poetry of an erratic personality un-nerves him. He grew up in a family with one: his father, a man who was never one thing if he could be two. Even so, Trevor starts to anticipate her return. As they say, *eagerly*. Because he also likes difference, and he is a curious man even though his first act after she has gone is to check his public liability plan.

Her name is Elizabeth but he didn't ask and she doesn't come back.

Sometimes mornings just get worse. Most mornings Elizabeth rakes not only her front garden, she scrabbles her implement over the small verge ostensibly her own and her two neighbours'. She performs like a film extra, pointlessly, wordlessly. Speech is not required. She is scraping marginalia into the verge and she does it with concentration.

If people approach her she may stop raking and say hello. They may stop and make a comment, because she is friendly and because her dog gives them an excuse. If they are men. Women simply stop and say hello. Her medium-sized dog is a brown guardian and ruff-fluff with large eyes. Gordon. And Gordon is a setter, or mostly setter, in some degree at least kelpie, and Elizabeth would have preferred a Labrador-kelpie had she chosen the dog. Her daughter bought and pampered, then abandoned, this dog for a dog-blind boyfriend, so Elizabeth has inherited both the dog and the dog's bloody name. He's a Gordon setter, duh, golden and with a limp. Children are so embarrassing.

'Oh isn't that terrible, limping like that.'

'Oh you poor thing.'

Gordon slumps and waggles and lays it on like a hypochondriac. He is a fat dog and this is a lot of acting. But Elizabeth plays up to people just as much as her dog and she is noisier. She has noticed how genuinely touched people are by animal injuries, especially any concerning limbs. It is sad. They think of cars and broken legs and the animal's mute suffering. A dog she once had with a front leg missing. It was running around one minute then a car hit it like a pack of Staffies. People are sad when she tells them the neighbour's young cat is half blind. When it jumps it misses.

Sometimes a man stops and stares at her. She has sworn at him before. He might be unstable, or he might be sad. Gordon does a Humphrey Bogart snarl and the man walks on past, remembering the dog has a mind of its own and is not on a leash. If Gordon is older in dog years than the woman is, he is at least brushed and glossy, whereas her hair is wrenched back into tufts. Her hair is terrible.

She has been a publishing editor for years. She no longer worries if authors frown when they read in their margins her sudden notes and outlines of character shifts. Corrections, possibilities. C and P. She never let authors know how ferally invigorating she finds her job. When she thinks up phrases to embolden the anxious types who brood too little and drink too much. There are a lot of them. Whether they write too much or they write too little they agonise with a sad intensity over their words and over writers who are feted. Not her: every book she edits has its virtues.

More or less. When she worked in-house, she had worked on big books and sometimes manuscripts from the wildest, if not-quite-realised writers. Now she is working part-time she admits some manuscripts bother her. The lack of challenge. Not for her so much as in the writer's habitual conformity. Like a lover who does nothing unexpected, ever, and keeps on doing it. She aches for some radical disturbance.

There is something nervous and noticeable about the thinned areas of her scalp showing where the clips have pinched her hair too severely. Perhaps for all her precision with the text, then, she is indifferent to personal finish, to decorum; she is a dag, because she can be if she works from home, and no one 'sees' editors anyway, which suits her perfectly. Her attitude is simple: why shouldn't people be invisible?

So Elizabeth rakes and scrapes. Although this is not mind-fulness – even the term makes her groan – the air above her is clear and fresh, one of the main reasons she chose this elevated street in North Melbourne, with its crisp wind blowing off the bay and its effortless eucalypts and the sudden batik of lorikeets. Just her and all this. And, parked against the kerb, her car.

She drives a 1965 long-bonnet EH Holden, a car born in the same decade as herself. Or thereabouts. A manual, of course, in immaculate steel grey bodywork and red vinyl bench seats, a collector's piece parked on a public street. The car is more handsome in her mind than her erstwhile husband ever was. And she still has it. Most of her driving involves trips out of town to see her ageing mother in Ballarat, and the ageing EH motor roars and the differential whines as she shoves the column shift up and down through the three long gears, accelerating firmly to get the most out of the big six. She loves the sound and the strange prestige of this phrase *the big six*. She is a Holden nut.

As for driving, this woman is not subtle, but the car is less so, it needs a bit of a shove these days. The clutch is heavy, everything is manual, mechanical, a disadvantage few drivers would believe, but Elizabeth has calf muscles like a squash player's. She drives properly with both hands on the steering wheel, which has a modern steering wheel cover to make it thicker and more sensual and not as odd as holding the original rim, as skinny as a whippet. Ah, the old EH Holden is a thing of beauty: with its column gear shift and bench seats so Gordon can walk from side window to side window without stepping over anything except the driver.

To Ballarat. Until she clears the city this kind of driving is an ordeal, braking for traffic lights, sitting in neutral then pushing hard to keep the clutch in until she eases off from the lights then gunning the old thing. The car revs and hisses, and yes, it rattles from the dashboard, from the tray, from joints hidden inside the doors or the boot, and scary banging noises jolt up from the hard, inflexible world of its suspension. The car is filled with eccentric noise.

Her old mother's house faces west along the short road past the Lake Wendouree that is always Wendouree if not always a lake. She drove up a week ago, a habit of visiting. Familiarities. As she turned in at the driveway she heard that crunch of blue metal under her tyres and felt the car's warmth and smell, like a dog lying in the sun, the old vinyl of the seats and dashboard rising over her like good humour. She can always be certain of this ritual of contentment: her unusual car, arriving, the sound of blue metal. Then reaching for the key, and waiting. She always waits until she sees the curtains move.

'Now, Elizabeth,' her mother had said, 'I want you to promise me, when the time is right, to contact that good Dr Nitschke. You know the man, he's famous. And let me arrange a dignified end. Nothing, nothing could be worse than shrinking into something awful, gowned and gaga, me, after all the holy things that I have seen, to become a blob in a corridor of some shithole of a nursing home.'

Oh, and how she had seen. Gods. Elizabeth's mother has been a religious tramp all her life. From a hippie in the dope years of

Fremantle to a fully self-centred Rajneeshee in Poona. People have forgotten the Rajneeshees but they live on in Wikipedia. Her mother met God in the deep eyes of the Bhagwan (or was it Bhagwan in the deep eyes of God?). Then her mother had sought a lesser deity: she married a publican in Ballarat. Sometimes her talk is joltingly retrospective: Bhagwan, Ballarat and the front bar. Then back to the good old Roman Catholic Church of her childhood.

Now, self-extinction? Isn't that a mortal sin?

As she drove home, this particular request was difficult to un-remember. An ear-worm. Or like something sitting on the front bench seat beside her, not wearing its seatbelt. Elizabeth drove back to the city half-singing 'Exit International' as if it were *The Internationale*, like an old leftie in a beery voice. It made the old EH leap ahead, though that might just have been the downhill trip. And then she imagined the Philip Nitschke Doctor Death dance-and-chorus line, all the old folk too weak to kick up their heels but happy enough to die.

What Elizabeth began to think of were the man's scary machines, how over the years they had changed from an attaché-sized aluminium case of packs and tubes, to a computer-and-box set-up, to the gas bottle and its small red case – each looking padded and coffin-suggestive – to the recent container no larger than a toiletry bag. Cold and canned. For travelling not very far but one way only.

How bloody macabre.

She had kissed her mother and hugged her for reassurance.

In theory, if she had to, Elizabeth could live in Ballarat and look after her mother. By doing her editing work from home, as she already does, nothing much would change apart from the distance. Instead of driving up to Ballarat every week she could drive down to the city when required for meetings.

If she has looked after ailing pets, will an ageing mother be different, simply feed her by the hour to keep her weight up, pay her more attention without quite caring, watch her chewing slow down in front of you, her cat's-eye weeping and her dog-legs dragging until ...? Therefore Elizabeth knows putting the final matter off is quite possible until Death will not leave the room. Drifting, as she had, inevitably, as she grew older, back to the theatre of Rome. If not to serve, then to feel important. The wafer and wine, the Catholic communion of her youth. God drinks in mysterious ways.

But Dr Nitschke?

Sometimes, standing in the sun, Elizabeth admires the softly skeletal cirrus: even if she feels the sky high above her under the central beam of a long roof, it is not a religious feeling. If the air is blue, or at night a shot of green, this is secular. Unlike her mother, whose waves of religious craziness broke around her during childhood, she has never been formally religious or inclined to exaggerations of consciousness. It just seems there are moments akin to a special promise made to a child looking up into the face above her. *Elizabeth. ... when the time is right ...*

Verge-raking over, she walks back inside to call the local council. Elizabeth uses her cordless landline, walking around in her loose dress, trying to convince the city council to adjudicate on the matter of the broken fence behind her house. The broken fence and the broken neighbour. She stands on her verandah looking over at the evidence, broken pickets, clinging viny growth hanging from *his* side, a threatening long-handled shovel leaning across the boundary line. The council is represented by a thin voice inside a vast office somewhere in the city, like Rob Brydon's Man in a Box skit on TV, except this voice is indifferent, barely conscious, judging from the evidence of yes and no and *yairs* and sighs and moments of other conversations held concurrently with other members of the office, mobile held to some part of the chest to muffle Elizabeth's hearing.

Even as she tries to make her allegation the man walks through the gap in the fence, raises the shovel above his head and grimaces at her. He doesn't move after that, just holds this ugly pose, cursing something she cannot hear. Behind him the darkness reaches towards his boots. The front of him is dimly lit, the rest shadowed.

Becoming more normal, albeit thin and soprano, the council voice says Elizabeth is worried for no reason, it happens all the time, disputes do, and suggests she consult the council's internet material more closely. Contact them again only, and only, if the communication breakdown with her neighbour to which she refers has reached an impasse. He says *imp-arse*. A new fence is a joint agreement and cost – it will cost, won't it? – and everyone has to agree.

'The neighbour is a fuckwit,' she explains, which is not council internet or telephone terminology. The man is a bully. He is standing there now, eyeballing her from her own fence-line. What can she do if he insists on building the fence then billing her for the bigger half? ('That's an ironic joke,' she explains.) The man is scary and aggressive, and she thinks he won't fix the fence at all (his solution to the problem so far) after having pulled the bloody thing down. Then what does she do?

'Like I said,' says the voice …

Elizabeth's face is what one might call strong. The cheekbones, the full lips, the way her head is held (her mother going on about good posture, and her early gymnastics training) and the confidence this signifies. Some people prefer women who are manly rather than pretty. Even with her big glasses and vague degree of make-up she has a face that attracts attention. If she were to speak at a meeting. If she stood. If she had a Facebook page. Likes arriving every time she changed her profile picture.

Except she doesn't believe in this stuff any more than her mother's religiosity, and she knows how they are related. Privacy is her friend and it plays hard, stubbornly, as private people know. She listens to the secrets others have, the editor privy to an author's early and less disguised imaginings. Her mind, so free to relax, is also free to stew on things, yes, to *dwell* as her mother says.

The man has disappeared. If only he stayed that way.

She finishes the call and sits down to humph. This she does by staring into her bookcase for solace. The bookshelves were made by her father and have absolutely no more religious affiliation than he did. They cover an entire wall of her lounge room. Her father liked to read, though, unusually for a carpenter, and this was another bond between them. He would have sorted out the guy at the back fence.

The novel she is editing is mercifully removed from daily reality. It centres on two eccentric characters called Berra and Box. Berra and Box are voices without bodies or careers and, to be honest at this stage of her reading, page 57, no identifiable gender. Berra and Bex worry about food. They laugh about men. They cry over TV series. They are wordy voices without apparent occupation or physical representation in the world, thus the anonymous archetypal feel of Berra and Box, regardless of a vernacular that is ribald and barely middle-class. She notes in the margin: *They sound suspiciously like voices derived from Samuel Beckett.*

It has struck her before that un-gendered names and voices are suggestive of the male, not only through male as a default but also from their lack of gender-specific conversation and exchange, something more likely with women. Their conviviality, their shared emotions. Food concerns in a text are not really man talk. There is something female and enlivening and very un-literary about food talk, something like a happy neurosis which connects people.

Berra and Box are not very real, they are schemata like much else in literature and this, conceptualising it thus, satisfies her. They are embodied in words she can recognise because she recognises their characters not their faces. There is no possibility of meeting in the street or at a social event where Elizabeth will almost certainly blank out and embarrass herself and offend them. B and B, she is already convinced, are a lesbian couple with close-cut, white-bleached hair.

Alongside the food-talk para, Elizabeth writes a question in the margin regarding gender. Just in case the author is unaware. Editing like this fills her with a double version of the present tense. Sometimes she feels double as a consciousness, as if her dreams live on during the day.

Sometimes she wakes and there she is sitting, editing, at her desk. Oh, she thinks, *Here I am, the world is happening, life goes on.* Then continues reading.

For the next three hours Elizabeth stays with the manuscript. No lunch. Until B and B get onto end-of-life thoughts and Elizabeth is sent veering back to her ridiculous mother and her euthanasia talk. She can't unhear it, even though she knows her mother will forget about it within a few weeks. During her publican years her mother decided she was an astrologer. Talking Pisces and pouring pints. *How could she?* But, like the sannyasin she had been, she treated the eating body as the temple. No alcohol! Decades of vegetarianism.

Elizabeth walks into her back garden to light up an evil ciggie. Relief, the neighbour man isn't to be seen. Her backyard is brightly lit by afternoon sun whereas the neighbour's yard is as dark as a bat cave. It is always dark on his side. There is nothing colourful, nothing that looks alive, just a tree with black limbs hanging low over the space between the broken fence and the back wall of his house. Sometimes she hears children, followed by the sound of him shouting.

She is standing out there in her garden. Above her she can sense the weather changing.

One cigarette. As a uni student she supplemented her diet with cigarettes. Her diet was black coffee, fruit and vegetables. In that order. Her mother had tried years earlier to make her a vegan. Her diet was performed as a morality test. It never occurred to Elizabeth until years later when she became gluttonous then bulimic that her erratic then overly purist eating not only failed her body, it made her appallingly guilty. But she could not live out a vegan's grainy strictures, its worthy lack of pleasure. All these years later when the Paleo diet hit the TV screens and magazines she leapt into the cave mouth. Besides, she had been slicing up fresh meat for Gordon all along. Nothing like putting the blade into something.

Yes, but then it went the other way. No grains at all? No legumes and pulses? No cheese! That isn't eating, that's getting paranoid. How can she live without ever again swooning eyes shut in bliss over indulgently buttery and salty mashed potato? Why are diets so joyless? Why do diets carry such impressive black holes? Still, as a parallel black hole, she can eat all she wants and it stays down.

Still, that fainting episode, how awful. *Lizzie must be sickening for something*, her grandmother used to say. Despite positive moods – she has recently thought of taking up running – she is ending her day tired and dull before mealtimes. Instead of yet another singular activity she has thought of something more social: and decided to sign up for the local choir.

From inside the car Elizabeth hears the roar of wind approaching through the trees, the closest trees swirling with it, until sudden hail volleys over the street and is striking hundreds of rooftops in cold swathes. The hail falls like a sheet of white atoms, a street-sized window breaking over everything. It scares her by its otherness, its unstoppable fury of white and bouncing everywhere. The car roof above her is deafening and dinting, her early-model car all sheet steel without soundproofing.

Hail is bouncing on the roofs and smacking against the windows hard enough to worry the glass.

And the traffic. She is blinded and in panic. Unable to clear her windscreen with the old Holden wipers clunking across and back, and dulled by the dark light, she veers to her left until she bangs into and bounces from the kerb, stalling the car. Just hopes it hasn't blown the tyre.

The house numbers are just visible. The choirmaster's place must be nearby.

Just then her rear window smashes in.

For Christ's sake! She puts her hands over her face.

The street is speckled white and bouncing. Then she turns to see tiny cubes of glass falling onto the back seat and the clumpy hail collect among it and spread over the upholstery.

It being Melbourne, this storm of energy flails then finishes. Gone. A brief scattering of tiny hail returns for an echoing minute, a shifting afterthought as the sun cracks open the sky and the street shines in front of her car. *Utterly amazing* is all she can think, *hard to believe how beautiful it looks*.

Car roofs and bonnets will be dinted, one thing her steel panels will not be. She can see a smashed rear window like a fist-hole and feels a momentary sense of community. Not that it lasts long. There are geometrical shapes of glass crystallised on the pavement, cubist and shiny among the opaque balls of hail.

When the choirmaster opens his door she is standing there completely dry but looking drenched. The look on her face, the slump of her shoulders. Then again, Jackson the choirmaster is a nerd. He won't have noticed. Even before she enters he is telling *her* what has happened here. The sky has fallen in. He was watching it all the time from his balcony. *The Pastoral Symphony*. He is wide-eyed, still worried his windows were going to burst.

'Mine did,' she says.

They go both outside with his brush and pan and she leans into the back of her car and collects the loose glass. The pan full, she steps back out of the car and he surprises himself, actually comprehends her mute question, runs back inside then emerges with a double plastic bag. Nothing makes the job anything other than awkward, though saying *Fucking hail* seems helpful (she thinks swearing is cathartic).

The sopped-up damp is going to leave pale watermarks everywhere, depending on the salt content of the rain and the porosity of the old upholstery. Few people have ever sat in the back of her car. Gordon has vomited in it before, a suspect sausage or two sluicing out of his mouth onto the vinyl and sliding over the edge. To his great surprise. *Who did that? It wasn't him.*

1965 rear window, what's the bet it'll cost! *Is she insured by Shannon's?*

Back inside she resumes the purpose of her visit: he is Jackson, social choir- master, and she is signing up for his choir. *Can she read music?* She can. *Has she sung in a choir before?* She has. *Can she sing longer passages unaccompanied?* Only in the shower.

Will she be another guess-and-gasp style of singer always following the lead of someone who can? Each voice group needs at least two people who can actually sing, who lead in on cue, on correct pitch and who once started keep going. Elizabeth is an alto, like most women, but can also sing the tenor line so Jackson is glad she bothered to drive across town. 'Tenors are always in short supply,' he tells her, and most who claim to be tenors are mere whisperers.

Afterwards, when she fills in the form and writes down her email, she notices her handwriting is as shaky as the others on the list.

'That hail,' she says, 'I can't stop thinking about it. Absolutely frightening. Like being stuck inside a timpani tuned high. Do you, by any chance, have any aspirin?'

He does. She watches it fizz in the handsome square-based glass, its white particles and bubbles like gently reversing hail. She doesn't drink it down until it has fully dissolved. Placebo choruses start playing in her brain.

On the way home she acknowledges that this is 'Elizabeth's next dabble', the choir. That she may or may not continue. She tends to collect ventures, beginning with a rush then forgetting why she bothered. A book she had edited several months earlier made reference to *The Dice Man*, a big seller in the 1970s. US author Luke Rhinehart proposed a daring method of breaking through the repression and habits of your everyday self. Create six outrageous options every day, choose one by a throw of the dice, then do it. Elizabeth is not that stupid. She has, instead, decided to do two things. Take a lodger, again, to … help with the bills and, if she can just admit it, for some company? And join this choir. She knows Luke Rhinehart doesn't even exist, the book was written by a novelist called … George Powers Cockcroft. Who ever heard of him?

With a name like that. Enough to make your day.

She finishes her day by dragging out the wheelie bin – along the side path, past the darkened porch, its front light defunct for weeks, through the front gate and then bang, setting it down behind her car. Time to stop and not think about anybloodything.

Over towards the city the blueish shadows are even and windowed yet a full moon has stalled and is pressing down on top of several tall buildings, their stems like pale asparagus.

～

P-T-S-D were four letters he hated. Leaving his government job provided Trevor with superannuation and sanity. Peace. He has set up a bookshop like his grandparents had. It skipped a generation – God knows what his over-emphatic father would have thought. Now he is attracted to easeful commerce. He leans back in a shop where the days pass as regularly as weather and as differently as weather but where the environment stays warm and well lit. He loves books. He loves the sitting as much as the reading. Sitting is the easiest thing in the world, but sitting and continuing to grow is more difficult.

As a business, that is. Judging from Trevor's shape, he has done it literally. In the last year his waist has widened, his features become muffin-like. His face had been normal in his 20s: he had cheek-bones. He is surrounded by shelves of books selling diets, and more diets but different diets, and torturous detoxes, and liver-flushing rituals or devices, even the appalling colonic irrigation, where the suckers sit on a sucker they will never forget. Not once has he practised any of these cures.

Curing what exactly? His life had stalled and doing more of a stalled life is a very ambiguous option. Many people take that option or, rather, avoid the worrying option of change. How do you cure that? By bringing a sudden but emphatic end to the years of running workshops and role-playing and talks about cultural (multi-)practices, prejudices and, worst of all, attempting to lead front-line men and women through this devastating trauma of the workplace. His main problem now is a bell.

When the next customer opens the shop door the bell tinkles. For weeks he thought he liked the tinkling sound of customers opening the door. Then, accustomed to it, he failed to hear it. Now it is becoming annoying. He pulls back the long drawer under his counter and removes a new screwdriver.

Leaving the door wide open, a man with a very long neck has entered and is staring at the walls, at central bookshelves, at the trendily designed covers of the latest fiction and non-fiction and usual bookshop books.

'Fark me,' he says, head jerking back on its stalk. He leans on the shop step-ladder then sees Trevor behind the counter and waves his arms at him.

'Jesus Christ, what's happened to the bloody shop? Cookery books!'

The man is frowning.

'It's a bookshop,' says Trevor, walking over to him.

'Yeah, but what happened to Jonesy? What the fuck is all this stuff? It's looken like a fucken library.'

'You know, it's a funny thing: a bookshop is a shop that sells books.'

'Ha ha, yeah, nah, it sort of was before too, but different sorta …'

The man has a throat like a turkey and swivels around in alarm.

'Hey, what are ya doin' with that fucken thing!?'

Trevor lifts the screwdriver as if surprised to be holding it. The man relaxes a bit.

'Do you have any videos and DVDs? Nah, you don't, I can tell. What happened to bloody Jonesy?'

'I'm pretty sure he's ash by now. On someone's shelf.'

A few seconds before this sinks in. The man gapes.

'Jesus, you mean he died and never told anyone? Farkin' hell.'

The man turns around, bangs the door as he walks out and leans into a skinny, uphill kind of walk, even though the pavement is flat. Trevor watches him reach the lights and stop. Well, you can't keep all the customers happy. He slides the stepladder under the door and aims the screwdriver up as if to draw blood. He unscrews the offending object and lobs it into the bin. He performs a test: the door opens with a faint clicking sound and shuts firmly.

Most customers do shut the door behind them. It's a small shop and he thinks that quietens people down, library rules, especially if they walk in by themselves: in a small shop they are made self-conscious. Crowd control. Maybe book fans are better house-trained.

He has many theories now. He has the time for it in the long hours of waiting for customers, then watching customers, as they browse, as he asks them questions, noting how they ask him questions, how they talk about books, which books they want or do not want, how and when they read, and then these same customers leave without buying this, or that, or any other kind of bloody book.

There are supersellers, somewhere, who get into the minds of ordinary people and turn them into customers. Trevor is more the sort of man who puts his hands in his pockets. He is a man of location. It's all in his head: he retains the title of any book *and* its location on the shelf. He remembers what a customer looked like and where they stood and what they asked for. His memory is freakishly retentive.

'Yes, we have a copy of that,' he says, then walks straight to the book. People are impressed, and impressed people are impulsive. Showing off pushes his sales. And yet his gift is that of a savant: uncanny accuracy without attachment to the actual book. He can find any book immediately but some customers notice he doesn't follow through with details about said book. He's a bluffer. He's a fox not a hedgehog.

Otherwise, his mind sits in alert emptiness; is collective not analytical. He would be just as good in spare parts. When he was young he had worked in bookshops, so a bookshop it is. He is introverted but isn't anxious and does not talk to himself excessively. He may be wrong about this.

The shop has a small rectangular floor plan. Shelved high up on both side walls. And dividing it from the front door to his counter at the rear is a large double-sided shelving stand which obscures the counter so no one entering can see him sitting behind the counter, nor he them. Except he can, he sees all from above – in the circular mirror perched near the ceiling like a shiny eagle. He sees them from the top of their heads down. They stand for hours, sometimes he thinks they stand there for days. He looks up and sees their hairstyles, their foreheads, their vertical standing selves. Their tiny feet.

The rear wall, behind the counter, is painted a rich dark blue. This colour, this blue, he considers his magic touch. He keeps the lights on above it so the wall is beautiful and harbour-deep like John Olsen's mural of *Five Bells* around the Opera House. Trevor sits there with the light gleaming on his pate. He might almost be a Buddha figure, the effect one of warmth and welcome.

People find themselves turning towards him and approaching his Eftpos machine.

A girl of about 5 is staring at him through the shop window. She tilts her head and he tilts his. Someone grabs her hand and pulls her sideways out of view.

But the problem of establishing the shop has nothing to do with where people stand or where books are located, only which books are there at all. If Trevor is confident there are good readers, he is also confident of this: good books are always changing, and give more. A good reader, he said to his accountant, is flexible and finds more, good and bad, in every book, good and bad. Uptight readers read everything the same. The trick is to provide for both.

The accountant sucked lemony air from this. His books are binary – they are simply good *or* bad.

Customers will gather in front of self-help shelves like groupies. It does something to their breathing. Breathe, stop, sigh, breathe, pause … Trevor stocks these books not because he believes they help people change but because they have the biggest miracle you can sell – placebo effect. They become addictive. Like naughty books, except as clean books about naughty thoughts. Not for him, though. Too much reason – or unreason – disturbs him. His own tendency is to abundance and eclecticism and a kind of demented largesse – his mind is too wide, too catholic.

Trevor is a wide man.

In the narrow room behind the bookshop a kettle shrieks. It is a soprano and he is a bass. The highest he reaches is for the leaf tea on the shelf. He spoons out a generous serve, empties the rough-cut black tea into a coffee infuser and fills the glass with water, then balances the plunger in the un-plunged position. He reseals the jar of leaves and lifts it back into position on the shelf, placing it exactly where it had been. A habit. He places the spoon

22

beside the kettle as he always does. He is as orderly as a single conventional sentence.

Like anyone with minor addictions, he considers them habits. He cannot smoke inside the shop, he cannot smoke outside the shop, and he shouldn't smoke at all if his customers, when they arrive, are to be free of his smoky-stuffy clothing near them. People are so judgemental.

Yet here he is now, standing outside, drinking from his mug and having a cigarette. He is admiring his new chalkboard sign on the pavement outside the shop. It reads:

Knausgård is fascinating even when he's boring.

A woman in her early 20s, tending roundish, olive-skinned, with a dramatic face, is peering at the display of books in the front window. Eventually she looks up at him.

'Hello,' he says, and indicates the front door with his mug hand. 'Can I recommend you a book, or is there something in particular ...? Family sagas, latest fiction, Marxist theory?' (It is student territory, he sells more of those than the jeweller next door sells jewels.)

Inclining his head in a dated gentlemanly way.

Her make-up startles. Her eyes shine. But not at him.

'It's this memoir,' she says, pointing to it. 'I read it recently and I totally love it. I'm recommending it to everyone I know. It changed my life. After I'd finished crying I realised I had to make up to my family. And turn vegan.'

'The power of literature is always surprising,' he smiles, drawing on his cigarette. 'And did you?'

'Did I ...?'

'Change your life, go vegan.'

'I did, I did. It was the best thing I've ever done. Books are so totally true.'

'Well, true, um. You didn't buy it here?'

'No, no, I bought it online.'

'You should definitely see our shelf of memoirs,' he says, stubbing his ciggie and then opening the door. Thinking that *our* is a bit much, which he only said because *online* is worse.

'One shelf of books,' he adds, 'and whole new ways of life are there for the taking. I have life stories here you wouldn't believe.'

Meaning she probably would. She's one of the elect. She knows reading is a gift unlike any other, and she lives it. Other people might live in money. And regarding money a real estate man once told him bookshelves in houses lower the asking price. All that wasted space. Before Trevor could say anything the man asked, *How often have you been in someone's house and not seen a single book? (Cookbooks not included.)*

As the two of them stand outside the shop, the strongly seductive smell of roasting coffee beans drifts over from the auction rooms. Ambience. Cars, trams, pedestrians and the ever-present aroma of coffee beans.

Trevor tries imagining a world where anything that moves us changes us.

The woman moves in close behind him and he waves his hand towards the Memoir section, every bookshop's second biggest seller. Fame, celebrity, anything about celebrities. Every inspiring truth – and illusion – under the sun. For non-readers it has strangely slipped into reality TV, the reality swap that takes a healthy mind and undignifies it.

The stepladder is in her way so he places it under the section on Home Improvements. People love this section, too: they sigh and frown and think about TV shows like *The Block* and *Grand Designs* and how life will be shiny and new once they've renovated it. Then they proceed to wreck the little that worked and never finish the job.

He watches the woman turn several books to the back cover and read before replacing them and wondering which. She consults her iPhone, looking perhaps for email. Or what to do next. If she moves towards the door he will make a recommendation. It pays to realise: many people do not read their purchases to the end, and surprisingly many don't even distress the pages beyond 100.

To explain his sign, he relates the outrageous success of Karl Ove Knausgård whose novels have sold millions even though one of his books burdens the hand at 1000 pages. His epic *My Struggle* is in six volumes, nearly 4000 pages. She hasn't heard of him. Trevor says he watched the author speaking on British TV. At a bookshop. He tells her the author is a lanky and likeable self-deprecating man who exposes endless, humiliating personal details. His books are a 100 per cent energetic monologue with grabs of dialogue. He admits to being a cry-baby and a masturbator and a dud in bed. It's crazy: an author who bullies himself until readers adore him. 'I think,' says Trevor, 'his teeth are made of the same stuff as Richard Branson's.'

She is only briefly alarmed. She purchases a copy of Knausgård's *A Death in the Family*. Why not? It lies ahead for everyone. She offers her card to his cordless Eftpos machine, they exchange her receipt and a final moment of talk. He hopes she enjoys it and becomes a happy customer. She says she's sure it's true. She pulls her hair back and up and ties a band around it, says her name is Kathy. As she leaves, her smile undoes him. Sometimes the simplest of things are absolute.

Except she turns back and stands in front of him, feels as if she is expanding. She realises he is smiling at her, is waiting, so she begins.

She was older, her siblings were much younger and her father was a butcher. He worked every morning in the abattoir and spent afternoons in the shop. Her mother ran the shop, and even played the stereotype: the jovial, jokey, extroverted bloke who sells chops and sausages to the ladies. Her mother was funny, whereas her father was silent, almost passive, but he slaughtered the animals. He did all the boning work, wearing a steel-mesh glove on his left hand, and the sweaty suffocating glove made his fingers and fingernails grotesque, soft and wet. They were like toe infections. She began to find this physically repulsive. She dreamt his hand had changed into dry rot like the wood under houses. In her teens she realised she was ashamed of both parents: she had become obsessed with celebrities and glamour and the beautiful people. Except she was trapped with the weirdly back-to-front parents, the blokey mother and the half soft animal-killer father. The silent children. After some ugly arguments, her own doing, she left home. They were heartbroken. Anyway, the book, the memoir she read, was about a woman who scorned her own family and finally, after years of shame and guilt, reconciled with them. The author said she had to do one thing for the family and one thing for herself. What she did, in turn, this shining, now teary woman standing in Trevor's gaze, was apologise to her parents and her brother and sister, and never again eat meat. She accepted them and released herself from them. Properly.

Assuming she has finished, Trevor smiles.

She lifts her right hand with the book in it, looking suggestively like swearing an oath.

'A few days later,' she continues, 'my mother rang me. She said my father's hand was changing. It was healing, after all those years. Can you imagine, by the end of the week his hand was normal. Whatever he had wasn't natural, something was wrong. And now … it was cured.'

(*Well*, thinks Trevor, *that sure beats placebo.*)

'Thank you,' says the woman, 'for listening. You know everyone has a story inside them.'

'It has elements of the Brothers Grimm,' he adds.

'No, it's …' Then she smiles, shakes her head and leaves.

Bookselling day in and day out is not what he expected. It is more like dreaming of love and waking on the wrong side of the road. Then stumbling back. A bookseller is not a stranger, but a familiar. There are strange sounds. Just now he isn't sure if the shop is lit up or sinking into shadow, whether he has been elevated or embarrassed. Just briefly, he leans forwards onto the counter and holds his head in his hands.

Some shops put a cat in the front window. Maybe he should even have cats on the shelves. Everyone loves cats. Unlike dogs, who beg to go outside, cats and reading go together. Or, yes, sell bloody coffee. Gather a single-origin crowd. *Where's this book from?* The northeast coast of South America. Guyana. *Wow, it smells great.*

His accountant simply wants results. His only question to Trevor: 'Why would a public servant sitting on a firm salary (no innuendo intended) quit to … be a bookseller?' To this only question Trevor gave an only answer: 'It was change or die.' This was met with silence. The accountant is a finger tapper, unless he hears the money coming in – and then he grins. *I believe you up to a point*, his tapping says, and *absolutely*, say his grins.

Anyway, no one pays an accountant to be a wit.

Trevor told him the money could go into a shaky share portfolio, and he knows nothing about shares except how financial managers diddle their clients over them, or into a slow-running-profit-and-low-tax business like a bookshop. He will never lose the shop like a share fiasco. 2008? The shop is a good investment, meaning it costs less than expected. Then he can get on with his real passion: art. Painting. Talk of literature and painting makes no sense in the greatly indifferent land of accounting – where the only book is the one of red and black.

Painting? (This time the accountant had laughed.) 'Well, you won't need me for that. I only deal with money.'

The truth is, the money that changed Trevor's life was not his superannuation. The shop was funded from the substantial estate of his long-disappeared father. Real money in sober bonds, not capricious shares. His father, a self-regarding man who made a fuss every day of his life then was never seen again and who, after three silent decades, was finally declared dead. If he'd been famous his disappearance would have been a legend. But he wasn't. All he left was money. For Trevor, no ordinary money, but that shameful inheritance money no one refuses yet everyone is cagey about receiving.

Gifts never come clean from the gods, they have repercussions.

Trevor is watching the TV news, a large glass more than half full of shiraz in his left hand, the remote in his right, and his mind holding less than either. Diana still not home. The meal still not cooked. He is the cook.

Budget time. Wincing at their statements: conservative governments hate giving money to people who aren't doing well in life. The Treasurer's breathless logic. The people at the bottom should help the bottom line.

Something bangs outside on the street. A dog begins barking and Trevor stands up to see why. There is nothing obvious on the road or pavement nor in the buildings opposite, other than above their roofs the stupid observation wheel at Docklands is colour-lit like a kitschy glass bowl from the '60s. Its patterns change silently in sequence. A dumb chameleon.

Trevor should cook dinner. Put gentle food in the grouchy stomach. Habits must be fed. Instead he watches a story showing vaguely river-type scenes and the tiresome dialogue between the studio and the riverbank. 'What is the latest from this finding, Graham?' 'Well, Peter, the police have found a body or, more correctly, several parts of a body, assuming the parts were from the same person. The arm or leg is tattooed.'

Christ, thinks Trevor. *So much for the afterlife.*

He has no tattoos to be identified with. It isn't this that makes him stare into his red wine for a while. The things that come back on the tide. How to identify a failed marriage? It's obviously not a forensic problem identifying the difference between an arm and a leg and a battered head, just the person involved. Wounds. In the news it's whoever sat under the ink-gun. To cap if off:

'Their teeth, Graham?'

'No teeth, Peter.'

This puts him off thoughts of food. He sits on the lounge thinking of Diana and for more reasons than the dietary his empty stomach continues to be unhappy. Their marriage is over.

Eventually Diana answers her mobile.

'Where are you?' Trevor is asking, a very long way off.

'I'm at a pub having a drink with workmates.'

'Again. Why are you doing that?'

'Because that's what workmates do. You wouldn't know, sitting by yourself all day in the dark like a book. Like dust on a bookshelf!' she laughs.

'Are you trying to be poetic or is that an insult slipping out?'

'Make of it what you will,' she says, her consonants sluggish. 'Bookman. You're an antisocial, angry sort of ... boring man.'

'Well, books aren't boring, so what *or who* ... is boring me, eh?'

She hangs up. The mobile version of. ...

From the balcony Trevor can see three then four cars driving up the street. They look ominous in some ridiculous way, a cavalcade, a cortege, a gang ... as the first car jerks over the speed hump its headlights flash blueish-white. *Xenon bulbs*, he thinks. He imagines wearing a black suit, sitting alone in the back seat looking out at the houses and apartments, the day over and, later that night, something terminal yet to come. He turns to face forward. The driver is a head-and-shoulders target at the range.

A minute later the street is empty again.

Inside the spare room, fortunately large, he is working on a metre-square painting. He is gluing photo images from a magazine onto a square canvas. The left half satisfies him, not yet the right. The gouache he then paints onto them shimmers at first, the surface providing no grip. Eventually enough paint dries and thickens, and his smudging and colouring lift and subdue areas of the given images until he finds the random, then controlled meanings he wants. Highlighting, and obscuring. Noticing, and ignoring.

Like not noticing the single bed on the other side of the room. Trying, anyway.

Later still, his mobile buzzes. Diana. He volunteers to pick her up from the city (insists, more like) after she has missed the last tram and would otherwise rely on a cab, expensively, or a male friend from the group she had been with. So he pockets his keys and leaves.

Given the hour is late, and the streets are darker than usual from the last hour's heavy rain, it might seem normal there is no conversation between them in the car. Just two people driving home after her night out. The air is winey but without poetry.

So when something flashing from the left side of the street hits them with a dull bang the two of them are alarmed. A howl is it, or a shriek? It could be a child, a drunk (*Jesus, how much has he drunk?*), it could be … he has struck and probably injured someone. Trevor pulls over to the kerb, then runs back to where it might be. Rain falls over his face and he keeps wiping it clear of his eyes to see better. Nothing.

Behind him he hears the car door thump shut. He walks across to the vehicles parked on the other side of the road in case the impact has … Heart slowing, his clothes rapidly becoming sodden, and half blinded by the constant rain on his face, he hears a whimper. *Jesus, it's a dog, he has hit a dog.* A light tan golden retriever or some such breed, the kind one associates with the open fire and the kids, the carpet glowing, happiness all round, not soaked and bloody in a gutter running with stormwater.

The dog has a tag with his name and address: Adam, 37 Harcourt St. *This* is Harcourt St. so Trevor searches for numbers on the side he was driving. *No. 37 is where?* – he stares at a letterbox seeing even numbers – *but of course it has to be the other side of the street – panicked, the dog was running home.* Just then his mobile rings. *Who could it be at this hour?*

'Trevor, are you coming back to the car or do I drive myself home?'

He looks down at the dog, its eyes are open, it is breathing, he looks down at his shirtfront dark with water still dripping from his pate and his forehead onto the dog's coat, the street surface bubbling with rainwater and wet leaves. It cannot stand. A feeling of hopelessness comes over him.

Should he pick up the dog? Or knock on their door first? What if the dog, if Adam the dog, tries to get up and escape from him? What should he do? In what order? Still undecided until he realises No. 35 is visible from the streetlight so he picks up the dog, carefully, holds it with its spine as straight as possible and carries it across to the house and knocks on the door of 37 with his foot. Then again, for longer, kicking the door, the poor animal in his arms. A man comes to the door looking obviously wary. Trevor explains as quickly as possible and the man, frowning and angry, stares down at the dog.

'It's my daughter's dog,' he says. 'She isn't here.'

They see a car in the street U-turn and approach then stop beside them. It is Diana. Tooting him. But they ignore her even as she is watching them and shouting out that if he doesn't fucking well hurry up, pissed or not pissed, she will drive home.

'Christ, is that ya missus?' says the man. 'She's gotta lotta heart.'

She has her reasons, says Trevor. Then realises he hasn't said anything at all.

She won't drive off, though, he knows that. Nothing to do with being half pissed. She hates driving. He knows why she will stay in the car. She imagines the animal is dead. He passes the animal across to the man. It is alive. The man shuts the door.

The car's engine still running.

The night, streetlight, rain.

The silent drive home. That in his thoughts he must face leaving and not avoid it through anguish and utter difficulty. He doesn't even know *how* to leave.

Some people have firewalls in their minds which silence the drama, some dream stories anyone could interpret, and others wake to jagged imagery which taunts like an ugly schoolteacher. Trevor dreams of a dark room where several animals are calling out, some of them bleeding, some wet from no obvious injury, others hiding and whining, all of them distressed. It wakes him shaking and he cannot return to sleep. It isn't a nightmare, he isn't scared or disordered, what beats through like bad adrenaline is a kind of self-loathing. Anguish born of desertion. And the end of summer.

The following morning, he pauses under the awning as he opens the shop. The fainting woman's handprints are still visible on the front window. The woman who never came back. He returns with a dampened tea towel and wipes at the prints. They resist. He wipes again. The prints are still there. He stares at them then goes back inside and ignores everything he possibly can.

From outside comes a terrible thump, another thump, glass falling onto the bitumen. Two cars crash without screeching tyres, without people screaming, into a parked car. If the car behind didn't brake, it didn't see the car in front. It can now. The car in front sees the parked car all too well.

Jesus, Trevor thinks, *not again.*

A radiator sighs. Water pools beneath the car and a rivulet heads off towards the gutter. This water is what bad luck looks like. Also what mobile-phone driving looks like. Until a few people gather there is stasis in the cars. Eventually one of the drivers shoves open his door. A black BMW. The prestige of the car and, by association, its owner is completely reduced by the absurd white airbag pressed against his face, and then pushed aside as he crouches and edges out. Other drivers are slowing to rubberneck speed. A few on mobiles go right past without noticing.

Two women, perhaps a mother and daughter, remain in their small white car, the older woman crying and the younger one shaking her head as if disentangling cobwebs. Her eyes, when she turns to stare at the onlookers, are huge. The BMW has tail-ended them.

A man all but canters into the bookshop and breathes out audibly. It makes Trevor think of stables. The man says there's a bloody crash out there. Trevor nods and continues checking through his online lists. Crashes un-nerve him.

'I mean that's three cars in a row,' the man insists, staring through the window.

'The Beamer driver,' he says, 'looks like that shifty deputy-mayor bloke in Sydney. Auburn. Ex-, that is. You know, the Narcissistic idiot who stopped the traffic to hold his wedding.'

'Well, this guy certainly stopped the traffic,' says Trevor. 'It's a stupid intersection, it tricks drivers all the time. The number of minor prangs I've heard out there ... and near misses when I'm crossing the street.'

'But what about the lights?'

'Drivers go straight through them. And I don't use them. I have a jaywalking gene in me. Luckily there is some other kind of gene that allows drivers to miss me.'

Selling rule No. 1: don't scare the customers. So Trevor asks the man what he is actually looking for. In the way of a book, that is. Or books.

The man wants to browse. Or recover.

Settling down into browsing does calm a person. Eventually, the man asks for *The Hypochondriacs*.

'Ah,' says Trevor, 'great choice.' The book is faintly medical or psychological but it's also *Schadenfreude*, the famous are brought down to be laughed at. Still, who wants to read of ordinary old next-door neighbours turning their underwear inside out to protect against *divils*?

'It's not in stock,' he adds. 'But I can have it here in a week or so.'

'I was worried it would be months.'

'Ah, you see, you're feeling better already. Placebo effect.'

It is possible the customer thinks the bookseller is strange.

Trevor steps outside to watch the aftermath of the accident. Drivers and cars, at least, are cause and effect. How sad and old the left-over debris seems, pieces of glass from high-tech halogen and xenon lights, bits of plastic bumper and other fragments scattered on the bitumen. They have no identity.

The police are taking statements: from the driver of the black BMW SUV, a man who for the sake of impressing them has pushed aside the airbag to retrieve and then wear his suit coat; and from the rather shattered women in the little white car which is seemingly without its boot, and looking more like a football, deflated. Crumple-zones may save lives, but they sure make a joke of a small car.

It's true the driver looks like the crooked ex-deputy mayor of Auburn, Salim Mehajer. He is raising his voice, trying to be important. He is not behaving like the driver at fault, which in the case of one car driving up the back of another he surely is. From a distance it appears his expensive car and suit are making a claim – on that basis – to higher status and lesser culpability. He is complaining about his neck. He is over-groomed, with gelled black hair and shapely stubble, a young man whose trousers are too tight over his thighs and crotch and who wants everybody to see how unimpressed he is.

The parked car, a poor third, is deeply concave on its street side. It hadn't been five minutes earlier. No one is shouting and swearing over this damage yet. They will be inside a shop, or posting a parcel, unaware.

There is a faint smell of petrol.

The policewoman makes soothing talk to the two women and they are relaxing somewhat, tears finished for the time being. A tow truck appears for their car. The big BMW is barely scratched but enough to infuriate the young man. It is the women who will check for possible whiplash, whose car needs repairing, leaving them car-less for a week or more, whose vehicle will bear the signs of crash repair for those who know how to look. They will have to fight for insurance cover from the obnoxious other.

Not for the first time Trevor shudders over such damage. The idiots who cannot drive but can crash. *Is it likely a car could career under the awning and into his front window?* A car wedged halfway through the front wall, its bonnet covered with books, and the floor with glass all the way up to the counter.

One of the cops, the older bloke, closes his notebook and walks over to him.

'Hey, don't I know you?'

The past, in a police uniform. It feels as if someone has walked across a time zone. It makes Trevor feel freaky and sci-fi.

'Yeah, I remember,' says the cop. 'Those groups you ran about the African kids and our not so bloody useful prejudices. Can't say I've improved much, and it's not from trying. It's bloody difficult changing. As a cop you have to trust your instinct, and if someone tells you that instinct is wrong, I mean, whatdoya do?'

Trevor used to tell cops how prejudice masquerades as instinct. The cop hasn't forgotten. He looks at the shop again. *A bloody bookshop?* It seems Trevor is one of the few who have changed: then again, he was never one of *them*. The cop gives him a thumbs up and turns away, before turning back.

'Once it was idiot fucking drivers, and now it's fucking idiots on their mobiles. Did you see it happen?'

Trevor says he heard it from inside. He had a customer, so he only came out a minute or two ago. The cop looks at the bookshop again and raises his eyebrows without comment.

Because Diana is a designer and works long hours he usually makes the evening meal. A simple standing pleasure after a day of sitting surrounded by ideas. Cooking became his hobby without him quite noticing. Which means he enjoys cooking the meals that in many houses are made grudgingly. Tonight he is three glasses into a bottle of shiraz. He keeps remembering the poor old dog, and the car smash outside the shop.

'Hello honey,' she calls, arriving home close to 9 pm, and then:

'Trevor, open the windows, you're stinking the place out.'

The house is filling with oven fumes from the square of pork belly he is trying to crisp up. More to blame than his special spice rub is the smell of crackling and fat simmering into smoke on the tray under the meat. The end result will be excellent, he knows, the fatty meat and crunchy skin tasting of salt and Sichuan pepper. *Ah, to have a house with a separate kitchen.*

'Jesus,' she adds, winding open the windows near the table, 'I should have come home much earlier or much later.'

'Thank you for cooking dinner, darling,' he says.

Diana is a medium-height woman with dark hair and brown eyes. Almost his favourite colour scheme in a woman. Right now she is scowling.

'I had a shit of a day. Shit and more shit, bullies and idiots.'

She slumps into the lounge and looks as if she's there for the rest of the week, then she stands and walks to the fridge and pulls out the bottle of wine left from two nights earlier, unplugs its vacuum seal and pours herself a large glass. Hers, not his, a pinot gris. She and he are similar and different: his wine red, her wine white; her figure roundish and his figure dumpy; her satellite of discontent, his centre of gravity.

Back on the lounge she says her boss has begun acting out the blame game, giving everybody reason to feel challenged, humiliated and even exposed, accusations made in front of other staff. The power of under-estimation. She is waiting for this pattern to spread far enough for the CEO to sack the man. But CEOs are too used to letting shit behaviour prosper until they get what *they* want. *And who knows what they want?*

That said, she stands, loosens her blouse and then reaches inside to undo her bra and slip it off her left shoulder, stretch it down her arm and then off, repeating this on her right side until she pulls the limp thing out and drops it onto the lounge. Her prominent breasts sag into comfort. She looks over at him.

'Oh Trevor, it really does stink.'

'So you said. Perhaps the word "stink" is …?'

'No,' she laughs. ' "Stink" is the right word.' And she gulps the rest of her wine.

'What is it you're cooking? Oh, let me guess, something completely unhealthy – crispy pork belly?'

'Pork belly it is. The problem is the oven.'

'It's the oven's fault?'

'We need to think about getting an oven seal. In which case, I could be cooking seal belly. They're equally fatty.'

Despite herself she laughs.

'Like the Inuit?' he adds. 'Can you imagine the stink inside igloos?'

In discussions of this sort cholesterol and longevity are as mysterious a couple as the couple having the discussion. At least Trevor's culinary smoke is successful. It has taken her mind off the bastards at work. (He knows she loves her work, and her bastards.)

There he is, scooping out the cooked rice and thinking of his and her likes and dislikes. And how angry he sometimes gets just thinking. The two clenched fists of his brain.

After dinner she comes back into the lounge room. She watches him rise from his kneeling position on the floor where he has been sifting through newspaper images, which he has been cutting out very carefully with a large pair of scissors. He makes getting up look awkward.

'They can gauge a person's fitness,' she announces, 'by the number of times or points they lean on or push on to get themselves up. You have just used both hands on three points of contact.'

'Jesus, Diana, are you serious?'

'You should only use one hand at most.'

'But who does?'

'Huh.'

'And how do you allow for a person with a leg injury?'

This makes him sound more personal than ergonomic. He is. Her not answering doesn't help.

She reminds him he has mentioned renting closer to the bookshop, that he has done a reconnaissance of the area in his lunchtimes while trying not to smoke. Has he found anything yet? she asks. First good opportunity, he tells her, and he'll be off.

She smiles, as they say, she thinks, winningly. And strokes his forearm.

'Do it. Last time you said it you didn't.'

'Um …?' Meaning he doesn't know what this means other than *Move Out Now*.

'Oh. You're hesitating over the answer.'

'No, I'm hesitating over the question.'

'My God, you sound like a philosopher.'

But he is serious.

'You want me to do it … now?'

She is aware of how withdrawn she has been, so this flush of connection, more, actually *stroking* him, is worrying. She has decided to cut him off, yes, overboard and adrift. For him, her acting by design is the old joke at her expense, or her occupation, long past any use-by date. It has been too loaded with irony: Trevor very past present and Diana frustrated by future absent. Infuriating to be in the middle. Unable to respond to either.

So, with that decided, small intimacies have resumed.

'Go on,' she says. 'Go and find a girl.'

'I'll find a girl like you, except younger, and prettier, and with poor eyesight … That what guys do.'

She laughs, moves in for a kiss, at the last moment offering an averted cheek. Stupid habit, and/or vestigial feelings. *Pathetic really. She shouldn't.* But they are both like this – they keep forgetting they aren't together.

He holds her around the waist – she will one day be more than plump but now she still has a waist – and he says he might, why not? Inevitably, her remark about his physical awkwardness has stung him. Especially given her own fitness is roundish.

Diana is right about his recurrent glooms. It makes him a mordant humorist and she likes that in him. That essentially is his full case. Full, which means it furthers nothing. They are in the friendly, dead place where nothing matters. Until something hurts.

~

On Elizabeth's next trip to Ballarat there is something different to talk about. To help her practice for the choir Elizabeth will take back her electric keyboard, the Casio. Her mother, old Mrs Sermon, had loved singing when she was young. She found the only regular place for singing she liked was in the church, where mid-voice tones and easy tunes were carried by eager faces. She was reassured by Christian emotions – nothing too worldly and nothing too Godly. But she lost her love for God, until she met Him again, years later, as a bearded, brown Hindu among the Orange People and His holy exercise of free love. That sort of singing. Now her voice is old – no breath control, an irritable cough. So she cannot sing but, God, can she talk.

The problem will be finding the Casio. Mrs Sermon is a hoarder. Nothing that enters her house ever leaves it, whether once important or hardly noticed, however briefly or superficially, nothing is allowed to leave. The two of them always sit surrounded by newspapers in unsteady stacks two metres high. All that keeps them vertical is their leaning on the stacks alongside, like trees in a densely vertical forest.

The only thing Mrs Sermon doesn't keep is silence. Between the stacks of hoarding and the constant talking there is no room in the airspace for anything else.

Every time Elizabeth visits her mother's home the floor space is noticeably less. Logically, a time will come when she rings the doorbell and will not be able to open the door. Or must squeeze in sideways like a cartoon character flattened by a roller. Those architectural drawings of floor plans with a semi-circle to indicate a door and its sweep are already incorrect, the truth more a thin slice of the pie chart. If front and back doors end this way, even her mother's kitchen mess will be trapped inside and left to rot, which is not hoarding, or retaining, or keeping, but colonising because bacterial creep will be catastrophic and take over completely. The world of invisible bugs will grow all over her home.

As if the clutter is somehow disconnected from her, her wayward mother shrugs and dissembles, the hoarding seems to have occurred all by itself, the result of some obscure law in the soul of an ageing person.

'Now listen, Mum,' says Elizabeth, 'it was bad enough when you began, and that was years ago. You at least used to do it neatly. Now the place looks more like a paddock after a tornado has dropped its load … All you need is mud, and a few branches, and a current-affairs film crew …'

'I am always neat, you can fit more in if you fold. You just have to be careful.'

'… and broken fences and a few hundred sheep. Then an entire supermarket is emptied in here. And then everything is compacted by bulldozers. Where does all this crap come from?'

Her mother is not listening. Listening is not one of her qualities. Why bother, when talking about her past is so dramatic, so full of names, and herself, of course, so revealing of her charismatic self, through all those well-lit years of mysticism and undressed days … of Kundalini rising? She hoards objects like she once hoarded gurus. 'Mum,' but she has to laugh, 'you're chucking it into rooms like a madwoman. There's no room for anything else. It's beginning to stink, Mum. The only thing stopping you being worse is you have a girly throwing action. God, what the place would look like if you were built like Dani Samuels!'

'Like who?'

'She's a shot-put champion. And discus. You could hurl bags of junk into every high corner, you could aim rubbish into that gap under the ceiling and beside the shelves and wedge in it there like a slagball.'

'A what? Why do you insist on talking in that funny way?'

'A spitball, you know, like kids chew paper into a wet blob then splat it onto a wall or the ceiling. Just as well you can't do that – or you would do it. Everyone would think you lived in a cave with a colony of bats.'

Batwoman, she thinks. She wonders if since her last visit her mother has forgotten all about dying and the nice Dr Nitschke.

'Why is your hair that awful lolly colour?' asks her mother. 'You were never a pretty girl, Elizabeth, but then again …'

'Thanks, Mum. Then again what?'

'Oh, I don't know. That purple hair colouring and how bloody awful. Even at my age those batty old ladies with thin, pink and blue hair, the fairy-floss brigade I call them, you'd think they and you …'

She directs a long, mad stare at Elizabeth.

'Look at you. Time you learnt to eat properly, too. I can't work you out. You're starving! Don't they make you eat at work? You have a lunchtime, don't you? Don't you go out and eat like everyone else?'

'Mum, how many times do I have to say it? I work from home.'

'Were you sacked?' Mrs Sermon leans forward in her chair. 'Was it because of the way you looked? Or your strange ways with men?'

'Jesus, Mum. You of all people.'

'What's that supposed to mean?'

'For fuck's sake, Mum!' (Her mother is used to this by now. The Bhagwan approved of swearing.) 'You gushed over any half-good-looking guru who came along. Every one of them the only true guru, of course. At the time. Gurus are always a bloody *man*, too, with your hardly-there cheesecloth with your tits hanging out for them to snicker over. You were fortysomething *girls* and you threw yourselves under him! Professional women. Well, the others were.'

Mrs Sermon is good at ignoring people.

'Mum, I gave up full-time *professional* work because of low-level bullying, not my looks, nor for being a weirdo, thank you very much. I work at least three or four days a week, in the same job, and at a high level, but from *home*. I resigned from full-time. It almost rhymes with … Alzheim.'

Her mother winces.

Elizabeth gets up and squeezes past the unwieldy paper stacks and the almost religious mess, slightly fearful of spiders legging it around the corners, or leaping onto her from above, until she manages to enter the kitchen. She pushes aside coloured bags of plastic containers which make the plinky clatter of Tupperware. *So useful these, so handy, one always needs containers, you never know when you might need them*, the mantra of hoarders, and they are never once removed from their bags. They are the lightest items of hoarding but most awkward and most empty, just taking up space. Like her mother's incessant talking.

The kitchen counter and stovetop, the sink. A rare space of sanity. Clear, or near enough. Books to the sides, everywhere, and clips of recipes cut from magazines. But the bloody magazines still on the table.

She fills the kettle. Before she can return the jug to the base there's a slew of recipe books covering it. She pushes them aside and switches it on. There are several cups out but she washes them anyway, to make sure the old eyes haven't missed soup gobs or porridge over the last weeks. You can't see bacteria but they fill up a house. Any house.

Once, years ago and before hoarding became a public TV event, she met a man who had collected so many comics and journals in his rooms and corridors his old weatherboard house collapsed on its stumps.

'Mum,' she calls from the kitchen. 'It's hard to think you were once so anti-Establishment. All this,' she sweeps her arms out in melodramatic arcs, 'is a great big diary of ... capitalist consumption.'

When she comes back out again she says:

'Did you know hoarding is now considered a mental disorder?'

'Don't talk such nonsense. I just keep a few things I maybe shouldn't.'

'A few things! You're a hoarder. It's in the *DSM*. And anyone entering your house must be petrified. If your stacks don't crush them the air will infect them.'

The keyboard.

Elizabeth sighs, it was half the reason she came and she has nearly forgotten it: time to get polite again. Her return trip will yield not her mother's forgotten dreams of Dr Nitschke but the keyboard. Her mother will understand her needing it for the choir, surely. Such a diligent thing to do, getting a few steps ahead of the required rehearsals, offering her lead to the choristers who need it.

'What,' asks her mother, 'is the *DSM*?'

'*The Diagnostic and Statistical Manual* ... for, um, mental disorders.'

'Elizabeth! I really wonder about you. You're saying I'm mental?'

'It's in there, Mum. Hoarding is now officially considered a disorder. And it's not of the body, is it?'

'Huh.'

It draws Elizabeth across to stand beside her, one hand on her shoulder.

Because there is one eccentricity or impure clause in her mother's hoarding: while Mrs Sermon never throws anything out, she will sometimes try to give things away. As if the item remains, by proxy, in the extended family. Not lost, not abandoned, and albeit immediately forgotten … until she needs it, which of course she never does. So over their cups of tea Elizabeth convinces her mother the keyboard has a home to be out-hoarded in.

Strangely enough they cannot find the box the keyboard came in. This is a paradox because it must be in the house. At least they have found the adaptor, the block-heavy item that *is* more often lost, even in carefully contained households. The box dilemma takes her mum up a level of oddity and takes Elizabeth another hour to resolve downwards. Up against the laundry ceiling on a box full of tinned soup she finds two rolls of bubble wrap. Thus the Casio returns to the world in five layers of green bubble wrap and looking like a 3-D bubble bath.

Or a coffin.

Elizabeth is wistful about her health. She knows it, she is as strict about her diet as a girl of 19 might be, and at times just as careless. Whereas she has by now staggered across 40 worry-years, is within sight of the scary 50 and doesn't like the sound of that. The sound of age is terrible. Luckily, she looks younger. Eat well and you'll age well, meaning slowly.

She is standing in her garden. Beside her is the abandoned bed where she grew vegetables. Ate them and left them.

None of this health-think stops her having a guilty ciggie. High up in the night-blue darkness of the sky she sees white summer clouds gathering like a model's bony chest and ribs, even sees collarbones and a single trailing arm, briefly, until the slow upper winds drag all shape apart.

Despite her mother's comment, her pelvic bones, her hips, no longer show and a small pinch of flesh has developed on her belly, the kind an Egyptian lady would be proud of. At other times, she is surely lighter. Thinking of, and then deciding against, making a doctor's visit. Then, prompted afresh by her fainting moment, her embarrassing window-pressing experience at the bookshop.

Back inside she fossicks through her boxes of has-beens. Years ago, her ex had left behind a blood pressure monitor, which is a fact though not sufficient to explain why it's still here. She pulls it out from the bottom shelf of her shoe cupboard, and then stands. *Is she swaying slightly … or is it the power lead swinging underneath the machine?* Over their final years she had watched him place his bare arm through this sleeve and pull the Velcro around to wrap and clasp, then press the button. She recalls the electric pump whining up to its pressure limit. Then begin beeping, the low hiss as it released. A healthy cardiovascular system should operate at systolic and diastolic pressures – it's written on the outside of the casing – of 120 over 80.

She sits at her dining table, pushes plates and papers up against the wall to clear some space and arranges the small machine. Irritable. *The rubber air-tube isn't perished* (she thinks, after a quick inspection). It feels oddly engaging to be attaching the sleeve, as he had done, and relaxing, briefly, before pushing the start button.

The thing hums uphill busily for several seconds then stops. She waits for it to beep and hiss. But it begins humming again and the sleeve tightens on her arm until it hurts. Then stops, then silence, then the release. That unexpected pain will have driven her blood pressure up, her few seconds of panic.

It blinks and shows 85/62. *No, it can't be, she'd be dead.*

'Fuck!'

Gordon comes waggling over.

'Fuck.'

It could almost be the dog's name for all the fuss he's making.

~

Trevor is daydreaming until level with the alleyside door of his shop, which he checks now every morning. A week or so earlier the dark green paint was gashed near the lock, exposing raw wood. Why some silly bastard would try to smash his door down he couldn't fathom. The damage looked out of date: *burglars with a hessian sack and a jemmy? They should have used a portable drill.*

Then he noticed a thick chalk line drawn on the brick wall around the doorframe. It looked like the white outline drawn on the floor after the body had been removed.

Then he couldn't get his key into the lock. It wasn't until he entered through the front door and came out the side door that he was able to insert it properly.

When he rang the police he received the laconic accent as Aussie as it was doubtful, or indifferent. Female *um* and *er* noises and possibly *mate* and *When we have time, mate.* There was a sound that he discerned as the policewoman drinking from what was no doubt a take-away coffee in a cardboard cup. He knows cops well. He could *see* her drinking it, and rolling her eyes at a fellow cop on the other side of the desk.

Today he relaxes into his leather chair, the upholstery shining like a much-held wallet. As he goes through the rest of his new orders onscreen he hears a strange bird-call, a rhythmic squawking outside the shop. He realises he has heard it before, maybe on Friday. But what sort of bird makes a sound like that, so high and regular? Perhaps it has been caught by a cat or run over like the poor dog he hit that terrible night. That poor dog, the shame of meeting the owner.

Outside on the pavement he looks both ways, then as he walks towards the sound it stops with a clunk. The bird he has been worrying about has jolted up into its fixed position for the day: it is a roller door. Pinched and tight from the cold. Unless it is oiled it will cry out every morning of autumn and winter. His mind has been tricked by a door. On his way back he walks past the shop next door to his own. The jeweller's window displays of necklaces and rings are not convincingly real to a man like himself, living in his undecorated universe.

The jeweller looks like a cassowary. His high forehead is peaked, his black hair is pitched upwards and gelled. He is tall and his black beard, shaved to pencil lines along his jaw, makes him appear vain and hard-hearted at the same time. On his ring-finger is a large diamond. (A tax deduction – advertising.)

Trevor decides to tell him about the door-gouging incident.

The man is not happy to hear this, even less so when he realises it was weeks ago.

'Well, have you had any break-ins?' Trevor asks him.

The jeweller shrugs in the manner of a *Yes, no, I'm not saying, I have a reputation to protect.* His name is Allen, he has a smile that operates his lips independently from the rest of his face. *He can sell things looking like this?*

'Every jewellery shop has attempts,' he says. 'It's a basic reality, and that's why we have sophisticated detection and alarm systems. You hardly need worry.'

Trevor looks up into the corners at ceiling level. Some small sensors with opaque faces. Plastic aliens, eyeless eyes. He supposes they are pretty good if they work. If they are connected to the system.

'I don't have anything,' he says.

The man is appalled.

Trevor says all he has is books. How that in itself usually puts people off.

The man shuffles inwardly and almost coughs as he accuses Trevor of risking the security of his jewellery shop by having none in his.

'You don't have *anything*?'

'But, Allen, I keep the lights on all night!'

They stare at each other across more than just the jeweller's over-elaborate counter and sense of taste. Against his side wall there is a kind of vault bricked into the corner and against the back wall in battleship grey a steel safe as big as a fireplace. A digital pad and a handle, and a combination lock, just like the movies.

'My jewels are high-quality,' says Allen, 'and I keep exclusive items in the safe and the vault. I'm telling you. I'm not an amateur. If you had anything of value in your shop you'd have security too.'

'Allen, you are such a charmer.'

Trevor meets all manner of philistines.

'Let me say, my shop is connected to a highly sophisticated system. And the fewer people who know the better. The best security is a set-up no one can anticipate.'

'Well, Allen, seventy years ago the local North Melbourne jeweller showed his security to some crooks – by shooting at them with a revolver. In the '30s. He fired half a dozen shots up Errol St. Blam blam. That's the way to do it.'

'He *shot* them?'

'Nah, they got away.'

'Very funny.'

'I'm sure you're very up with high tech.'

When the man smiles the jewelled ear-stud glints more than usual.

'The safe weighs two and a half tons, Trevor. It's simply not going to be carried away. Or cracked in situ. No one is capable of fiddling their way through the combinations in less than a week.'

'Then why are you so bloody worried about my security?'

Trevor leaves feeling more pissed off than before. What a pompous prat. His face like a manicure. That pencil-line beard. Narcissism and anal retention gripped so tightly they'd need an Allen key to unscrew them.

The chalk line around the door is still on his mind. The oddity remains. The cops haven't rung back to check the complaint. Then again, he knows what cops are like. Avoid trivial matters. That used to include domestic violence, unbelievably, once the lowest rung on their ladder. Even car collisions rated higher.

For the last few days he has been receiving emails from someone. He should log these. The email account name makes no sense – returntime@gmail.com – one more of the ubiquitous Gmail accounts that might be a robot, a code, a kid, a mistake, a person hiding or even a person who is simply (the apt adverb) an idiot. More likely it is someone after money, or a data scam. The messages are not revealing:

You are Trevor Novak? You were living in Upwey? This is urgent, we must talk about the money.

I see you have a shop. Books? Why are you selling books? Anyway you let me know. I will explain about the financial situation. Urgent.

Things are safer these days. Not so many crooks out there. They're all in the city! They used to be … Contact me now.

If the sender is sentient, probably Russian – they sound Russian – they must know a sane person will not answer these cryptic approaches. Not even any sexy pics. Money. The suffix on the account is generic. Though why Upwey? An old schoolfriend?

As he dims the night-lights and locks the shop it comes back to him that the woman's handprints are still on the window. He decides to leave them. *What was that all about? Starving, by the look of her. Diet, she'd said, or had she said it wasn't her diet? Making her hair thin out, too. Warfarin?* Or some other scary medication he can only guess at. The stuff from Big Pharma.

After he has deposited the daily cash in the bank deposit box he walks to the pub for a quick pint. Another of his habits.

A friend once said Trevor walked with an invisible limp. It annoyed Trevor, who isn't romantic, or poetic, like a damaged type for films and novels, well, as long as they are upper-class. As long as they don't dribble. His is a genuine limp, though, because sometimes it gets much worse, visible like a hop, as Diana likes to say. Gout pain hurts the foot in one big toe so the good leg makes a big stride to protect the other one, which must always be following, like the woman in a waltz. But Trevor's good leg over-compensates in its lift so the forward movement is closer to a hop. It comes and goes. As the worst ghosts do, it re-emerges. Nerve damage done long ago.

There are people with damage. Along the street a few men sit against the walls of shops and banks. They sit there for hours. When you look back they are still there. At some point they all leave, like birds from a tree at sunset. Mostly they are gaunt and down in the gums. Half of them wear drab or garish clothes that do not fit them. No hours spent in front of the mirror. If these men are walking they yell to each other across the street and carry tinnies and saunter down laneways, emerging lanky and forlorn and asking in registers of twitch and pathos: 'Could you spare some …?'

When walking in two and threes beyond the main street they talk in voices held together by the word "fuck" and without the begging tone. They sound much happier and moderately better off.

The word "fuck" might just do a lot of good in the world. And it's free.

What to make of the young woman who mumbles and stares at everyone as she sits on the pavement outside the IGA wearing shorts (denim) skimpy enough in summer to expose her shapely legs? A thin gold chain on her right ankle. Sometimes her hair hangs and she wears pink trackies, sometimes her hair is tied up and she wears a variety of clean, fitting clothes; and she swaps between smoking, drinking and mobile-phone calls and intervals of ducking into the TAB. His conscience travels around in zigzags when she is there. Never outside his shop, of course: too few people. Beg where the traffic is. Her face blotchy from exposure.

Months ago a gaunt black-eyed man with a hanging shoulder grabbed onto Trevor as he was jaywalking and grunted for money, and Trevor thought for seconds they'd both be run down. He shook the man free. Later he saw the man hold a woman against the post-office wall until she found the dollars he wanted. The man had fallen out of a Dostoevsky novel and was never seen again.

Sometimes the street stops. No one moves. Perhaps they feel the presence of others among them, or perhaps they have been given time to reconsider. Sometimes an everyday street is so everyday it feels unreal.

Never mind. What would he know? He contemplates his Guinness. This may not be what he works for but by God it helps. Drinking alone doesn't worry him. Divorce, money, aloneness, drinking. It's a sequence. When he was young he enjoyed driving too fast, hence the limp. Now he is older, his inner dialogues rush through him like cars around corners, not much control but much churning up of the dust. He hates the glib statement "If you think things are bad just look around, there is someone worse off than you." The heartlessness of it.

Today, to his right, a man sitting on a crate has been playing sets of blues harmonica without pause for fifty minutes. Old-fashioned work ethic. The man's musical endurance is helped by sleight of hand, or mouth – having no teeth he clamps on the harmonica like a wobbegong and is able to suck on the in-notes without pause. This appeals to Trevor. Once as he saw the man approaching, he simply held a $5 note out behind him. As the man passed, he saw the gesture, took the note, said 'Fanks' and went on his way.

From the kitchen he hears Diana arrive.

'Now today,' she sighs as she walks in, 'I had to discuss book covers with crazy bloody writers. God they're a pain. You'd think they would just be grateful to get into print, the otherwise luckless sods, but no, they are experts in design, every one of them. I tell you, our designs are pretty bloody cool and dramatic and eye-catching one way or the other and there are lots of ways, from tonal patterning to print and fonts, to images, and combinations more sophisticated than these know-alls know. Sometimes you meet one who does but by Christ that's a rarity.'

'On the other hand,' he says, 'some cover designers never read the books.'

'Author No. 1,' she says, 'wants his name in lettering an inch high and nothing less than his own original photography in the background. Author 2 wants a total ban on images like a bloody Muslim and insists on having ornate letters, her name, the title and a prominent blurb saying how fucking wonderful she is. Where's that bottle of wine? Is this one yours or mine? They don't like the font, they don't like the composition, don't like the *semiotics*, one said. They don't like colours and they do want red, or they don't like colours, full stop, they want white. White covers, I ask you. Jesus. You of all people know what happens to white covers. They get shop-soiled before they even get to the shop.'

She is so annoyed she leaves her bra on.

It's not anger that makes her attractive, she just is. The pang in him. The irritation. She kicks off her shoes and laughs at him standing there with his hands on his hips and grinning.

'What are you smirking about?'

She walks over and gives him a peck on the cheek. He tries to wrap his big arms around her.

Trevor has a *conspicuous* head, as Diana has termed it. Everyone notices because it is shaved, and shines, and at some moment when he is close in they realise it is … Diana once told him his big face is reassuring, full of protection, which is a strange compliment, lacking the frisson he would have preferred. At least, thank God, he is not pasty. If anything, his complexion is the kind they once referred to as olive. Nothing Mediterranean, nothing indigenous, nothing even obvious, and just a small degree sexy, so perhaps Diana was withholding something from her compliment.

Now he is hoping and knowing it's hopeless.

'A day with nothing quite as it should be,' he says into her hair.

'I don't think that tops mine,' she says, pulling away.

Since Trevor and Diana have been living in separate rooms this kind of static neutrality has been undoing them both. So the two-voice thing in his head is becoming insistent.

It's sort of comfortable. You could stay, people do.

You have to go.

Something he has known before: once the break has occurred the two beings turn their attention away from each other, not exactly *off*, though off it can seem – when they lose the suspension of disbelief over each other.

He's checked the figures: 38,000 people in Australian *do* live, estranged, under the same roof. This is cognitive dissonance in human form, one of his inner voices announces, and then it says:

You can't go on living like this.

He wonders what happened to the dog.

After several years working at design firms, Diana had never quite settled in. Too many jobs under the cynical managerial style of pitting one worker against the other. A Rupert Murdoch technique. The shark pool, they called it, used for promotion or redundancy, a blood-in-the-water metaphor for management keeping its hands clean. Survival of the most brutal.

At night Trevor amused her by acting out the bodily turmoil of her worst imaginings: her revenge soap opera and his deliberately overdone role-playing. He pulled faces and bent into silly shapes and performed melodramatic role-play of her two senior designers getting horribly pissed, then glassed inside a nightclub and losing their looks (not easy doing this, splayed fingers gripping his face) or whatever looks they once had (even harder doing a before-and-after). He invented another boss collapsing with a stroke, as she narrated – in a dirty, vengeful voice – that his face was as purple as a fat cock. Left alone now in a stroke home, unable to tie his tie. Sitting on the floor grappling with his shoes, dribbling.

Her mordant fantasies. His theatre. Back when she thought he was fun. Back when they used to fuck a lot.

She crunched the tactics and dollars and applied for new jobs. Quite soon she was re-employed. To her surprise she began to rise rapidly into a double position of hands-on design plus management of design staff. The cake and the cutlery. With no one ordering her into blank corners and her ideas increasingly hitting the brief, her corporate contracts became successful projects.

There were few women in the firm, which was a problem, perhaps, when male colleagues saw her striking qualities extending beyond the brief. They were doers too, and doing sometimes took place on in-service retreats in the hills. On full bonus pay, of course. After a few years of running her design department she discovered the level above her was in fact a boys' club and, despite its sophisticated vocabulary, its trendy design terms, its gung-ho hold-your-game concepts, the glass ceiling was just as unbreakable as anywhere else.

This was a conundrum. Form raised her and function kept her at bay.

Yet after one weekend work retreat it changed. The man was too important to ignore. He wanted her, he wanted to fuck her as much as Trevor did. He ran another design firm. Lust, so much sexier if you're getting ahead.

Back at work it was still in her, not anything fluid, a light-headedness. She was distracted enough to spend too much time and at home, Trevor noticed, emailing someone. He heard her typing, he couldn't unhear it, and she was typing to *someone*. He asked her. Did she have a lover? Or was she becoming a novelist? A new job, a new company, she told him.

She wasn't becoming a novelist.

Then came his anger phase, like dying, but a grief all the same. He was never a company, he was a bodily person. Eventually she told him she no longer loved him. When the emotions had died down, over several weeks, a dull, bloodless understanding happened between them, the body became a metaphor, exsanguinated.

Time is a trickster: being nothing, it promises everything. For Trevor and Diana it is passing between them differently. Their time lines are uneven, unaligned.

Diana recalls getting home half out of her mind with the tension of working with colleagues, when he asked her if they were, these colleagues, reacting to the fault she had described her old bosses of having – a dismissive attitude. Too bossy. But she is rightly proud of her tolerance, her willingness to lead and take the blame if her team makes mistakes. It made her furious.

'The only trouble facing you,' Trevor once said, 'is growing into the likeness of your old bosses.'

Back then it was simply a joke. But when he said it again he meant it.

'Bullshit!' she yelled at him. 'Really?' he said. Disingenuously. No, she said, he was intolerant and couldn't even wait to hear what she was saying. She screamed and he said, 'Don't go nuts at me, I was just doing what ...' She widened her eyes in aggression: 'I'm going nuts, am I?' And rushed for the door before he could answer.

She left like this so he, her once-lover and her friend, couldn't answer.

Someone must receive the daily fallout. This is a ritual relationships take on faith.

If the colleagues at work are to be lived with, the anger necessarily comes home. Or the bosses will tell an over-reacting worker she is out of control. She can't win without damage somewhere. They may be right. It doesn't mean she is wrong. What they forget in Diana's case is how conscientious a boss she really is. If she is awful she is also a saint.

But at night there is that liver-killer of the immediate glasses of white wine, escape from the hierarchy in her work mind and then, in time, it is projected onto him. She admits that.

~

When the fainting woman comes into the shop he remembers that she hadn't earlier. *What will she say this time?* She turns to her left and looks at the corner of his window display he has left for public ads. Or it might be shyness making her turn left while moving forward, like a diffident horse. He is the one with the limp.

Trevor is standing beside a man who is a big fan of Irish fiction and especially of Dermot Healy and the new star Eimear McBride. 'A man of good taste,' says Trevor. They have been discussing linguistic tangles and how and when or if they are appropriate in the novel and how this book by McBride was thrown aside by umpteen publishers, umpteen meaning for nine years, before it was finally taken, sold and immediately made her famous. A very French outcome for an Irish book.

They turn to look at her.

'Hello,' she says. 'Do you remember me?'

The fainting woman is addressing the customer.

Because no one is sitting in the armchair behind the counter, Elizabeth is forced to guess. She hadn't thought to ask his name before and, though he doesn't know this yet, she is bereft of any facial recognition. She is responding to bulk, which she remembers. And his bald head. Then she looks at the second man. They are both big. They are both bald. She recalls his voice is deep.

'Hello. Well, you look happier than last time,' Trevor says, thinking she is still a little strange. 'You recovered from whatever it was …?' He recalls her using that phrase.

'Oh hi, it's you. I was wondering if I could place an ad in your window,' she says.

Which isn't the answer he expected.

'An ad. For …?'

'And yes. I'm fine thank you. I have been feeling a bit … you know.'

Being men who are confused, they wait.

'I have a spare room I want to rent,' she says, holding up a sheet of paper with bold printing on it. 'Well, it's a basement, but I'm keener to have someone apply first rather than put them off with boring details. It's a good room, ensuite, very neat and tidy. And I won't be charging them like a landlord and I won't start bothering them like a sudden mother.'

It makes him think. *Why not? Why not, then?*

He nods (he likes the mother bit) and fetches some Blu-tack from a drawer underneath the counter. She is ash-white today and shorter than before. It suits her. Her glasses have lime-green frames, fashionable, not to his liking. As she positions the A5 page Trevor decides she had been a dancer. Who gave up dancing because of occasional but uncontrollable fainting. And getting on a bit. *How old was Margot Fonteyn when she removed the smelly pumps and told Rudi to bugger off, which in Rudi's case …?* A woman of her size living alone probably eats very little, lives on wafers and sunlight like old Saint Thérèse.

Her kitchen will be spotless.

He asks her address and she hesitates, looks down at her sheet of paper – her ad only has a mobile number, a perfectly reasonable precaution – until he suggests it may help if he can let customers with rental interests know roughly where the place is, or the street at least. Especially if it's nearby. He won't be exact.

'And if it's not?'

'I can always lie. How keen are you to rent it?'

'It's nearby.'

She tells him and he writes it down, writes her name, Elizabeth, her number, and slips the paper into the drawer.

'Done it, finally,' she laughs. Without looking at him. Pleased with herself.

'I have a shed at the back, too. Near the back door, quiet there. It's not liveable so I can't advertise it as such. But it's weatherproof.

'OK, yes,' she adds … 'and I'm sorry I nearly fainted on your doorstep. You were very chivalrous. Took me in like a knight, etc.'

She is tilting towards him as if he is one. Then she laughs, loudly.

'Glad to help,' he says. 'Good luck with the window ad, though people tend to walk past without reading them. My name's Trevor.'

'Ah, Trevor. I'm Elizabeth.'

He smiles and she turns to leave.

'Have a look at this,' he says, following her to the door.

And he shows her the two handprints on the shop window. Right next to the STOP ADANI posters.

'I have your ID,' he laughs. She looks back at him, uncertain. Then walks up to the main street.

Anyway, he thinks as he watches her, *she is too tall to have been a ballerina.*

As soon as she has left, Trevor reads her Room To Let note. Very neat, readable, bold, well-spaced printing – and the room sounds good. It mentions extras. *Now what might a person make of that? Was he being too intrusive showing her the stubborn handprints?* He goes inside and returns with a tea towel.

This time as soon as he wipes them they disappear.

The shop is doing reasonable business. Which means he has been thinking of his painting again, needing more space for that and much more space, like it or not, for himself *sans* Diana. To fetch back the wayward artist of his 20s. To fetch back the bachelor, too. Yet again he worries over the interaction between accidental and deliberate. How he had deliberated over his desire to paint, become a student and exhibit, and how, accidentally, his life changed and he stopped.

How accident and coincident also interact. Most people won't believe in coincidence but an ensuite basement and a shed are throwing waves of sunlight and shadow through his brain. It's not impossible.

A customer once asked him about Patrick White. 'The curmudgeon,' she said. She was holding a big hardback reprint of *The Eye of the Storm*. She liked Geoffrey Rush in the film of it.

'White's very mannered,' he told her, 'but poetic in a roguish way, so if you play along with his bossy narration he can be a real pleasure and a dry old comic at that.'

'You mean he's funny?'

'Yeah, very deadpan. He's an ironist.'

'So you rate him then.'

'He's a great writer, full of ironic insight. That can seem curmudgeonly, and as a person he was. What I respect most of all is, he's not just after beauty. He's old-fashioned enough to want truth. Capital T.'

She waggled her head. And stood breathing.

'I owe Patrick White,' he said. 'When I was about 20, just drifting about in the country, someone gave me *The Vivisector* to read. Because I'd begun painting, or was trying to. The novel knocked me out. Hurtle Duffield is a rough artist-loner. Old-school expressionist, Romantic at dark heart, looking for transcendence, all that … It changed my life.'

God, he thought, *I sound like that eager young woman who went vegan and whose family … the father who worked in the abattoir. Now there was an unlikely link to vivisection.*

'It convinced me to pack up drinking and dole-induced boredom and move to the city, enrol in art school. I began to think like an artist, not just a viewer.'

'You made that up,' she laughed.

'No, not at all.'

'But now you run a bookshop.'

'Yes. I …'

She was waiting. Or reading her bullshit meter. She might not buy his story, but she bought the book.

She's not wrong, of course, he might have made it up. He told a story with a romantic beginning and a humdrum end. His humdrum end, he's desperately hoping now, is only the middle.

For the next hour or so he watches the time on his laptop. If he had a wall clock his head would turn to it by habit like a schoolkid waiting for the bell. Like his old job, where the days were Public Service and always 9 to 5 – unless they were longer.

When he looks up he notices two people standing on the pavement inspecting his window display of books. The man is balding and whiskery, a big man wearing a long green dress, and his hairy wrists protrude from the sleeves of a stretched cardigan. She is slightly plump and wearing tight blue jeans and a shirt buttoned all the way to her throat. He is pointing to the books, each in turn, and talking to the small woman beside him like the clichéd man explaining "art" to his female companion in a gallery.

Except this man is clutching a shiny red handbag.

In the storey above the shop there are two rooms but no facilities for domestic camping. A man would go feral very quickly, especially through lack of hygiene. There is arguably enough available space for a camp bed of some kind among the boxes of books and the left-over shelving and the nagging corners of bits and pieces (or crap as he calls it) he hasn't binned.

People are greedy for rooms and forget space, an architect once told him. When their mansion is built, the five bedrooms are so tiny they can't open the built-in robes unless the bed is a single. To check the floor space Trevor clears the clutter back and lies down on the floor like a corpse. That chalked outline of the body in old crime movies. That chalk line around his side door.

Measure for measure, just enough. Pathetic as it feels, sleeping in his shop might be preferable to the shame of sleeping in the doghouse in your own home. Think about it. Sadder, lonelier, more despairing, check. Or this really would be taking Hurtle Duffield too far. Next, brushes, turps, tubes of indigo … shitting in the corner like a possum.

As he stands there he remembers when he left home to attend university he boarded with an older woman who struck him as having the demeanour of a model. Meaning she couldn't walk past a mirror without stopping to touch her hair and admire her face, her figure, her posture. A private smile always came to her lips. There was something approving in her expression before she moved on to do whatever it was she was doing. There was a wide mirror in her lounge room, which was form for that era, and another one in her dining room, which was not.

Silly as it seemed, he found her agreeably mysterious. She was the first person he met who was entranced, who would stand for minutes without moving.

If ever she came into his own room, after a faint, too faint, knock on his door, she would engage in conversation with him while studying herself in his full-length wardrobe mirror. This made for a strangely otherworldly kind of dialogue, her voice not merely averted but wistful, he thought, for the young woman of her past speaking from the image of her present.

Eventually he asked if she had ever married. Oh no, she said, she'd never met a man good enough. He thought she was being arch or self-deprecating (ironic?). She wasn't.

Then again, why not remain independent if you prefer it? The alternative would be intolerable, as many well know. Eventually his company was too much and even his money not enough, and she asked him to leave.

Now the thing he doesn't want to think about comes back as it must. It is himself. Not the shop, its orders and accounts, its visitors or lack of them, the break-in, if that's what it was, or his tenuous running margin, and not this strange Elizabeth with the room, not his cousin and his gripes, not even his own view of the world, his own sense of a life lived waywardly, no, none of these. Diana. Himself. That spare room in their own apartment where guests have slept and where he now sleeps.

~

Sometimes she has just woken up and is already out raking her verge. Therapeutically this morning, trying to erase the voices of the endless never-listening talk, Elizabeth's inner track runs with characters not horses. She is using her rake as a baton to the ground, she is conducting them into silence. ... Someone in the street has ordered a skip and very generously, like the local scavengers and like the old cockney song, spilt some on the step.

Pieces of plastic and ugly wooden boarding. Too lazy even to load the stuff into the steel hull and have it chug off into the Ocean of Waste Items. The whirlpool of plastic etc. Whether it's the droll blokes from the rooming house or students or hipsters or good citizens in German cars and well-appointed houses, the result is careless scatter and drift. Frayed chipboard stained from something old and damp and cut in semi-circular shapes you don't normally see, perhaps as a fitting around something flue-like or ducted, removed carelessly and just left as geometry in the sun, and of what possible use to anyone?

She realises a man is standing beside her. She just wakes. He might have been there for an hour or so.

She doesn't look up, she uses her peripheral vision. He is large and overcast and standing near her like weather.

It seems he is about to say something, and yet no words arrive as her rake hesitates then moves, under some rhythm of yes-no-yes-like accompaniment, then *who cares*, as she herself stays silent. *Is this an eccentric invitation perhaps?*

'Excuse me,' he says and now she straightens up, as if surprised.

'Ah, good,' she says. 'Do you think you could help me load this stuff into the skip? You look as if you could lift a fridge …'

Gordon waggles over from the gate towards the man. The man nods, amused, and helps her lift and drop the wood into the skip.

'Nice day,' he says, 'and for walking about with a dog.'

'Yes. Good exercise. Not that I care for goody-two-shoes health advice. I'm more of a fidget, and according to the experts that's meant to burn calories.'

'Fidgeting?'

'It works for me.'

The man laughs, looks at her, then at Gordon.

'Yes,' she says. 'Hello then.'

'I know it'll seem odd that I've come,' he says, bending to pat then push away the dog jumping around him. 'I wondered if I could see that spare room?'

'Oh good. You saw my ad in the bookshop?'

'Yes, of course …?'

'Good, you noticed it, the guy in the shop said people just walk right on past.'

'That was me,' he frowns at her. 'I told you.' (*That's twice now,* he thinks.)

'Oh. Oh, of course, your voice! I'm so sorry. What *is* your name again? How embarrassing.'

'*Trevor*. Look, I just helped you with ...?'

He points to the skip but is asking much more.

'Trevor, I'm sorry, I'm so sorry. I have this ridiculous condition that I've spent my whole life apologising for. Prosopagnosia, weird as that sounds.'

'Face-blindness ...?'

'You know it then? Yes, I'm sorry. Oh, there I go again. Most people make horrible expressions when I say it. I'm incapable of remembering and recognising people by their faces.'

'Oliver Sacks had it.'

'Oliver Sacks! *The Man Who Mistook His Wife for a Hat*. ... Really? I didn't know that. What a great big happy bear of a man he was. So sad he died.'

'Yeah. He was as odd as his patients. Which is pretty endearing. I often hear his phrase in my head: *neurological deficit*s.'

'Neurological deficits,' she smiles at him. 'One of my favourites.'

'Most people,' she adds, 'think prosopagnosia is some kind of brain rot. Or a twisted spine, like scoliosis, or worse – something to do with the uterus.'

'Did you know,' he says, 'that magpies have facial recognition? Of humans.'

She sags slightly.

'Is that meant to make me feel better?'

But then it occurs to her:

'Why do you want to see the room?'

If he suggests he can recommend the room better for having seen it he will look silly taking it himself. She might even think he's stalking her.

'I might want it. For myself, I mean. My wife and I have been living together but we're separated. If that's any way of putting it. There, I've said it, embarrassing.'

He is relieved to have said it.

Only now she realises her ad hasn't specified a preference for a woman. She had thought maybe some younger man, hardly more than a boy perhaps, might just be possible, but a woman is what she has imagined happening and, as she thinks about it again, younger. And Trevor is Paul Robesonish, only white.

'And the shed studio thing too,' he is saying, as they walk inside, 'could be very interesting. I used to paint, a long time ago, nearly twenty years or so, I was certain I'd be an artist. Then I stopped. But I've kept working at it on and off. I've decided to go crazy and push it again. I have to … give it a year or two. If it works out, well …'

'Gordon,' she calls. 'Come on!'

So the dog rushes past him as she turns back inside, hoping the man is not hitting a midlife crisis. Which he probably is. Then Gordon reappears, looking at this new man, watching with the right degree of wariness.

'I wondered why you commented on the blue wall in my shop.'

Opposite the window and behind her lounge and armchairs is a wide blue expanse, as if the sky has leant down and entered by camera obscura. *Did she comment on his wall? She can't remember.* It wasn't her best day.

The room, when he sees it, is downstairs, something he hadn't anticipated, thinking the house was instead a single storey. Still, she had admitted it was a basement. Being lower than the ground level of the street he would, in effect, lie there half buried. Many houses in the street have basements, hers the modest variety, she adds, just a room with its own bathroom and toilet. Otherwise she wouldn't be renting, on her own floor, would she, people in her personal space. Sharing her bathroom and toilet.

They look at each other in silence. It makes sense. The room is easily large enough, with robes and a desk under a double corner window onto the side lawn and fence, and a decent bed. All this takes him back. Student days. Except better. The toilet and bathroom, best of all.

He wants to see the studio.

She says it's just a shed but, yes, it could be converted into a studio.

First, there is a smaller room across the way, which they move towards, only she uses it for storage. They stand there at the doorway looking in at boxes and cobwebs for longer than necessary. He *is* big, she thinks. He occupies a doorway. *Rodin was a big man but he used hammers.*

As if attuned to her thoughts he suddenly steps away.

They walk outside, down the small lawn area to the shed, as rusty now as an old farm shack.

'What's happening to your back fence?'

They stare at the wreckage of tall pickets, the left and right sides still up, the centre gone, the wood strewn on her side of the border, the horizontal timber frame between the posts left as is.

'Arrrgggh, my neighbour's a bit of a bastard,' she says, biting on the words like a dog chewing fence pickets. 'I shouldn't call him *my* neighbour because that suggests some degree of affection ... I call him "The Creep". And he is. Apparently he has the right to insist on a new fence but he wrecked it before asking. You can see he's chucked the old wood on my side of the fence, not his own.'

'He sounds like a complete shit.'

She smiles with relief to hear it.

Inside the shed Trevor is impressed to see solid benches and a clean space lit from above by three corrugated acrylic roof panels. He checks for power points.

'Does it have power?' he asks, still looking. This place has every potential to be a studio or a workshop or just about anything – if it has power.

'Um, I don't know. I think it's still connected. I can check.'

'Well,' he says, '*I* really like the place. And your dog, was it Gordon?'

As dogs go, as dogs who live with single women, Gordon is a good canary: he knows men. And he immediately wags his way over to Trevor. No Bogart behaviour from him today.

'Yes, Gordon. He has a bit of a limp.'

'Hello, old Gordon with a limp. I feel onside with Gordon already. A car accident, I suppose.'

'He's not really that old,' she says, 'about 8, I think. Yes, it was a car. It's always a car.'

'Cars,' he says to the dog. 'A car got me, too, except I was driving it.'

Crouching down and gently stroking Gordon's head. It reminds him of the dog he ran over. Gordon immediately sits and gazes from the depths of that melancholy brown world of dogs.

She is surprised to see this man looking sad. Not being *Oh dearish* and making sorry noises like most people, but empathetic. He is a surprise.

'He wobbles,' she says, 'but I love him, wobble and all.'

He says he understands that she must love her limpy dog, maybe even more so for his vulnerability. He feels the same; and 'as everyone says, and it's true, isn't it, dogs give unconditional love?'

'Well,' standing over him, Elizabeth lifts a finger to make a point, briefly the pedant, 'yes,' she says, 'they do – more importantly, animals allow humans to give unconditional love *back*. No neuroses or anxieties to get in the way. No human obligations. If you are even halfway selfless you can love a dog ... absolutely. Or a cat, any animal.'

She knows without animal love a person might not have love at all. It's the selfless bit that matters. The worrying thing is that people let you down. They have failings, plural. A dog might only have one, like eating the hose.

So they both look at Gordon and Gordon feels twice the love.

Trevor is also feeling estranged. Continues patting a dog in a backyard of rusty roofing and busted pickets, staring into the empty shed and hearing his own voice asking about the power. It is a complicated pain. This place feels right, even if he cannot for the life of him work out why it should.

Serendipity. He needs it, it is here. He'd be a fool not to.

Even if Elizabeth cannot recognise this man's face as the face-of-Trevor she can recognise shifts of feeling on his face. Any face. Recognition is not allowed her but empathy is. Time is moving slowly. There are some big feelings going on within him: they are imbedded in his surface.

Back inside, he inspects her kitchen and the newish appliances, the clean uncluttered surfaces. (Elizabeth is never her mother.) *So he was right about her kitchen being spotless.*

'Ah, what a great kitchen. No,' he says, 'I'm not recommending your place to anyone.'

She is startled.

'No,' he adds, 'I want it for myself. I would like to move in, if you're happy with the idea. I have money and I'm self-sufficient and my wife is encouraging me to move. Yes, and that studio … it's ideal. Just what I want. What do you think?'

Her shock rises. And so she suggests some time to think it over, for both of them that is, a day or two, and to be fair if anyone else comes around and wants the room … he asks her – he tells her in fact – to ring him. Please let him have first option. If they want to offer more (they have wealthy parents …) he will counter their offer. As long as she is happy with him.

From within his thin wallet Trevor plucks a business card and hands it to her. Business cards have always appealed to him, and now he has one. A minor vanity. Respectability.

'You said you were a book editor,' he says. 'Do you work into the city?'

'Freelance,' she explains, 'so work comes directly to me, *sans* office and tea lady. I am text-bound not desk-bound. I am my own boss and timekeeper.'

'Good for you,' he says.

Then she relaxes and says she has her eye on a new manuscript which she has just heard about. Martina, an editor friend of hers, has broken house rules and texted her the details of what could eventually be a very interesting book. A young new novelist. Something about sects – and Elizabeth had been brought up in a sect.

Trevor is impressed. 'A sect?'

'The Rajneeshees.'

'Ah yes. Haven't heard anything of them lately. Well, you'll have to move fast, then,' he says, 'invent something, anything. Don't let anyone else get it.'

When a stranger moves so quickly to your defence he is either genuine or astutely insincere. His voice, Elizabeth's main register for discernment, sounds genuine. Not breathy, not the lower-case tones of a liar.

'Yes, you're right.'

'Good, then.'

He is leaning on the counter as if it were his kitchen. Then she simply stops talking. He straightens up.

'I like to cook,' he says. 'If you don't object. I could cook for both of us sometimes. Asian, European. A bit of everything. What do you eat?'

What to say? With her strange habits? She is still thinking about the manuscript. Her mother. The Bhagwan Shree Rajneesh. Nothing comes to her. It has only been half an hour since she opened her front door and let this man in – he's befriending her dog, giving her professional advice and already seeing casseroles on the table and a bottle of wine.

'Er … can you do Japanese?'

'At a pinch. Yes. Crispy tempura batter. Soya and sugar. Salty raw flesh, or black sauce and white flesh.'

'Put like that, Japanese cooking sounds a bit kinky. Like geisha make-up.'

In the Realm of the Senses. And think of the writers. Mishima in a white nappy committing hara-kiri. Or seppuku. Kawabata writing about old men very like old Kawabata, staying awake alongside the geishas who were drugged to sleep by the mistress, and how the old men can do anything, anything, except put their fingers in a girl's mouth. Moths bunting against the lampshade.'

My God, she thinks. They are both silent, the moment to leave.

When Trevor has gone she sits in the lounge and watches the very normal, very unsurprising light fade across the blue wall they now have in common.

Her last lodger was a Chinese accounting student who made endless cups of tea, smiled desperately when asked anything and only ate take-away pizzas. While making no demands of Elizabeth, she seemed to consider the house her own. The pizza boxes she stacked in the kitchen. Never in the wheelie bin. The girl had to be told.

It is her home, after all. Sometimes she wonders who lived in it all the years before. She wonders what they looked like, and how they used the rooms, whether there had been children running around and shouting or being surly and untrustworthy and hating their parents. It is so quiet with just her and Gordon and if there is one stranger living with them, one lodger, that hardly makes a family and most houses are made homes by family, however noisy or fractious or goody-two-shoes they might have been.

After waiting several days for Elizabeth to ring him, and with rain appearing on the horizon if not yet in the street, he is climatically worried. Maybe it was stupid to delay after immediate liking her, and the room, and especially the vacant shed he has ever since been imagining as his studio. Stupid of him to have talked too much. So he is ringing her from the shop.

A pause. It could be a telemarketing company pause, no reason except the delay of connection when they ring over the internet, except this isn't the internet.

Then her voice. He asks straight off, and adds:

'It's ideal and it's so close to my shop. I hope you haven't seen many other applicants yet.'

'*Any* others.'

'What? Oh good. I really want the room.'

He can hear lorikeets chiacking in the background at Elizabeth's place. She must be outside as the birds wind up the volume in the late afternoon. Another plus for the place, the birds. They screech and whistle at multiple intensities, they sound like their colours. Some trees are already looking bare, so the birds are brilliant.

'I suppose so,' she says. She can see rain is about to fall in the street: the trees' sudden wavering, the screeching unstoppable. She is standing by the partially dismantled fence. She nods, wasted on the mobile. And makes a noise in her throat.

'Is that a yes? Elizabeth?'

'Yes. A few months, let's see how it works out. Then more, if …'

'Good! All right, yes, but it has to be long enough for me to bother moving out of my place and into yours. Six months, please.'

'Three, Trevor. If you like the room, take it. Look at it this way, I've never had a man staying in my house before who wasn't a you-know-what and most women would never take the risk, so three months it is. I have to be honest, and,' she laughs, 'you're a try-out.'

Probation, he thinks. *Fair enough*. He likes her and he wants to get on with her.

'Good thing you rang,' she says. 'I thought you were going to weasel out of it.'

'Me?? I thought *you* were.'

She makes a humph noise and says she's merely vague. And that she has no liking for weasels. Or ferrets. Or any of that toothy lot. As a kid she saw them tearing into rabbit burrows, and rabbits. They're not sentimentalists, those creatures.

He can't imagine anyone resisting her for long. She might have considered another tenant for all he knows. Nothing will make him ask, even if he feels the pressure to do so. *How did they get on to ferrets?*

'My full name is Trevor Novak, by the way.'

'Like Djokovic? I'm a tennis groupie.'

There is simply no way for him to avoid this. '15-love.'

'Novak translates as new man,' he tells her. 'I'm trying to be New Man before I'm an old man. In that shed of yours. Even if moving's a pain.'

'Is it the problem with your leg?' she asks, walking up the shed and peering through its filthy window. Not seeing faces makes her especially observant of the body. She has to be. All the same, she knows she doesn't have to be so blunt.

'Being metaphoric. I mean just the bother of moving. My leg's just a left-over limp. I scare children.'

She laughs, uncertainly, sounds unsympathetic. The birds are making a din above her.

'About your back fence,' he adds. 'I'll help you with your Creep. I can be extremely insincere when it's called for.'

'Um? What?'

'I will smile at him then make threats. Most people weaken at that point.'

How, she wonders, *does he know she is outside, thinking about her busted fence?*

'By the way,' he adds, 'about your prosopagnosia. Talking of metaphors. I was thinking the other night how the Labor Premier is tall and stooped, like a big black beetle with a face and ears.'

'And glasses.'

'Yes, and glasses. Whereas the Liberal stands there like a money-suit – with a Modigliani face where the man should be.'

'Similes, Trevor.'

'And no eyes. Well, similes then.'

He can already see himself in the mental move unloading items from a hired van: a virtual table here, a rug there and, hmmm, one too many toasters, beds and mattresses ... making a house with two of everything. Divorce's Ark.

If Elizabeth has been bothered by a mature-aged man gazumping any potential young woman (in truth she had vaguely thought Asian again, her stereotype for polite) she shows no sign of it when he rings to arrange a moving-in time. She finds herself accommodating. And so he moves in. If he gets too much he will have to go, it's that simple.

Over the weekend he keeps making trips, with bags, cases, boxes and that face. A face she also knows as him when he's there and forgets when he's not. She will have to do more than that, she must memorise his walk, his outline, his clothing and especially the deep timbre of his voice. The shiny pate. She will enjoy regular payments and less of the generational differences of her daughter, now inter-state, thank God. Meaning the man is housebroken, of conventional appearance and has no speed-gabbling incomprehensible friends.

Just hope he isn't a disguised sad sack. The wife stories. God, no. Scratching over things like a self-obsessed chook. Like her own ex became, what a carry-on that was.

She will invite Martina over to get a second opinion. She hasn't signed anything yet but will get him to. Besides, if Trevor is going to live here it will mean contact between him and Martina too, given she is Elizabeth's friend. If anyone can tell a suss bloke, it's Martina. Any sniff of inconsistency.

~

Sometimes she has just woken up and is already out raking her verge. She is in the world. Crisp air, light, mess. Beautiful leaves they may be, falling daily like gentle fractures from colour, but they dampen overnight and are a bastard to rake up.

As if by Newton's law of equal and opposite, as Trevor moves in at the back of her house, two people move out of a flat across the street, leaving stacked neatly tied bags of domestic items plus oddments of furniture on the median strip. Normally a bunch of crows patrols this area, crows and those vicious little Indian mynah birds, but overnight more human crows got stuck into the bags, untying them and sorting through the items by dropping them on the ground. A mirror is broken in several nasty pieces showing green angular reflections of the foliage above them, boxes of loose paper have been spilt on the grass, furniture is scattered. After the wind gets up, the place looks like a tip.

Sod them, thinks Elizabeth. She the neat and tidy.

Until she realises from his shape the man approaching along the pavement is her cantankerous neighbour. The Creep. Over her back fence. In his case she can discern his profile and the face which she likes to think is so angular it must have been broken then reset, but is in fact annoyingly handsome; mostly, she recognises the way, oddly for a man with a narrow face, his paunch spreads around his hips like a woman's. Perhaps that's his irritant, because something is.

And he is always dressed in black.

'I see you're good for something, then,' he says, as he walks past. 'A coolie, ha.'

This time Gordon is growling his judgement, and his judgement is good: she has to hold him back or he will leap at the man as he walks past.

'And keep that dog of yours on a leash, why don't you.'

'Right,' she calls out. 'I see you're one of those people that my dog distrusts. Dogs can always tell.'

He stops, without turning, then walks on.

Men, she thinks. Having just accepted a new one into her house. It has to be said that Gordon trusts him. But you never know, dogs *can* be wrong. During the rest of the day she and Trevor talk about the room, the shed, the weather, the parking restrictions in her street. From such casual conversation she can tell he won't be a problem. But people can be wrong, too.

When the last of Trevor's clothing is lifted out of the boxes and dumped-if-not-hung in the wardrobe, and his books are arranged, and his CDs clacked into rows on the IKEA shelving he has bought, he stands back and looks at it. The old room in the basement had seemed like a forgotten space, dull as an empty caravan. Fading fabrics. He has draped a dramatic throw rug over the spare chair and the narrow desk glows under the reading lamp he always uses. Even the bedside box has a small lamp on it. Trevor is not a man for a ceiling fluoro. It has to be his room now.

A new place, where he is alone, seems to have a thinner atmosphere. The room spaces, the specific smells, his hyper-consciousness. It is not that the light is less, it is somehow not fully present, unused to him being there. Spaces feel empty even though he is in them.

With Trevor occupied in his room, Elizabeth transforms into a manic worker – entering and cleaning the shed, waking its interior back from sleepy anonymity. She wears a cloth around her nose and mouth like a mask, she works like some people who don't enjoy regular gardening but every twelve months rush in like attack troops to shoot and burn everything in sight. While he is tamely carrying belongings into his room and arranging them, she is ripping down the dusty bags covering windows and dragging into daylight the cracked and long, curling layer of heavy linoleum. It groans and aahs like an animal trying to put off pain. She has filled her two wheelie bins. She is relentless.

When the rubbish is swept up and shovelled back outside, the doors open, and the windows cleaned, you can actually see the back wall from the front. Amazing. She looks up. The roof iron is somewhat thin towards the rear. No signs of water damage on the floor.

What a sharp and exhausting job she has done. Cathartic. She will tell Dr Chen, her latest GP, how good this has made her feel. Until twenty minutes later she clutches at the dining-room table and sits in a hurry, bright speckles gathering in her vision.

On his final trip he is caught in traffic by a slow tram which eventually stops. It takes the queue of cars a few minutes to begin passing. Only then can they see it's an unmarked terminus and the driver is standing outside at the front smoking a cigarette. And it's school pick-up time: parents' vehicles cram the roads and some jump out into the traffic like rabbits rushing from a gunshot.

As he parks in Elizabeth's street he remembers he must apply for a parking permit. All those houses of continuous frontage and no rear parking. Even the expensive terrace houses, with bedrooms going all the way back, so handsomely renovated, so two-million-dollarish. But no garage.

He's used to managing for himself, he says to her. Diana more the salary worker than DIY at home. He says his father was a geologist working away from home. He had been born in Poland and was a charismatic but very selfish man mixed up, they later discovered, in suspect mining deals. He disappeared decades ago and therefore Trevor had to help his mother at home, a strange legacy of helping and independence. His mother died, without them ever being sure about his father. Except his father, officially lost in the desert, or possibly murdered – no one knew – was eventually moved from being a Missing Person to being declared dead. There was no body.

This takes Elizabeth by surprise. Amazed. *It's a book!*

As usual Trevor is unable to explain any man disappearing like that. Going, going, gone. Whereas the Freudian father must live on: the symbolic figure remains even if there are no human remains.

She says *her* father was a practical man and he looked after her. In her case it was her mother who disappeared. And remained. Because she was still alive and kicking. She had joined the Orange People. Her desire for enlightenment and rampant sexual "sharing" pushed ahead of banal routines. Like school lunches, dropping off and picking up, weekends … Her mother was a self-centred crowd-pleaser.

'We have something in common,' he says. 'We are the offspring of Narcissists.'

Sitting on her tiny back verandah they watch the shadows collect over the shed. It is a mild evening. Elizabeth is smoking the second, she states, of her two, at most, ciggies a day. Her reward for clearing out the shed after earlier having read and then correcting or tweaking several thousand words by the next big thing. She says they are all the next big thing unless they already are the big thing. He is sampling his newly purchased wine.

'My wife,' he tells this woman who is now his landlady, 'drinks white wines and has joined the trend to pinot gris and *peenoohh greegio*. It's not wine, it's cat widdle.'

'And acidic,' she tells this man who is now her lodger.

'She can be that, too,' he says. 'But she is very sociable at work. Whereas I'm turning into a stay-at-home.'

'Does your wife warrant a name? It will get pretty tedious if we keep referring to your wife as your wife. Given you seem to want to talk about her.'

'Diana.'

'More to the point, Trevor, are you over her?'

'I only left her at lunchtime.'

'Ha. You said you've been living in separate rooms. Healthy to get out of that, much healthier. Feel more yourself. Frankly, I say the less of exes the better.'

They view each other through long and short durations of separation. Hers and his, respectively, marital. The temperatures are not the same. There is a skin-coloured light above his mind's horizon, no light at all near hers.

After a short pause she says:

'Let's ex the ex.'

It makes her laugh her bigger-than-a-ballerina laugh. But Elizabeth has always been embarrassed about her drinking tastes. How she must now admit to preferring the tired old gin and tonic. Cliché. Unadventurous. She admits it.

'And yours?'

'Anything alcoholic that isn't Southern Comfort – or over-junipered gin. Shiraz mainly. A single malt sometimes.'

She says gin is back in fashion, it's distilled locally, albeit by hipsters. What could be cooler than that? Trevor tells her he only ever uses Aussie olive oil. Because it *is* olive oil, and true as labelled. Italian and Spanish, many are not, as they claim, cold-pressed, not virgin and, frighteningly, not even olive oil.

Trevor is suddenly happy. She too. Unexpected, contingent. Words. She was right about bookish. *It wouldn't have happened with a 20-year-old girl from Guangzhou.*

'If I drink more than my usual few glasses,' he begins, then pauses for a count of four, 'I get the urge to go and do something. You've seen the STOP ADANI posters in my shop window. I'm going to paint a mural on my side wall, the alley wall. A landscape of the Galilee Basin and STOP ADANI. After a few drinks.'

'And when Adani gets the axe?'

'I'll replace it. Protest is never out of date. As long as there is a future, and bloody mining companies. My real painting, though? Well, we'll see.'

She concentrates on him, trying for a mug shot, if there is one. *Front: quite large head, shaven. Nose, um, noticeable. Big upper body yet normal legs in tight trousers. The time will come when this looks absurd. That voice.*

'I have a daughter,' she announces. 'She usually stays in the basement.'

'Like a demented cousin? I haven't noticed her.'

'Ha. When she stays here. Not sure what to do next time.'

Before he can ask the question Trevor considers it several times for the plain factualness of it, the biological.

'Did you only have one child?'

'Yes, one. Only? What's wrong with one? I have replaced myself. If she comes anytime soon,' says Elizabeth, 'she can have my study. It used to be her bedroom when I was full-time.'

It occurs to Elizabeth she hadn't thought this through. Her daughter will only stay for a night or two, preferring her friends' houses to her mother's. What she does enjoy is being picked up from the airport and saving the $50-plus taxi fare or whatever it is Uber-ing into town, the EH Holden with its retro coolness and wide bench seats encouraging a kind of movie-star gesture, her body draped sideways, arm over the vinyl and her big sunnies like black code in the pale interior. Even if no one she knows sees her, it feels fantastic. And a bed when she wants it.

'How old is she?'

'Well, she's, um (lots of arm-waving and general vagueness in a very *Ab Fab* manner) – look, I had her disastrously young. It was an accident, some sort of passive sex and pregnancy hangover from my hippie mother. I blame her.'

'As in passive smoking?'

'She's about 23. Despite all her anti-family melodramatics my mother was thrilled to her tits when Yvonne was born, until she realised some maternal help and support might be required. Let's face it, she could hardly be bothered looking after me. Yvonne's father hung around for longer than I expected.'

'How long is longer?'

'Oh, about ten years?'

Again, Trevor hears this word "about". *Is knowing numbers a lost skill? Relativity does not extend to time, unless you're Einstein.*

'It could have been worse,' she says. 'His name was Ian, a carpenter. He was completely indecisive. Not sure where he is now, and I don't have to care, as long as he calls Yvonne. Sometimes. I had to make him leave. He had the boringly proverbial seven-year itch, but it took him three more to do something about it. My father looked after me and my mother didn't, then I looked after Yvonne and her father didn't.'

'You know, I love her and everything,' she adds, 'it's just that I'm not … the cluckiest woman on the planet.'

'Besides, men are always leaving.'

Ah yes, he thinks. *Or being pushed.*

(Big inhalation on her third cigarette.) Of course she still thinks about Ian and in some ways still misses him. Or the home life of couples. Those times of the year, like birthdays and summer holidays and Christmas or New Year when the old emotional system goes wanting. She lifts her feet up onto the bench in front of her. *Such a casual woman*, he thinks, imagining Diana sitting there with them, *her back straight, her hair in place, still sexy after their ten years together, but so … well-comported.*

He had wanted to believe he loved Diana enough for her to say something reconciling, even if he has felt forced to leave. If he could hear her. If he is that man.

Families. 'I gather,' he says, just for the fun of it, 'that family photo albums don't mean very much to you, though?'

She looks at him, not following.

'I mean you wouldn't be able to recognise anyone in the photos?'

'You're a funny man, Trevor. No one has thought of that one before.'

'Similarly, selfies would be a waste of time.'

'No, no, even I like doing selfies! That's fun. I just don't look at them afterwards.'

'Like most people, then.'

It makes him remember. The days of Diana resting her head on his shoulder are past; his days of remembering her head resting are not. One thing he knows, though, his feelings are slowly subsumed into a conversation like this one. They are fading, they are losing form, like a bunch of old colour photos.

'If your daughter is about 23,' he says, 'how come you haven't returned to full-time work?'

What can she say to this, this time with this person, the question she often puts to herself? She sighs and considers it.

'Something happened. Me being me. I was working on a manuscript with a major novelist, a man – I'm not going to name him, shouldn't have said man, let's say it was a person – a person with a big readership. I told him the manuscript wasn't working. It had one *great* character but not much else going for it. I suggested they keep the character and … start all over again.'

'Wow.'

'Yeah. I got in the shit, of course. That's the only way to put it. The person complained to the big boss and things were never the same at work. It was overreach on my part.'

'They sacked you?'

'No. A few colleagues just made things uncomfortable. It affected my health, I think. But – and it's a monumental but – the author took my advice. Without telling me and without me having any further contact with him, he re-wrote the book as I had suggested. It became a major success.'

'Bloody hell. That deserves a monumental wow. So in fact you had the last laugh, and they knew. They couldn't un-know it. A case of gainsaid.'

Elizabeth enjoys telling this story this way. Opening the body to see what's inside is how she thinks of it, the process.

'You don't have any?' she asks. 'Children?'

He pauses for longer than expected. As if he has never been asked before.

'No,' he says.

Just to be safe, Elizabeth leaves the small kitchen light on overnight. In case he wants to, well, have a drink of water. Though there is water in the downstairs bathroom. Anyway, just to be sure. And so her house isn't left in complete darkness. It is very dark at night.

She lies alone listening for any unexpected sounds.

It occurs to Elizabeth that she has missed talking like this, forgotten its pleasures. In this spirit of exchange, she will have to tell Trevor about her years with Ian, the man she took to complement her coffee and cigarettes and then her life. He thought he was a husband, she thought she was a wife. A tradie and a bookworm. Beginning from when she was at uni, when she became pregnant. Knocked up by a carpenter, as if she were a sideboard.

Her bedroom door is shut and Gordon is inside with her, something she hadn't anticipated, given she usually sleeps with the door open and the cheerful dog moves freely here or there in the house. It was OK with the girl from Guangzhou. At first Gordon scratches at the door, wanting to go downstairs to visit Trevor. She makes him sit on her bed and as she strokes him she listens to the sound this makes, impossible to describe, of her hand caressing his coat. A sound she loves, leaning in against him to hear it.

The shower downstairs is running. He is under the water, naked, somewhat overweight. She could creep down and do a reverse

Psycho. Slash, slash. *Does he have a towel? Ah, well, that's his problem, unless he comes back up.*

What an odd evening. So far she likes him, feels trust has been growing immediately he began moving his things in. Strangers often stayed in the house when she was a girl, her mother's lovers, friends. Orange men, women, after all that dynamic meditation during the afternoon. The sannyasin. Veils and all clothes orange until they shifted into maroon for whatever reason. *Rending the veil, to meet what exactly ...?* She never quite knew how to take them, or trust them.

Their guru sat in Poona surrounded by US and Australian worshippers. When the family lived in Fremantle her young mother went looking for enlightenment with the Orange People, the sannyasin of Bhagwan Shree Rajneesh. Many of them lived in a commune, or, if they worked, spent as much time there as possible. They were renouncing their worldly passions. Elizabeth was 14. She watched the light passing through her mother's diaphanous orange clothing, over and around her mother's body, her mother's tall, endlessly moving silhouette, often naked inside the see-through cloth. Her mother was slim. Her mother was having sex.

Everyone was having sex. Sometimes with people they knew.

The sannyasin all dressed in orange. They were famous for it, and laughed at.

As a teenager Elizabeth and her mother lived in Fremantle close to, not amid, the Rajneeshee commune. Fourteen years old, trainee gymnast, schoolkid. The routines she performed every day in her gymnastic endurance were beyond the merely personal – they were universal and heartless. Fremantle had been undergoing its own rigour. The council painted the old harbour town in gauche pastels and divided loyalties in preparation for the America's Cup, and smooth-talking Alan Bond had been celebrated and reviled and, as far any anyone knew, still owed shitloads of money to local businesses. Bond's dictum, one sannyasin said, belonged at the rock bottom of simple: never pay a debt until, and unless, they take you to court and are likely to beat you. In other words, the sannyasin said (and he was a lawyer) the man is a complete shit and should be in jail. It came to be.

Elizabeth's favourite male sannyasin was called Mali whose new name, meaning "gardener", belied his reality as an architect in civilian life. He laughed, as he often laughed, resting a hand on her shoulder and telling her about the movement. On Sunday the group was involved in the various and quite different meditations the Bhagwan had developed for his followers. Most seemed to prefer the dynamic meditation, or it seemed so to her, perhaps because of the lurid imagery this group action left.

They kicked and jumped and leapt up and down like hyper kangaroos who'd lost all forward direction. And, because they were dressed in such thin clothing without underwear, she could see the men bumping and flopping in jumpy bulges under the clothing, and the women's tits – it looked as if it hurt – bumping and jolting. The men, their bouncing cocks and sometimes their erections; some small, some big; until it became embarrassing. She was embarrassed. But they kept at it. Earnestly. They screamed for catharsis.

From her point of view, after years of exacting practices and routines, keeping the body compact and highly focussed, they looked like apes set loose in a lounge room. They were not gymnasts. Nor were all of them were as good-humoured as Mali, she had come to realise, and some took themselves so seriously, she had heard from her mother, they told the newer men, and the women especially, how they, not the newbies, were advanced souls. Yes, they had been around and around many times. *Oh then*, she thought, *they are advanced. Egotists. What happened to renunciation?*

She and Mali were sitting side by side on the old bench beside the main hall the meditations were performed in. They could hear shouting and singing coming from the sannyasin group inside.

'Your mother is quite a woman,' Mali had said. He, as dark-skinned now as his name, from all the outdoor work in WA's relentless sunlight. Skin cancer was in God's hands, it seemed. And gardening was what God needed, now, the weekend work of hoeing and planting vegetables for the endless supply of vegetarian food, steaming platters of which, in Elizabeth's view, the sannyasin ate their way through like furious orange caterpillars. Peculiar when she thought about them with her friends, yet normal when she simply sat there, as she often did, among them.

His beard remained untrimmed, which Elizabeth liked; the wispy everywhereatonce of his facial hair looked sexier and cooler than that of the local folk-singers and more recently the daggy bush-band members who performed at public functions in Freo. Shovel beards. How these contrasts made any kind of sense was beyond her. Fremantle had become a mixed bag of lifestyles since the re-painting and tidying up for the America's Cup. She did not consciously regard the similar beards of the homeless men she occasionally saw in the parks.

'There's no pressure on you to join the Rajneeshees,' Mali had said, 'but if you do we'll find a name for you.'

Like her mother – *Amitabha*, she thinks.

Having a Sanskrit name would absolutely improve her peer love at school. She could guess the extra passion it would put into their bullying: a form of dynamic meditation her mother would not imagine. But then, her mother was oblivious to most things not immediately concerning herself. Having a mother wafting around Fremantle in Orange garb and picking you up from school, the rare times she did that, was confronting enough. Though Orange People were increasingly common in Fremantle, they were a sex cult, a guru sex cult, everyone said at school. Cool and uncool at the same time.

Her mother was bully enough. Her mother wanted more power in the movement, not for power itself, but to impress her wonderfulness upon everyone. Her mother expected love and, possibly, in a desiring reflection from the big man, her share of worship.

Except her mother had also decided to renounce the worldly nonsense of washing and deodorising. She stank. Social mixing with the plebs, whether in the school car park or the shops, was therefore a standoff for more reasons than her religious differences. A few of Elizabeth's friends had already left school and taken up exotic names (so cool as long as you're not at school) and, unless they made a law against it, attracted a succession of lanky undressed Orange men. They were under-age even if they were quasi-children of a quasi-god who had a wavy beard, mesmerising eyes and a sense of humour. Also, in years to come, ninety Rolls-Royces.

Mali enjoyed dynamic meditation as much as the rest of them and she felt shy sitting with him, talking, except she liked him the way she liked her father: working at something direct, honest, hands-on, a physical job. And, after all, not unlike architecture. She never thought of him as a bullshitter.

Why hadn't he become a Christian? asked Elizabeth. Even her mum had given that a go. The real RC, she was. Loved the rituals. Had to keep her clothes on.

Mali smiled at this girl. He moved closer to her, their thighs touching.

'I was never interested in Christianity,' he explained, 'but it works for many. Which means there is something deep about Jesus. What he was,' he said. 'And it wasn't the meek and humble moral man of God. Intelligent people didn't wear that, not any more, not for themselves, though the general idea of a moral life was there in Christ by example – for people who never read philosophers!'

He laughed.

No. Well, until he knew any better he had thought myth and religion were about truth and meaning, and how the world was made, that stuff. Now he thought they were speaking about power. The paradox was: Christ, with all his personal charisma, must have been like the Bhagwan, except greater, lived and then died powerless against the Romans. The only power the Church had fed its followers was Resurrection, eternal-life bullshit. Suffer now and then you'll be fine. *That was just giving in, didn't she think?* A sign of defeat and so a sign of weakness. Most people should learn how to live with each other, to suffer and to think about how they live before their lives waste away. Never just throw it in.

'They waste away?' This made Elizabeth jump. 'Why?'

'They have a problem with sex,' he said to her. 'The Bhagwan speaks always of love. From the heart. It's the Sufi way.'

But he was staring at her mother.

Her mother, the embarrassing one. She had been dancing topless and now she sat in the garden area with her orange merely draped in her lap.

'And towards the heart,' he had said, looking into Elizabeth's eyes. 'Amitabha. She attracts desire.'

'She has a great body. Is that a Sufi thing?'

Mali thought this girl was too young to be so cynical.

'It's embarrassing to have you kind of rub this in my face,' she added. 'It doesn't look like love, it looks like no-rules sex. It's not normal.'

'No, no,' he said. '*We* are the normal people, we have learnt that so-called normal people are not, at all, they are insane in certain ways. Or robots. They can't *see*. They want to be told what to do, or they want power, to push people around.'

'And she doesn't? She pushes me around. She pushes everyone around. There's a lot of coercion going on here. And a lot of being *told what to do*, Mali, just that it's not by force. You think you're not conforming? To the Bhagwan ...'

'You're very articulate, Elizabeth.'

'I'm at high school, Mali. I'm trying to work out my values.'

But Mali was besotted. And there was no avoiding her mother, she was everywhere. He said Amitabha was supposed to mean

Boundless Lustre. Elizabeth laughed. Boundless Lust, more like. Her mother seemed to be with a different man every time Elizabeth managed to find her. She could not resist the swirling cloth and beads and the energies of the Orange flock: more to the point, the men couldn't resist her. Her mother had no limits. She slept around and meditated on a level of forgetfulness far above normal life.

According to her mother, the Bhagwan stated that they have to work through the blockages in their sexual energies, that women are faced with both catharsis and generous supplies of male antidote. Hence the fucking. No holding back, never. Her mother admitted she loved fucking, it made her a better person, closer to God; closer to you, too, my darling. Her daughter shrank.

'What if the men want sex with me,' she'd asked. 'I'm only 14.'

'Don't be silly, that's not …'

'Some of them have been a bit touchy-feely. Hugging and kissing. I'm not stupid, Mum, and I'm not making it up.'

'Oh, don't be silly, they like you because you're my daughter.'

Even a 14-year-old had to gasp at this. Especially a 14-year-old.

Her mother wouldn't hear of any problem. No. (She was deaf as well as blind.) They were renouncing orthodoxies, ordinary stupid same-same people, boring everyday life, for bouts of group dancing, elevated bliss-creep (from jumping exhaustion, drugs, the pleasures of the chosen), *taiko*-drum-sized-cooking-pot meals and the eternal class of superior beings.

Except, for young Elizabeth, sitting or wandering amongst them, they all blurred in together. All the sannyasin looked the same. Every one of them. They were not special. She was the nadir of an irony. They knew about Elizabeth's rare neurological condition of prosopagnosia, and yet it surprised them, these humble and not so humble seekers after God, to realise this condition rendered her so face-blind she couldn't distinguish one sannyasin from another. They were rendered equal. Prosopagnosia had reduced them to the same level of advancement. Their souls were all the same.

If God and the Bhagwan and her father had sat side by side in the same orange robes, she could not tell them apart. Instead, she had to memorise them by other means. When they were all long-haired and bearded (men) and all long-haired and blossoming (women) they were astonishing similar, impossible for her to tell apart. Her mother's voice had always been the main identifier and then, one new difference, her hair was close-cropped, sometimes shorn.

Elizabeth told Mali she had a private joke about this blank-face thing. He asked what and she told him: 'God has prosopagnosia too,' she said, 'all His children are equal, they are the same.' No one was any better than another.

'You are a chip off the old block,' he said, somewhat startled. Given he meant her mother, this sounded decidedly inept to Elizabeth.

She told him she at least knew what irony was. And how it was brought on by having a mother.

She noticed he stopped laughing.

So it was her father, the tradesman the cult looked down upon, who had taken care of her. His work may have been in joinery but he was not a joiner. In fact, he said the Orange lot were not into self-renunciation either, just self-indulgence. These educated people, mostly professionals, treated anyone who wasn't a Rajneeshee with disdain. He was a mere tradesman, his kind of work/life a discipline the sannyasin were not inclined to value and would fail to achieve. Every morning he rose early and went to work regardless of weather or personal vision or thoughts of *any fucking guru*.

He would say to Elizabeth, if a room full of intelligent people insisted the Bhagwan's games were rigorous enough to grant them union with God, why wouldn't they work hard, as Christ the fisherman, the carpenter, had; and focus, being patient and to sufficiently without ego, in order to become enlightened through work of that kind?

The care he took involved picking Elizabeth up from her gymnastics lessons, and taking her to performances and weekend camps, while she trained and trained. Until she literally grew out of it. No tall gymnasts.

Her mother hardly noticed, though enough to say *How nice, dear* sometimes, and *How bourgeois* at others.

Then too soon after uni Elizabeth announced she was pregnant. *Her little girl was having a baby!* There was no offer from her mother to help. This pregnancy, her mother had said, is something Elizabeth shouldn't have let happen. As if her own example ever helped.

As before, her mother's quest came first, and Elizabeth's anger followed.

After the Orange People split up or flew to America her mother packed off to Victoria because she hadn't time for babies, even her own grandbaby. Far away geographically and even further personally, her mother said she was *between lives*.

So yes, Elizabeth does know about sects.

An ambulance siren seems to lean towards the street then veer off, and while Elizabeth lies straight and stationary in her bed an injured person similarly prone is tilted left and right by G forces inside the lit vehicle. Life is seeking some direction but is indecisive.

The siren diminishes and thins out entirely. Her street, another street, any street where trees do, and houses don't, move in the wind and rain but become less with any person lost.

She realises she has been drifting. Back to WA where her memories seem only to have one season: summer. Summer outside and inside the warm house inside her dreams. Perth's usual weather, or maybe it is something about her. Nothing sentimental, or idealistic, nothing like that, something generic. Except for her mother.

The house is silent.

One new customer presumes to tell him – the bookseller as passive audience of one – that a super-ministry run by Dutton is a great idea. That the Government needs to stop things (the man almost says *everything*). Trevor is just hoping the miserable sod will buy a book. The man chats away as if programmed to stand in shops and pronounce on such matters, as no doubt he does (and does with no doubt). Trevor says Dutton the ex-Queensland copper reminds him of the primary-school kid working up a huge effort in a dull voice just to make a simple-minded statement.

Only days earlier a young man dressed like a share-house floor came into the shop and asked him to sell copies of *Social Alternatives*. Trevor said sorry, no. He explained that he chose whatever political works or posters were displayed and wasn't going to read through every *Social Alternatives* they brought in.

'Why not?' objected the young man. 'Are you a fucking Tory?'

'The word "no",' said Trevor, 'is not a political persuasion.'

Two more emails arrive with a ping from returntime@gmail .com, an address that disclaims identity even as the email itself is cryptically personal. The writer seems over-familiar with Trevor and even keener to know about the shop. It occurs to Trevor this might be from one of Jonesy's confused customers. The messages are intrusive, they ask about turnover. An offer for the shop? Or is there a very strange 12-year-old who hasn't yet leant about online porn?

An hour or so later he stands and walks back into his tearoom, fills the kettle with water, then clicks it on. He feels embarrassed by his half loving, half leaving behaviour with Diana. His collection of ironic acts. The manner need not be heavy but the matter must at some point be heartfelt. Every clown knows pathos.

The day drags on. Customers. Most are quiet and purposeful even when they browse and delay and do or don't buy. When they pester and preen, show off or patronise him then leave empty-handed, that's when the man behind the counter is a genre: the murder novel. But he knows most customers will buy something rather than waste, or seem to be wasting, their coming in spending time. How human to want a result, something to carry from experience. Given that most books bought remain unread, or at least unfinished, and many never even opened. His custom is now his usual experience but not his nourishment. From now on he works within five minutes of the house and wants to get back there. He wants his new life to begin.

Not over at all, the past, but now the time comes – simple to say, complex in feeling – to unpack the rolled-up canvases, boards, painting materials. Study them. Wait for them to *want* him, not taunt him. To join time.

These objects have gravity; and challenge. The shed is redefined; it is a studio. They make him feel very sober. Stacked on the bench are his boxes of paints. Eager to save his pride he has arranged the used tubes of oils on top of the unopened ones to give Elizabeth the impression he has been working at these canvases for years. Mess equals serious practice. These squashed tubes of paint, so beloved of artists and their voyeurs, are surely proof enough, covering for the many others that are embarrassingly pristine. His brushes, though, who could argue with *them*? They are clearly old, most of them soft, some of them hardening, and wrapped in stained rags. His turps, being turps, merely stinks.

In a different way, everything looks old. He feels old. Old and unrelated.

He once spent several weeks renovating, re-painting and then setting up a studio only to prowl in it like an angry cat. Finally he slumped in a corner in the single armchair, unable to work. Sitting for hours, days, in the armchair. It was a disaster. Nothing much came, and nothing of the work that came worked. No narrative, not images. He was half the Coen brothers, not a whole film in his head.

Then he fixed it. Or by chance he woke from it. He raided offcuts from the carpet bins and laid them on the floor, three wooden bookshelves not from IKEA propped against the walls, two standing lamps. This is how he broke his emptiness – by making the outside well lit, and comfortable, with places to sit, and read, a shelf for books. It was not him, it was the space. It simply began to exist in its own sense: to function, that is, by making itself welcoming for his work to emerge *into*.

Looking back on this he wonders if this hiatus was a precursor to the breakdown of his talent, not its breakthrough as he'd once thought. Now all that matters is his own feng shui. He is moving more than house, he is moving the unseen shapes of himself. He must find an armchair for this place.

Elizabeth is watching him now, curious to see how he is setting up.

'I don't know anything much about painting,' she sighs. 'Just the usual portraiture, which in my case is a joke, given I can't even make out actual likenesses, but it is interesting … forensically. And, of course, creaky old landscape painting.'

'It is creaky. I like that. Reminds me, when I was at art school one of the students was absolutely obsessed with painting landscapes. You know, realist ones. The painting lecturer kept telling her not to. In the final student crit he stopped in front of her sunny eucalypts and screamed: "Fuck it! No more trees!" After that we called it the Fuck It, No Trees School.'

Before he fully wakes the next morning, his right leg is numb and inert. Not cramped, just leaden. It feels profoundly the wrong weight and shape. Like the heavy door to the shed. As he stands to get dressed the first shocks of hot nerves rush down from hip to foot. In the darkness of his leg is a sudden, contained lightning. He recognises, and feels, his right leg collapse under sudden weight.

What comes now is what has stopped him before. The problem will ease and go, as long as he is careful. He knows it. His memory and his body. The accident when he was nearly 30, breaking his leg and hip when the car rolled. Usually young men with leg injuries have been dragged under motorbikes. The joints break down and the vascular system hardens.

The trauma returns internally. It can make him feel catatonic, but in mind only. The leg works.

Walking upstairs from his new basement room is easy: it is regular legwork against gravity, the focussed resistance of climbing, co-ordinated muscle shifts from one leg to the other. Choose the right position of his foot on the step, the lift, and the muscles will choose themselves. He knows walking downstairs is the problem. It is un-supported, it requires foot-eye co-ordination and the reading of distances. It should be automatic, as reflex as catching a ball, but his mind has lost that faculty and now he must think his feet into position. He might think of this as proprioception.

For Trevor, walking downstairs is controlled dropping.

Before he leaves their apartment with a last box of books, Diana holds his arm, snuggles up against him. She can hardly keep a huge smile from her face, her mouth exaggerating enough to pout. *This is our goodbye*, he thinks, *softer than expected. Much softer.* He can feel her plush body against him.

'Why don't we,' she says, 'have one last fuck? Would you like that?'

What can he say? That he'd like to? That the offer sounds patronising? That he thought they'd had their last fuck a few weeks ago.

She led him into the bedroom (*her bedroom now*, she thought but never said) as if he were no longer Trevor but a lover. Where they did what they had over the years found they did best, this time warmly and slowly, savouring it, each other, then fervently, knowing it was their last-ever fuck, she was surprised to feel huge waves of erotic feeling. The illicit urge to have him inside her when they were estranged? But still, what? In love? 'Ooh Trevor,' she said, 'this is good. Ooh yes, you should move out all the time!'

Not quite regretfully, but she was enjoying it more than him. Her legs were shaking. He went for it like a sweaty racehorse and came, through her slippery and coming, finally, finally. That was then.

'Why not?' she says. 'Eh? The sex still works.'

'Yeah. A lot of good that's done us. So maybe not?'

A kind of anger reddens her, like a sudden rash.

~

In his shop the following day he sits under the glowing overhead light, in front of the striking blue wall, feeling deathly still but empty. Not anything like Buddha. The brutal, patronising irony of it: parting intimately, erotically, only when they know there is no return. Just an ego trap that he set off. He, both bait and prey.

When they achieve the independence they've worked so hard to get, some people feel useless. He will not let this happen.

A few customers arrive and leave. With a smile and a nod and a few words he goes through the motions of greeting and selling. (*Buy some books!*) Seated and annoyed now, he begins thinking about his return to painting as something quite different, less intimate than interrupted, less calm than angry: that you don't become an artist to test the hypothesis of talent, or some expected aesthetic, or a kind of public sexiness. Such things are sentimental, Romantic, there only at the beginning, if at all; thereafter, you work with your art to discover its trust, because then the practice itself morphs into results, and torments even. Intensities. Heat. These things change you. The practice will make you an offer. You take its white drug of Otherness.

Perhaps. Always perhaps.

Today's chalkboard sign is longer than usual:

When you read Extreme Tattoos *your skin will scream but you won't be able to put the book down until it's over. Pauline Trove explores the fashions and the cult of tattoo expression like a woman brandishing a nail gun.*

Trevor walks from the back room with a box of books. Cuts around the edges with a Stanley knife. Deciding earlier against DVDs, Trevor has instead been visiting second-hand bookshops looking for bargains – interesting books in good condition, only editions with modern print and design, with pencilled prices he thinks he can erase and improve on when shelved in his own shop. A modest collection has resulted from this enterprise, plus he has picked up a small box of books from a garage sale.

Now, opening the garage sale box, he flips through one book, then another and another. Then, with increasing amazement, all of them. Someone has neatly, in black texta ink, scribbled out the swearwords. The words are guessable but gone. The scribble is in cramped up-and-down wiggles, as if a tiny lie-detector arm has travelled through the book finding the naughty bits. Obsessive censorship. Words never intended as swearing get similar treatment. In one paragraph the mushroom word *shitake* has the *shit* scribbled out, the *ake* remaining. The "texta censor" has gone through every book.

In books of little dialogue most of the narration remains intact but whenever the characters speak, *dzzzt dzzzt dzzzt* goes the ink. *Who? Why?* However many books Trevor takes from the box, they are *all* marked like this. Then they were offered back to the public at the garage sale, probably dropped on the pavement to clear a deceased estate, the texta censor dead now, gone off into the black texta land of the dead, not a single voice raised in bad taste. They are reasonable books he might otherwise have placed on his newly cleared second-hand-books shelf. When he bought the box it was the titles and the age of publication he looked at. What a brilliant find, even if he can't display it! *Who*, he can't stop imagining, *would be deranged enough to do this?*

He is behind his counter and still thinking about it when a lanky man with Keith Richards cheeks pushes the door open and sniggers at the shelves of books.

'Jesus,' the man says.

He swivels around like the turkey-throated man of a month earlier, scanning the entire shop as if it is the most extraordinary thing he has seen for years. His mouth hangs open, his hair dangles. Amazement is not a drug you stay addicted to, but it has its moments.

Eventually he sees Trevor.

'Mate,' he says. 'Mate, I've never seen anythun like it. How long you been here? Shit, all these books. You must, fuck me, have books on every fucken thing.'

Trevor is imagining the pen and neat finger movements inking out the man's speech ... *dzzzt me, have books on every dzzzten thing ...*

'Hey, you can't smoke in here.'

The man is about to light a cigarette. He stops, spreads his arms in appeal.

'Fucken hell. Jonesy never minded. I ...'

'Mate,' says the bloke, still holding the unlit ciggie, 'you're looken at me as if I've never read anythun but you'd be dead wrong. I read books like *Sin City* by that Yankee guy Somebodyorother. They made a film about it with Bruce Willis in black and white, with freaky white blood when people got shot. Have ya any by him?'

'I can't check if you don't know his name.'

'So it was sorta literary, eh, if you get a film made of a book?'

If Trevor is surprised he is probably showing it. He thought the film was gratuitously violent – and he enjoyed every moment of it.

An older customer over near the biographies is staring. The man ignores her.

'Do a fucken search, then, ya dumdum, you know, just look up *Sin City* the movie and Whoverheis I'll come runnen. Nah, sorry mate, sorry mate, I don't mean to tell you ya job …'

The man wanders off to look at the books displayed with their front cover showing. He walks a circuit, saying 'G'day, love' as he passes the woman, and returns to the counter.

'Frank Miller,' says Trevor. He is not looking at his laptop, his memory as usual cutting the mustard. Graphic novels.

'That's him! You got the guy.'

And only then does a screen search.

'It says here … (Trevor measures it out like dried poison) that Miller's work overall is … misogynist … homophobic … fascist … and that *300* is a Spartan vs. Athenian battle with spears and arrows and more blood than … In its film form, at least, it's racist and … he denigrates disabled people.'

The guy moves across to the counter and shows his teeth in a grin. A few teeth, a hollow grin.

'That sounds *great*. I dunno what some of those words mean but order him in for me, will ya, eh?'

'You want me to order a book or a DVD?'

'Yeah. Jesus. Isn't that what you do?'

'But which? One of the books?'

'Yeah. Yeah. Nah, the DVD.'

'Can you leave a deposit? Or pay for it now?'

The man frowns.

'Is that what everyone does?'

'I mean, are you going to come back for it? I don't want to … make an order only to be stuck with it.'

'Are you havin' a go at me? That's discrimination.'

The man is disgusted. While he is trying for eye contact, Trevor looks up at the ceiling mirror to avoid him.

'You're an arsehole, do ya know that? A real shit.'

The man glares at him now, his arms spread wide, and then he makes a my-head-is-exploding gesture. Happy to mix his metaphors in every way. As he leaves he drags a row of books off the New Books shelf and slams the door. The books lie in a heap on the floor. Old Books now. Outside, he lights his cigarette and walks casually away.

The woman turns to Trevor, her face like a frightened spider.

'Never mind,' he says. 'The man probably learnt to read in prison.'

Maybe he shouldn't say that but the man is a complete *dzzzt*. Trevor could, while it was happening, texta out the man's swear-words and see him standing there with a black scribble coming from his mouth every few seconds.

After waiting out the hours he closes for the day. Only when he's inside the car park and searching for his car does he remember he walks to work now. His memory is stressed. At this rate his inner passwords are probably jumbled.

Back on the street somebody's dog has run free. It runs towards him as he heads into the right street. He cannot tell if it wants his love or his leg. Gordon is different, being a setter he is simply floppy ears and running and eating, then more running and especially more eating.

At Elizabeth's he is ready to knock as if merely visiting. He pauses, then uses his key and tries to convince himself this is where he lives now, walking through the short corridor into the shadowy lounge room; and more, not merely where he lives but what he must call *home*. This, meant to be the least strange of words, estranges him.

She isn't there, or is in her room working on a manuscript. Probably out, given his recent noise and her silence. Either way she doesn't appear. But when he calls her and asks if she wants a yardarm drink she says no from inside her study. *Too much work to do.*

Surprised by this, more by his disappointment, he stays for twenty minutes or so before convincing himself that what he really needs is a drink with someone to tell his daily absurdities to. No more Diana rituals at end-of-day. He wastes some time by stumping downstairs to his room, staring at himself in the bathroom mirror and seeing a man who looks to be simply him/ not him, the familiar image with an unfamiliar background. How many hours of any day, and any life therefore, do we stand or sit un-occupied? Living vacantly, daydreaming, blanked out in front of TV or screen information, or waiting, and waiting as always for a desired intervention, a *gratification*, for God's sake …?

So he walks back to the main street. He will order a drink then ring his friend Lester.

Lester is an ex-detective. They don't usually drink in the same pub. Trevor's favourite pub is not gentrified, or retro, it's dark and sticky, as lacking in coolness as sticky pubs have ever been. Plus a bit. Not a dollar has been spent on its appearance since the dollar came into existence, 1966. A few posters of recent concerts have been glued to the wall, though it's hard to tell given the gloom and the walls being completely obscured with old vinyl LP covers. A section of carpet has been prised up from the floor – probably with a crowbar – not to reveal some trendy floor-boards but to expel the circular burn marks that date from some years earlier. Nothing has been laid down as replacement. The bar area is beer-hard underfoot, is shadowy and poky and many locals who are not hipsters but who are perhaps hip and love old heavy-metal bands and Sunday afternoon guitars, collectively, have found, like a German verb in a grimy sentence, it's this pub they love.

Despite these no-nonsense attractions, Trevor finds a table outside. When he reaches the bar, Lester is standing there. Two pints of Guinness are lined up in front of him.

'About time,' he says, without looking up.

'I never rang you.'

'No, you didn't. Have your bloody pint.'

Once outside, Trevor recounts his meeting with the bony-faced man in his shop. And mentions Frank Miller, the novelist, and the film of his novel *Sin City* shot in stark black-and-white graphics, some frames almost fully blacked out. Bruce Willis as the hard/soft man like a cop, an ex-cop even, a kind of Lester.

'I've never had any trouble with my customers,' says Lester, 'except return fire.'

'They were probably afraid of the dark.'

Lester had been famous for night work.

'It probably won't surprise you,' says Lester, 'that I have a DVD of that film. It's great action, it's kinda nuts and it's melodramatic. The vigilante prostitutes are some guys' fetish of hard bitches in black leather with automatic weapons! What's not to like?'

Trevor has to laugh, this man of the night likes dark action scenes in make-believe movies. Lester has a long nose with a friendly bend in it. Peaceful as it looks, when the man was off-duty someone swung a left hook at him and made contact with the nose. After that, Lester made considerable contact with the man. He's not really friendly. He belongs in a DVD of *Sin City*.

One thing he has maintained is his fitness; Trevor not. He knows he must address his very average physical state. He must take on his own rehabilitation. Possibly with resistance work? Weights. More than active exercise, real weights, pressing, pushing, the boring battle against inert muscles. He could, but again he has been saying to himself: not yet.

Resistance training begins with resisting.

'I'm off to a club tonight,' says Lester. 'Instead of using Tinder. Old-school. Why don't you come?'

'C'mon, Lester, you do the night-birding. I just can't do the talk: "Hi-beautiful-wouldya-like-to-come-home-with-me" kind of spiel. Anyway, I'm too old ...'

He means he is not like this.

'Bullshit. You wouldn't know. It's all about bluffing. How can you sell books if you can't sell yourself?'

'That's so bloody American.'

'Come to think of it, you are looking a bit shopworn. A night out will do you good.'

'I'm tired. Being tired is good for me.'

Trevor thinks nightclubs are like Paradise, where biffo St Peters stand shouldering the Gates, but inside all is Hell in high heels and pills and fools in flashing lights. Getting wasted on industrial cocktails before trading migraines in the back seat of taxis. Lester has a different and wilder way about him. He can change places. And Lester has a bit of Koori blood, which he claims when he feels like it. Dark brown eyes, a certain look. His own man. He doesn't suffer fools.

A man approaches the tables. He is tall and, despite his walking stick and an alarming lurch to the left every few paces, is casually dressed, and his dog seems well fed. (If the man is gaunt and the dog is fat, so we see fast dogs paired with slow owners.) He stops beside one of the tables where a man is drinking alone and he cackles hello, then leans hard on his stick.

'Didja see the fucken Roos on the weekend, mate?' he says, a genetic utterance for all Roo fans as they stagger from the weekend in bitter delirium.

The other man laughs and sucks on his ciggie.

'Too fucken right, I did.'

'Couldn't believe my fucken eyes seein' those useless fucken bastards playing in the rain, it wasn't footy it was shit and fucken mudslides, mate, kiddie stuff, that greasy turd of a ball they couldn't get a grab of, the limp bastards, Jesus, they woz tryen to fucken kick and tryen and fucken trying but where woz the kicken?'

The two men smile in sad agreement. Even in the IGA between pale Aussie customers and the brown Indian staff it's not community and it's not world music that unites, it's bloody football. The man keeps on.

'Yeah. What an arse, what in gentle fucken Jesus was I doin watching it, eh? I never seen any fucken playen as fucken bad as that. And that big cunt with the fucken contract, millionaire bastard, fucken what's-his-name, ah shit, what a waste a space, him … you know him, mate.'

'Johnson?' the other man says. 'Useless bastard.'

'Nah, that's the other cunt, nah, I got it, fucken Geoff Hollins, *that* fucker, me head's on back ta front since I seen him with his moneybags in his eyes and not a fucken ounce a talent in his hands. Or feet. Arse-about kicker, gentle fucken Jesus.'

Lester is squinting. How many silly buggers like this has he seen in his shortened professional time? The motley lot.

'Now that,' says Trevor, leaning towards him, 'is gift of the gab.'

'Yep,' Lester says. 'Shit and fucken mudslides. And arse-about kicker and gentle fucking Jesus in the same sentence? The man's a bloody poet.'

'Oi,' calls the man, 'you two over there.'

He is pointing at them with an angry finger.

'Think footy's funny, do ya? Yeah, well, you're probably arse-end Collingwood fans. On the piss like a coupla fucken alkies. Yeah, mate,' to Trevor, 'I seen you smacken 'em down by ya sad self. Got a another pisshead friend with ya just for the day?'

His moment and he hits it. If he knew his stuff he might see the look in Lester's eyes. He doesn't. Lester doesn't mind him. He leans on his stick and moves off down the street. His fag is almost out but, tight-lipped now, he is sucking from it like a lord.

'Local colour,' says Trevor. 'Whatever that guy thinks comes straight out of his mouth. Most of it unpublishable. Talking of which …'

He tells Lester about the blotted-out words in the books he has found.

'I should show you. Each blot is a kind of *dzzzt*,' he says. 'Our friend here would be all *dzzzt*, non-stop *dzzzt*. He would sound like a tattooist.'

'You know,' he adds, 'I read somewhere that wharfies are introducing a non-swearing policy at meetings.'

'*The wharfies?* It'll be the cops next. Of course, you know I prefer the company of well-spoken crims.'

They sit for minutes without talking. Lester goes through the texts on his phone. From the sidewalk table they can inspect the locals. Given our two men are sedentary during the day, perving counts as exercise. By nature they see the world differently – one as a detective, one merely voyeuristically. The pub's customers, the alms-gatherers. Sleek-haired men in black Maseratis up by the cafés, who they both think are probably crooked.

Customers are constantly entering and leaving the door of the gym. It looks so easy, they go in cool and come out hot, sweaty in patches and clutching towels. Not one of them is fat; some are slim and shapely. Some are muscle-trucks, NRL monsters who spend hours shaking off beads of sweat like flies.

In complete contrast, a group of African women in long dresses and head coverings wander down Errol St., swaying like fine giraffes above most people, who can't help looking as they pass.

Lester is someone Trevor has met again only recently. A male voice growled a hello while Trevor was deciding if the IGA's runner beans were fresh enough to buy in handfuls or needed to be chosen. 'Don't tell me you select green beans one at a time,' said the voice. It was Lester. Now retired. It seems Lester lives close by, so he can walk over to Errol St. instead of feeling historical over a bottle of whisky at home. That kind of retired, he once said, takes it out of you.

He is an ironic man behind his trim beard. Too old to be a hipster, too young for a bearded hippie, too ironic for either, Lester displays a beard all his own, *sui generis*, the lower edge of which is cut squarish on the chin. It is dark and cut … like a tiny boxing glove. Between blinks he looks like Robert Downey Jnr, though his beard is beginning to show a dash of white, like splits in the leather. Within ten years the effect on Lester the hard man will be decidedly unusual. He will look like a doctor.

He has a sober temperament, come of long drinking practice and a habit, akin to a tic, of sizing everyone up. For men as much as women, this can be obvious and unsettling. He's a Tinder *sans* Tinder.

'How's your new home?' he asks. 'Though I think it's a bit strange, Trevor, you living with a woman young enough to be your missus. Or old enough.'

'Did I tell you I was moving? Come on, you and Sherlock.'

'It's the house dust all over your sleeves.'

'Unlike yours. She's smart, good sense of humour, agreeably weird. What more can a lost soul ask of his landlady?'

'Breakfast in bed?'

Across the street Trevor notices the blonde woman begging as usual outside the IGA. Her voice will be in dying cadences or everywhere in a rush. She converts alms into fast or slow slur. Sometimes she stands, and jitters about, more usually sits on the pavement, abject and blotchy-faced from the weather. Dressed in black, she is without her little fluffy dog. The man who plays harmonica hasn't been around for weeks. He was last seen carrying a battered little amplifier to boost his appeal, blues harp all the way down the pavement.

So today the woman has the street to herself. Trevor sees her whirling down the pavement towards them. He never saw her stand up. Despite her weathered face her hair is freshly streaked and curled and she wears a long black dress. Closer now, he sees it is a black fabric trimmed with gold, surprisingly striking on her hardly fed figure; except the woman is berating people and shouting. She sounds ludicrously Russian in conversation with someone or something unseen, impossible to understand. Drunk. No, she is high, or manic, or all three. Is she even the same woman?

She is taking very small steps but swings from side to side like someone taking large ones. She almost falls on the back of Lester's chair and as he turns she sweeps her handbag just over his head then calls out to the other side of the street where nobody is taking the slightest notice. Then she's off on her downhill lap of the street, until several minutes later she sways back past them still mumbling and calling out in Slavic whatever, as fully preoccupied as before. She may be falling into something but doesn't land in it.

'I had my DNA done,' announces Trevor. 'The results show a group of red dots over Poland.'

'Your invisible father is showing up for once.'

'They look like a tight grouping in shooting practice, which seems appropriate.' Gunshots into Poland. His lost father.

He thinks of his jeweller tease: of two men running up Errol St. towards the pub, one man running some distance behind them blasting shots from a revolver.

'There's another grouping over in the UK, my mum's lot, but there are patches in the Middle East and Italy … like little grubs on my grapevine. We hatch out everywhere. Think of those eugenics fuckwits around the country. Even with bits of European DNA flying about, Indigenous kids are the purest race on the planet. More evidence every year.'

Lester sighs and nods. But he is old-school. Which is why psychologists are necessary in the police force. The daily world, even in the streets of Melbourne, is more various than pies and policemen.

'DNA is scary,' says Trevor. 'What's inside our bodies is not us. Biologically, from conception until death, we are *packed* with flat-out genius on the inside.'

'I haven't seen much of it.'

'Yeah … That's because we're dopey fuckers on the outside.'

'Nurture. It's a joke,' says Lester. 'Talking of dopey, I had a crim who'd lived in shitholes half his life, came into the station so often he'd lost all the molars on the left side of his face – logical given most police are right-handed. Which meant he had to chew on his right, and maybe if people are right-handed they chew right-handed so chewing on the right felt normal. But then the bloke said' (Lester puts on the guy's voice) ' "I got that Bell's fucken palsy on the right side of me face, didn't I, so I couldn't fucken chew any fucken thing on any fucken side.'"

The street is changing shifts, the dead phase between shops closing for the day and others opening for the evening. The two of them decide to walk back to Lester's place for a sundowner – well, *sans* yacht – a glass of single malt with a glimpse of sunlight through it. Before he changes to go out. As they pass his shop Trevor explains his Big Idea.

'Imagine,' he says to Lester, 'a phone app that customers could use to check book reviews, in real time, and then be linked to my bookshop. Come in or order it immediately. A Yes or a No. A Tinder for book readers, meaning book sales for me.'

'Sounds good. Bloody do it.'

Due west, the two men walk, slap-bang into the sun. At the intersection they squint into the circular glare at the end of the long street. The tram cables overhead follow down the slope then disappear to the right like thin black air trails of birds sweeping out of view.

'I did. I discussed the app idea with Diana. She's the designer. I made her promise to take the idea to work and see about developing it.'

The cables keep sweeping above them. The staves. When he's talking like this Trevor fails to notice real birds let alone metaphoric ones.

'They paid me a basic rights fee, like film rights for a book. Nothing happened. Months later I heard of an app that reviewed books and gave a star rating to each title, as up to date as the search engines were. The company made shitloads.'

'Crooks whatever the colour of their shit.'

'Yeah. They said it wasn't my work, it was the form the app operated through, which was their invention. They had patented the form, not the function.'

'They cheated you, all right. You should have rung me up.'

'They ripped me off and hardly took breath. A different sort of crim from the kind you fronted. Hardly great for a failing marriage, though, is it?'

'Fuck the bookshop and that app stuff,' says Lester. 'Settle in with your landlady like that old Pommy artist Turner, and just paint. I saw some of your paintings years ago. It was,' he grins, 'good enough to sell.'

'I never showed you anything. Why would I show you, a hard-arsed cop?'

'You bloody did. You, the guy with the great memory.'

Lester's home is a rundown terrace with an iron filigree frontage above the porch and the first-floor balcony. It is Gothic, as in rusty, unpainted and untended. Unlike any other in the street. Inheritance, he says, his parents. How about that! That it looks more like a rooming house than a terrace makes Trevor unexpect-edly happy. It belongs to someone he knows. Usually these buildings are so renovated they are rounded up to the extra million by some hateable stranger who strides from the front door and drives off in a BMbloodyW.

Inside, the house is warm but empty. Heat not homeliness. Trevor stops in surprise. The corridor is hung with paintings: con-temporary work, some of it. There are more in the open lounge area.

'Lester! Do you collect art? You sly bastard. You of all people, it just doesn't … You were playing me.'

'Jesus, Trevor, and here I am thinking you're the one who reckons there's more to people. Not just black and white, like most coppers.'

'Most people.'

'Yeah, as it happens, I collect paintings.'

'What about this triptych? I've never seen that style before. It's really strange. Who's that by?'

'Not really a triptych, mate, more a naughty threesome. Yeah, well, what do you think of them?'

Trevor stands where the three paintings are hanging together. They are dark, almost grimy from a profusion of lines criss-crossed into their surfaces, with a mosaic of sudden colours somehow escaping or nearly escaping from this net. It looks like a Bacchanalian orgy. Bodies, tables, faces?

'Hard work doing this, obsessive work. Such a small scale, almost miniature. The detail, though, not so much tight images, as … tight.'

'Intense focus, almost primitive in style. They work together.'

'You might be surprised, or maybe not, to know that I painted them.'

'You what? *You* did?'

'Yep.'

If Lester is unexpectedly pleased with this bit of entrapment, wrong-footing Trevor, he is also displeased to have his talent questioned. Except it isn't, and the unexpected, which is, is its own reality.

'Come on,' he says.

He walks through to the rear level overlooking the garden and they stand in the sunlight. Next door he hears and sees what looks like universal family chaos. Loud voices, as children run around and complain and call out for food and yell at Mrs Next-door who is just audible, too, wherever she is and someone explains something with great irony and impatience and a radio begins and a girl with black hair says 'Hello Dad' and rushes into another room.

'Bit of an orgy been happening here, too. I can't remember if you had any children, Lester?' Trevor asks over the lessening din. He sees for the first time that the man's face is quite lined, oddly noticeable in this late sunlight.

'Don't need 'em, I've got a dozen next door.'

'Sure.'

'Oh, one or two, somewhere about. Lost contact. My biggest sin. Par for the course in cop work, as you know. If someone does a Koori genealogy around my line a few names will pop up.'

And that style of painting. ... 'What do you mean *about*, why does everyone say *about* about children, I mean the specific numbers? My landlady's daughter is *about* 23, and she lived with her husband for *about* ... You can't have *about* one or two kids. Sin? You're not a Catholic.'

'Why? I'm not, as you know, a stay-at-home kind of man.'

'Well, your neighbours are. They need these multi-storey terraces just to house them all. How many children do they have?'

'Nine, I think, from 16 all the way down to 3.'

'It's a rabbit hutch.'

'Yeah. Depressing, eh?'

Lester checks the glasses by holding them up to the sunlight. The back door opens next door and a boy in high-school uniform saunters into view, backpack slung over one shoulder, mobile in his right hand.

On his walk back Trevor passes the pub he's never been to: a UFC pub, with loads of patrons dressed in singlets and swearing and music way louder than his head likes. None of it being what he likes. Two kids the size of dining-room chairs fly round the corner as if someone has chucked them, and after stumbling into him run back to where they came from.

'Carm'ere, you bloody kids,' yells a female voice. When Trevor turns the corner he sees a woman in white slacks rising awkwardly from a pavement stool which looks like a toadstool under her massive bottom, and she big all over, hunched forward with a bag strap pressing between two vast breasts in a shrunk-on mauve T-shirt. She stands with legs planted apart like a bloke drinking a stubbie with his mates.

'Carm'ere, you little brats, you bloody well do like I say. Hey!' she shouts as one boy runs past her towards the cul-de-sac beside the pub. Trevor continues on. It is in fact perfectly safe there, few cars appear except occasionally to do a slow T-turn.

'Keep 'em in order, will ya,' says a bloke sitting near her, half in a growl and half in resignation, his belly large with beers and issuing sundry 'G'day, mate's.

Up to her then. She smiles at Trevor as he passes, sucks heavily on her fag. *Oh, suffer the little children.*

Today there is no one eating inside the pub, just UFC posters on the windows showing absurdly aggro faces, and advertisements for gambling nights repeated alongside him for the twelve paces it takes him to walk past the four windows. Trevor knows there is disproportion in the world or else no one would know anything. *Comparisons*, his head says to him, *are decisions. Not always good ones.*

Lester can actually paint, and they are good paintings. This opens a gap in Trevor he hasn't felt before. It astounds him, it also makes him feel naïve. Naïve is also the style of the paintings, knowingly or not. Lester has said he was never trained; he's more like the crims he's put behind bars who take up painting in their cells. Full of emotion and grunt. Over time, something more distinctive emerges.

Before going home, Trevor visits the IGA. And there she is again, in her black dress, the Russian woman who isn't. She is sitting with her legs tucked to one side of her like an artist's model, next to the wide doorway. Her face is mottled with dust or sun or something he cannot explain.

Perhaps she thinks people don't see her when they walk past without stopping, or they see her too well and she haunts them.

She is, perhaps they are, ghosts of the divide, where having/not having makes everyone defensive. He's no different. Except she is no one's neighbour, hasn't half a dozen kids, has no address to write down.

He shuffles his bags as he speaks to her, though what to say? She knows more about the weather than anyone. When he pulls out and gives her $10 she grabs the note and shoves it into her sleeve. And starts crying.

～

The publisher has given her number to the new author Martina had recommended Elizabeth edit. Shia Newman. She is keen to pick Elizabeth's brains and will, by the sound of it, be ringing her very soon. This means Elizabeth is going to have the manuscript after all. She is *happy*, so happy she grabs Gordon up onto her chest and hugs him until he struggles to be released. This is not his preferred form of love.

Elizabeth's mobile plays its short waltz tune and Gordon is, even worse, briefly swung around in waltz time until she lowers him to the floor and he skitters off. Yes, it's her: this Shia girl is in a hurry. To introduce herself and, she explains, because they have told her Elizabeth was brought up in a sect, which is awesome, so valuable as a primary source.

If it were true, and if the sect had been the abusive and mind-robbing kind, then her wording might have been unfortunate. Zeal is single-minded.

Elizabeth begins to correct Shia's understanding, which she realises has come through Martina selling the idea, but she must do so without losing the conversation, especially this early.

'My mother was a sannyasin,' she says. 'I was among them for a year or two even if I didn't live on the commune. I can tell you everything I know. Use whatever you find useful. I don't mind, and I'll be reading it through anyway. I wasn't captive in any way, the Rajneeshees weren't that kind of sect, or cult, and that's where the issue immediately gets messy. Those terms "sect" and "cult". They don't always help.'

'Ah, I'm so glad you say that. It's totally confusing,' says Shia, her voice almost jumping through the phone. Because some groups are simply *sui generis*, like The Family, children who were being groomed by the woman who said she was Jesus Christ. Anne Hamilton-Byrne. She stole children and drugged them with LSD and huge doses of psychiatric drugs. She bleached their hair white and cut it in a bob so the children would think they were siblings. They looked like aliens.

'God knows how they survived, and being starved, and beaten. It wasn't religion, they were meant to re-educate the world after the Apocalypse. That's a kind of Doomsday scenario, or it seems to be, except the woman was a sociopath who couldn't have children of her own and who stole millions from the servile adults. Just another crook.

'Have you read it yet?' she adds.

'No, I haven't even received it. Things usually move … more slowly. They gave you my number because it's a work in progress, so to speak, and because I was OK with … discussing it so soon.'

'I'm jumping in too fast.'

'No, not really,' Elizabeth laughs. 'Maybe a bit. Are you including that sort of detail you mentioned? You will need to be clear about what kind of narrative you're writing if you want to fit … information in.'

'That's why I'm making it a novel, so anything goes, doesn't it?!'

Elizabeth doesn't say anything. But she explains her mother, the Rajneesh phenomenon. How sects are seen to be offshoots of mainstream religions, heretical or purist or alternative … whereas cults are based around the deep belief and following of a charismatic person with religious, political or social vision. Or mystical.

Or terrorist. They both emanate from powerful leaders so it blurs the difference. Neither option quite defined the Orange People. Charismatic leader, yes, but the Bhagwan encouraged his sannyasin to question their lives and religion, and follow him only if they wanted to. It was subversive socially *and* religiously because they talked mysticism but practised non-stop fucking. No one went out bombing the public, but they disdained the public. People were free to come and go, no one was brainwashed unless they were just susceptible. Lots were: he ran a cult of personality worship. Yes. He mesmerised them. Absolutely.

Sects have rules and punishments to enforce obedience, like the stories of members being chastised, ostracised, even beaten, and children being punished. The Bhagwan was being dreamy in India and if the sannyasin neglected children it was by having *no* boundaries at all, *no* rules, nothing. Her mother just ignored her. Elizabeth observed them in their Narcissism and drug-taking and knew they were high on it, but the personal and sexual wildness they called exploration often resulted in dramas of disloyalty and hurt (which had to be played down) and pregnancies for the women. *And were the children preyed upon? Ah ...*

In bed that night she replays their conversation, aware Shia had been writing it all down. The shock of Hamilton-Byrne, who she'd forgotten about. The Bhagwan seemed mild in comparison. The long-haired, oversexed men and women, her mother, the children. That dismissive attitude of the Rajneeshees, worse if they were in your face like that, and how it jarred with her wanting to be a gymnast. When her mother decided to join the ashram in the southwest it became intolerable. 'The Bhagwan is coming!' her mother had cried. She had to go. Elizabeth had to go, everyone had to go! To live in the children's shed where just about anything might happen, and live among the risk of some men who enjoyed grooming girls (not that "grooming" was a term used back then, and not for post-Apocalyptic but pre-adult sex). Or, in a judgemental tone, her mother saying if that's what she felt then bloody well stay in Fremantle with the other kids, it hardly mattered which.

What mattered was the adults' path with the Bhagwan.

As if Elizabeth should simply abandon gymnastics because her mother saw God in the guru's inverted commas.

Life and death among the holy people. What begins in freedom ends in force.

Part Two

Part Two

NOW TREVOR RE-WORKS the apartment canvases to revive them. And himself. He had worked as well as he could in the spare room, it had begun to feel like searching for the high he was sure was still there. Like opening the lid of a tin of house paint to discover how the blood red thrills him again. Like a surgeon said: if you don't feel a thrill when the scalpel slices into the skin, you shouldn't be a surgeon. Yes, Trevor uses house paint. Uses oils and gouache. And photomontage.

Montage is not like still life or portrait or figure painting, a mental image projected onto canvas, not Lucien Fried and his putty colours, a primary factual shape, which the artist imposes then modifies; Trevor finds his imagery with random and chosen edits from publications (not the scalpel, the scissors) and from his careful or slashing drawings, bringing these into collision like words shuffled against each other make unexpected meanings. Unavoidably, not merely shuffling but shunting though photos piques him and freaks him, their wanton emptiness. Magazines, anything that carries illustrations, the larger the better. To make something sharp or serious of them is their punishment. Glossy pics of models, high-rise architecture, traffic, figures in normal poses – normal, the hardest thing to find – why look normal when you can look glamorous and pouting? Trevor glues them down, their glamour momentary, or gone under glam as he paints them in half and mocks them.

The colour vibrates at him, some images lift and others fall back.

This gives him sudden starts, and it risks every false start, as fragments in the physical space shift in the temporal one, the moments of line and shape or mere flurry expose a potential work. Only by this much making, by this much willingness to keep shifting, in however many stages it takes. Open the lid, see it. Keep opening lids. Use the knife on the skin. Then he paints the parts into an emerging whole.

The confined space of that room embarrassed him, especially if Diana stopped at the door to watch. The drop sheet he used was actually a plastic tarpaulin covered with an old sheet, so it crinkled underfoot and annoyed him, until he kept working and was able to ignore it.

There was no ignoring how cramped he was, how awkward he felt having no room to make the required degree of mess. There he was painting in his cell like one of those prisoners who take up painting, or like Lester. Except Trevor, in theory, knew how to.

The fingers, the genius of the wrist, the forearm, the brain. The larger movements. Then the Braille, the actual detail. These cityscapes, loosely geometric and oddly smudged – he's big on smudge – begun then, in the months before he left her. Some areas left raw, the primed canvas showing through. Fitting, really. As is obscuring faces, bodies, settings. Painting into a kind of paint-streaked shock of half realist, half nightmare memory. Or something like haunting.

Now, for longer hours then were possible before, he paints in Elizabeth's shed. The studio. Big changes. He cannot do any of this as an amateur, to crimp down into naivety, to have that excuse. He knows too much – and therefore he must succeed or fail as a professional. *Bloody Lester, what would he know?*

Sometimes the long auburn shape of Gordon sits with Trevor when he paints. And he has been painting most nights, the labours of painting are concentrating him into imagery and carrying the past out and dumping it on the median strip. Elizabeth hasn't mentioned his probation once, which he presumes is a good thing.

At first he wanted the paint uniform, smooth. He can't stand the Australian trowelling style. Ben Quilty, the Porridge Expressionist. So much of it. Trevor plunges his wide house-painting brush into pots of paint, lays some thick, some in washes. Gashes, gaps, lines of hiatus. No one pretty uniformity.

Qualia, the raw, sensory experience. He is trying to force breaks in the space-time the imagery refers to – people frozen, or speeding – so the static images are smudged, interrupted, people in streets of the '40s get contemporary fashion poses, and repeated so often they drown in commonality.

Some canvases look sexual, some industrial, media-arty-type. His fusions blended thus can have a crime-scene feel. Frank Miller. A mash-up of glam and industry and sleaze. This retraces his imagery from years behind a desk he doesn't tell anyone about. Strange human faces seem to hover nearby like wilder things from Hollywood or *Doctor Who*. Not ghouls, souls. Some faces are living, emotional, some zombified.

It was genealogy of a kind, like those gunshots into Poland. Diasporas. Uncanny, perhaps. Sufficiently visible to discern human features but somehow vaporous, ambiguous and, set against the solidity of solid objects, un-nerving.

If his work were compared to tailoring, his shapes are not close-fitting suits, immaculately cut, but oddments from a Salvos store.

If he is excited, he is also panicked: the familiar adrenaline begins to surge in him. Even when turning back to reckon through this imagery of his rebirth it *is* exciting, it irrupts through his armchair-in-a-bookshop life, the sedentary of sedentary.

Thank God painting became respectable again. Space for artists who go by feel, intuition, colour. The usual. Artists need intelligence but some painters just find it. Some are dim and find it. They get there. If there is a there. His getting there wasn't an accident, he chose to do this; it *was* an accident that scrambled his head and stopped him.

Some days earlier Elizabeth had sneaked a look at his work. No one is expecting Trevor to bloom as a backyard Van Gogh. Not even Trevor. But what *has* he been doing? If he was doing any-thing. *Perhaps he was out there reading.* There are paintings, someone did them.

Now, for the first time Elizabeth comes out to watch him actually painting. Several works are turned away and several more exposed.

His brush is turning in orange paint like stirring a tiny pot of sauce. As he upturns it to inspect the load, she suddenly says:

'There are so *many* faces! It's … bewildering. I like the textures especially, the sensuousness of the actual paint.'

Of the paint, he thinks, still looking at the brush. There are faces, and in clear view, and different, but of no one in particular if *she* is looking. He asks her if she reads his faces as libidinous or concerned or, well, what …? For instance, he notes, the woman he has placed in the foreground of one painting who looks like a blind person, in dislocation from the social world of the people around her. She is sitting like that woman at the IGA, she has a chain. There is a small dog, or something like a dog. All just paint.

'Yes, I can see all that,' she says. 'It's objective.'

Then how does it make her feel?

She says the impact of his work banks up in her. Each painting is so big. And busy. She says how a painting is all there at once, at attention, everywhere you look and you can look everywhere! It's a tautology of itself, being all present all the time. Whereas you read one sentence at a time, running page by page, linear. These moments are fairly seamless, like consciousness is, moving forwards in time. You comprehend its cause and effect and its coherence. Whenever you pause, or put the book down, the awareness of what came before returns into awareness. Reading is always this elegant moving forward then catching up. It accretes.

As if in answer, one painting is skewing shelf above shelf of book spines into something like twisted laddering or fragments of cuneiform. His shop, his shape-changing.

'The faces are of public people,' he says, 'and people I've seen from around here. So each face in the overall picture has a story. They're barely even likenesses. Tell me if you can recognise anyone.'

Are they faces Elizabeth knows but cannot name? Are some of her? What does a portrait of her look like to her?

Then she sees him smirking.

'Jesus, Trevor,' she says, and walks inside.

Above them the clouds are slowly moving south. He feels the autumn sunlight increase through the acrylic section of sheer roof. Cool, white radiance, no heat in it.

A beam of light stands brightly in front of him like a girder, or a rafter that has fallen loose at one end. Dust floats in the light then out of range, enough lit motes for Trevor to sense this light beam, this standing rafter, as a light body within the soft body of the darkness. Its negative space. The more he stares at the light the less he sees of the studio and nothing at all of his canvases. It is embarrassing: the light/darkness effect is more powerful, more strange, than anything is making.

The lack of speech is where mystery is. Wordlessness.

He walks into the glow. His bald head glowing, eyelashes and brows glowing. The light accepts him, eternal and indifferent.

Inside again, in her familiar spaces, for some reason she remembers standing out there, in her backyard at dawn, and hearing the hot-air balloons overhead. Then they appeared. They were brightly striped and amazingly exuberant for things so silent, and almost intangible, but every so often she heard the soft roar of the gas flaming up, the sigh as the balloons moved further off, then another one or two came drifting over, then more. Her neck began to hurt. *God knows how anyone would cope if the aliens came.* All that happened was Trevor came.

She remembers standing close against the large glass windows on the 30th floor of a tower in the city and seeing maybe as many as ten or twelve hot-air balloons moving slowly towards her. It was the week her long-range boyfriend Richard's novel had been announced on the shortlist of a major book prize and it was an early morning photo shoot of the authors and because she was incidental to this she stood aside, and for half an hour was mesmerised by the balloons as they drifted towards her as if coming straight in, before passing over, above and out of sight.

Elizabeth's wood-floored study is wired for essential uses. It hums and clatters plastically from morning to evening as she pounds her (she is a pounder) PC keyboard with questions, deletions and, occasionally, carefully worded psalms to the authors she is reading over the shoulders of. If they have earned them. Her room is busy with typing and thinking and flurring through pages of the already read and now rewritten, the zipping singsong of her printer and her dappled kinds of correcting.

The room is only just big enough for arguing over stylistic problems – and yet a novel's assorted characters blunder around as well. These men and women occupy a great deal of space in the room.

As an editor she necessarily tinkers. Words, phrases, punctuation. Tenses. Most clichéd of all, and yet visceral as a paper cut, is the editorial cut. Cut! cut! cut! Immediacy is not at the expense of ideas or descriptions, it makes them. And now she will be mindfully inside the authoritarian psyche of sects.

Sometimes the tinkering returns in code at night. This morning she woke holding a dream, of a small cotton bag, inside it a metal plate with about fifteen loose screws and tiny loose bars. The problem was, Did she have a micro-screwdriver to assemble it, something like a watchmaker's or optician's tool? She had the same dream again, this time a worn leather pouch, inside it dozens of tiny gold chains and several small screws, a wristwatch wheel with a ruby hub.

Another kind comes back to her: she is sitting alone at her desk and a stern author stands behind her talking onto the top of her head. *How dare she make these marks they are both staring at, cuts and scratches, in the desk, like a cyborg mouse desperate for food?*

Sometimes she imagines her manuscripts as essential services, like the water which began as high rain pours down into the reservoirs and aquifers before streaming through pipes and stations until she stands beneath it, still on its way elsewhere, falling from the shower rose.

Sometimes it *is* emergency services. Heavy rain, a broken roof. Clearing the kerbside mess. Pulling bodies out of wrecks.

~

The subdued dawn light above the long park and the trees is quietly amazing and seeing it is humbling without any search for meaning, it might be said. Magpies warble their counterpoint in the branches. An occasional crow sounds lazy even this early in the day. Elizabeth and Trevor are taking Gordon to his usual Royal Park track and to meet, as always, the neighbourhood dogs. After the first weeks she has talked Trevor into accompanying her. 'Think of it as exercise. As a way of getting to know each other,' she said, 'without sitting down and drinking anything.' For his company, in fact. She is taking more liberties as she becomes more used to him. *What a quickly accepted habit*, she thinks, *on her part at least*, meaning she was lonely after all.

By now she even knows Trevor's body smell. Sharing a kitchen, handing him a drink, brief but olfactory moments. When clothes at certain movements are further from the skin and the now familiar scents waft out. Which most people don't notice. She does. Occasionally, inevitably, they bump together, reach across each other, touch. It can happen showing a stranger a map on a mobile phone, so in a shared kitchen the floor size of a double bed it is routine.

Walking the dog, to be fair, means only if he wants to, but in these windless autumn mornings what could be more beautiful? The sun, the cool air, sounds of dogs and calls of conversation, a walker's laugh from a hundred metres away, the grunts and footfalls of a woman running up behind them then passing, the material of her tights shining. Elizabeth and Trevor, two uncoupled adults, then, are playing a twosome as they walk around the park, and who would think otherwise, as they talk or don't talk, and as the brown dog keeps racing far away from them, then back, like the arguments and agreements of couples? Their worthwhile and slightly uncomfortable joke. On the way back home he lets her get slightly ahead and observes her.

She walks as if the sunlight moves with her down the path and the shadow stays well behind. Only then does he become aware of the smile on his face, as if nodding his head in agreement to some unasked question.

What Trevor has been adjusting to – after their initial and mutual awkwardness –feeling less than free wandering anywhere at any time in the house, in any state of undress. This is especially the case in summer, his season of walking unclothed or in a *longyi* as the body thrives on skin-to-air contact. At first Elizabeth was nervously territorial. *Comic, really*, he thinks, *given it was her idea, that she has advertised to have a complete stranger enter her world.* 'Enter her fold,' she once said. You don't have to be a linguist to know that sounds a bit Freudian. His grin was smothered just in time.

He finds himself sitting on the edge of his bed, considering a room when once he had a house. At least he has all of the basement floor. He still feels a dullness which he puts down to grief for a marriage winding off its centre. Or off his centre. It is heavy and embarrassing, the irrevocable shame of it.

On and off, then, he is feeling estranged. Then becalmed. On these same tree- and bird-lined streets. Lorikeets and fruit bats, day shriekers and night flappers. If not exactly bird flights, then winged possums, flapping mammals in the darkened streets, so very odd to think about at night. He is now an inner-city dweller and cohabiter. It is a new form of self-consciousness. Being with Elizabeth prevents him becoming an isolate.

So, after closing the shop at the end of each day, he comes home and they sit and talk. The days pass regardless. He becomes accustomed to living in her house. There is an invisible space he moves into and it calms him, at times he feels like a tourist skimming effortlessly along pavements on a Segway, moving and talking, seemingly unreal.

Trevor is sitting on her back verandah – he has a chair now, beside hers – when the phone rings. She goes inside briefly then returns with a large bowl of crisps and the cordless phone pinched under her right ear and shoulder like a tiny violin.

She points at Trevor then at the chips, then nods and murmurs and says words such as 'Is that so?' or 'Amazing' or even the extended 'Really, he didn't, did he?' The caller is obviously her mother. Mrs Sermon can provoke 'Yes, Mum, I completely agree, Mum' by punishing at a mundane level, preaching the beauties of a flat life. Her calls are one-directional – they feature the weather and the nice neighbour with little kiddies, not the awful neighbours with the boat and the welding machine and what the little kiddies wear and what they were thinking of doing on the weekend. But whereas most phone hogs gab on without listening, Mrs Sermon will stop without warning, to ask Elizabeth her opinion, checking she is still there and following this eccentric waffle.

Every few minutes Elizabeth walks over, picks up a crisp, crunches it noisily and with her mouth open. God only knows what powers of self-absorption her mother has not to notice the acoustics. As the bowl of crisps empties, this casual mischief becomes very funny, then annoying, then funny again. She doesn't always do it.

Elizabeth places the cordless on loudspeaker, while she checks something on her laptop. Lately her mother's memory has been haphazard, she spoke in non sequiturs before recovering. It was unexpected and sudden. Now she complains she has mislaid her Casio, the lovely Casio keyboard she wanted for singing something the other day and went searching for and couldn't find it anywhere and, do you know, for the first time she realised just how hard it is finding anything amongst the carefully collected items, not clothing, not in boxes but among the appliances otherwise not musical. *If Elizabeth has seen the Casio on her visits could she let her old mum know where ...*

Elizabeth is silent. The constant brand name is annoying her.

She tells herself: *My mother is a talkbot.*

Silent, but not from duty or boredom as usual, from this question regarding the keyboard, its worrying amnesia. Nor does her mother remember when Elizabeth reminds her, she borrowed (the bloody Casio) and wrapped it in *green* bubble wrap – she makes much of the colour, her mother likes colour – such an elaborate parcel, like a coffin, remember? *She* had said it looked like a green coffin ... and it's now here. *Wasn't this memorable? Unforgettable?* Nothing.

Maybe her mother is losing her grip. Old people can wake one morning feeling much the same as the morning before, unaware that during the night the bureaucratic sidekick of Death has come to their brain and left a permanent black redaction. Elizabeth blows air through her lips. She has full lips and would never make this exasperated pout in public even if she can do it almost silently. It is for her relief alone.

In ten minutes her old mother (so long ago *née* randy sannyasin) has forgotten she rang about the keyboard and begins going over the little kiddies again and her sciatica corns irritable cough and how there is nothing there really is nothing worth watching on television any more. This universal complaint by old people.

Someone is knocking at the house next door. Barking from Gordon. Saved by the chance to tell a fib, Elizabeth says she has a visitor and her mother, who is annoyed to be interrupted so soon, changes her tone (hearing 'Shut-tup … Gordon!') after a bump ('Gordon!') and (I'm coming!) keeps talking. Elizabeth is forced to stall her, say 'Someone is here, Mum'; *she has to go, she will ring back tomorrow*. Intending nothing of the sort, she shuts down the call.

'Sorry about that,' she calls out to Trevor, when she resumes her seat. He has gone back into the studio.

'Oh God. Over for another week. The old fucking tyrant.'

Which makes him jump with laughter.

'A world of dissatisfaction,' she explains. 'The state of the weather. You know that saying "All good", for her it's "All bad". It's this or that or this *and* that … Even the way the locals drive too close to her when she wanders down to the shops.'

Trevor looks around the edge of the studio door at her, then walks back to the house.

'They drive too close to her?' he repeats. 'On the pavement?'

'Oh, no. The road. She always walks on the road.'

'What?'

'She thinks pavements are too uneven, she might have a fall and be lying there for hours before anyone finds her.'

'Worse than someone running her over? How old is your mother? She sounds ancient.'

'Yeah, she does. Oh, I don't know.'

Her resistance to admitting ages. Her daughter's. Now her mother's. Therefore, by simple calculation, her own. Journalists called it being *triangulated*, a word she cuts from any manuscript.

'Mum carries on like a nervous goat sometimes and I get confused,' she says, vaguely. Eightysomething? Seventysomething? She's probably about 75.'

Trevor's eyebrows lift and stay lifted.

'That's a ten-year difference. I've been picturing a batty old hoarding kind of woman with pressure stockings and worrying teeth. I thought she must be nearly 90. Didn't you say she is con-templating euthanasia?'

'Yeah, well, she faffed around when she was young, refused to act her age – then got old quickly.'

She peers into the crisps packet, which is now empty. She explains the memory glitch about the Casio. Then says nothing, preoccupied with the thought of sudden decline. Aged care.

This mother-complaining amuses him. He likes to listen to Elizabeth complaining and the dutiful anarchy of her saying unkind things she both means and doesn't mean about her eccentric, bothersome mother. His own mother had not provided much conversation or eccentricity and had become increasingly cynical. And fat. This he found alarming as he too grew larger than expected. He couldn't complain: hypocrisy is ugly. All the same, why isn't there a label, a warning, on the wrist? *You will get fat.*

Still, Trevor admits one-sided conversations like Mrs Sermon's, which customers indulge in, make him feel like a taxi driver as the doors open and the mad, bland, garrulous, tall, short, fat as bean-bags, sit there raving, and the some who stay silent and seemingly disassociated are, some of them, drunk. At least he never has to hose out the back seat.

'Well, Trevor,' she says, 'now you know what women feel like most of the time.'

She moves back inside, stepping to one side and over the opportunist Gordon who is lying flat in the doorway for maximum attention and nuisance. She returns, stepping neatly back over Gordon while balancing two bottles and a tray of dips. She is so fast on her feet, at handling things, at everything. Hand-eye co-ordination. She must have been …

So finally he asks her if she had been a dancer.

'Not bad,' she says, 'pretty close, most people think so.'

'You're so light and fast and co-ordinated.'

'Not thin and nervy and fussy, then?'

'It's OK by me if you want to be thin and nervous. Just as long as I can be fat and slow and you don't ask me to run around the park chasing Gordon.'

'God, the last thing Gordon wants to do. He'd prefer to stay out here and chew a bone. Eating. Anyway, you're not fat and slow. You're … stocky.'

They laugh at the euphemism.

'Well, Trevor, thinking of the male gaze: when you're young they call you girlish, or willowy, then in your 30s they say slim, by your 40s it's skinny, but a skinny older woman is fast on her way to being a scrag.'

'I like you as you are.'

'You're being very gracious, Trevor. No, when I was young I was a gymnast.'

'Ah. I never even thought of that.'

'No one does. It's much the same. Training and training and more fucking training, and calluses and broken toes and frightening bruises from hitting things and falling off things. And the constant stink – you, them, everyone. Just like ballerinas. They get you young. My mother was off with the bloody Rajneeshees so I got nothing but discouragement from her. My father was a tradie, more physical, and he sort of pushed me. At least it wasn't pole dancing.'

'Your guru-susceptible mother married a tradie?'

She liked sexy men, she tells him. Charismatic men even more than sexy men because the charisma was of a higher level, her mother would say, with such a man she is as perhaps at no other time, able to relinquish her ego. A man like her wonderful bloody Bhagwan Shree Rajneesh. She said he was as smooth as honey but he promised wildness. He talked non-stop and made people's teeth chatter. It should have been from irritation but she said and they all said it was from nervous adoration. Their Kundalini rising. Elizabeth thought it might have been more basic than that. When she was young a sannyasin told her the Bhagwan mentioned love and the Sufis all the time, not the real Sufis – who were famous for rejecting personality worship and spiritual hubris – but the virtual Sufis he projected from his "inner Sufi" over the swooning sannyasin. Her father was more acerbic: he said it was bullshit, they wanted gorgeous gurus, not Sufi tough guys. She had fallen for the wild side.

'She is the colourful one, then, your mum?'

For a while Elizabeth isn't sure if this means she is not. But he is smiling at her like a friend, not a sannyasin. *He meant to use the indefinite article.* She tells him again about the new manuscript she will be developing and how it merges with her own past. Though some sannyasin remained parental and considerate, many of them were so pre-occupied they were guilty of neglect. How she escaped then was only a matter of age and changing circumstances. No authoritarian obedience. Hard to think about it now. In fact her mother could be very loving when she felt like it, and her irreverence made her a lot of fun when other parents, not in the cult, were so po-faced and conventional.

'Mind you,' she adds, 'my mother kept talking about Bhagwan's love. Then she said I was a disappointment, just a boring kid doing bar exercises.'

'Whereas she might have admired your discipline, rigour …?'

'If I had been a Buddhist in a cave, maybe. It's too straight. You are so young when you begin. Then your hormone system goes out of whack. Hardly exploring my sexuality. I didn't even *start* getting tits until I was 17.'

He tries to keep focussed on her eyes.

'Yes, I know, I hardly got them when I did. But I kept growing taller.'

'I don't especially like big tits on a woman.'

'Are you saying my tits are small?' But she is laughing.

'No, they're very nice, probably, just not big.'

She laughs even louder.

'How about your wife?'

'She's got really big tits.'

They are laughing like drunks. Elizabeth bumps back and forth in her chair and her eyes run with tears. They know what her mother said wasn't about love.

She realises she looks forward to Trevor's arrival at the end of each workday. It is satisfying, even flattering. After his shopping beforehand in the local IGA with its ferocious prices for meat and its unhappy girls on the checkouts, walking home and cooking their meal most nights.

Nor, by now, is he in her way, nor she in his. As far as she can tell. Sometimes they hardly see each other after they talk and he has cooked dinner. He stays downstairs, painting. Elizabeth is usually in her study reading through the manuscripts her several publishers send her. Work is never done for the freelancer, who must always say Yes to ensure there is never No. Years ago she learnt that sad truth. The professional parataxis: availability, reliability, slave.

The tenancy deal is working. They get on, they talk, there is no worrying attempt to go further.

Even better – though she doesn't know it – each night, if he gets the chance, Trevor emerges from his studio or the basement, walks over the lawn to the broken-open fence and, checking the neighbour's house is in darkness, empties his bladder in looping streams of piss onto the man's backyard.

~

Over the next few days Elizabeth is feeling unwell. Low blood pressure again. There is something wrong with her. Surely. Like last time, unless she bothers to think about it, when she slumped from internal mysteries, viral probably or, worse, amoebic. Yes, they must have been amoebic.

She begins to worry about the water, the sprinkler she has briefly used in the back garden, inhaling the spray perhaps. Water sitting in the hose warmed up by the sun. Was there something she contracted in the shed when she cleaned it out for Trevor? Her balance is off, she begins to wobble like her glossy setter, like Trevor, which is truly unsettling. If they walked around the park they would all wobble. Again, she worries, she will have to go through her doctor giving her that doubting look and hear those doubting words. *GPs are such a pain, they are so incredulous.*

To blur the indignity a little, she makes an appointment with the optometrist first, doctor second. The optometrist is an optimist, he'll make her feel better. She has to decide whether she will eat something before her appointment or after it, or not at all.

Down in the optometrist's gloomy eye-testing room there is little that is new. The cream-coloured machines are latent with age, hulking, poetic things which suggest nostalgia rather than pain, so never as bad as the brightly lit tools and structures in a dentist's. Which she finds alienating. It is her first visit to actually discuss laser surgery. Normally she shunts this question aside but given this visit is itself a displacement ...

Elizabeth tells him she is pretty anxious about the whole laser surgery thing. She only has two eyes, she says.

He says anxiety is pretty normal – over eyes or teeth, it makes little difference – and her situation hardly compares with those of some patients he's seen. *No, he shouldn't be telling her but …* A particular patient has been seeing him for years. Since the man's right eye is all but useless from the rubella he'd suffered as a child – his dud eye, he calls it – his visits are half the work for the optometrist, but a double anxiety for the patient: rubella predisposes people to early-onset glaucoma.

Recently the man made an emergency appointment to see the optometrist. He was led in by his wife. His good eye was completely plastered over and a bandage was wrapped around his head. He looked like a man from a bombed-out village.

The man explained: when he had driven off from the eighth tee his shot hit the women's tee marker and the ball flew straight back into his eye. His good eye. Now he's truly worried.

Elizabeth finds it hard not to laugh at this weirdly absurdist drama, which makes her eyes well up.

'Now,' says the optometrist, 'that is anxiety. Elizabeth, wipe your eyes' – he hands her a tissue – 'and don't blink. Good. Again. Good. Sooner or later everyone needs glasses. Now, sit over here.'

Elizabeth sits under the testing frame as he swaps lenses.

'Is it better like this? Or like this?'

Slide and click, slide and click as the lenses are rotated in the frame.

'The man looked more like a Francis Bacon,' he says, 'than a man.'

'Great story, but should you be telling me? However, (she points at her eyes) how are mine?'

'Yours are fine. If you're happy with glasses you don't need surgery.'

As if optometry isn't worrying enough, Elizabeth knows she must convince her new doctor. No, she is not a hypochondriac. Her previous doctor thought so. There is something wrong with her system, something she judges or intuits, nothing specific. Fatigue. Then manic energy. Uncertain digestion. On her walk to the local medical centre her thoughts are rolling over in variations of *I can't be sure* and *I can't recall* and *Yes but* ... to avoid incriminating herself, her own Fifth Amendment, as if she were facing a committee. The day is sunny, without warmth unless you're a lizard on a fence. By the time she is there it has become overcast and the southwesterly starts blowing off the Bay. *Cold as calamity. Nothing like a cold day in Melbourne*, she thinks, as if the cold is a harbinger of this malaise she is worrying over.

In the waiting room she sits and reads a silly glossy magazine of Photoshopped women pouting, and more pouting, or with diamonds and coffee and pouting. *Has she been bitten by one of those white-tailed-spider things during her burst of shed clearing?* No, she can't feel any bites on her skin. *Has she succumbed to a food allergy?* Her bowel habits haven't changed – they are always odd – so that's ambiguous. *Lyme disease? Malaria? Are there bloody mosquitoes in the neighbour's backyard, in the pools near the taps where even tadpoles wouldn't procreate?*

Above her the TV channel describes how women recovering from endometrial cancers do better on placebos than on universally ingested herbal cures. In fact they don't do anything on the herbal cure. Except lose their money. *Why*, she thinks, *doesn't the herbal cure have at the very least its own placebo effect?*

She is to see Dr Eli Chen. Not as young as Elizabeth expected. Being Chinese, Dr Chen asks about everything her patients do from walking to shitting. She is thorough and what she perceives sitting in front of her is a strangely controlled woman. Blood pressure very low but variable and, given the "white coat effect", as she explains, this is very unusual. *Diet?*

And so the saga begins.

Elizabeth leans into it: describes her food, its presentation and when she eats, how much and the difficulty of sticking to this tested and, she is certain, excellent regimen. Healthy, happy, almost wise. Her wild dietary history. She means her diet before Trevor arrived. Eating his food in the last weeks is just an indulgence and she isn't going to any more.

'Elizabeth,' says her doctor, 'you may have an adrenal problem. Or thyroid. Have you been gaining weight recently?'

Her patient is unwilling to say so at first, then admits that she is, she cannot understand why, putting on weight. It makes her feel, er, guilty. *Since when is doing the right thing the wrong thing? Or is this the Trevor effect?*

'Have you,' asks Dr Chen, 'ever heard of anorexia nervosa?'

'Come on, I don't have anything like that. I'm not like that. I'm careful – OK, determined, not demented.'

'Yes, I see, yes, however, I asked because there is another somewhat related condition or syndrome. Known as orthorexia nervosa.'

'Ortho- as in ...' she almost coughs '... orthodox?'

'Quite so. Perhaps you obsess over the correctness of your diet and then worry if you can't keep up. You feel you must at all times be eating the right food? Do you ever feel like that? Ah. You do. Lapses aren't like sins, unless they make you feel that way! Elizabeth, you might be worrying about healthy eating so much it's making you unhealthy.'

The paradoxical absurdity of this sinks in. *She is a food moralist?? She eats with an overly strict sense of the right and wrong ways of foods, ways of eating, when and how much and ...? What a ridiculous thing, let alone a ridiculous thing to suffer from. She is both puppeteer and puppet?*

'So, do you blame yourself if you aren't keeping to it?'

'I might do.'

If no one had suggested this of Elizabeth she might have considered other people weird enough to have it. But not herself. *Is she inclined to feel bad after breaking her regimen?* No. Well, yes. *Could this be deemed a form of ... self-loathing?* Guilt, maybe. *Guilt comes from where?*

She bends forwards and puts her head in her hands. *She is making herself sick? Jesus Christ, no faffing about with this doctor.*

'I feel pretty up all the time,' says Elizabeth, sitting up to prove it. 'Bouncing, in fact. I have, someone said, a bounding insouciance.'

Her working-with-it doctor has never heard of bounding insouciance. It makes her smile. She types it into Elizabeth's file then turns back to her.

'Yes, that's a danger sign.'

'You're *joking*. Of what?'

'Excessive adrenaline in your system. You're high. I strongly suggest you add more carbohydrates to your meals. No, no, don't shake your head. Paleo, for example, is not a proven nutritional diet even if celebrity chefs spruik it. The Chinese have been eating healthily for millennia and – we eat anything! But in balance. Yin and yang, yes? Not God and certainly not any caveman nonsense.'

'It's not God with me. Or caveman.'

'OK. You've never had a, um, religious attitude to food? Has your family?'

'Not recently.'

Why, oh why, must the adrenalised image of the Bhagwan leap into attention, or is he a guru with thyroidal brown eyes? A long white beard. Beads and beans. Platters of vegetarian food. Beans, grains, the '80s pre-cooking show offerings plated without any gritty piles of ancient grains, exotic grains, South American grains. Her mother's life and the current editing. This will keep on recurring now, she supposes. *Flashbacks. Returns.*

On the way home Elizabeth walks around the corner of the hotel with serviced apartments. A young couple are shouting at each other.

He: 'You care more about a photo of you now than you did about a photo of my brother who was dying.'

She: 'But he didn't die, did he, so it's not the same.'

He: 'That is so selfish. I still feel so bad about that.'

She: 'It isn't the same.'

He: 'You just want to make an argument out of everything.'

She: 'What? You started this by jumping back in time to your brother. Two years ago! We're here, Joe, in the street. It's fucking Friday!'

Elizabeth hurries away, still hearing the crossfire if not the words. The scary unseen things. For some reason she begins seeing the dark leather pouch she dreamt of recently, and inside it tiny chains, or were they lengths of the finest necklace, links like golden quinoa? *To be walking in the fresh morning air and see this shadowy, intimate image. Quinoa!*

Not that she tells anyone. She has many dreams like this. She is sure the imagery represents the fine interlocking worry of editing. Pouches and delicate chainwork are not for sharing, they will fall apart upon speaking.

Elizabeth turns and looks at Trevor without reaction, her arms full of books. She places them in two piles on a swivel chair. Trevor is standing there after closing the front door. She looks blank. His arm goes back and he throws a plasticky dog toy across to her, but instead of catching it she bats it away into the kitchen.

'What the hell is that?' she shouts. 'For fuck's sake.'

'It's me,' he says, waving his hand. 'Trevor. It's a fetch toy I bought for Gordon on his walks. Is your face thing still happening?'

'Jesus, Trevor! You could have given me some warning before throwing the bloody thing at me! You, I could recognise you anywhere. You're easy.'

Not for the first time he isn't sure if she is being affectionate or belittling him. He is aware of simply standing there, watching her, looking away, looking back, as she shoves the books on the chair. The dog toy is abandoned in the kitchen. *Where is Gordon when you need him?*

'How?' he asks her.

She makes a hand gesture like slurring Auslan down towards his leg.

'And you tilt your head to the right. You smile too much.'

'I what?'

But she shrugs. Then she pushes the swivel chair on castors all the way into her study and begins unpacking the books. She isn't well. She tends to be blunt. She is woman enough to admit it, without deciding if perhaps she shouldn't do it. People can't see themselves much or are blind to the little they can see. She didn't say his head was big and shiny.

'Did you know there are super-recognisers?' Trevor says to her, rather loudly to make sure she hears, and to recover some balance. 'Like supertasters in the wine business.'

No reaction.

'Who remember *every* face they've seen. Even decades later. Even from passing someone in the street. Even out of context.'

'It's a spectrum then?' she says, emerging again.

'Facial recognition? Yeah. Must be.'

'Like autism.'

'Well. Yes, I suppose so. It turns out – funny, eh – that you're at the bottom end and I'm at the top end. I seem to have high visual retention.'

'So do I, Trevor. Just not for faces.'

Her voice is as edged as the hardbacks she has been shifting.

'And what's this thing about top and bottom? I don't like hierarchical metaphors. A spectrum is horizontal and it's about time people – you – realised it.'

He looks at her for a few seconds, her expression fierce, then nods: her voice was as sure as her distinction. *His own silly fault*, she thinks, *trying one-upmanship and this time it's worse than his comment about magpies having facial recognition. Fucking magpies? And super-bloody-recognisers? Is he trying to be funny by making some point?*

'OK,' he says. 'We are … at opposite ends.'

'For faces.'

Downstairs he is uncertain what to make of this. It matters that he does. By the time he has re-emerged Elizabeth is unconcerned, trying to arrange some flowers in a vase for her room. Over the days he will learn her better, and consider his place in this. That she is tart at times means little, he comes to see that she is quickly buoyant, melding into equanimity as if nothing has happened. *Just carry on, Trevor*, says his keeper self.

Within days he is pestering her about eating more. Perhaps she shouldn't have told him what the doctor said. Now there *is* someone to cook the meals she might as well succumb, as against crunching her rye bread and tahini paste or green salad and nuts and/or a sliver of steamed fish, or splurging on too much steak. He has been cooking every night and joshing her to eat as much as she likes, playing the TV chef 'Come on, you'll love it, mm, mmm, delicious if I say so myself'.

'When I first saw you, you were weak from hunger.'

'I was not.'

'You were in a faint. You collapsed against my shop window like one of those poor starving women in Dickens' London. You were a waif.'

He looks her up and down.

'I am suggesting food, not salvation. You have JWs doing their endless door-knocking around here if you want that. Mind you – they might be wowsers but even they look well fed.

'And,' he adds, 'remember you told me you didn't drink.'

'When did I tell you that?'

'When you collapsed on my window.'

'Stop saying I collapsed. I said I didn't drink brandy.'

She knows if she eats more of his meals she will enjoy it, even if it is the wrong food, and therefore she gets annoyed with him.

Feeling guilty is something she will have to get over. It tastes of weakness, a niggling sense of being trapped.

With him cooking every night the kitchen has become territory – his – and he behaves as if she must queue to use it. Insidious usurpation. Something as chemical-sounding as that, the chemistry of ooze. He complains about her ladles, or lack of them, her knives. The new Dick knife she has bought.

'Why did you buy another vegie knife?' he said recently, testing the blade for sharpness against his thumb. 'Instead of something useful.'

'Because you keep using it to cut up garlic.'

'I do not – it's for fruit and nothing else.'

'Nonsense, I cut a banana recently and it stank of garlic. Garlic and fruit do not go together and it's my kitchen.'

'You probably cut it on the garlic corner of the cutting-up board.'

'On what? *The garlic corner* ? On my cutting-up board? I can't believe we're having this conversation.'

'You like things being done your way?'

'Trevor, I have lived alone for … years. With no one else here to do things, they *are* done my way.' (She knows she is fudging it.)

'You hardly use the board. I cook most of the meals. By now.'

In fact he keeps all the knives in a high state of sharpness. Like his tricks.

When cooking an Indonesian rendang he always browns the meat in dazzling oil before adding it to the mix, always cooks the garlic/onion/ginger and a knob of intensely smelly belacan shrimp paste (his optional addition) for twenty minutes to remove the raw flavour which home cooks leave behind in curries.

Thus he makes the house stink. He always does. Just a different house.

He places the casserole in the oven, lid on at first, then off, then reduces the sauce on the stovetop. Down to a rich palm-sugar pleasure. The other meals he cooks are Chinese-style or European.

He has restocked her cupboards with spices and bottles of sauces, different kinds of soya.

'I knew someone who called their dog Soya Sauce,' she says, watching him select a bottle. The colour. 'It ended up as Soyuz, like the Russian rockets. Which means "union", apparently ...'

It's just the dodging around him in her small kitchen that tires her. He is always cooking something. Worse than having a mother or an in-law take over. Her own mother calls her a caterpillar. No wonder: she tends to eat raw and green. Grab it, eat it. Otherwise the stupid guilty feelings.

He makes her his Sichuan variation on Hainanese chicken rice. To a pot of water he adds sliced and bruised ginger, garlic, a cinnamon stick and a handful of star anise. *Lovely little star anise*, he always thinks, so geometrical he is reluctant to use the neatest ones – but what else are they for, craftwork?). Finally he adds soya light sauce, rice wine, spring onions, a shake or so of five-spice powder. And several dried chillies. He loves these dried chillies even more than star anise, less perfect in form but far more sensuous: the depth of their reddish colours, the full curve of the seed case. Rubies.

Once the liquid has simmered for several minutes he reduces the temperature, eases a whole chicken into the liquid (or a portioned duck if he feels like duck) and simmers it for twenty minutes before turning the heat off, covering the pot and leaving the chicken to take in all the flavours. The proteins cook without firming, the flesh is succulent yet safe.

Waiting to one side are his chopping block and heavy steel cleaver.

For the meal he serves the chicken brushed with sesame oil then chopped through Chinese-style, with rice and a bowl of the chicken broth. Greens steamed on the side. He makes his own chilli sauce and a ginger, spring onion and rice vinegar sauce. A dash of sugar.

Too awkward to be on opposite sides of the table, she sits at the end and he on her left. As it's a chopsticks-and-bowls meal the table is set with the chicken in the middle alongside the steamed greens, and rice between them. He positions the ginger sauce near her and a small bowl of his chilli sauce in front of him.

It looks simple and smells too beautiful to feel trapped – 'The broth alone will cure you of everything!' he says – so Elizabeth has agreed to eat. Only half coerced, only half trapped. Yes, Doctor. (But what will she feel like in the morning?)

This is where my life is, she thinks, *a point halfway?*

On Sunday Martina stops off to pick up Elizabeth before they drive up to Trentham for the traditional-crafts festival. At Elizabeth's suggestion, Martina has come inside to inspect Trevor. She is a colleague, an editor of non-fiction books for one of the big publishers. They have known each other for years. *She can run her editorial eye over the man*, thinks Elizabeth, *looking for fact not fiction.*

From his basement room Trevor has heard Martina's arrival and the sound of voices. He moves up the stairs then stops and sits. They are in the lounge discussing a friend they have in common, a journalist dying from some kind of brain cancer. Too many stressful overseas postings, in his case. How long has it taken for authorities to recognise that foreign correspondents and city journalists may suffer from – Elizabeth has already uttered the words "post-traumatic stress disorder" – that condition again?

'Diet can't help him now,' she adds. 'There are tumour-like tiny headphones in his brain.'

She is ignoring the possibility her own kind of stress might originate in her eating regimen. It's a wayward kind of contrast. *Orthorexia nervosa. Brilliant. She might be in the next* DSM!

Elizabeth is dodging in and out of denial.

No, she doesn't over-control her eating, not really, not for a minute did she think Dr Chen ate "just anything". Dr Chen was, and it suited her, slightly plump. Controlled not obsessive eating, her body was saying to Elizabeth. See, *I am what I eat*, happy happy cliché. Her previous doctor was Indian, and plump. She explains all this to Martina, whose body has softened with early middle age. Which is sexy, not skinny and not fat. What does *she* eat?

'Doctors have it in for slim women who come to see them,' Martina says. 'And they are not a sensual people, the Chinese.'

'I'd keep that one quiet. Anyway, Dr Chen isn't. She's very serious. I call her The Chen. Did I tell you her first name is Elizabeth? She calls herself Eli. My previous doctor smiled a lot and that has to mean something. Though exactly what I'm not sure. It was reassuring. Just as well, given all the places she looked.'

'I usually prefer doctors who don't have Caucasian backgrounds. I never went to your Indian doctor. What happened to her?'

'Oh, I felt like a change.'

Martina tilts her head and says nothing. Elizabeth pretends not to notice.

'Now I can't even remember her name. Pria something something something. Sort of sensual.'

'Oh, good,' says Martina, 'if it's true. I heard somewhere that Indian people are way more uptight than their erotic forebears. As far as I can see, *Tantra* is for women's magazines.'

'Or in those New Agey bookshops where the incense is enough to kill you.'

Somehow this conversation has digressed, which seems to suit both women.

'And they don't eat meat,' says Elizabeth.

'They do eat meat, sweetie, they don't eat cattle. They love big brown eyes, like yours and mine.'

Martina knows what Elizabeth knows and between them they know men fall for their eyes fast. Her own face is curvy and fleshy now, quite different from Elizabeth's strikingly straight features. If anyone tends to the bovine and sacred it is herself, and given her olive skin she could, almost, look Indian.

'We are fine women, Elizabeth,' she adds. 'So what if you are slim and I am plump? Well, good for us. All the same, you should listen to this new doctor.'

Martina has always seemed so strong. All that regular diet of facts. And working with writers, she has said to Elizabeth as a tease, who are not simply making it up.

'I meant the religious orders don't,' adds Elizabeth. 'Eat meat. Hindus, Sikhs. After years of me worrying about food, The Chen is saying, or she *implies*, that I have some anxiety issue. I am either neurotic and have turned it into my diet, or my dieting has turned me into a neurotic! Jesus wept.'

She realises this is the bind.

'Fish, olive oil, red wine,' Martina sighs. 'Lean meat, salads and carbs, and pickled things too, maybe. Healthy food, beans, not spiritual enlightenment.'

'OK, OK, I will try adding more carbs. The Chen says if I don't my system will crash.'

'You're not a computer, darling.'

Trevor smiles at this. Listening in is a skill he has practised equally upon the whispering customers who are hushed and church-like in the shop and those who proclaim their erudition at length. While the shopkeeper sits behind his counter. Given his retentive memory, he is his own CCTV.

On a whimsy Elizabeth imagines a laptop and staring into the screen of herself staring back, a scream forming on the face. It doesn't crash. Diets. A hard drive of lists and "Do nots" with barely a *like* or a *just for the hell of it* in sight. *Change this and you will change your life*, or some such psycho-babble is running down the column beside her. *But is that an opportunity or a threat?*

She stands up to look for a plain old unenlightened apple.

'Trevor,' she calls, 'stop hiding in the bloody kitchen. Oh, he's not here.'

At which point Trevor emerges from below and enters the lounge.

'Hello,' he says to Martina. 'I'm … Trevor.'

'Well, well, so you're her new man about the house. Popping up from nowhere.'

'No, no. Just the lodger. Which sounds pretty old-fashioned.'

'It does. Don't you have a home to go to?'

'I'm a lost soul. My wife asked me to leave, or maybe I asked myself. Elizabeth has taken me in, at a price. So I'm more around the house than about the house.'

'You like talking, I can see that,' Martina says, with a kind of sexy smile. She stretches out a dark leg. 'Of course, Elizabeth has told me all about you. You'll be good for her. She loves talking, too.'

'Yes, I've noticed,' he says, looking over at Elizabeth, who is still standing. 'We, um, have a drink and analyse the world most workdays. After the day's work, that is, not before. Though that might be interesting. And I feed her. I am her feeder.'

'Ah.'

Martina and Elizabeth laugh differently at this. Martina looks him over.

'So, Trevor, and you're an artist.'

'Well, I was. I am trying to resurrect it. Back then, and it was way back then, I was young enough to puff myself up and stupid enough to ignore advice and, even if it sounds too biblical, I lost my way.'

'Me too. I thought about writing. I fell for a ridiculous man. I discovered I was better at editing and then I found a better man. Sounds easier than it was. Mind you, editing isn't about making but it is about finding. It's not unusual for writers to make but not find.'

'I'm sure you're right,' he says.

He is a bit smitten.

'Oh, good', says Elizabeth. 'Now that we've solved that.'

She sounds annoyed.

He watches them leave – up and gone in a rush, it seems.

They drive away in Martina's newish car, a Mazda. It may not have car-collector value but it does have a suspension. If only to tease Elizabeth, Martina delays referring to Trevor and concentrates on zigzagging between the constipated little chicanes traffic planners get their kicks from in the 40 zone – left-right-straighten, then left-right-straighten except clearly some vehicles don't bother and have bent the steel dividers over into sorry signs.

'Martina, you promised.'

'OK, what do I think of your new indoor plant? I hope you water him well.'

'You know what I'm like with plants.'

'That's why I said it every time I'm in your house I remember that lovely, and I have to say, virile dracaena you ruined by over-watering. Or under-watering.'

'Both, I think.'

'It didn't even recover when you took it outside. I can still see it out by the side fence, drooping.'

'My God, girl, can you drop the innuendo?'

Martina's car is an automatic which she drives smoothly, almost indifferently, certainly without apparent effort, in contrast to Elizabeth in the EH, whose style is more a shove and twist and low-level fighting. The invisible favours of power-assisted every-thing over manual madness. Having working steering and brakes makes the fifty-year age difference proof of some kind of progress in the world. Which is just as well when the rain sweeps over the highway.

'I like him,' says Martina. 'He listens, he seems amused, anyway he smiles a lot. He's not exactly handsome but he's OK-looking. I bet he's a pushover. And not a Narcissist, that's the thing. Or a bully.'

'Well, he can be a bit of a prat.'

'He's a man. But it's good to have a bit of man smell around the place.'

She sounds somewhat whimsical saying this. *Her own man so often absent.* Elizabeth looks at her and laughs.

'And now he's nagging me about eating more – of his meals. They smell too.'

'Well. Lucky you.'

'Yeah, but you know, he's boring. He goes to work in his boring shop and then he comes home and stands there for a while staring at his bloody paintings, comes back up to cook dinner, then goes outside and stands in front of his paintings again.'

'But he must be painting?'

'God knows, all I ever see is him standing.'

'It is likely Martina is unimpressed by this or simply thinks her friend isn't being serious. Not that it really matters. The trip takes nearly an hour and the queueing takes nearly an hour so they are full of bladder and empty of stomach by the time they get inside. The racecourse area where the festival is set up looks small in displays and stalls but huge with people. A success, then, even as it starts raining again, a lighter fall this time, as they stand waiting for the bratwurst stall to pump through its endless orders.

Each display is a craft made true: beauty has many forms. Leatherwork and plaster-form and letterpress ... wood-turning, tool-sharpening, shingle-splitting from wood blocks ... Most traditional crafts seem to be hyphenated practices. Making garden walls with dry-stone techniques, where the shape and the interlocking position of stones triumphs over the need for mortar; wooden sheds where the boards and rafters are connected by dowel-joints to avoid the need for bolts or brackets. One stall is hung with tanned materials, from traditional leathers to large swatches of fish skins tanned and dyed and ending soft despite the enduring impression of scales. Even more amazing is to see the young woman wearing these and soft thin leathers as her only clothing.

Two bearded hipster lads, one tall and one short, display and demonstrate their hand-made kitchen knives. These are beautiful, especially beautiful, sized in each step from short and delicate vegie knives up to 16-inch blades of major cheffy menace. Because Trevor is a kitchen nerd, Elizabeth stops to inspect the way these men have carved the wooden handles so smoothly, the metal studs finished and polished flush with the surface so the knife rests in your hand like love. It is more natural than anything natural.

Elizabeth notices the blades are very thin and taper to their edge without apparent bevelling. She asks the shorter men about this, explaining that she has recently bought a Dick knife and, when comparing it with her much older Dick knife, noticed the new blade is distinctly bevelled.

The man looks at her, his expression asking the question.

'The old blade is thinner,' she explains, 'it's sharper. And it slices even if it isn't sharp. The new blade is thicker and requires more pressure. Is it the bevelling?'

'What do you mean, bevelling?' he asks. Water is still dripping from the edge of the awning.

'The blade is thicker but the cutting edge is forged at an angle. Isn't that a bevel? Yours aren't.' She holds up his vegie knife and points to the taper. 'I really, really like these. Your blades are thinner ...'

Martina has been watching this young man. They are surrounded by a wall of noise from the equipment kept running all afternoon, the music box's pretty melodies on wind-up from the waistcoated and top-hatted men, and the endless blabbering crowd noise, and yet she cannot tell if the Craftsman of Knives cannot hear Elizabeth clearly or simply, oddly, doesn't know the term.

'These are crafted on the Japanese model,' he explains, 'with very thin steel so they slice through anything as if it was butter.'

'Lovely. How much are they?'

He explains and her mind immediately wanders to the next stall. She could buy a TV for that.

'Thin blades feel gorgeous but they do chip, don't they?'

'You shouldn't *ever*,' he says, 'cut anything *hard* … with such a knife.'

They leave him to his knives and move on. But they do chip.

Just as the two women are walking back towards the exit and designated car park Elizabeth notices a well-known publisher and his wife and three children arriving.

'Nothing much for the kids here,' she says, 'but there are animals. And wind-up music boxes. Are you a crafty sort of person, book deals excepted?'

'Not much.' The man is tall and clean-shaven and wrapped in a long rakish scarf arrangement. He never once looks her in the eye.

'And you?'

'We had a great time. There's even a hand-and-foot-operated printing press.'

When he doesn't respond she continues:

'I see your new latest imprint has sold well. 'A good idea having this line of international authors. I've enjoyed some of them but I haven't seen many reviews.'

'It doesn't need them. Reprints of the canon sell themselves.'

'This is my friend Martina,' she adds. 'She works for your rivals.'

'Oh, yes.'

'Hello,' says Martina.

The man looks at her, nods, then looks at his wife but doesn't reciprocate. He stares over her head at the crowd, at the restored steam-driven carousel, at the food stalls, at his kids already standing in the hot-chips queue.

'Yes,' she admits, 'the carousel, your kids will enjoy that. How old …?'

She hadn't taken much notice of them.

He stares at anything except her, or even Martina, and that must be a first. If nothing else, he is facing two very attractive women. Elizabeth makes another pointless comment or two, until he very obviously tries to walk away without saying anything. Then does.

'And that,' she announces to Martina, 'is how our lovely literary world operates. Look past you for a better option, for *any* option, then leave.'

'The man has a mental problem. I've heard about him.'

'Nah, he's just a shit.'

The car is hotter inside than expected. Martina smiles the way a driver can when the passenger is twisted to her left, looking at the late angles of sunlight across the paddocks. Elizabeth is saying how much she'd have enjoyed a hands-on craft of some sort. Something mute and physical, not words. A structure you can actually see, as against imagine. 'Carpentry, pottery, quilting ... OK, maybe not quilting. You,' she says to Martina, 'are more hands-on because the book has to make sense, be testable in a way, fact-based, and only then opinion'.

'You have no interest in factual writing, Elizabeth. ...'

'Maybe I do. Really.'

'Apropos of which, then ... That young writer I mentioned to you a few weeks ago: she has accepted our offer. She is writing about sects, and has decided to bring much more research into it. Most of which she has already done, which we didn't quite realise. Because she wants her book to be a *novel*. You were brought up in a sect, weren't you?

'It wasn't quite a sect and I wasn't ...'

'Well, that Orange People mess you talk often about, and your wanton mother. So, what do you reckon, your money where your mouth is? ... Shia has asked for you. We have to confirm it.'

'Are you serious?'

'Why not? We haven't appointed an editor yet. It's all about men with ideas and power controlling women. Then, sadly, how women play into it. I think she is wanting as an adult child to find some absolution, maybe. When I was young my mother was terminally ill but my father was the charismatic man who had grand ideas and made the rules. He ordered me to look after her so I did.

Women's business, you know, these Mediterranean men. They love their women but they love their manliness more. It took all that for me to accept that it's up to women to care, up to women to forgive. Not that they should, that *they can*.'

Elizabeth keeps forgetting that Martina is a Catholic.

When she arrives home, Elizabeth tells him of their encounters with the short knife-man and the tall publisher. Trevor pulls open the drawer and checks the two knives. It had been *his* observation regarding the edges, the bevel. And the chipping, a known drawback of finely bladed Japanese knives.

'It was wet but not cold,' says Elizabeth. 'Still, the publisher looked as if someone had just taken him out of the deep freeze. And his bloody wife. Jesus, what a fun pair they are. Martina called him a retiree. From humanity. He's about 40.'

Back in the kitchen he calls out, asking what kind of editing Martina does. He has been thinking about her during the day. While he waits for Elizabeth's answer, he starts trimming runner beans for the evening meal.

'She's been editing non-fiction for years – and she sits on the editorial board too. She can influence decisions.'

Elizabeth tells him about the new writer. How she and Martina have been discussing hands-on sort of work.

He knows. The chillies he has begun de-seeding are stinging his fingers. He washes then wipes his hands, steps around the corner towards her.

'She's sort of beguiling.'

Elizabeth is staring at him. She lays her reading down on the table in front of her. Trevor is leaning against the doorframe, the paperwork is on the table, Gordon sprawled beside her chair.

'Trevor, she's only a few years younger than me.'

'Yes, but she …'

'But what?'

Even he knows he's said the wrong thing. Anything he says now will only emphasise it. Yet again, a moment crashes after a but.

In this situation, sharing the house, the kitchen, the conversation and her friends, her work talk, his vagaries, they hardly know each other. It feels as if there should be rules, but there are none. Unlike a real relationship, they can't say what they want to. And what does she want? It's her house.

'Look,' she says after a while, 'I may have this bloody face-blindness, but to make up for it I'm a great listener. I listen very carefully to people, so when you say …'

'OK, OK. You think I'm being disparaging about her?'

'Of her. No.'

'What then?'

'I hear that you fancy my girlfriend. Well, you can't. So stop it.'

'I had the impression she liked me. Or was she only teasing?'

'You? Such a blokey thing to say. She's married.'

'Oh?'

'He's a troubleshooter in the corporate world, so he's often interstate or overseas. Someone who comes in to sort out businesses that aren't performing. He's like a fixer without a gun in his bag.'

'Lops off heads in one company before moving on to the next? With a bonus. A tough guy.'

'Mmm … something like that. Look, for all that, he's a very urbane man. She doesn't mention his work, or him, very much.'

He lifts both hands to express, what? Her substance, allure, presence, the soulless fixer.

'Uh huh.'

Just before he showers, his mobile rings. It's Diana, saying hello briefly before saying she has just received a strange call on the landline. A man with an accent asked if Trevor lived there because he'd like to speak to him. When she asked, the man wouldn't explain himself, no power-company talk, or telcos, or charities, none of that, he tried to charm her. 'He was like a perve at a seedy pub.'

'What kind of accent?'

'I don't know, it wasn't a long call because I hung up. It wasn't Americanised Filipino, more like a movie version of a Russian.'

Diana. As he undresses he is thinking of her. He stands in front of the bathroom mirror and sways so his penis moves left and right. This strange pleasure of watching your own genitals and that feeling which is visual, and the visual that feels of the very thin skin of the penis. His own, his hanging shape. Filling with blood and becoming heavy. Below it the puckered scarring down his right leg.

She can hear the downstairs shower running. Her own shower is also a grooming session, removing the outlying fuzz of her pubes in preparation for her night with novelist and sometime lover Richard. For him? Trimming a panty line is fine, but how much to trim after that? She is not a young woman waxing or shaving, the skin left bare. The goose bumps left after depilation. Funny, though, that they shower at much the same time, often. Often enough.

Standing, naked, under the water, aware she is in the top shower and he is standing, naked, under the water, immediately below her in the basement shower. Like two lifts in the same lift well. Standing, facing forward, in the passive stance of showering, the in-between moments where new ideas form. Though it couldn't be two different lifts in the same shaft, they must be in the one, together, passive, he behind, she standing facing the doors as the moments pass.

In bed Elizabeth is annoyed by the conversation with Trevor. There's no denying the subtle exoticism Martina gives off. Even her name. Elizabeth has been thinking of her friends and colleagues, her inner worry-list of too few friends. If she must make more effort, at this moment she is dropping into sadness. Above the doona her bare arms are crossed more in containment than in easeful pre-sleep. The bedside lamp gleams on the bedding, its light tending more to white than gold, better for reading under.

She will be seeing Richard soon. Perhaps it will be better not to mention the new writer and her own involvement. She will see her colleagues again, too; some huggable, others cool; the dramatis personae at one remove, friends at work only. Except, as per Richard, she will be seeing them dressed for pleasure not work, at the literary prize night. The writers she knows better than others, those she has edited, others she enjoys meeting every so often. Talented, witty, grumpy, or these combined in mordancy.

She wants to feel young and sexy.

She also knows in the morning she will wake and think: *I am still here. It is still happening. The little we actually know of it. The world, its beginnings, all the things that begin to happen here … then finish, if they finish, somewhere else. Whether we know it or not.*

During the night another hailstorm swathes the street. It wakes Elizabeth, she hears the heavy sound arriving, the surging then diminishing to a light toccata, then suddenly crashing down, she thinks, like truckloads emptying. It is a strange cold music. Again she frets about her car, the damage, the old un-reinforced glass windows.

Downstairs in his basement Trevor hears little of this, having no roof above him. But he wakes alert and shocked by a powerful fall of hail clamouring outside on what must be the metal roof of the shed. It is taking a beating.

~

Most of the time, even if he is head up in selling or talking, or head down in his sales accounts, Trevor notices his customers arrive, but sometimes they enter like air or light. Sometimes they leave in the same way.

This time an older man has come in looking to left and right at the shelves in a way that suggests he has no interest in books whatsoever, is just wasting time until … a table becomes available at the coolest café on the street? Not by the look of him, so Trevor stops what he is doing. If anything, the man seems energised post-coffee, not in need of. … Then he walks up to the counter and inspects Trevor so closely he might be a dermatologist. What is this, yet another crazy, more proof of Trevor's charisma for attracting customers on the wrong side of the status quo? The man is not classy but too well dressed for crime and too old for the cool café. He is white-haired and bearded, he looks like the author pics of Irish novelist Dermot Healy when he was sunk in his cups.

'Trevvy!' the man shouts at last. 'It is you. My boy is all grown up!'

His father? No, no. It's impossible.

'Trevvy, it's your old father. I know, I know, it's hard to believe but here I am.'

'What?' Trevor coughs at this. 'No.'

Trevor stands so abruptly his big chair bangs against the wall. Fathers don't shift from young and dead to old and alive.

'Now look,' he says with a tight mouth, 'my father died years ago. OK, maybe you knew him, maybe you worked with him back then, because it was *back then*. But my father is dead. He's been dead for thirty years.'

'No, it's me, Trevvy, your old *tatus* come back from … being away. Of course you're surprised, it's confusing and I should have come earlier. I search for you on the internet and I find you. Here you are. You saw my emails and every one emails these days. I told you to expect me. Ha ha.'

'Being *away*! Don't be bloody ridiculous. Didn't you hear me? My father's dead.'

He sits down again. The man is behaving like a clown. An old clown. He is *short*. And Trevor has had enough of these continual intrusions by people who are not customers, who are suddenly there in front of him, his counter not enough barrier or authority to make them behave. Yet this man, still smiling at him and somehow familiar, is giving him the half fright and awfulness of being trapped in a dream.

'No, it is me, Trevvy. I've come back from hiding, yes, I admit it. I'm getting old and not very well, I had to see you again before I ... you know. Come here, my boy, and give me a hug.'

'You're crazy and you're making me ...'

'I am not crazy, please no, don't say that.' (His tone is suddenly pathetic, or is it wheedling?) 'I'm your *tatus*.'

'My *tatus*. My *tatus was* crazy.' (Though this logic hardly helps.) 'Yes, I saw some pretty confused emails that said nothing. They were your emails? Oh, God, it was you, wasn't it, who rang my wife?'

'I tried to ring you. Some woman answered.'

What survives of a fly-in, fly-out black-haired father from thirty-five years ago? Trevor's brain is falling a long way down the recognition spectrum. Off the spectrum altogether for a child who has lost a father – and had an old pretender return as if from a prank. Then again, his father *had* been a pretender, he'd been every sort of weird.

'Yes, I email you for weeks. You never answered. Rude,' I thought, 'you are not a good boy.'

Why would I answer emails that say nothing and are probably from internet crooks in Russia? Or Nigeria?'

The older man steps in around the counter and reaches at Trevor for a hug and there is an embarrassing tangle of push and pull like a punchless tussle in the pub but with one man awkwardly seated.

'Jesus, get off me, will you!'

The air is ringing in Trevor's ears with as much tinnitus as *Tatus*. *Jesus Christ, is it his father come back for redemption?*

'Listen to me, my boy I show you. I tell all about you.'

He does. Trevor stays sitting in his armchair and so the old man stands there beside him rambling through details of life in the family home. Back in sleepy Upwey, almost-country Poland, he says, peasant town. Making big gestures and then with un-nerving hoots of excessive laughter. The bookshop his wife's parents owned, his many trips away on mining exploration. The disappearance. Trevor listens, dazed, remembering his father's antics always had been crass and theatrical. Then the man is talking about his wife as if he had been her great love, ah yes. Her great love, not his.

Not once does he acknowledge that she is dead.

'Mum's dead, she died years ago. She probably died because of you.'

'Don't say that!' The man puts on a sad face. Trevor sighs back at him, the bathos ridiculous. It must be his father. He feels sick.

'You knew we'd think you were dead.' Trevor grinds this out. 'You are that cold-blooded. You were never going to tell us. Except now you're back and it's all OK, right? Like hell it is.'

'Ah, don't get so angry, don't worry about that,' his father says. 'I will explain it. They were going to kill me.'

His shoulders lift in mock vulnerability. The man can't act.

'You know, body left out in the desert, yes, yes, dead of thirst, you see how easy it was. You know what was happening. They were bad men. I had to escape.'

Trevor tries to interrupt, but the old man has been rehearsing for too long and nothing will stop him now. So much running around in Europe, back to Poland, yes, yes. He lays it on, he weeps and sighs. Different jobs but nothing as cushy as good old Oz. Until he came back in Australia. Work in Queensland, more crooks there than under the stones in WA though who cares if you have work. Some work, not enough work. No money. Now, though … he is old, he has come to see his boy.

There is an unpleasant edge to this only Trevor could detect. The Narcissism. The unnecessary intensity. A man capable of turning nasty.

But Trevor is a head taller than the old man. His father was always a big man, a character, a show-off, who never played small or short or … Now Trevor stands again, towers over him. From the old man's expression he is no less surprised to see this tall son. Of normal height at 15 years of age, Trevor grew rapidly in his late teens. And it's not as if the old man can open his shirt and display a tattoo across his chest saying: *I am Trevor's father.*

Trevor is shaking his head. He cannot hear past the sound of the man's Polish accent to where truth might actually be. To where he does not want to meet it.

'I have to leave again, my boy. I'm sorry. For a few weeks, have somethings to sort out. Legal. I just wanted to see you first before I go again but I'll be back in a … maybe a month? I had to … I'm most impressed that you have a shop. Very good to be in business. You own it, of course?'

'You're leaving? After just arriving? So much for saying hello to your long-unseen son. Just a hug, eh? Then after thirty years you're leaving again?'

'No, but I mean do you own the shop?'

Trevor can only stare. He places his palms flat on the wooden counter. Something real.

'You see, my boy, you won't believe it, those official bastards have told me something horrible. You remember I always hate authorities. They say I am officially dead.'

'Who? What are you talking about?'

'The authorities, they say I am dead and I can't apply to be alive again. It's madness. Officially I am not standing here in front of you, my own son. It was too long ago, they tell me. I don't exist.'

'But you must have a passport.'

'Polish passport. I was born in Krakow.'

He bangs his fist on the counter, making Trevor pull his hands away.

'I went to see them, I said' "Look, do I stand in front of you like a dead man!?" Those bastards. So much money I left for you and your mother, if I died, yes, yes, but I'm here and she died before me. Well, sad she died, but now you know. You have a duty to your old dad.'

Like a man being confronted with a gun, there are people who don't always run, they freeze. Trevor freezes. Until the absurd ruling insults his intelligence:

'You can't apply to be alive again,' Trevor mimics him, and then his shock pours into laughter.

'You must think seriously, my boy,' says his father, looking serious. 'I will be back soon.'

The old man turns to leave.

'What is this STOP ADANI poster in the window?' he scowls. 'I see these things everywhere. Not up in Queensland, too smart those people to behave like this. When I came everyone says Australia was built on the sheep's back, eh, all the time. When I come back the sheep is iron and coal. Anyone can sell this stuff you have so much of, and here *you* are, you don't even *want* to sell it.'

For a few seconds it seems he is going to reach across and tear the poster from the glass. As he leaves he wrenches the door back so hard it jams open.

'My own son!'

Trevor hesitates then follows the man out, sees him get into a car parked nose-first in the alleyway beside the shop, blocking the entire pavement. Pedestrians have been walking out onto the street to get past.

Impossible to think when his stomach is cramped, when his father is like electric discharges in his brain. *Who else could know the trivia and the detail of what the old man has recounted? His outrageous behaviour. Anyone pretending, any impostor, would surely be all charm itself, they wouldn't dare be aggressive and contrary. No, it is his father all over.*

His father can't apply to be alive again. It couldn't happen to a worthier man.

Just before dusk there is sometimes a particular lack of colour in the sky above the houses, and in the shadows seeping under houses, which makes Trevor think of a Beckett character low on words, uncertain of location, hoping onwards into the hopelessness. *Cold. His father. Not as a father, as a force. The man had not seemed very interested in him, just the money. This tightens his skin. It is blanching.*

Mostly he is angry. Then the awfulness of everything returns and pushes mere anger aside. His father. He has begun Googling the man and found nothing. Of course. He doesn't exist. The whole thing is grotesque. Not any kind of sweet return, nor the spooky not-quite-right return of a changed child, no dissociated person come back sane and too-frightened-sober to believe the worst of whatever it was.

You're a naughty boy!
Your father is here.
He is dead.

He remembers the woman who came into his bookshop desiring a memoir, and change, whose father was a butcher with softened, disgusting hands and the sullen children. Then his hands healing after she has made her peace with him. Possessed by the apparent clarity of a fairytale. *How much of a person is a child, and how much a set of puzzles?* Trevor is closing in on 50 years old. He feels it like accessing another world. Like recalling dreams, some people remember each moment in high resolution while others live and die as if very little is clear.

How absurd, too, that he is living in a house with a woman who, if he were to stand still in front of her and remain silent, would not recognise him. Making him a ghost. Father. Son. Artist who stopped being. Now his blank father stands in front of him.

The world has other kinds of prosopagnosia.

No, Trevor has no love left for this old man. It isn't biology, it's choice. He *will not* recognise him.

The rain is falling vertically through the purpling sunset. Melbourne rain without wind, the soft side of the gusting hail of the night before. No sooner has Trevor arrived home from the shop and removed his wet coat than he meets Elizabeth, bag swinging, with her going-out face on. She is wearing bright red and actually showing some cleavage in a classy, tight-fitting dress. No more green-framed glasses, she must be wearing contacts. And, amazingly, she has applied a very exact liner of kohl around her eyes, and is wearing lipstick. Her hair, bleached blonde since the day before, is brushed and loose. She is looking young and fresh and sort of sexy. It startles him.

'Elizabeth, you're looking … great. Where are you off to?'

'Oh, great? Do you think so?'

She hoists her bag over her shoulder as deliberately as her phrasing. He is smiling, in that way, and she knows she has succeeded.

'Everyone scrubs up well if they make the effort, Trevor.'

She is trying to balance suggestion with press-down. It's all in the tone. (That he was so obvious when Martina was here …) Then she grins at him. She *is* feeling good.

'I'm meeting my publishing people at the pub,' she says, 'then, while everyone is upright, on to the awards night. We have some books in the running, and we must be there if they win! A celebration with staff, all gratis, hey, and with our shortlisted authors.'

'Right. OK.'

'One of whom is sort of a boyfriend.'

'A *sort of* boyfriend?'

'Kind of a boyfriend. Richard. I really hope he wins. Either way, I probably won't see you till tomorrow night. Could you feed Gordon for me? Maybe take him for his morning walk? Talk to the magpies, grin at the happy chappy who carries on with the three women?'

This is all provocation. Her newly blonde hair glows on her, and without her glasses, her brown eyes … She may not be immediately attractive, but she is … something … He is staring, and she is smiling as if such things happen every day.

'And, *and*, today I read through that manuscript, the one about sects I told you about. It arrived this morning and it's mine. Martina just rang to ask me what I thought of it. Lots of work to be done on it, I can't wait. This is big, Trevor!'

Suddenly she grabs him, and almost hugs him as she had Gordon.

'I'm, ah … What do you mean?' he says, meaning the author but feeling the pressure of her body.

'That manuscript by Shia Newman. I'm sure I told you about her, rising star, young but talented, looking into cults and sects. It'll be a good book when I've finished with it. Trevor, they appointed *me*.'

'Congratulations, I have something too …'

'I've been told she's a bit strange. All good. Most authors are.'

Trevor raises an imaginary glass of champagne.

'Huh, strange? That's nothing. My father has reappeared from the dead, or someone claiming to be him has.'

She tilts her head like a bird.

'From the …? I have no idea what you're talking about.'

'He just walked into the shop, this afternoon, as if it was a completely normal thing to do, after thirty bloody years. I told you, didn't I, that my father is officially dead.'

'Ah, you did. That *is* surreal. Sorry, I have to use that word … Bloody hell. I'm sorry Trevor but I really have to go, I'm late and it's important so, sorry, it'll have to wait. Don't forget to feed Gordon. Bye.'

'You're going to be cold!'

'I have a taxi.'

And off she goes.

He thinks about it. *It's her night. Good. She's a professional unseen. Editing, the job that disappears itself.* Like a father, or *his* father. And his own efforts, out in the shed painting canvases no one will ever see. The ironies dissolve the paint in him.

He raises his arm and the imaginary champagne again. The imaginary bubbles rising up and emptying.

As soon as she has gone he walks downstairs and sprints across the lawn. When he pulls open the door of the shed and turns the lights on he has to stop and look again to make sure it's real. The roof iron at the rear is peppered with holes. Rain is falling through and *tinking* onto the lids of the paint tins and several of the acrylic paintings are in rivulets from water dripping down their surfaces.

The main shed is dry, the rear of the shed is raining. It has its own weather.

An hour later, rain over, wanting to be doing anything but this, he unpacks the plastic tarpaulin he had used as a drop cloth in the apartment and, on the stepladder, slowly drags it over the gable, covering the damaged roofing. He throws two ropes over the tarp and ties them down to four garden stakes he has found against her side fence. She must have been growing tomatoes in the abandoned bed.

～

Her anticipated literary night is not the old-style deal: one of the hyper-nights of dress-up and dinner. Not like the Oscars. Not any more the long nights of pre-dinner drinks, a big dinner, awards announcements and waywardly witty speeches from writers, sometimes catty speeches like *Why the fuck hadn't they won the prize before?*

'It was my chance to eat and drink at their expense,' she had told Trevor.

'But you don't like eating,' he replied.

'A means of expression. It's the attitude that counts.'

'So what happens at these events now?'

'Now it's fucking canapés and bubbles.'

'I want a full report.'

Still, it's her chance to drink at their expense. And she does. During the presentations a right-wing historian no one had ever heard of is given a prize (when a politician intervened) and then stands and rants for twenty-five minutes without even being drunk. Elizabeth sees a so-called senior novelist who isn't shortlisted for anything so must have been a judge. This man is welcoming and witty, sure to impress with anecdotes of things literary and famous people who … he's a name-dropper. This famous figure had impressed her when she first met him, or met his charming manner, until she realised he was a younger-woman player.

There are many younger women.

This famous man is no longer, if he ever was, a conventional seducer. It's reciprocal advantage: he fawns upon them and promotes them, and their fame keeps him in public view. Meanwhile, his books appear every few years, polished to the limits of his considerable facility, heavily mannered, because by now it is locked in, a personal style he cannot escape from. His characters all sound like him. Even his punctuation sounds like him.

The best work of fiction is by an attractive young woman for her debut novel, a startling new talent according to the Judges' Report. She is writing about landscape and identity, a white person's version of Country. *Very topical, very young, very likely.*

As a shortlisted writer who hasn't won, Richard is ghosted at the exact moment the actual winner is announced. Years ago if writers and editors won they drank to celebrate, and if they lost they drank to drink. Now it sobers his publisher. It is all very well for poetry publishers to be impressed with a shortlisting but in the real world of fiction the author must *win*.

It had been a year between drinks with Richard, when he attended without having a book eligible. Part of seeing her. Now the way to transcend the night's disappointment is with some lively and affectionate sex. They aren't even in bed before she begins to make joking references to a recent US novel called *I Love Dick*, which Richard puts down to her natural warmth and sense of celebration at recognition by her peer group. It is nothing about boy slang of loving dick but Elizabeth is teasing him. Richard is easily flattered, so why not a bit of flattery and play-acting? Use of the mouth.

He is a lawyer after all.

Once in his room she pulls the pillows out of the awkward bed-cover pouch they so annoyingly fold them into, then drags the cover onto the floor. Richard smiles, remembering this from other times. She undoes the zip of her dress. When she turns back to face him he caresses her from her shoulders, down her waist to her thighs in her sensual tight-fitting dress. She knows he wants to see her skin, he wants to pull the red dress up and reveal her long body. She lifts her arms above her head.

There is something erotic about the clinical design of hotel rooms, their poor-man bedside fittings and plain paintings or photos, the heaviness of the curtains and the wardrobe with its fridge cupboard and glary white fluoro. The mirror. The room is generic, tacky and scented, for having sex in. Elizabeth always thinks so, unless she is crashing alone. This room has a globe blown in one bedside lamp, which in her rare hotel moments seems to be *de rigueur*, and there on the wall beside the TV set is a wild scar in the paint where someone has thrown a bottle at it and missed. Perhaps.

Richard is a quiet well-behaved man; in her experience most writers are quiet and well-behaved, introverts, dull even, nothing like the off-the-wall stereotype, unless they are like the poets who take too many drugs, as proof of their authenticity, and lack house-training.

Richard is her tipsy indulgence, sex without tomorrows.

Halfway or thereabouts through their happy fucking his mobile rings. In such situations he might let it ring and to his credit he tries but, he knows who it will be. Given it is after 2 am he has to be in his room, so his wife assumes he'll answer or else he isn't in his room, meaning he is in someone else's room. Or that he's fallen over in the street.

He answers. It goes on too long, the empathy and understanding, the consolation and how she suggests they have a romantic meal out when he returns, to make up for the stupid judges. What happened during her workday, the kids.

Luckily he finishes the call before Elizabeth's phone rings. That would have been hard to explain.

Elizabeth's mother is ringing out of late-night neediness.

After that their night of sex is rather slower. But in the morning, well, come the morning.

The following morning Trevor does the right thing and takes Gordon out around the damp Royal Park circuit, busy every morning with doggers and joggers and overfed magpies singing in groups like a family of gleaners. Some birds remain in the trees beside the track singing about the many things clever magpies know, or just imagine, while they inspect and recognise every face among the regulars walking around the track. Even if Elizabeth can't. Others stalk, head to one side, then the other, listening for insects and grubs just below the surface of the ground.

Little else is black and white. *His father, the man in the shop. A madman.* So like his mad father, the man who maybe never played but actually *was* a clown, loud most of the time, scary when he felt like it.

Un-nerving now. The reappearance – and, unless he's lost his intuition entirely, Trevor is sure it's about his money. Having both Gordon and the walk to himself feels, despite this, surprisingly enjoyable, even if the mornings are colder now and thoughts of his father aren't exactly warming. He should do it more often, he should do any kind of exercise more often. Gordon treats him like a true owner. It is quite touching, and wet. Trevor even half tolerates the talkative man with tattoos who walks with the three women and their dogs. *Oh so bloody jovial, he is.*

Under the trees on the west side of the track he notices someone. It looks like the woman from outside the IGA with her little dog, her bleached hair and real tan. Even if he's not her mate, a bloke with grey hair and glasses who sells *The Big Issue* outside the IGA is standing with her. Trevor has watched this man wavering on the pavement like a grey tree in the wind.

One day he asked if the woman was on ice or anything, and whether he should give her any money. *The Big Issue* guy stayed silent, eventually saying it wasn't up to him to say anything: Trevor would have to decide for himself. *Commendable loyalty*, Trevor thought. The *Big Issue* guy did say she'd just been kicked out of her accommodation. Into the weather. The hail.

Gordon rushes at the magpies, which ignore him. At such times conscience and circumstance make Trevor feel bare. He promises next time he'll give her something more. Say something. But not impose. Then the talk-talk man and women approach again and the man grins and nods, suffering perhaps from happy amnesia, or even prosopagnosia, and provoking Trevor and his dog to break the pattern and head away towards the tram track and the walk home.

By the time he has changed and eaten something, Elizabeth opens the front door and enters. She is still wearing her contacts.

'Just look at you,' she says, 'looking healthy for once. Off to work? You can sit against your blue wall and meditate for the day.'

He supposes this means she had a very lusty evening. It doesn't make him happy.

She tells him which book won – no, not the boyfriend's. It prompts Trevor to say he hasn't sold a single copy of it. She says she will text that news to Richard. That isn't what Trevor meant. 'Ah,' she says, 'but *Schadenfreude* is the one bit of German all writers understand. And can't get enough of.'

So he tells her about his father. He trims his voice like a piece of paper.

How his father went to WA for work, up in the North West on a mining survey. He was a geologist, working for mining companies of the kind Gina Rinehart descended from. He went to the North West so often he had a postal box up there for mail. Back in the '80s when there used to be mail.

'I wrote to him when I was little,' says Trevor. 'Every week. He never replied.'

Trevor is staring out through the front window as if, through this clean, clear glass he might see further than the empty street with its trees and tidy median strip, to his father standing beside a Land Rover, to his right the straight road in the crooked heat, to his left the ocean. In the heat shimmer over red dirt, the man is reading his son's hand-written letter.

Then, he tells Elizabeth, his father never came back and no one ever found him. The aliens got him.

Out in the heat-shimmer. Then more shimmer and no man.

There were shonky people doing shonky deals, he tells her. Over mining leases and payoffs. Iron ore. Nickel. Fortunes being made, potentially billions, and – that's what happened. His father had a knack for getting into trouble. So when he disappeared no one knew if he had died or was killed or had done a runner.

'That's horrible,' she frowns. 'How did your poor mother take it?'

Trevor turns back and looks at Elizabeth, her large eyes naked with amazement.

'We both … cried … I was 15, at high school, I didn't want to be crying over anything, but if your own father dies … Crying is something real anyway. More than he was. Otherwise it was all endless and empty. He was larger than life, but someone who couldn't care less. Like most "characters", it's never much fun living with them.'

'I left my husband,' she says, '*because* he couldn't care less. And he wasn't much fun either. I did it the other way around.'

Trevor walks into the kitchen out of habit.

'You read accounts of clothes being left on the beach,' she says. 'Suicide.'

'Not him.'

'So what happened next?'

'Without a body and a death certificate it's up to the courts. You have to wait for decades. The coroner said there was no reasonable likelihood that he was alive, that there was a low probability he intentionally remained *in the wilderness* – ha, very dramatic – but, given the lack of any contact with family, or with anyone else for that matter, he concluded that death had been established to his satisfaction, i.e. on the balance of probabilities.'

'My God. There you have death in prose.'

'My mother worked in her parents' bookshop. She hated him and she missed him and ... she never quite believed he was dead. It was like some smart-arse game he was playing. Unless the person is found, dead or alive, or fugitive, you have a story without an ending. Whereas fiction promises a neat ending and usually provides it.'

'Except tragedy.'

He nods. In the silence before he responds they watch the people walking past the window. The other-end-of-work rush. Everyone is walking to a destination. A neat ending.

'In tragedy,' he adds, 'you have a body. Or bodies. Grief has a body to farewell. His was a book with a character disappearing at the end, like an abruptly ended dream. You wake up. You can't go back to see what happened.'

'But this bloke claims he's your father. No wonder you were so worked up yesterday.'

'Yeah. I can't tell if I'm happy or bloody furious. Yes, I can I'm both.'

'Sorry I was in such a hurry before. I did wonder about it. Well, a bit, anyway. After that I was lost to self-indulgence. As maybe

Mark Twain said, "Too much of a good thing is never enough." Or was he talking about whiskey?'

At work, the next day passes slowly against the blue wall.

It occurs to him that Elizabeth's hair seems to have settled down. It usually has the nature of an excited teenager. Maybe it's sexual. This thought happens concurrently with his standing as he likes to do immediately in front of his electric kettle, the place in the back room where the counter is worn down in a casual curve, as if someone for many years used this area as a cutting board for bread or tomatoes or … There is something wordless and consoling about this worn area. He hardly waits to stands there, but when he stands there he waits – until the kettle has boiled. Then he never thinks of it again, not once, until the next time.

His pavement notice today says:

When you have finished reading Seating Arrangements *your family reunion will never be the same. The best memoirs are often of the worst families. This book is not for the ethically faint-hearted.*

Exactly. To think he typed up this flash review three days ago. What ironic timing. *Seating Arrangements* allows for several family members to be present at the same table, something far from Trevor's experience, and yet the irony of his thoughts remains. Under no circumstances will he let this stranger sit for a meal. This day of all days he wants peace and quiet. Sometimes the thought of customers reduces him to a catlike aversion. Of having to be so fucking polite to everybloodybody. It's the love-hate dependency comedians speak of. It growls in the shadow of the spectrum and won't come out to play.

Just when the evening is becoming dark the door is swung open and stays jammed open against the threshold. Cold air blows into the shop. A bloke strides towards Trevor at his counter. He is Keith Richards without the grin.

'Well, mate,' he says, 'have ya got my DVD then?'

He is alarming, gaunt cheeks and outdoor tan and bone from his skull to his elbows. He is a hammer.

'I beg your pardon?'

'Don't tell me ya forgot. I was in here about a month ago and I ordered that cartoon-book novel thing, the DVD of it, you remember now, eh? You were bloody rude to me.'

The Frank Miller thing. The man who swiped his books onto the floor. *How to tell or not tell the man he never ordered it, never meant to order it, then forgot about it completely yet stayed angry with the man? On principle.* A shop is open, as in family: you can't choose your customers. He'd never thought of that. This bloke was all snarl and snap and now he is back amazingly like a real customer.

'Ya think I don't bloody read but ya wrong,' says the man. 'I'm kinda professional.'

'What in?'

'I specialise in taking the piss outta fuckers like you. Ha. Anyway, didja get my fucken DVD for me or not?'

'It was out of stock,' Trevor lies.

They stare at each other, given it could be true. The man hasn't thought of DVDs or books being anything other than for sale. Sort of all the time. *It doesn't make sense otherwise, does it?* The tattoo on his neck and throat seems to be alive and feral.

'So can ya order it from a second-hand place?'

'No. I only sell new items.' (Also not true.)

He stands and shows the bloke his nearest shelf. The neat spines and clean-cut edges of the pages. The man is taller than him.

'New books. Are you paying for the books you damaged last time? No. So the answer is no.'

'You dick,' the man says. 'You fucken …'

Seeing the man turn to leave, Trevor returns to the counter. But the man, suddenly angry as all hell, reaches for Trevor's neck then pushes him hard against the shelves.

'You never fucken ordered it, ya bastard!'

Trevor's foot catches on the stepladder and his leg buckles, he goes down hard on his right side, and the ladder and books hit the floor. Then nothing. Both of them freeze in the silence and the loud shunting of nerves.

From out of his depth to such a decision. The man's act has a kind of warped grandeur. Which ends as he suddenly slides down a bookshelf. Trevor has kicked out with his good leg, knocking the man's feet from under him. For several seconds they are both struggling on the floor, then both are scrambling up together; they are as clumsy as two crabs on a glassy floor. Until the man clambers up, gets to the door and is gone.

Of all things, Trevor's bad leg. Without moving from the floor, now that it hardly matters, he uses both arms to prop himself against the counter. Then eases the leg out from under him and into an outstretched position. *Jesus. The leg.* An object it may be, but the pain is all of him.

Emotions can hit without escape routes, the less dramatic, unkind ones: like humiliation. If never as big or as hopeless as grief, being belittled is a loss. The shame of it. Thank God no one was in the shop. Better than having a witness, because Trevor can do that, his facial scanning like a magpie's. The man's colour and staring face inside its bone. The cheap deodorant as embarrassing as the hurt.

Turning his back on the bloke like that, he must be losing his touch. Even if it was a man who looks like many others. Only a few of whom take down booksellers from behind. He didn't anticipate it. He wishes he could have hit the guy. Still, it was a hard fall. It's a Saturday, he should have stayed at home. What was it Bruce Lee said? *If a mad guy wants to bite your nose off, you won't be able to stop him. Short of killing him.*

He can't remember the exact book or the DVD. Oh yeah, he can, fuck it, he always remembers. He wishes he didn't, to make a point, to refuse the bloke that small concession but no, it was *300* by Frank Miller. Spartans vs. Athenians. One reviewer called it *a piece of shit*. Trevor hears the words. Bragging, is he, to himself?

Except Trevor is a fallen Spartan, or Athenian, lying on the floor with his armour crooked and a leg so damaged he cannot rise. Completely vulnerable. So displaced he feels as much an idiot as the idiot who shoved him down.

No, no, no. His father, now this. After years of calm routine and slow dissolve. He could laugh if he made an effort. Limping. *Gordon and Trevor together limping around the park, no, it is too ridiculous. Trevor is variously a shit, an arsehole and now a dick.*

Jesus, Elizabeth had only just mentioned *Schadenfreude*. He must get up. He rolls onto his knees and pauses in a Gordon position, oh how pathetic he is, shifting from Spartan to dog. *If he were a dog, people might take pity on him and offer him biscuits.*

Even if he normally walks like an ungrammatical sentence, he is not disabled. He stands up, gets himself into the armchair behind the counter.

At least he has ibuprofen. The Spartans didn't. Maybe they didn't need it.

With every movement more bad memories come to him. Murky thoughts and not imaginings, they rise and wallow to un-nerve him physically, like waking from a night's heavy drinking or feeling faint after standing too suddenly.

It is guilt and recurrence, the old bad lore come back to get him.

They are driving flat out on the gravel and the dust ahead of them means another car they have to catch. When you are young you see the extra possibilities of speed. So you speed. No much wind to blow the dust aside. The road is flying towards them like a driver-view video on YouTube, air rushing past the windscreen in through the open window as he slides the car left enough on the long curving road to hear gravel fly up underneath the wheel arches and behind them, and now he is not ordinary any more, he is speed: he is more alive, more alert, more like the swooping eagles across the open paddock. It is pure power in him, better than Buddha. Until the dust, a wall of stationary dust, and suddenly on the other side of it a bloody right-angled corner. He slews the car in a half circle but it kicks back on a crossing gutter, lurching onto its side then head-jarringly into a tree. Trevor's right hip is rammed against the door and his leg crunches. Dust fills smothering inside the car, his navigator mate is screaming. All that dust, thick, choking and slowly thinning around him, his left arm angled through the steering wheel, his hand gripping the protruding edge of the dash. Seconds, minutes? A second car, its brakes on hard and grinding the gravel, smashes into them. They're thrown up against the dash as the second car somersaults into the fence.

How many years of trying to repress this dread have failed him.

His mate's car, upside down on the fence, steel posts, barbed wire. The navigator's side. He can forget, until he sometimes sees the same car on a street, a white Mazda 1800 designed by Bertone. Whenever he leans unexpectedly fast into a left-hand corner. Whenever the vehicle tilts down to the right. There is a long silence, memory has lost the soundtrack, the other men are caught under the white car tilted on the shitty unforgiving fence, the brownish underbelly and the four wheels with gravel-stained tyres.

When a local farmer drove up, Trevor's passenger was holding a cigarette – he was still dazed, he was a smoker – so the farmer was as worried about him starting a fire as he was about the two cars crashed against his boundary fence. It was summer. As the media say, bone-dry.

The cars were dead, but there was, he can still remember it, petrol leaking from one of them. He thought of it when the cars crashed outside his shop not long ago. The smell.

He reaches up for the counter and manages to stand. Manages a few painful steps. His neck hurts. There is no option: he rings Elizabeth. Because he has no option he rings until she eventually answers. Faffing about in the backyard, she tells him, and not that she has been walking back and forth examining his paintings. 'I'll tell you why when you arrive,' he says to her, not wanting to alarm her or put her off either.

Then he sees the blood on the floor. It surprises him, he hadn't noticed the guy's face but he must have cracked his mouth, or nose, against the floor. Or a bookshelf. The jolt eases into an unforgiving laugh.

By the time Elizabeth parks outside the shop he has locked up and is sitting carefully on the steel-rung bench on the pavement.

'You've hurt your leg again,' she says as he drags the door open and arranges himself, wincing and grunting, on the bench seat of her Holden.

'Sorry, Trevor, but it is pretty obvious. Do you want to go home or to Emergency?'

'No. Home. Thanks. I slipped stepping down from the ladder. Which ended up with me on the floor.'

'It wasn't your father?'

'No.' *Jesus. What a thought.*

As Elizabeth works the old column shift through the gears it keeps taking him back to the accident. In his foul mood and pain he had forgotten her EH Holden is *circa* the years of his mate's car and the accident. The dust that never settles.

'Why the EH?' he asks her.

'It was my father's, talking of fathers. He renovated it years ago and I have a good garage looking after it. The mechanics want to buy it. They put the word on me every time I take it in. That's why it's in such good condition. The buggers. They helped me find a replacement back window after a hailstorm shattered it. I love it too much to sell it.'

Car love. At some point Trevor will need to tell her what happened. All he wants to do now is swallow ibuprofen and strong drink, and blot out everything.

'Anyway,' he asks, 'anyway,' turning way off the pain track, 'how did your night with the author go? This morning you looked (he is about to say *shagged out*) ...'

She makes a high-pitched humphing sound, like a dog dreaming and barking with its jaws shut.

'Well?'

'Are you sure you're not hurt?'

'It really fucking hurts, so tell me, how did it go?'

'I spoilt things a bit over the meal,' she says, 'by telling him how excited I was about this new manuscript and author. After the prize letdown it was the last thing he wanted to hear. I forget how competitive writers are. I only see them one to one, if I ever see them at all. It's always about them, so they're happy. I sometimes edit the whole thing without meeting them face to face. It was tactless of me.'

'Sounds more like ...'

'So I had to *seduce* him.'

They both laugh. He so much wants to laugh.

'He's a bloke,' he says, 'which means after sex he's all smiles.'

'Except his wife rang and he had to answer ...'

'Sure, but then ...?'

'Yeah, then my bloody mother rang ...'

He tells her about the roof of the shed, how he threw a tarpaulin over it. She hasn't been outside to notice. Once home, he sits on the lounge while she fetches water and painkillers and makes him a strong coffee.

He shouldn't really drink but to make matters worse she pours far too much whisky into his usual glass and brings it over.

'Isn't that what you wanted?' she asks. Unsure of why he is staring at the drink as if there is a hair in it, she bends to see.

He looks up at her and smiles. She's there beside him, it's night-time, the mood is calm, intimate even, in a way they are both relaxed with. He is not going to spoil things by telling her what really happened with his leg. Or embarrass himself.

'Is Richard your only boyfriend?' he asks. He knows he shouldn't. Surely he's vulnerable enough tonight to be unthreatening. Not the actual question, which is simply the prompt; having to answer at all. There are several lines forming around her eyes, and lines curve on either side of her mouth like a pair of brackets. When she smiles this makes whatever she says seems gentler and softer and more endearing.

She says she has occasional boyfriends. She isn't concerned about the casual sound of this. After all, her mother's frenetically sexual days as a sannyasin were an early model: they were also an indelible one.

'When you've watched your naked mother,' she says rather dramatically, 'fucking a man in the open while other people are walking past, you don't forget. You're forced into a frankness that is not like other people's. The sex cult they half denied and half boasted of being was all around us, they wanted us to see. You do know what sex is, from very early on.'

Talking like this with Trevor is good. She holds his gaze. Her reaction to open sexuality, she explains, was to become frank in action but reserved in discussion. Therefore, in her own estimation, she remains prone to embarrassment.

'Me too,' he says, 'mainly by not getting enough. Anyway, look at me. I'm hardly up to clubbing with you tonight. Unless you changed into something …'

'Naughty,' she says, laughing. 'You've had too much of your remedy. You should go online, do Tinder.'

Though she is less than convincing. She rubs her bare arm as if swiping back and forth over some impossibly good-looking face.

'Tinder? Online seduction?'

'Until you're able to walk again.'

'Ha. I'd end up feeling like an ex-cop I know, he says. Everyone seems to use it, and that one with a losing name – Bumble?'

'It's not that bad,' she shrugs.

'How does it work with your condition?' he says. 'Suppose you swipe someone a week after you'd decided never to go with them again. Because you didn't recognise them.'

She takes a deep breath before not answering him.

Not long after the fall Trevor's body starts entering returns in its pain diary. Reality. Where, after the date of onset, it demands appointments. It is not seducible. If no painkiller is ruthless enough to defeat it, not reducible either. Nurofen being half fake anyway.

He is forced to close the shop for appointments, limping through a sequence of diminishing sentience: from GP to specialists to joint and tissue scanners. Old territory, old route, very old in fact, back to the car crash, back when X-rays and CAT scans ruled, whereas now the MRI reigns over all, and costs a car crash of its own to prove it.

When not waiting for expert advice and its expert invoice, he stays for hours reading in his room. It doesn't help to remember his bloody father, or the shame of the fall. By now he has told Elizabeth what really happened, and watched her alarm. She can see he is still angry.

Then he lets go, and she sees he is depressed.

His leg hurts while he sits in the shop and it hurts every night. Like a guilty conscience. Humiliation. Pains enlarge in the dark and govern the weak body of sleep. His leg is like a character: it hurts and makes him vulnerable. Waking, he feels pushed down by the windowless walls and the ceiling above him. When he sits up and turns on the bedside lamp it hurts. And again when he twists over to turn it off.

Nothing to be done, or denied, or left for another time, he has to get well again, he has to *get fit*.

He dreams from inside the car. For some reason the person in the passenger seat hands him a lolly of some sort in such a way as to hide it from someone sitting in the back. As he puts the lolly in his mouth the car seems to drive itself off the road to the left and then quite effortlessly begins to roll. Quietly and without fear, he sees outside on the hillside, in great detail, the earth banking has been cut open and the extensive root system of a tree has been exposed. The roots are bulbous and huge and covered in red earth, though some have been sliced open by excavation equipment. Then the car rolls over and he is awake again, shaking.

The next morning Trevor stands on the pavement outside her house. The air is cold but quite still, beautiful in its simplicity. There is a faint smell of wood smoke in the air. His head clears. This is perfect, as close to eternity as any moment gets. As long as he doesn't move. As long as he remains still, feeling the crisp air on his face and his bare head, and smelling the easy woodsmoke. If he doesn't move, his leg doesn't hurt. Just stand here all day. He notices how rough the surface of the road is. The silence, which means the lorikeets are in some other street.

He has emerged, he is lucky.

Thereafter, for three evenings a week instead of walking home with a continual limp, and sometimes arriving wet through and feeling weak, he goes to the gym for physio and customised exercises and, with their possum-screeching sounds in his head, he pushes and pulls and bends against the weight machines. The relief when it stops. The sweat. The possums. He'll never be the same.

Before his next few months of rent or probation arrive he should be – and will be pissed off if he isn't – expansive of lung and muscular of limb. His chest can do with some work, for a start, and the muffin problem, from face to the dark fleece of his stomach, obviously needs improving. One day he will be a better-looking man so, yes, let vanity drive necessity. In his 30s he was a much tougher and leaner unit: not all of his days were lost behind a desk.

That bastard who pushed him was a wreck. The man had jumped him from behind. No pity for him. Resisting empathy, then. Probably a man much worn down by a shit life worse by far than anything Trevor could imagine.

You don't choose empathy. Every day some heartless sod wants to rake you over. Empathy is for loved ones, isn't it? But who are *his* loved ones?

He watches a small plane echo across towards the city. Propeller engine, sightseeing. That agreeable sound of props churning through the air when in fact it's the bite of heavy engines. Combustion. The upper floors of thin buildings are glowing in whitish sunlight, the sky behind them frigate grey. The city is a flotilla of kitsch.

Diana has told him there is something wrong with him. She has told him (she is not one to merely suggest) that he is still grieving. She refers to the era of Gestalt psychology and Fritz Perls, whose acolytes suspected everyone of having holes. Holes in their whole, and that such holes were the carryover of unfinished grief.

His father was emotional but it was normal for him, he was Polish.

When he gets home that night he walks straight through to the house and downstairs and out to the studio. It's very satisfying, navigating the house like a warm breeze. He is wondering what next, where to shift the balance of the painting, or not, with his latest colours, or not, or paste more images … when he hears clapping sounds like wooden boards being dropped. Outside he sees the back fence leaning inwards. The neighbour is breaking pickets off the crossbars and dropping them onto the pile on her side. The man has a wide, soft stomach and a hard face. There are bags of his rubbish, too.

It is the first time Trevor has encountered the man directly. His mobile is in his pocket so he walks down and takes several pics of the rubbish. And of The Creep.

'And what do you think you're doing?' says The Creep. 'Entering a photography exhibition?'

Trevor stands near the fence-line. The pickets to the left and right sides are like gateposts, the gate wide and bare and open, and the man is standing in the middle of it.

'Yeah,' says Trevor, 'inner-city ugliness.'

'The fence is a heap of shit and that's why I'm pulling it down.'

'I wasn't referring to the fence.'

'And who the fuck are you?'

'I'm renting a room here.'

'Oh right, poor woman. Poor you.'

'Poor fucking neighbour you are. Stop chucking your crap on Elizabeth's lawn.'

'No one would call that a lawn!'

The bloke starts breaking off pickets. Then he turns to look at Trevor.

'It's none of your fucking business, buddy.'

Trevor hates being called buddy. Americanism. Heat rises through him and his jaw clenches.

'Now look, mate,' (his voice low and angry) 'just leave this shit' (he points to it) 'on your side. Is that too complicated for you?'

Pudgy though he is around the middle, the man's angular face through the gap in the fence is disconcertingly good-looking.

'I'm not discussing this with you,' says the man. 'I'm not even discussing it with her. I might come over and kick your wonky leg so you'll never dance again. Tell the woman this fence is gunna cost her ...'

Trevor shakes his head at the gall. He thinks of *Good fences make good neighbours* – and feels like throttling Robert Frost.

He takes a few steps towards the man, stares at him hard.

'I get it,' he says to the man and the fence and the hole in the fence. 'I think you're a crim. I know the look and the attitude. And …'

He adds a few more words. Then a few more.

The bloke grunts and, heads off inside. *Well, Robert, bad men make bad neighbours*. He heaves the bags back through the fence.

Elizabeth has been watching the end of this. *So much for diplomacy*, she thinks. She prefers the aggro or whatever it was; it is thrilling. She feels like whooping.

The man does not return.

The gap in the fence darkens like lights turned off, and Trevor sees Elizabeth has been standing outside.

'What did you say to him at the end?' she calls out. 'I couldn't quite hear.'

'Nothing much.'

His face is like a road. She raises her eyebrows.

'The man is reasonable,' he says, 'so we talked and he went away happy.'

Back in his studio he knows he's just had a delayed reaction to the Frank Miller bloke. Arseholes. He is like that, some things rinse him out like the yearly event when the mother in Duras' *The Lover* swashes out the house. He inspects the images he has been painting. Barrels, drums, boxes, objects with swirling centres and a complete lack of foundation. They stagger but are still. Yes. The man has made him angrier than he'd expected.

Perhaps it's the smell of too much turpentine. At least turps thins out his oils, better than adrenaline ever could. It was satisfying, though, pretending to be the hard man. Real hard men are different. They are like Lester.

Normally Trevor walks home the same way every evening. Lunch-time walks are different. If it is sunnier walking around the block, and cold in the shadows, he walks in the sun. If it is hot and he is carrying food, he walks in the shadows. Walking off the workday's cabin fever he enters a pub he hasn't visited before. A bloke sitting alone by the window. Lester. Well, well, the cop turned outsider artist just like the crims in *Maximum*. The deeply lined face. The ambiguous person he is.

It seems Lester drinks in a fancy pub, gentrified, young, innocent staff in white shirts, shiny surfaces. To contrast with his state of mind.

'Trauma,' says Lester. 'Yeah, I copped a bit of that. As you well know. We always said you used to look as frazzled as we did. Front-line trauma, though, that's something you never got.'

'Did it come from crims or from your own higher-ups, that's what I couldn't work out. You'd never say.'

'Mate, I had a job at the time. I wanted to keep it. But being shot at, that's takes top position. Being shot at does leave you traumatised, if you're a breathing human. If you're still breathing afterwards, that is. Takes a while for anyone to adjust to. Imagine if some fucker is staring straight at you and lets rip with a big fucking hollow-point. Bang. It was after you left, mate.'

He pulls his collar aside and shows Trevor a horizontal scar deep on the side of his neck near his collarbone. He swipes with his hand like a front-to-back version of cutting his throat.

'Jesus, Lester. They nearly got you.'

'Nearly! They fucking *got* me, Trevor, just didn't kill me. An inch to the left and I'd a gushed blood for half a minute then carked it. The slug would've torn half my throat out and left it hanging over my shoulder. A bit further over and it'd have blown my head off. OK for you in your fucking desk job.'

'Yeah, no guns in the office. Some people don't need them. Like your boss.'

'Yeah, he was a right cunt. One of many. I might well have ended up down an alley with a big hole in me because of him.'

'Do cops shoot each other?'

If Lester knows, and he must, he isn't saying because not saying is the best act for a man who has been tough until tripped up by his own mind, let alone by crooked cops with or without big calibres. Or as he had always said: it's like small cocks and big cars.

'Well, you could say,' he says, 'that some of my wounds were self-inflicted, by a self beholden to no one and to nothing. And a lot of bloody good it did me.'

'I'm almost as bad,' says Trevor, then downs his drink. 'Do you have any undercover work or are you just painting strange little things and reading John Silvester in *The Saturday Age*?'

'Funny bastard. I was superannuated out, and on a disability gig like a great many people in this suburb. Some of whom look self-inflicted too. I'm just more burnt out and that's saying something. At least I earned it. Ha.'

'How's the painting going?'

'Huh.'

Though why is he asking the old cop and not the other way round? As he leaves he feels the sunlight lean across from the west. The wounds we all carry sometimes go cold in him and, it being unusually warm today, he walks on the sunny side of every street for as long as possible. He needs it. Instead of walking through the house he walks along the side path Elizabeth uses for the wheelie bin. There he sees her, lying on the lawn with Gordon, her face in the last sunlight, eyes closed, her wide lips in a huge and private smile. Sunlight is holding her blonde hair in a loose bob around her face, but it is her wide smile of happiness, even satisfaction, that entrances him.

He stands there watching her, then quietly retreats.

~

After thinking about it for a few days, Elizabeth asks him a favour.

'It won't be for long,' she says, 'it's just that I get bored driving up to see Mum by myself and then back by myself. If you potter about in the garden that'll be OK, Mum won't mind and, as I said, it'll be a quick trip.'

A division is happening in him: to go because it is different and he likes her and driving up to Ballarat like this might make a change – and the deadening thought of being trapped in conversation with an old parent who will ask him all sorts of clichéd questions expecting their clichéd answers, while he sits on the edge of an ergonomic nightmare of a lounge chair made in the early '70s.

'I'll shout you a couple of pints afterwards,' she adds.

'Let's see. How about before?'

Elizabeth explains that, yes, although her mother was a publican once, she doesn't approve of people drinking during the day. Daft as that sounds. Her mother knows Trevor is the lodger and will worry if her daughter has a lodger who drinks during the day.

'Now,' he laughs, 'why would that sound daft? A publican who opened at 10 am to sell booze to customers she didn't approve of because they drank during the day?'

There is no answer to this, as Elizabeth well knows.

'How about you leave me at the pub while you see her? I'll sit in the beer garden with a book until you pack me into your car for the drive home.'

'She wants to meet you.'

He returns to the kitchen and stays there. His chilli-and-ginger sauce is ready. After simmering the pork belly in his six-month master sauce the day before, he has kept it overnight in the fridge, a slab of dark something. He adjusts the gas under the oil and as he waits he stares at the rice cooker and inspects the broccolini for blemishes. His life is all inconsequential *and*s.

Then Elizabeth leans on the other side of the bench. And smiles at him.

The introductions are over quickly. Trevor sits down in the spare chair in Mrs Sermon's lounge. Not that anyone would seriously describe it as a lounge. The chair presents a posture hazard, as expected, but he is also at risk of being crushed by cliffs of newspaper collapsing on him. Every surface in the house is sticky. The woman is kind of crazy. She has been talking about him without once addressing him.

'So,' says Mrs Sermon, 'has your lodger been settling in comfortably?'

'Yes, Mum. Trevor, that's his name.'

Trevor clears his throat. Elizabeth has remained standing; there isn't room for a third chair.

'Um, Mrs Sermon, I am only, ah, renting the room for a few months.'

Elizabeth shakes her head at him.

The old woman isn't very old-biddy-like, and she smiles the smile of conspirators throughout history. Without once looking in his direction.

'It's all right, dear, I practised free love as only the Orange People could do it, I went off to live in Poona with everyone who was sexually enlightened, so there's no need to be discreet.'

'About … what?'

'I'm very pleased Elizabeth has found someone. It's been so long.'

Trevor is peering at Elizabeth now, who is nodding at him like someone on happy pills, smiling and doing something fussy with her hands. *God, how slow is he? What a set-up. This is worth much more than a few pints.* Elizabeth is looking so cheerful and yet desperate he feels tempted to hold her to some of her own implications. *Jump into her bed?*

'What happened to your father, Trevor?' asks Mrs Sermon. 'I know fathers are as weak as piss, excuse the expression, with hers (she flicks her head towards Elizabeth) clearing out years ago and, from what I've heard, yours did too.'

'It was Yvonne's father who left,' says Elizabeth, 'not my dad. *You* left.'

'No, no, you're wrong.'

'My father died,' says Trevor. 'Or he went missing, presumed dead. A death without a body, it confuses everyone. For thirty years. Then, a week or so ago, he re-appeared.'

He stops. She is looking past him rather than at him, unfocussed. She begins rubbing her nose and keeps it up for longer than usual. She has been inspecting Trevor as closely. His rounded stomach and his shaven dome. Perhaps he has been something powerful in an earlier life before falling back. There is something unfinished about him. But he is strong, he sits still, he is a good man.

'Oh,' she says, finally. 'Well, that's … bad luck.'

It makes him laugh. Bad luck is the least of it.

'What was your name again?'

'Trevor.'

'Ah yes. Trevor,' she says. 'You should eat less. You're fat.'

They are travelling in the grey EH across Ballarat to the shops and what Elizabeth still thinks of as Dan Murphy's as if denying to herself it's actually Woolworths. The lure of cheap booze quashes any deeper principles. Her mother shuffles on the red vinyl bench seat in the back and complains about its lack of support. Trevor is in the front. If he could, he'd project himself completely out of time and space altogether. *Elizabeth owes him.*

'Well, your father had taste,' he does say, 'maintaining a car like this. You have to let me drive it one day.'

From the back seat he hears the old woman muttering.

'He was a loser,' she says.

Elizabeth turns around to address her mother.

'Now, now, *towards the heart*, remember. *Love and compassion.*'

'Oh, shut up.'

'By the way, Mum, changing the subject, did you see the news item about a hoarder dying in a house fire? It was horrific.'

'Never seen a house fire. The pub I had burnt down after I'd left. They said bikies lit a barbecue in the front bar.'

'The hoarder shouldn't have died. The fire crew couldn't get into the house to save him, they had to break windows to get access. It was his own fault.'

The old woman clears her throat and says:

'No one was fooled about that fire, they knew he wanted to collect the insurance. The place never made a profit after I left.'

'Because of all his rubbish, Mum,' stresses Elizabeth. 'Being in the way of access, and then catching fire. The firies couldn't find a path through the house. All those stacked rows of newspaper – just imagine it – a maze of flames inside the house.'

'A house fire, dear? Some people are so careless.'

'Another man was found in a mummified state hidden under his junk inside his house. He'd been there for ten years.'

'Obviously he wasn't a nice man or someone would have found him.'

Trevor finds the old woman's obliqueness amusing. The fire image is pretty good, all the same. But then so is the mummy.

'He was on the floor,' says Elizabeth. 'Under piles of junk,' she adds. 'By the time they found him they were lucky to be alive themselves. He wasn't. He inhaled all of his rubbish in the form of toxic smoke. God, what it must have been like …'

'And your point is?'

'Mum, you must be joking. You're getting worse at collecting. You're out of control.'

'What are you telling me this for?'

'You want to know why? You, a hoarder of newspapers?'

Another minute passes before her mother responds.

'Well, it would save me fumbling around with the good doctor's do-it-yourself kit. Would it not?'

'Would it not,' says Elizabeth.

She drags at the heavy manual steering to enter the car park, this lack of power assistance the only gripe she has with the car. That and the turning circle from here to the footy boundary.

'Your house is a firetrap, that's what. And then, *then*, it's a person trap. You're simply not mobile enough and if your place went up it'd be a fiery maze too. You're my mother and, though you're as stubborn as (she grunts at the wheel), I'd prefer you ... alive.'

'Very kind of you, I'm sure.'

Despite her minimalism her mother's head is nodding and, while it might be from the heat, it's more probably with suppressed emotion.

Which mustn't be on Elizabeth's mind when she curses the old man who has nearly reversed his car into her beautiful car doors. 'Fuck you,' she shouts out the window and bangs the horn. Trevor wakes up, straightens beside her. From the back seat they hear her ex-publican mother.

'Yeah, fuck the old guy,' she growls. And Trevor laughs. They all laugh.

The old guy pulls back into his parking space then, unbelievably, begins reversing again. They are still behind him. Elizabeth doesn't just toot again, she holds in the horn inserts on the steering wheel. The old mechanical device keeps blaring and people stop, stare, until the old guy drives in again. 'What an idiot!' Elizabeth can handle herself. And doesn't the old man wish she wouldn't.

Her mother can walk unaided, just. The walking frame is something she loathes even as she leans on it to keep her balance. It is better that she suffer this and stay conscious of her balance than stumble and fall. Broken hip, end of life. Sign-off for the good or bad doctor. Death in Dan Murphy's.

Instead, as she wheels herself in slight wobbles, Mrs Sermon waylays the customers with aisle rage.

'Come on, let me get past. Do you mind? When I was your age I let older people have right of way and I never gave it a thought. Don't you scowl at me, it looks terrible, if you could only see yourself. What is it with people nowadays?'

The customers know what to do. Like seeing an erratic driver on a highway, people mostly dodge lanes and avoid them. She's lucky there is such decorum around un-drunk alcohol. The old publican in her knew better when the stuff was flowing. Stern hand needed.

'Elizabeth. Where are you? Don't go so far ahead. Where's what's-his-name?'

As soon as they walked through the shiny bar entrance Trevor had veered away to the whisky shelves. As he inspects the single malts he can hear her voice carrying above the aisles. Booze may make people excessive and noisy but when they search for it among the shelves they remain modest and quiet. She is wearing loose slacks and her favourite green cardigan, her hair as pinched up as Elizabeth's used to be and carrying on like a regular, which is no doubt what the customers think she is.

A woman in the shop's khaki uniform asks her if she needs any help, which means placating the normal people in the shop. Except she accidentally bumps the walking frame and it digs into the old woman's shin.

'Ouch!' she cries, 'Oh oh!'

And she sits down on the floor to examine her leg. The staff woman bends over her. By now Elizabeth is pushing back towards her mother with her trolley in front of her. Trevor is approaching from behind. It looks like a traffic accident.

'I want my daughter to come back and … ah, there you are. This stupid woman has hurt me,' she says. 'Look, I'm bleeding. She pushed me down.'

If Elizabeth is ever worried about her mother it doesn't show, or perhaps she dare not show her pleasure as these out-of-kilter moments occur. Her mother's obstinacy shines on and off like a wonky beacon.

'You're showing off in public again, Mum. I bleed more than that when I brush my teeth.'

Her mother squashes her mouth down like an old woman without any teeth.

'It's stopped now. I've been holding my shin so tightly my hands are hurting. Don't just stand there,' she says to Trevor, 'help me up.'

First he was set up as the new boyfriend (she didn't say he wasn't) and now she has another scheme. Monitoring the elderly. Therefore the long way through her debt is via Guinness. It's far from over. She is sitting opposite him, or in front of him, a single glass of white wine in front of her.

'Do I think your mother is demented? Let's see: she can't remember names, she's tactless.'

'She always has been.'

'Do I think she's a bit on the crazy side? Or just old? Or undernourished? You are a family of dedicated starvers.'

He is on his third pint.

'And you want her to stay in *our* place for a week, while you study her. While *we* study her …? For what? Symptoms?'

'More or less. It's no good asking her, she's full of crap.'

'Like her house. I've heard of hoarders but, Jesus, it's a nightmare. All that rubbish on top of rubbish, like a cave full of bat shit.'

'Would you believe her sannyasin name was Amitabha, which means Boundless Lustre. She thought it made her sound tubby, so she shortened it to Amit, which still dignifies her.'

'How?'

'It means Endless Infinitude.'

'And she bloody well called me fat.' He takes another gulp. 'She behaved like an ageing drama queen in the booze barn. That poor woman she berated. If she stays with us for a week ...'

This may encourage more sympathy in Elizabeth. Or less, which he hasn't thought of. In truth, the "fat" comment has been more useful than hurtful, or useful and hurtful: in the gym he has been pushing his pain threshold, something he used to consider neurotic in others.

Elizabeth has driven her mother home and left Trevor at the pub with some money, before returning to sit beside him looking out across the street and the large median strip to the shops on the far side. Ballarat is so wide. All the subterfuge has made her tired.

She had thought of bringing her mother down to the city several months ago before he arrived, thus the room problem. That is, Trevor. She can't ask him to move out of his paid room to allow an old woman to sleep in it for a week. (She'd like to.) *Where would he live?* Her daughter was different. If she came for a few nights she could sleep on the roll-out mattress in the study, but she hasn't. Then if Trevor volunteered his room it would only make it worse, but he hasn't. Elizabeth will leave her room for her mother and sleep in the study herself. It strikes her again how the pleasure of giving or yielding can be that person's indulgence. Almost sinfully so. Altruism is an open pit.

She knows her mother might be in fear of dementia. Given that her poor balance and confusion are not unique, and that she is diagnosed with hyperthyroidism, her fear of Alzheimer's is already a displacement. If she lets dying happen she will die from her glands or, like most people, from her tired old heart.

So much life, so much resistance. A few weeks earlier she had told Trevor how she worked hard during her marriage, wanting to live and work and keep ahead of the accidental Yvonne. *So many women fell behind.* Her fear of what could happen to their daughter. *At any moment.* But Ian was too easygoing, he was being rubbed away by her energy and concentration, he left before she rubbed him out. Some people just want to amble along.

After sharing a ciggie with Trevor, they drive back to the city in silence. Like a real couple. There is no way he can drive after his drinks barter has been consumed. Full of the black stuff he is. For all his curiosity about the car he sits there as passenger, more the passive than the passing, ambling along, so relaxed he hums to old songs in his head as she eases the old car through several corners and on to the road out of Ballarat until they are free-riding down the highway to Melbourne. Hoping it won't rain, though that isn't likely – clouds too pale and grey, more light in them than water, more stage design than downpour. The odometer shows 198,000 and this, he realises, is miles, a long past which means one major engine reconditioning, gallons of oil blacker even than Guinness and boxes of all-but-obsolete linings for the old drum brakes.

Watching her drive is his consolation. And she can drive, no doubt about it, a car that many people couldn't or wouldn't. The gears aren't easy, having long throws and a jolting movement which she makes smooth in two barely perceptible movements: out of one gear into neutral, pause, then up or down into the next gear. Smart. Pausing just enough to allow the leverage and gearing to align, then on to the accelerator. On to the gas, as the Yanks say, but never would of this iconic Aussie car. From the back of the car he hears the familiar Holden sound of the diff whining. It is sending him to sleep.

~

Trevor arrives home from the gym in his sweaty singlet and black tights to find the room-shuffling in progress. In the house there is almost as much lifting and stumbling being done as in the gym, just nothing lifted is shiny steel and instead of musclemen it features auto-vocalising by Elizabeth as she mumbles and grunts and bundles doonas and pillows in her arms until she can barely see over them. She hasn't noticed him. He attempts the joke he has thought of a few minutes earlier, putting on a high-pitched US accent.

'Hi, honey, I'm home ...'

Elizabeth turns and looks at him without reaction, still holding the doonas. She has been setting up her room and not listening to the monologue of her mother's, now suddenly ended.

'It's me,' he says, 'Trevor. You can tell by my smile.'

She moves into the room, returns pushing a swivel chair on castors all the way into her study. Of course she knows it's him. His body is changing shape, enough to discern, more to admire. His arms, his freer movement, or is she just imagining? That he is here in her house. At least she hasn't told him she recognises his body scent, the warm bread of his skin. Not that he alone smells like this. She is aware of several types of body scent whether she wants to or not, from bread or yeast and earthy and fruity all the way across to wet towels, and sharper heat stinks of *people like coalmines* as she once told Martina. Or gymnasts.

She drags a small mattress and some blankets into the study and scrapes the chairs on the wooden floorboards. This time she stops, lets him see her appraise his relative nakedness. She raises her eyebrows, then continues.

'What do you think of my public legs?' he says.

'Huh.'

What she sees is the extensive scarring. He is bright and lively and going to keep talking. It's as if he has forgotten, unable to see the leg for the limp.

'I've been going to the Fairfield boat shed. I hire a rowing boat – notice, Ms Editor, my use of the -ing ending – and row an actual boat on the Yarra. Didn't I tell you?'

But she has disappeared again.

During this little ceremony of accommodation, Elizabeth's mother has been sitting in the lounge like a proudly feathered chief.

Watching him. Very upright. Her walking frame, ugly thing it is, beside her. She is not unattractive, Mrs Sermon, even at her age. More Red Cloud than Sitting Bull, judging from her ruddy features. Too much sun in the hippie days and a raddled later life of the skin. A scarf is wrapped untidily around her head. Hardly feathers, let alone full dramatic headdress, yet it does suggest qualities of repose, dignity, even wisdom. Three things her daughter claims her mother went in search of but came back without.

Trevor hasn't noticed her. Until she resumes talking.

Apropos of woollen blankets, perhaps, begins telling him of the sheep they saw, thousands of sheep in the paddocks on the way down and how, astonishingly, some had escaped onto the highway causing havoc, she says, havoc, as they, the newsreaders, always announce it. 'Havoc,' she repeats. 'What a great word.'

She likes his legs, it seems. Yes. She thinks legs are important and is proud of her own long pair, shapely as they used to be. Long they may be, but she refuses to admit they are no longer reliable. Either that or her hips have let her down, something she will almost accept.

In Elizabeth's roomy and better-lit rooms he sees she is not so old after all. Inclined to play old when it suits her, he suspects, watching as she calls to Elizabeth and asks for confirmation about the sheep. 'Remember, the sheep?'

'Oh yes,' she adds, 'we used to roast sheep on a spit during my childhood, when we lived in the country, on sports days you know, when the football teams had finished up at finals, or after show days. The men did all that and the women fussed about with cakes and salads on long trestle tables, all very divided worlds back then. Parents. That is before I grew up and became a vego with the Rajneesh organisation. Women were meant to be freer there, too, but it was the men who had it best, sex and more sex and the power, too. We were left, like women in communes the world over, with babies.'

'I don't recall you worrying about babies, Mum,' shouts Elizabeth from the other room.

Her mother pauses.

'Sheep. All those fat sheep. My goodness, what a roast they would have made. We nearly brought one back for you. Elizabeth says you are a carnivore.'

Elizabeth walks past, eyebrows raised. This is a revelation: her mother going at it with a young, well younger, man? Maybe not the walk, but the talk. 'What is this about sheep?'

'Nearly brought one back? A baby or a sheep?'

'That one you almost drove over.'

'Mum, you are exaggerating. Something you always accuse *me* of.'

'Yes, well, my exaggerations are more interesting than yours. Have you ever eaten sheep on a spit?' she says, looking at Trevor.

When Elizabeth returns he notices her skin is shining. She, too, is wearing a singlet. Her arms and shoulders are lean but there is smooth muscle tone there. Work suits her and she is aware of it, looking at him looking at her, and feeling the cloth tight against her upper body, her jeans the stretchy ones they now warn women not to wear if doing much bending and working or sitting for long periods. Cutting-off-the-circulation jeans. It's good to have a man around, for her sense of proprioception as much as her self-esteem. Her posture. She likes the way he notices her, that he is surprised by her. He has even enticed her mother to have a conversation, not a monologue.

To celebrate feeling good about herself and self-sacrificial, before the actual discomfort of a night on the floor, she goes into her room and returns with a bottle.

'Heathcote shiraz,' she announces, 'for everyone except you, mother dear.' And then she opens it and pours two glasses.

'I think I'm a bad influence on you,' Trevor says. 'I'm making you a red-blooded woman. Where previously you were gin. Resveratrol is good for the heart.'

Influence or not, he is soon relaxed. And yet how easy it is, making him feel slightly sheepish, old and fuddy-duddy. Recently it seems Elizabeth is fresher in appearance, she could pass for late 30s and that's, um, young. Except when she makes no effort and like him, like men, like many women beyond Instagram, why should she?

She throws half a biscuit to Gordon and misses him by miles. Then she is fumbling a plate. Her home pair of nerdy glasses, which she has taken off and clearly needs.

'If you're so short-sighted, Elizabeth, why not get your eyes fixed? When you go out on the razzle you wear contacts. When you were trying to get Richard going.'

'When I'm being a red-blooded woman, you mean? Trevor, you've noticed. It's to stop my eyes glowing red.'

'You could chuck the glasses altogether.'

If he is trying to be helpful she is trying to make him smile. And make him take an interest in *her*, not her weak eyesight. She knows, she knows.

'Bloody nuisance,' she adds, 'except I've had them all of my life.'

'Laser surgery is perfect for short-sighted people. Once it's done, no more glasses needed for anything. Go and see the optometrist in Errol …'

'Trevor, I know all about those laser operations.'

'OK. Well, not all. Otherwise you'd probably have it done.'

'What? I can't bring myself to have them cutting my eyes.'

'Or crossing your t's?'

Mrs Sermon interrupts to say she's had it done and to stop being such a wuss. It isn't the first time they've had this conversation, with its *I have/I can't* commentary. The old woman has the nerve to roll her eyes at Trevor. *She didn't*, he thinks, even if he's wrong.

'I've had it done too,' says Trevor. 'I can show you the DVD of my operation if you like.'

'That's grotesque,' growls Elizabeth, then makes a nervous laughing sound.

The following night Trevor again suggests she watch the DVD. Her TV sits in the lounge like a black blank because she rarely watches it. He has a small screen downstairs he occasionally uses. With an Apple TV he can watch On Demand from SBS.

Tonight her mother is sitting there watching without much interest.

So Elizabeth lets him slide in the DVD.

It's a silent movie – she has not expected that – which makes it even creepier. Even some mumbling between surgeon and assistants would provide some work-rumble to neutralise the slicing and replacing. At least there are no graveyard sutures.

The cornea is washed and wiped and then a stainless steel slicer is placed over it and positioned like a soft-boiled egg-cap remover. Trevor's slicer in close-up looks crudely constructed, hardly a Fabergé in finish – and is clearly numbered 140. Then it slices and withdraws and a small prong enters the image from the side, lifting the transparent eye flap back to the left where it is pressed flat and washed, wiped. A red light, which must be the laser, maps the clear surface exposed by the slicer, and in no time a section is presumably lasered off. The eye is washed, wiped, the slicer removed, the flap of cornea lifted back and carefully pressed into its home position, and again we see washing and wiping. In complete silence. Ghostly. Then the same with the second eye.

His blue eyes look grey and could in all truth be anyone's. Patients could have a collective film night and discover that their DVDs – for each eye colour – are all the same. That they are the same DVD given out to everyone according to team colours.

Anyway, his eyes reacted in reverse state: the long eye shortened and the short eye lengthened, and that was not the intention but he does not tell Elizabeth this as the operation is more truly designed to help short-sightedness and not lopsided sight like his was, and now is again, except reversed.

Mrs Sermon doesn't make it to the end of this eye-slicing discussion. The DVD bores her. Or perhaps she has fallen asleep with all the sheep talk. Delayed reaction. Yes, he does want to impress Elizabeth. Even if only by this modern and tamed version of Dali's film of the eye and the razor. It always sounds worse than it is. She has taken her glasses off now, turns to look at him, is very close. Except this isn't intimacy, it's an outburst of irritation. No, she does *not* want his eye operation and why did he insist on showing her? Her face is reddening.

He feels the hot water passing over his skin. The showerhead in the bottom bathroom delivers an impressive flow, newer in design than hers, the luxury of the recent renovation. Not that he has ever been in her shower. When he turns the taps off he hears her water running. Standing there, naked, water dripping from him as he listens, suddenly aware she is standing, naked, under the water, immediately above him in the upstairs shower.

As above, so below. Perhaps she will be his better consciousness. If she calms down.

Before he turns off the light the days shuffle through him as they always do. His leg is aching a bit and this will increase, he knows. The extra gym-work. Perhaps any single person lying half asleep at the end of any day is compressed on the other side, the dead end, of the achievement spectrum. Lacking recognition, of selves not faces, is all through it, and social awkwardness, lapsing outages of empathy, the kind in favour not of another's feelings but of having their feelings favour you.

It seems to him now, just now, that Diana is not very good at pleasure. Even sexually, between them it had become a routine she was content to let happen, not because it was exciting, or different, or unexpected, and therefore because she desired it.

Whereas her work is important. She needs focus, purpose, and that is her meaning.

Diana doesn't even know where he lives. And Elizabeth doesn't know who he is. Or what he intends. Still, if she can get that close and that annoyed over the eye stuff it's actually a good sign. There is a new sound in the house. The old mum is snoring from Elizabeth's room. He hasn't heard snoring before. Unless the old woman has left the door open. Yes, that must be it. He is quite impressed to know this. Or she is regressing to childhood and feels more secure in a new place if she can see some dim light from the lamp Elizabeth leaves on in the kitchen. The glow of long-gone parents. Safe traces of one life left in another, the next, and the next.

Continuity.

Sleep.

～

For several weeks now Elizabeth has been emailing Shia. For all her fascination with communal sects, Shia is a recluse, unusual for her age. The publishing staff call her "The Cavewoman". No one has seen her, there is only one image in the public domain, no presence whatsoever on social media (the marketing people will pester her about that). She only has phone contact with Elizabeth so only Elizabeth knows what she sounds like. Shia says little. This suggests something high-pitched about control. Either that or she has been watching the Elena Ferrante drama too closely. Perhaps she is Elena Ferrante, whoever *she* is.

Shia's emails, however, are over a page long and sometimes longer, including comments about the weather, her health, why she has been reluctant to trust editors – all of which make her sound like a grumpy male – with amendments and attachments full of unseen new paragraphs and their position in *The Collector*, details she might include if Elizabeth approves, though they are sudden and stylistically inconsistent. *Is she testing her? A woman strange enough to improvise her ideas through thousands of words for no other reason than to challenge?*

At times she departs from the manuscript entirely, digressing into a discourse on #MeToo and issues like land use or Indigenous rights. For a while she had considered comparing sect life with community life in central Australia. She knew that would tax her, she, the go-nowhere and probably well-educated middle-class white person, heading out to the central desert in a small Hyundai? She hates politicians and emperors like the loathsome Rupert Murdoch and barbarian Trump. But who doesn't? Her riffs carry something wild, and angry, some of it un-nerving.

The working title is a worry. When Elizabeth tells her John Fowles wrote a famous novel called *The Collector* in the '60s she doesn't respond (she's too young, she doesn't know, she doesn't care?) not even if Fowles' main character imprisons a young woman, pins her as if she were a butterfly, in his perverse collection. Still nothing.

Sects do collect and they do imprison, their killing bottles are sometimes drugs, like Hamilton-Byrne's doses of LSD injected into 12-year-olds who were then locked in a darkened room. Sometimes it is wildly gaseous rhetoric.

So Elizabeth has nicknamed the manuscript *K'lector* as in Hannibal Lecter. What she has uncovered in *K'lector* is a twisting contradiction in the characters. It has made her feel unwell. Though the contradictions are real enough, especially among manipulative personalities, sometimes the characters are impossible to disentangle. Her suggestion is to pull apart the structure and reorder the time line. And to let more of the character arise from the action, cathartically, finally, without so many unconvincing claims made by the author. It had to come clean, *earned*, like her own desire to see the book triumph.

Eventually she sends Cavewoman – in a hard-won bit of writing – a light-hearted scolding over her refusal to leave her hideaway and discuss her text face to face. No reply for at least a week. Elizabeth is worried enough to check the dates. Has she offended (*please, not that again*) another novelist? She emails a question mark.

It's ALL bullshit, replies Shia a day later, and forgive me for being non-sequiturial. The book publishing scene looks likes property management sometimes. Safe books in safe suburbs. I'm uncomfortable with all the bland media promotion of each literary darling as if they were celebrities. I am so far off liking any of that. Maybe I'm too dark for a writer, I feel stuck in this spiritual trap I'm trying to express. All those serious people reading every bullshit starofthemoment and festival directors and literary editors wanting to schmooze with them. Everyone in fact, so deadly earnest. But you're only an editor, so chill.

'Fuck, fuck, fuck!' Elizabeth shouts, eyes to the ceiling. The presumption of this hurts her breath. The one advantage of email: no body language. Also its disadvantage.

Again, some writer shits on a person who is working on their behalf. Sounds like a man.

And she has not addressed the suggestions.

Almost immediately she remembers the pithy response from T S Eliot when the definition was put to him that most editors are failed writers. Eliot's reply: *Perhaps, but so are most writers.* Brilliant. It helped her when she tried to write, long ago, and realised that, though she was good, she wasn't good enough. She is a better finder than maker – she discerns where the text is strongest and where it must concentrate. The raw text is unwell and she is its doctor.

So. Someone must have talked up Shia to the last person they should have – herself. All the more reason, therefore, to discuss the manuscript's faults. Not have this un-nuanced bloody email exchange with its crossover raves and crossings out and endlessly vexatious paragraphs.

A new email arrives on her screen.

Without any comment Shia agrees to the big shifts in her time line.

Towards the end of the day Elizabeth risks reinforcing her observations about the characters. Shia, she types, I assume you read my thoughts regarding the three sect leaders at the centre of Collectors. Ring me. A spunky lot and I'm impressed you've made them so. Verbally, that is … (I know psychological characterisation isn't your main concern …) but it seems to me these women (interesting that they are women, rare in sects) are like the Bronte sisters. Smart, headstrong and diversely talented, brilliant, but isolated. By choice in this case, cut off from the world in order to totalise their control over the group. They are dangerous. But why so samey? There's too much going on for them to be sounding so much the same. It's not psychological, it's the texture, the liveliness. We must discuss them.

Shia emails back in five minutes. Elizabeth's kettle hasn't had time to boil.

Just three versions, she replies, of the same sort of characterisation, is that what you're saying? I never thought of that. I could make it more so, on purpose, couldn't I? Make it creepier? Or vary them more?

Elizabeth again: Vary them. At the moment, whenever they speak, these three women, they're not sisters after all, whenever they speak (to each other or to others) they sound like … each other. Keep that incestuous kind of pact they have, which is terrific. I mean, parallel to them manipulating the children and younger adults, they have this sexually complex tangle of their own. Are they playing out their own sexual tensions on the followers?

Shia's next email arrives before she can finish.

So, I've missed a few tricks?

It sits there, alone and – incredibly – brief. Elizabeth stares at it, almost laughs. Somehow she has shut her up. She responds:

Motives: not always upfront or even 'evil'. My mother was indifferent and irresponsible and drove me crazy. She ended up wanting more power in the 'cult' – she was Narcissistic, blind, yes, controlling. She believed in her name of Boundless Lustre! She expected love and therefore obedience. Even so, it wasn't aggression, it was entitlement. She was up herself. You could keep in the back of your mind: these followers were not stupid or damaged, they were Narcissists.

When Shia asks for more of this mother-daughter detail, Elizabeth realises she is shedding any thoughts of writing it herself. Not such a good feeling.

Still. There is something Shia should use, not the melodramatic and psychological frights of gurus but the insidious spread of solipsism among their followers. Their attentions too often devoid of empathy. Empathy, such a contemporary issue even if a few years ago it was rarely discussed. Talking about her personal fallout from the Orange Blight, as Elizabeth once called it, comes back to catharsis. She needs it, so she tells it:

For six weeks of her school holidays Elizabeth travelled down to live in the ashram, to be briefly one of the Orange kids in Beedelup, playing near the lake under the karri trees, watching the adults meditate and talk earnestly and even have sex in the open, casually, for all the children to view if they wanted to, and what nearly pubescent child isn't curious? Except when she saw her own mother naked on all fours with a man slapping up behind her.

A few days later, her mother was squatting on a man and crying out as she tried to come. Elizabeth did not want to see this. She was angry and spent as much time avoiding her mother as going to her. Hardly a happy state, it was scary. Even if the other adults were warm and happy, who were they really? *Was she a communal child or an abandoned one?* Some other children felt the same way.

'You'll have to go back by yourself if you want to keep doing this silly being-a-gymnast thing,' her mother had said. 'My training under the Bhagwan is too important. The Bhagwan is coming here and I must be prepared.'

'Why did you even have me if you can't be bothered being my mother?'

'But I didn't have you, you were an accident, darling, just a flash in the pan, as it were! I was never any good at taking pills.'

'You mean sticking to a routine.'

Her 12-year-old bullshit meter had much to work on with her mother.

'Routines are for losers, darling.'

And she stared at her disappointing daughter.

One of the several dogs on the property ran across in front of them, wet and sandy from swimming in the lake. A second dog, mottled and mongrel, skidded around the corner of the building and chased after it.

'No, dear, it's work on ourselves that matters. And that's what I'm doing. When you get older you will realise how important this really is.'

'And what do you think I'm doing? Every day.'

'Just the body, sweetie, just the body. You are learning a discipline, of course, I admit that. That's good, but it's also a terrible limitation. I need my *mind* to be free.'

Her mind meant that much to her. Years before the Bhagwan she had enjoyed sitting topless and tanned in the full sunlight, with Elizabeth suckling from her breasts. She was aware of nature, of the sun, of a special, unearthly love in Elizabeth's eyes. It had to be more than thirst. Even sexual, of course, in the occasional orgasm she felt rising like Kundalini in her spine, come of her own flesh and blood sucking her nipples. Such a circular event is life. And from people watching? No, she was not as ordinary as that, she was spiritual.

More irony, then. To rephrase old Wordsworth: *The Child is mother of the Woman?*

Sometimes the Bhagwan said he didn't believe in God. It was all up for grabs. Or had they got that wrong? He had left the planet to his vicious sidekick Ma Sheela, the devil who had earlier groomed then doomed the ashram in Pemberton. Ma Sheela, who then tried to kill the Bhagwan's physician with poison in Oregon before she upped her ambition by trying to poison an entire township with salmonella, and nearly succeeded, just to prevent them voting for their preferred councillors in local elections.

By then, Elizabeth had a degree in English Literature, her own daughter was born and her mother had disappeared.

Even now the old mother prides herself on her sagacity. But to have been called a loser – so categorically – hurt Elizabeth in a way her mother never understood, never gave a minute to understand. This attitude of hers is quieter now, it hardly speaks its presence, or if so it is merely to patronise Elizabeth, which is ironic, even futile, considering the wreckage the old woman lives inside, the house crammed with objects and rubbish, the decaying carpet underneath.

But to have been called it ... And here is Elizabeth attending to the old judge. She knows how this drag on her time will only increase; as age and increasingly poor health, possibly dementia, bruise the Amitabha in dull phrases and wound the poor old fruit of her body.

As several days pass without a reply, Elizabeth remembers the story of Max Perkins, legendary editor at Scribner's, telling Thomas Wolfe he needed a line or two, or maybe a paragraph, to create a stronger transition between two scenes of *Look Homeward, Angel* – the original manuscript of which was so big it was delivered in a truck.

Two weeks passed in silence and Wolfe suddenly contacted him, announcing the delivery by taxi of the required transition, another 20,000 words!

Elizabeth does *not* want that.

She has in the past spent days text-editing a poor work of trivial writing or a highly competent work of no real interest. Just not sexy. Never a bad sentence, never a great one either.

Elizabeth used to hold editing workshops for the Writers' Centre and once, on the big blank whiteboard, she accidentally wrote *Story is a cumpulsion*. She couldn't stop laughing. There it was, a slip of the pen – the foreplay-arousal-orgasm model of the short story.

She told them even dreams aren't stories yet we tell them every night. Perhaps they had heard of that bloke who cut dreams into their fragments and then asked a workshop to reassemble them, *edit* them, back into "the story". So hard it was too hard. And no two the same. Stories are always going somewhere, and the fact is, we aren't. Like the dreams, we are fragmented, changing, returning, repeating.

When she goes outside to empty a rubbish bag into her wheelie her mood is broken. She notices the neighbour watching her through the broken fence and laughing. Just standing there, side-on, in a check shirt and long black trousers. The perverse thing is, creeps don't fail at being creeps. Perhaps she should say something. He has remained quiet for weeks, just the way he looks, then silence.

She walks back inside, but when she looks out again he is standing halfway in from the fence. He is standing in her garden. Worse, he seems to know she is watching him. Taunting her, like a small-town bully, and smirking.

Then he turns away and is gone.

That night she dreams of him. Darkness as always in the backyard near the man's fence. Something stirs in the shrubs on her side and she jumps away from it, fearing a snake or a dog waiting to attack and her being too close. The noise increases into a terrible scratching, and crunching somewhere in the blackness struggling up in front of her the neighbour, both eyes blackened, one long cut on his forehead, the blood which ran from his nose dried over his mouth and his cheeks where he has wiped it with his wrist.

Elizabeth does have a contradiction: her strong brown eyes are weak. Myopia. She is having trouble reading the much photocopied song sheets for the choir she has only attended twice, as if straining to see the notes tightens her voice, and the notes are fading in front of her. The choir. Another more or less abandoned venture.

Eye trouble is affecting her screen work, too, the endless work of her real work.

The day of her appointment to see the optometrist again.

The thing is, she tells him, since she saw him last she has kept wondering whether she should risk having laser surgery just to … relieve her of glasses? Her annoyingly persistent mother is suggesting it, so she's come in to establish for herself, once and for all, at the very least to shut her up. 'And now (*what does she call him?*) a friend … has stuck his nose in as well, says I should go ahead.'

'Ah. Everyone's an expert.'

'He showed me his DVD of them … doing it.'

'Did he really?'

'It made me feel queasy. Slicing each eye off like a soft-boiled egg. Anyway, in fact, this friend (*the word sounds all wrong*) had it done and it didn't go as planned.'

The optometrist is a cheery man with a lot of easy charm. He is wearing glasses.

'As far as I'm concerned, Elizabeth, your short-sightedness isn't a problem that requires an operation, because you're happy enough with corrective glasses. But they will need to get thicker and heavier as you get older. If laser surgery works, and it usually does, not always, you can dispense with the drag of wearing glasses' – he shrugs – 'and then why not? I can't be bothered having it myself.'

His hair wavers when he laughs.

When Trevor gets home carrying two bags of groceries she follows him into the kitchen. Before he has begun putting things away she tells him about The Creep's intrusion.

'I think he's trying to intimidate me,' she says. 'Just because he isn't doing anything doesn't mean he won't. Even if he doesn't, he's getting into my head. Which is exactly what he wants, has been all along. Just when I thought he'd gone to ground. What did you actually say to him that day?'

'What? That time through the fence?'

'I know you did, you said something to shut him up, I just couldn't hear it. You said he went away happy. As if. ...'

'It's in the eyes, Elizabeth. The stare,' he laughs, exaggerating his voice. 'Nothing really.'

He waits, but she isn't happy.

'Do you really want to know?'

'Of course I do'.

'I told him I can be a real cunt when I want to be.'

'Huh. Didn't work for long, did it. Can you be?'

'What does matter is that I told him. And that I have friends who are bigger problems than me, and they are ex-cops. I take it he knew what *that* meant.'

'I think he needs to be told again,' she says. 'I don't want him taunting me like that. He might be capable of anything. I'm starting to feel uneasy.'

~

Despite the new author, Elizabeth is taking medical time out for her mother. She has made an appointment with an orthopaedic specialist to discuss her mother's erratic mobility. Now her mother keeps insisting she has no social contact who isn't a bloody doctor of some sort. The specialist determines that her hips are a worry and so are her knees and, though it isn't his area, certainly not helping is the deterioration of muscle tissue in both her legs. She tells him she used to play tennis and for years performed strenuous physical meditations so what's this nonsense about her fitness? When did she last do daily exercise, he asks her, and she tells him she has always done a lot of walking and even the occasional bit of dancing and, when he asks when that was, she becomes grumpy and tells him he'd better take her word for it.

'Maybe it was the tennis. An old injury?'

On the way to do some food shopping Elizabeth says, 'Well, that wasn't a lot of help.' Her mother says the man was not only misguided, he was over-assertive. No, says Elizabeth, she meant her mother being so bloody-minded, wasting the opportunity by turning it into an expensive denial session. 'What was all that about tennis? Remember, Mum,' she says, 'how you pooh-poohed my gymnastics as a boring, routine body thing, nothing as free and fine as your mind? Look at how that turned out. Your body, I mean.'

She'd never have said that to her daughter about gymnastics.

Well, she had.

No, she hadn't.

At the shopping centre her mother decides she is coming in, using her stick this time, not that terrible walking thing. They argue. She insists. Inside it is busy, shoppers with trolleys and baskets and staff re-shelving for the evening. In the third aisle Mrs Sermon slips over and stumbles onto a trolley full of toilet paper. 'Oh fuck!' she growls, down on her side with one hand grasping the trolley. Elizabeth grabs the trolley just before it tips and spills the packages all over her mother.

The staff member is a small Indian man who leans over to help her up.

'Don't you dare touch me!' she wails. She pokes at him with her walking stick which she has managed to keep a grip on.

'And don't you touch me either.'

This directed to Elizabeth who is helping regardless. Her mother wobbles and flounders like a wobbegong shark cast up, mottled and unmanageable, on dry land. Until a tall, tanned person presumably not an Indian stops to help.

'Well,' she says, 'I suppose I could get up but I'll need a little help.'

She is all smiles as he reaches down.

Between Elizabeth and the man they lift her up, and she thumps her stick down onto the floor and leans on it as if shoving it down a hole. Now the smiles are no more. It hurts and there is no way to pretend it doesn't. The walker, when reversed, provides a seat to rest on, *so in future they must always use it.* She tells her mother to wait there, not move, she is going to fetch the walker from the car and her mother will just have to put up with it.

How it falls to the dutiful daughters. Not exclusively but usually.

On the weekends Trevor drives to the boathouse. Whenever he begins rowing, his childhood returns. As a kid he sometimes spent his school holidays on a farm that was, luckily, on his mother's side of the family. His father? Away, as always, on his field trips. After he had been shown how to manage the oars and keep the old rowing boat upright and moving more or less straight ahead, Trevor was free to untie the boat, get in, push off and row upriver, against the slow current. This meant he could row with the current on the way home, just in case he was too tired.

His rowing now is filled with its own peace, and rhythm, and the sound of the hull passing through water, along with the past memory of his father, in a good mood, rowing upriver to fish. Therefore Trevor, rowing on the gleaming water with two oars and two states of mind, is *double-dipping.* The pun makes him smile even if his father does not.

The slow-moving water. The peace. The banks curve back and around like any river left to its natural development. Above him the magpies carol and sometimes cry, small cranes lift above the water and lodge, shakily, in the higher branches. Ducks smooth past, these neck-and-beak birds defining the word "glide", besides the twitchy zigzagging waterhens, black-feathered and red-beaked, and the dabchicks and other species he isn't sure of and – because it has been a long warm spring and summer – the endless bush flies. On warmer days he knows flies will be clustering on his back.

Even when rowing against the flow his right leg remains untroubled by the exercise. Both legs bracing against the double stroke, and the even lean forward and pullback on the oars, means his body remains in symmetrical activity. *Keep the legs straight and knees flexing back and through, back and through.* The boat skimming ahead.

Not even rain discourages him, falling around him, pockmarking the water, soaking him as he leans and releases.

All this work and pride in feeling healthier has convinced Trevor he should make an appointment with a gallery. Bite the bullet, in the old-school saying. Be positive, as the motivators say. Visualise and it will come, they say. Request a showing of his work.

Online searching has given him a list of possible city galleries he could contact. *Where does he start, though, and what kind of work do they show?* His trips into town to look at works have had an indifferent effect. So many landscape spreads of glorious colour in styles he'd considered long dead. Tourist art. Galleries showing faint colour washes and even coffee-coloured surfaces, as if Melbourne's second biggest obsession has entered the room. He watches before turning away feeling dead inside too many inert videos that exist, just, interminably.

Flinders Lane. A rising street of galleries but possibly none for him.

He checks every room of a much promoted uni postgraduate show. The first room is filled, if not dominated, by someone working with coloured string and tinsel, wasting packets of pipe cleaners without twisting or shaping anything convincing, a technique so invisible he wonders if ineptness is the theme.

A video, yes, another video, plays the changing profundity of a blob.

He smiles at the young manager without anything moving inside his or her head. The second room makes him shudder. How many cutesy girls with stunned eyes and kiddie bodies can anyone look at closely, whether or not they are hanging in a gallery said to be 'exclusive'? They make him feel like a stressed-out voyeur of kiddie porn and zombie art, with or without the corporeal. Pale. Exsanguinated.

They are so bad, any sense of hope falls around him like doom. His shoulders and his mind tell him he is the idiot and this is the playroom of the status quo. Or has he missed something? No. Nothing as awful as this is superior to anything. If one room is technical kitsch, the other is just kitsch.

The twenty-year gap of his inactivity has been filled with this? It is a chasm of banality. Time has deserted him. Or he it.

At Flinders Street Station he dodges the homeless individuals huddled in sleeping bags and rugs, and at intervals along nearby pavements. Art along Flinders Lane, poverty along Flinders St. For the homeless the irony is that they have nothing as free in this world as time, and time offers them nothing.

Of all people to ask, he rings Lester. After all, he bought those paintings from galleries somewhere, he must know the likely places. Or will he? Trevor has noticed that when he talks about his painting, or other artists, Lester shows no interest at all. He truly is an outsider: it's what he does that obsesses him, to hell with artists. Since he began doing it himself. And he no longer has any interest in the public existence of artworks beyond those he purchased a decade ago.

This is disconcerting.

Lester, the outsider painter who began full of fascination but without any training; and Trevor, with all his training and early success falling to impostor syndrome. What ironies. Yes, Lester knows the galleries. Or he did. They may or may not still be in business.

After a week or so of procrastination – unhappily endured, just as unhappily ended – Trevor makes an appointment at Fifty Square Gallery. For once he will not open his shop until the afternoon. His problem is fixed by making a new sign to hang in the door. BACK AT 1 PM.

On the actual day he is trying too hard. And the manager is trying to explain her problem. It isn't working.

'OK, yes,' she deigns to swipe through several of the pics on his mobile, 'yes, um' and again 'yes, they are quite good. Um, umm, this one is quite well done.' *Quite?* Until she returns to her job title, and manages to blunt his ambition. Until he interrupts her.

'I can't get over the fact that you've hardly looked at the paintings. These phone images – how can you possibly judge them? I can easily bring some here. I can drive in, park just outside …?'

'The question, Trevor, is not your quality or oddity as an artist. I'm sorry if I've been giving you the wrong impression.'

She stops, lifts her head slightly.

'An artist of your age should have a reputation. You have no track record.'

'What about the paintings? We're not talking about my track record.'

'*We* are.'

A pause while she lets this sink in. A pause as his body does.

'No track record of exhibitions. At all.'

She is laying it on and he knows it.

'Which means you have no reputation, no network, no ability to attract … anyone to your work, and that's a risk *we* would have to take on. No potential buyers? Who will even bother to come here to write you up and or promote you? There are simply too many established artists around and thanks to the art schools we have postmodern and very well-read and prepared younger artists everywhere. Actually, it's embarrassing.'

The woman's hair is stylish and jet black, as dramatic as her answers are flat. There is no flaw in her lipstick, her couture, her elegant posture. She is money, all right, from somewhere. The gallery is high-ceilinged and as indifferent as she is.

'But, you know, my work looks more impressive if you're standing in front of it. It's not miniature.'

He lifts his mobile again and is peering down and sorting through the images until he sees her raising her palm like a policeman.

'Trevor. We wouldn't sell a single painting. Perhaps you don't realise, we survive on commissions from sales. We have to be able to guarantee sales.'

'Of course I know that. But don't you have a newsletter and a mail-out for exhibitions? Can't you *promote* the exhibition in a way that attracts your regular audience? How about people who walk in off the street?'

Even before she answers he is embarrassed to have shot off so many questions.

'People who walk in off the street don't buy paintings, Trevor. Hardly anyone buys paintings …'

The bookseller in him is waking in alarm, plus the ironic knowledge that no eccentric locals will ever walk in *here*. And what a bloody pity that is. She stares at him.

'Why are you working in two different styles? Colour and energy in one but in the other – your pieces are dark, aren't they? The early ones, as you put it, are somewhat dismal.'

'*Dismal?*'

'Let's stay with dark. Trevor, does nihilism work quite as well … in paint?'

Trevor was in his 20s when he used to walk in off the street at gallery openings. Quite the young nihilist. Uninvited, barefoot, alone, or with a girlfriend. He enjoyed the free booze, the food, and he studied the artworks the opening crowd had its back to. He never bought any paintings either.

Now he dresses well and is still out of place. There are dozens of private galleries and they'll all ask him the same questions: his name, exhibition background, reputation. The space his curriculum vitae is expected to occupy is blank – the twenty or so years since art school.

'I saw an exhibition you ran,' he says, 'of watercolours. Landscapes done flat and pastel and pale. They were amateurish, the artist gushed that glorious nature awakened all his senses and then the painting took over. Seriously, that naïve, and that conventional. *They* were dismal. Not in temperament, in quality of imagination. You exhibited *them.*'

She doesn't even answer him. Instead she says:

'Have a look at the graduate exhibition further up the street. They are the new artists and they show all the potential we want.'

Such talk is its own abstract art. He has lost, and not just this time in this place, he has lost altogether; the game is completely against him. This and not the plethora of art-school graduates is what's embarrassing. Twenty-year-olds. Not even as old as his blank c.v.

'What about my recent work?' he says. 'Colour and montage. I think they are strong enough under any circumstances. I know contemporary art. I've spent years in galleries, including yours. I am contemporary.'

'The smudgy montages are' (of course, he has annoyed her) 'too soft in outline and image. Too ambiguous. Really, all so blurry. It's what my husband,' she laughs, 'would call unmanly.'

'Your husband is an artist?

'No, he's a businessman.'

By now, having had her say, the manager is impatient:

'Well, thank you for thinking of us, Trevor.'

This covers him with such patronising hypocrisy he feels like slapping her. *A businessman.* When he suggests he will put up the money, being businesslike, and however much is required, she just looks at him and says nothing. He isn't there.

~

In anyone's life there is room for more embarrassment. Trevor receives a text message inviting him to Diana's birthday celebrations. From a friend of theirs, or is that half a friend now? Is he foolish enough to go?

He thinks he is. Gate-crasher, car-crasher, limper. The perversity of walking into your own apartment as a visitor, just a guest like all the others, ready to get drunk and say the wrong thing. Has he un-loved her enough to sustain such a visit surrounded by the friends they have in common no more, being hers now, and by others he will see for the first time and so be seen by, with their sly expressions, their impossible-to-read gestures?

As soon as he tries to make conversation he understands the old friends want to ease him into the condition of ex, some don't even realise, and her work-friends, all very much younger, look upon him as a random old bloke. These thirtysomethings glance briefly when he says anything, even hello, smiling as he waits for a cocktail. Former friends, who have chosen Diana as the *thing to do*, are polite without hiding an expression they seem to have imbibed with their martinis that says, in effect, *My God, what are you doing here?*

Time, is it, then, to count the night a defeat and leave? He'd asked Elizabeth to come, keep him company, sort of friend not Dutch courage. It would have worked, too, except she raised her eyebrows and made a *You what?* kind of noise with her mouth shut.

So he's drinking instead. Vodka, vodka everywhere.

The martinis are too good, meaning strong, like nothing wet and wan from the pop-up bar he last stopped at. Three waiters are concocting alcoholic magic from the chalkboard list of 1. to 5. and everyone seems intent of running this lap at least once. Two men dressed in black and white, and a woman dressed in red lipstick, pour and spin, shake and stir, making heads swing and lust very likely.

Therefore he is standing at his own table, bought only two years earlier, or his half of the table, drinking from his half of the cocktail glass, filled with her liquor. At least he is getting her booze for free. How strange. Estrange.

An old friend of theirs called Susan takes hold of his arm and says, 'You are a cruel man, you know, and a cruel man always comes to a bad end. Why did you leave her? But now that you have …'

'A bad end or abandoned,' he says, 'I was. But never cruel, Susan.'

'Oh, you are. You walked out on her.'

'What? She spent weekends at work sitting on what's-his-name. If he's tall, dark and handsome I have to live in the undergrowth. Though I've never met the man, thankfully. Is he here?'

'Trevor. Don't ask. You might have met him before, I don't know. She's had one or two, I mean. I'm as jealous as.'

She makes it alliterative and dozy, sibilant as esses and zzzz. *Dzzzt.*

Had Diana invited her lover to their house? *Fuck, fuck, fuck.* He is in freefall, though Susan is obvious and a bore and probably making this up to impress and depress him with her gossipy nous. And her fingers are gripping his arm with more than mere attention, or drunkenness. She is looking up at him with – no, it can't be. *From one room in the doghouse to the next.* Alcohol has grabbed Susan and cliché has grabbed him.

'This is half my house,' he whispers to her, 'but I'm glad to say we're drinking the whole of her booze.'

They are almost overbalancing when Diana walks towards them, giving him the cat's eyes, assuming he is being louche with her best work-friend. He mouths a *Help!*, a yelp. All it elicits is more intense frowning on her already disapproving face.

She moves away to the bar, ignoring him.

Later he encounters another friend in common, awkward small talk as the man makes excessive hand movements with his glass of wine. How awful. The man is as embarrassed as he bloody well should be, for saying not a word to Trevor over the last months while clearly staying in touch with Diana. Separation, divorce, what it does to your friends. Makes them *choose*.

The bills for his CAT scans and MRI were steep but here at the party he is being scanned free of charge. To be seen through. Flesh and bone. There is a man on the other side of the room watching him.

Diana approaches again.

'You seem to be favouring me, darling,' he says, getting in first. 'Your workmates will think we are having a fling. Your boyfriend will be wondering.'

'Trevor,' she whispers but not at all quietly. 'Don't be a bitch. If you're going to be a problem ...'

'No, no. Not a bitch, just an ex.'

Three younger women and an over-barbered, calf-trousered hipster man turn to look at Diana and smile the young and the cool. One of them has been talking about poetry, so Trevor disengages from his ex-wife and takes the casual steps needed to position himself alongside the poetry people.

'A poem is a problem that has to be solved,' she has just said, and the young man with hair cut asymmetrically is smiling, symmetrical in agreement. This is where thin lips are a fashion statement. His are fat.

'Oh,' says Trevor, 'surely that's too neat. As a statement it strikes me as being, well, rather glib?'

They almost manage to ignore him without looking at him, then fail out of rightful curiosity.

'This is my apartment,' he adds. 'I thought I'd like to contribute. I'm Trevor. I read poetry a lot.'

'You don't agree with me?' asks the young woman. 'That a poem is a problem to be solved? It sounded really cool to me.'

'I think it sounds American.'

'On what basis?' asks the young man.

'Because it sounds like a neat thing to say in Creative Writing classes. It sounds like advice from earnest tutors to earnest students who believe either that theory and poetry are arcane problems or that popular culture and porn "empower" us. Anyway, poetry is not as rational as that. Poetry is a trip, not a problem. Poetry is a drug. All good books are drugs. Books are controlled hallucinations.'

'Wow, what are you on? A book is just words.'

'Ouch, words.'

'So, what did you mean?' She puts it to this old bloke. *Let's see if he can.*

'Reading is the hallucination, but the book is the drug. It just works differently for different people. Some get high, some take the whole dose and nothing happens.'

'Are you a poet?'

'No, I'm more of a shit-stirrer. You look like a poet,' he says, turning then to smile at everyone.

'Oh, come on,' she laughs. 'What does a poet look like?'

'Good question. Did I say I was Diana's husband? Past tense intended. This is half my apartment we're in.'

'Really?' says the hipster, 'and how do you decide which half is yours and which half is Diana's?'

'Whichever half I'm standing in is my half. Her half is over there. If we move towards each other then the line dividing our halves is always between us. Unless one of us stands in a corner. Like life, it keeps shifting. Talk of the devil.'

Sees Diana striding towards him from the other side of the room, or her half. She knows all too well his likely behaviour around alcohol. Like some poets, he has the unlike tendencies of being inventive and obvious. Unexpected but not original. One look at him now and she can tell he's performing.

He knows his time is up. Wives, they can tell you're making trouble just by looking at you – exes even more so. At least they understand each other.

Synopsis: outnumbered and possibly in the sad gawps of tease. To think a man might in goodwill attend a party imagining a few months have lessened some of the difficulties his social relations have thrust upon him, only to get caught in the *mise-en-scène*. Jesus, even the hundreds of books on the bookshelves are his, and somehow not his, now that he doesn't live here.

Even his books have deserted him.

'You are going way over the line,' she hisses.

'No, I'm still on my side of the line. This is my half of the house until we decide otherwise. I refuse to yield.'

'What?'

'Tell me, how does anyone behave at a party fuelled by martinis and Polish vodka? Remember, *I* am Polish. Half of me.'

'More like a drunken smart arse.'

'Only *like*, the simile not the thing itself?'

'Perhaps you shouldn't have come.'

'I responded to an invitation. Diana, I have been talking about poetry. Imagine that, I'm usually prose. Am I hogging the floor?'

He should walk off. The man who was watching him still watches him. Or them.

'And,' she adds, 'you haven't wished me happy birthday.'

'Ah, right. I get it. Happy birthday.'

Yes, she knows him well enough, his problem is with her colleagues on the other side of the room. She asks if he's hurt his leg again, she saw him limp to the martini bar when he came in. And stayed there, by the look of him.

He is trying to find the comfort part of feeling uncomfortable. A final margarita, a dash of flamenco out on the wooden floorboards he and Diana paid so much to strip back and varnish. With the cocktail waitress in the red dress who hasn't once smiled at him despite serving him three times. On his one good leg flamenco heel-stamping would sound like: bang, blip, bang, blip. A sloppy tango? To be honest, the young male cocktail deviser with a squeaky voice does the banter better and made Trevor a special – a Twelve Mile Limit, a drink for beyond the national laws, the one civilised encounter of his evening.

Perhaps he should dance with him.

His own speciality is Defiant Gesture but the whack has gone out of it.

It is crisp outside. The surfaces are wet, the trees still. Every few minutes he squints back along the tram tracks to find the double lights of the next tram due. Forget the party, forget the land of other people and other people's friends. Forget the dope who punched him or pushed him, and the creep over the back fence. Remember instead the last painting with its long red spine as wide as his forearm. Remember his new day's-end conversations with Elizabeth. He may have been knocked down but he has fallen on his feet.

While he waits he sees the red spine painting. When he brushed in the first bloody line it made him think of the red scar on Lester's throat. The man's own paintings made Trevor shrink, the entrapment of the netting, its lines covering every square centimetre of the surface. Outsider art is self-referential and therefore weird. A cult of one. If that's a test for authenticity, then … all other art is derivative.

Trams are forgiving, though, trams suit Trevor's natural disposition to have mind and matter as one, the bulk of him and the sensual pleasure of tram rhythms, the wheel and rail sounds, the stopping and starting, acceleration from electric motors something he forgets until the driver pushes the pedals or levers or commands the lightning, whichever it is, his back jerks into the seat frame in pleasant forcefulness and the steel carriage rushes towards the next stop.

Earlier, instead of going straight into the party, he had moved out of time somehow, moved by a strange light over the city. And now, back out on the street near home, he remembers and looks up to see something vaguely like it still up there, down here. Again he is lifted by it, by that light over everything. It is a light effect after rain, light without lines, a wet paper-wash diffusing cloud-light back down onto the buildings, lighting everything equally. No one surface is favoured by it, no roof is highlighted, no new or old buildings or façades shine any less; and nothing as knee-jerk as '*Oh, it's surreal!*' occurs to him. But something has changed, shifted, from banality to beauty.

Part Three

S TUCK IN THE emotional ore of his father is the grind. The antagonism Trevor has always felt towards mining. His father made his money in WA from mining companies aided by politicians. He read the book about Noonkanbah in WA when the Premier Charles Court sent in the police – would have sent the SAS had it been possible – to push the Noonkanbah Station people off their land so drilling rigs could have access. Some miners were cartoon bastards, like Lang Hancock, who declared he'd mine iron ore by nuclear blasting. White bastards, a shameful era, the forefathers of people like his own father.

And the era continues. In Queensland the Indian Adani Group is resisting Indigenous groups, or paying some off, ignoring the farmers and the majority of people in Australia, to gouge out the Galilee Basin for the biggest coalmine in the world. Bugger the extensive Artesian Basin's groundwater. Bugger the Barrier Reef. Bugger the people. But make the people pay for it. Billion-dollar handouts, roads and rail, royalties negotiated down the throats of submissive governments. If this were sex it would be Sadist. Massive clean-ups walked away from in other countries, wreckage and poison that will leak (as they still leak in other countries) into the soil, the water, the sea, the coral.

Under that thick, smiling moustache of Gautam Adani lies the contempt Trevor's father approves of.

Time for some public art, then, time to paint that mural. A 50-year-old graffiti artist. He has a wall, he will paint it. His largest canvas yet. Already measured, on the alley side of his shop he has roughed out a horizontal image to fit. The only interruption is the side door and even that seems ironically appropriate. Walk in, walk out.

That night, anger and disruption annoying him, he carries a backpack of brushes and spray paint up to the shop. After midnight on a Monday night there is nothing happening, almost no traffic, no one on the pavements. Even the homeless men and the blonde woman have disappeared.

As a student Trevor had decided to paint a mural on the lounge-room wall of a share-house. Not wanting to waste his expensive paints and unsure of whether they'd wash free from the high-gloss surface, he completed the mural with something dramatic and washable – soya sauce. It was a jumble of images, great apes with the faces of the occupants of the house. Naked, naturally. Domestic objects, snakes and ladders, Chagall-like levitations. It was a mess.

You need a plan.

As he works he uses his wide house-painting brushes to move litres of acrylic paint back and forth across the horizontal space of the wall. Over this he sprays and sprays, walking from the pavement end to the top of the blind alley. What a joy, he thinks, if only canvases were this big and he wasn't some obvious dickhead trying to win the Archibald Prize by size alone, he could do this all day as well as all night. He thinks of Gulley Jimson in *The Horse's Mouth*. He sweeps spray and paint across the wall, walking sideways to expand his image across the wall's size and scale, his face under the mask cheeky with smiling. Stands back, adds, adjusts, squirts a highlight.

Spray, spray, spray ...

Wearing his white face-mask for safety he would, if seen from across the street, look like a ghost spitting vapour trails of colour in the darkness and onto the wall.

Then he constructs the letters.

This mural-making is like really strong dope. As long as you don't inhale.

The next morning he tells Elizabeth what he has done. They walk Gordon around the park and before going home walk up to the shop with him. There it is. He mutters something about touching it up (later that night). Some extra highlighting is needed to make better contrast in the daylight.

The wall is a wide-open plain of brown earth and green vegetation. Twisted round in a right-hand-side downward curve, bent away from any realist sense, is the Queensland coastline and the bright underwater jewels of the Barrier Reef. In the sky above all this, painted in the protest font and colours, is STOP ADANI.

'Trevor, you are naughty,' she laughs. 'Though should we be seen looking at it?'

'Do you think people will talk?'

'I bet. Did you get permission to do it?'

'Well ...'

'Ha. Thanks for showing me, I'd better get home but let me know what happens if anything happens.'

She notes his pavement sign:

The return of the repressed is true. Recurrence is true. It is all true.

She knows she must sneak down to get another look at his paintings. She has seen him standing in front of roughly scraped canvases, stationary, seen him sitting in his armchair holding a house-painting brush, just inspecting it, feeling its bristles, sitting there, doing paintings in his head perhaps. What she has noticed is how long, apart from time at the gym, he has been spending in the shed. This thing of standing still, or moving hardly at all, returning to the one position for what seems an hour or so. It would drive her loony. She has to move, move, keep the energy flowing through her meridians, unless of course she is sitting at her keyboard hearing the long speaking of a manuscript.

The mural has surprised her. So bold. He had mentioned his father often enough. She has never seen him so energised, intense, angry really. It can only be confusing. It would make her weep. Perhaps it has shifted something in him. At night he has been grumbling over the news.

She drags open the studio door. The canvases and boards are now dirty with art. He has been working all right, making things, maybe even making progress, not that she would know. Cleaned up after every session, she guesses, his brushes are wrapped in cloth like tiny mummies. Scattered over the workbenches are painting knives and dinky, springy little tools that seem to her more like puppet props, implements for gnome gardens. And pliers, bolts, trowels of huge size and powerful-looking duct tape, the type you see wound around the wrists and mouths of the innocent by villains in films. All that.

Canvases, surfaces, roughened then painted-over surfaces of wood, or is it metal? Scattered images, colours and textures.

Suffusing sepia and texture, the material of flatness this drugged imagery is dragged over or dragged from, it's hard to say which. Each of these faces is side-on and rushing to the left like the workers in John Brack's *Collins St., 5 pm* though here the place is placeless, more in the mind than the street, a reddish-purplish blur of media images she can recognise, collages from magazines and tabloid newspapers (good for something at last) destroyed by all this rubbing, rubbing back, and rendered indistinct. One face is turning towards the viewer. It is half blinded by paint.

She can't see what she is used to imagining, happening slowly over time in a manuscript, as narrative unfolding; she sees immediacy, a state, the all-at-once of paintings and it mostly gratifies but

at the same time confuses her. The feeling of rawness and achievement undermined by a lack of … Not his paintings, any paintings.
Too much abstraction? Too much explanation, or not enough?
Even so, many novels only give surface observation, surface as the
main frisson. For some, surface is the *only* frisson.

But it is shocking.

It is painting.

She prefers photography.

Still. The tone and intensity of these pieces. Or the suggestion?
He makes no particular claim, or counter-claim, for his work,
having no public to demand it of him.

Further back in the shed she finds his end-on series, which
has now clearly morphed into the beginning of the side-on series.
It makes her laugh. Painters, printmakers, how they push an idea
in several directions, if they're any good, if any of the directions
work and warrant the visit. For years. Entire lifetimes. She knows
novelists who write the same book over and over. Working with
the same publishers, editing the same writers for several books
in succession.

She prefers writers who shift ground, not shift around. The kind
of creative writing Creative Writing workshops might be named
after. As if. The term "Creative Writing" annoys her as much as
it does most writers. And Richard, the always-author but only
sometime lover, loathes the name, if not the money: he teaches
Creative Writing.

She is still looking at the paintings when Trevor walks across
from the house. She is astonished to be caught. *Why isn't he at
the shop?*

'Another art critic!' he says, waving his arms in a silly fashion.
Clearly unconcerned that she's there.

He says the shop smells of spray paint. Not a lot but enough
to worry people. He needs something like old home remedies.
Vinegar, was it, they used to spray around? She has some urine

ordure eliminator, she says. It works for dogs. And must work for neighbours, too. She hasn't seen him lately so perhaps he knows better at last. She hoped it would come to a confrontation and a fight he'd lose, though of course she shouldn't want that, but ...

He says nothing. She turns towards his paintings.

It would be surprising if she didn't look at his work. At home alone. Considering he has been telling her his overall and bitty insights. Which rattle around like a box of loose type. Then the spray job overnight. She admits there is something she cannot quite get in these works. Nothing tangible.

'Loneliness?' she wonders. Aloud, to him.

'Loneliness. ... This one?' he indicates the faces to the left, the single full-frontal.

'No, Trevor. All of them.'

This is serious. *All of them? Or does she mean aloneness, not the same thing at all? Affect*, what someone feels. The paintings stare back at them. Unrelenting. Loneliness. *Some kind of Grief she isn't articulating?* That big space open between Love and Death.

He is worried now, he says, that his paintings may have a repressed father-lack in them. *It's simplistic and what else is there to say? He would not have thought that a month ago.* Or just a dumb everyday and garden-shed melancholy. *Who gives a fuck anyway?*

It is not a problem to be solved, he had thought, as he painted the face.

It is the man who is desperate to return.

It is the man watching customers amble around his shop while he waits for 5.30.

It was the man speeding along country roads during summer with the air *miraging* and the approaching cars bubbled and distorted. Driving along straight roads in crooked heat. It is also the man in the other car that crashed.

It is the man who has left married life behind him.

It is a son.

It is all these men as one man.

'Do you see any hope in them?' He is asking her. Suggesting. (Hoping.)

'Hope?'

'Yes, hope.'

At first she isn't sure if he means hope in doing them or hope within them. What does hope look like?

'It's me,' he adds, 'this sombre feeling isn't all there is to *me*, because I feel hopeful, it's a personal trait, and I'm certain I feel hope is in the making, when I'm painting, when I'm the person creating them. Sort of detached and positive. Is it coming through in the paintings or is it dying in the brushwork? Very likely something else is painting.'

'You're all over the place!' she grins. 'But I see what you mean, I think. They're unsettling, and sad … but hopeful?'

'Techniques. Craft. These don't have emotional labels. An artist is working his medium before anything else.'

'Her medium.'

'I don't want them to look dismal.'

Elizabeth can only smile at his openness. It reminds her of something Shia has written:

This is a strange world

And impossible to tell

She's shouldn't let on that she sees less hope than he … hopes. She doesn't see dismal. A wound of some kind will open and out through her will rush the words of doubt. He says he just wants to push and pull without any demand to conceptualise it, unlike artistic practice within universities. That way intention disguises itself.

'Why did you ever stop?' she has to ask.

'Work took over,' he explains. He did a double degree in Art Practice and Psychology, met Diana there and then moved into Design. A doctorate in Design Psychology. What Trevor used to call implausible theory and unemployment. Except while he theorised about art she landed a solid job.

He took his paintings to several galleries and brought them all back again. He gate-crashed art openings and tried to network. But he wasn't any good at networking. He wasn't sure how it was done. He never wanted to be an Aussie Damien Hirst, sawing dead things in half, injecting formaldehyde and being a complete wanker. Then a gallery took his first exhibition and three paintings sold. No one knew of the Dada artists he most admired, the women Hannah Höch and Sophie Taeuber-Arp, their montages and constructed patterns. And yet he got really good reviews.

Then he recalls removing the unsold paintings from gallery walls and laboriously laying them out (so funereal) on bubble wrap which cost more than unsold paintings were worth (nothing) and folding each parcel of them, pulling the tape out into lengths, that *rark*ing sound of tape tearing free of the wheel, of itself, cutting or biting it, wrapping it tightly and finally stacking each anonymous and bubbly rectangle against the wall. Bubble wrap, he can hardly bear to touch the stuff.

After all that work, he tells her, nothing happened. A vacuum. He had no style of his own, even though he knew better than to believe in "originality". If you don't sell, don't bother. There is no private life the artist has tickets for. Then it happened: he had a car accident. His leg had to be rebuilt over two operations. Life ran him over.

One thing he doesn't feel: hard done by. It just happened.

But, he says to Elizabeth: nothing is *over* until you're dead and buried. Events recur, in one form or another. Even after you're dead and buried, who knows?

She can never tell him, then.

He's gabbling again. Remembering the messy British artist Frank Auerbach. Trevor Novak. Raw paint daubed everywhere. Even if it's deemed old-fashioned, he paints. If it's retro, he paints. He still paints. He wants to repeat, and repeat not the past but the medium, because he knows the difference between repeating into oblivion and turning repetition into ritual. And from ritual to discover new forms.

His words are rubbing like his rags and turps over just-painted canvases, the edges smudging the consonants inside the smudges, hardly resisting erasure but remaining there, words, just. He could be drunk for all this slurring. Call it passion. Or absinthe. Or fathers. One thing his father never suffered from was lack of self-belief. The man could talk all day, like a dictator.

'Trevor. I hate to be the dog biting your ankles. I hear what you're saying, I just want to say it's not easy to begin a public career in your 50s.'

'You think I don't know that? I'll have enough good work.'

'It doesn't matter about being good.'

'Why not?' (He can hear the gallery owner in her words.)

'Maybe it's not about being good, it's about being important. Even for writers. Being topical, engaging with the issues. There are so many issues you ...'

But he knows. Relevance. *It isn't the quality.*

'So someone can be talented and their work excellent and still ... not be, arrgh, I hate the word, *relevant?*'

It sounds too awful not to contain some weak and terrible truth. It calls up the other issue he squirms over – at what point does an amateur become an artist?

'I'm making a pot of tea. Do you want some?'

'No, thanks, I'd better get back.'

After he has gone she remembers a night she had come out of her room to see him watching TV and wiping tears from his eyes. At first she thought it was a soppy romance he'd been caught by, an emotional backwash from his separation. The program was a documentary, several women were crying about something. Trying to explain the horror of finding their young boy after a car accident, they kept breaking into grief, crying in gusts of weeping and saying *sorry* as if they must apologise for honest emotion.

When he noticed Elizabeth and wiped his eyes he seemed apologetic, too, just like the women had been. 'Being a sook,' he said. *Deaths get to him. A lot of things get to him.* Instead of watching any more he went into the kitchen to prepare dinner. Five minutes later she saw him exactly where she had last seen him, head down, unaware, standing in front of an open kitchen drawer.

Now he says he is trying to stay calm about his father, as if fathers die, are invisibly buried and then walk back into your shop through the front door wanting your money every day of your life ... How the one man he had wanted in his life has returned as a bastard.

Now, though, showing how normal he is, he collects a bottle of vinegar, two tea towels and the dog-piss spray, and goes back to the shop.

Under the studio lights, he reaches down for a small canvas at the back wall of the shed. Obscured by his big shadow, he grabs it and catches his hand on a sliced-back section of galvanised iron.

He cries 'Fuck!' and 'Fuck!' as he holds up his hand, the gash white and pink along its torn edges, his opened flesh shocked into a faint. Then blood overflows like a dam spill. Blood runs over the canvas. Onto the floor. A turps rag, nearly clean, is all he has close, so he wraps his right hand with his left, winding it around, feeling reversed.

Damn it, a trip to the doctor. If he washes it now, opens it to cold water, salts it, fills it with Savlon and wraps it in clean cloth – or sterile cloth if she has any – his tetanus shot can wait till tomorrow. And stitches? It doesn't even hurt yet but it will, it will, when the cold water pushes it open.

Inside he flushes out the flesh trying not to look, feeling faint, pain focussed in this one sliced moment. The depth, the length, actually not as bad as he'd thought. The pain alleviating in his relief. Not a serious cut.

There is still daylight in the sky, just. With his left hand he flicks away a rubber toy, or what's left of it, and watches Gordon race off, fetch it ('Fetch!') then rush back like an office boy, dripping dog love from his chops and dropping the sodden thing at his feet.

The fence is still open, nothing of the neighbour recently, just dog love in the form of needy play. Dogs are so single-minded, the routine a panting bliss. Throwing, returning, his left hand wet, his right wrapped, the double-happy dog, when Elizabeth re-appears. After a minute of silence she says:

'Poor old Trevor. Been in the wars, one thing after another. And still up to throwing toys for Gordie.'

'And,' she adds, 'it was very good of you to put up with my mother recently. I've suggested Yvonne come down for a few days and we drive up to see Mum. You know, it all helps. She's by herself, just in-home care visits, all that. So …'

'I have a feeling you're going to …'

'… say my daughter will be staying for a few days. It's no fun for me, either. The gods have decided I'm on the bloody floor again.'

'Why not make *her* go on the floor? She's not collapsing from tennis injuries like your mum.'

'Very funny. No, I don't want her taking over my workroom. Trevor, do you know anything about daughters?'

'But she'll be good company, won't she? Does she help out with cooking and cleaning up?'

'God, you're naïve. She's not staying here to do the housework! Other than the trip to Ballarat I'll hardly see her. You really have no idea,' she laughs.

'If it's only for a few days,' he says lamely, and shrugs.

He means, *No more.* He hopes it's less. Her old mother staying was tolerable, because in some odd way she was eccentric and rude without being awful, entertaining in a way. And … it was only for a few days. He'd not thought of these things before moving in.

More time in his room, in the shed. Right hand, left hand?

'She can be quite a lot of fun,' admits Elizabeth, 'especially when she doesn't mean to be. Thinking of cut hands … She had dressed up for a party in a bar in the city, and when she got home – here, that is – she was so pissed she couldn't get out of her onesie. She grabbed the scissors from the kitchen drawer and cut it down the front from neck to crotch. In the morning she freaked out seeing what she'd done. It was a very expensive onesie.'

His laughter is gratifying.

'Now that,' she adds, 'is a story that has been around the block a few times.'

'She's lucky she didn't cut anything on the way down.'

'Trevor.'

'Well, I'm half serious, cutting downwards, sort of backhanded. No, it's funny, isn't it, Gordon! Just lock the scissors away.'

He holds up his bandaged hand.

The next time he throws for Gordon he chooses the chewed fetch toy he bought especially, the one Elizabeth batted into the kitchen. Gordon remains standing and refuses to play. Silly when he wants to be, he can stare down silliness in humans without weakening. It's his chewing toy, not his fetch toy. Now he walks away, looking back over his shoulder at Trevor.

Gordon is one of those dogs that make people look stupid.

Trevor is trying to imagine this wild daughter of hers. *Onesies, what a term.*

'Yvonne. It sounds odd now,' he says.

'I named her after Evonne Goolagong. But with a Y.'

~

Out there on the Royal Park track there is no ragged Australia of droughts and sweeping plains, there are no broken sand dunes and stubborn scrub, not even a river or two flooding from Cyclone Mildred or thin as a snake now, brown and still with small fish dying on their hegemonic banks. Not that kind of nature at all. Not even a small town with one pub and a standing crew of drinkers in dusty work gear.

According to Elizabeth the walking track is close to a full 800 metres. Intrinsically part of Royal Park, because it is within the park's wide and undulating acreage, with three slatted benches and a few trees around it and a wide pancake of grass within it. But he thinks of the track as something other. It's an idea, a narrow zone laid not into so much as onto the park, a neutral place for walkers and joggers, the tall and the tubby, and dogs of all sorts. The lolloping, the little-legged, the flat-out racing dogs of any and every breed extending their thirty minutes off the leash by speed and sudden changes of direction. He sees a comic threesome in black coats of scratchy Chihuahua, dachshund and barrel-bodied Lab and knows the woman loves them the way someone loves their karaoke voice when all around are grimacing.

It feels very different at night. His eyes have adjusted to the darkness. And it is dark, a low cloud-cover blankets even the radiant glow from the city towers. No one else out there, not a dog or human. Sometimes on his night walks he hears voices from the middle of the grassy area and, walking across on the unofficial cycle short cut through its centre, he has smelt cigarette smoke for some way off then eventually found two or three twentysomethings drinking and talking quietly in the open space. Too dark even to see their faces, if they have faces, or his. They take not the slightest notice of a large man striding towards them, which always makes him wonder.

This is part of the park's nature. A time to limp if you must, or walk that rejuvenated body freely, tonight without effort. Cool air on his face, sometimes jogging but mainly walking, enjoying the discipline and pleasure of maintaining rhythmic strides, of muscles leading and following and this fluency as sound – his shoes beating evenly on the track. The night is dark but the track is even darker.

On his third lap he is surprised to see sitting on the bench ahead of him a couple obscured by the shadow of a large overhanging shrub. As he approaches they neither move nor speak. Passing them he glances peripherally and cannot see their faces. He is a dozen paces beyond them.

'Trevor,' a voice call out.

As if shot from behind, he staggers a few paces then stops. Turns.

Now he becomes acutely aware of them: a man and a woman in nondescript but dated clothing. But as he walks back he cannot see their faces in the shadow. Even when he stops in front of them he cannot.

'I'm so sorry, Trevor,' says the woman. 'It just broke my heart when he left, even if he was a man who cared little for us, who was hardly ever at home, who left me like a faithless lover who thinks he can get away with anything, over and over again. Then went off and we never saw him again. Now I'm dead I want to apologise ...'

Her blank face seems to move but there is only a blur not a mouth. She has no features.

'No,' says the man, 'I always came home. You can't say I didn't come home. Only the once, the last time. You know I had to get away and couldn't get back.'

No faces on either of them.

'Poland is so cold in winter,' he says. 'They have snow more than before when I was a kid. The streets are like Winter Games.'

'... I should have told you,' she continues, 'but for a long time I didn't know. He was so heartless. Then I knew, and then I made sure he couldn't come back for his money.'

'You killed me off,' curses the man. 'Murderer. Trevvy, she killed me, that's why I come and see you. I am dead, the law says I am dead. Seriously, I beg them but they say I don't exist. I can't prove I'm me, so legally I am dead. It happens, I read about it, a man in Romania, he's dead too. He asked them to change the law – but for one man? Impossible. And if they did I go to prison.'

Trevor rushes towards them. But they are gone.

Above him the possums are strangling their young, or that's what it sounds like. On and on. In each of the trees as he goes downhill on the exit tracks he can hear this terrible sound.

One of the last times he saw his father Kazimierz was the occasion of his mother's fortieth birthday. To celebrate she had been cooking all day, preparing for her own party. Not so unusual, this, her '70s hopes of liberation pushed aside by the Polish character she married. Trevor was helping. His father had driven off to buy drinks. *If he can't have a lot to drink it's no use having a party*, he always said. Ignoring the fact it was hers. At least his father was at home. For a few weeks he made trips into the city for work meetings, otherwise he locked himself away working in his study. This study, more often empty than occupied.

The family knew most of his life, like surveying and assaying, was performed elsewhere.

Trevor's nerdy 10-year-old brain had once nicknamed his father "Elsewhere". By his early teens calling his macho dad Elsie was subversively appealing but never a possibility. He had certainly called him Gone, because if people asked him if his father was home he'd say, *No, he's gone*. Gone *up north*, meaning the northwest of Western Australia usually, where much of his mining survey work was done. Gone – to Queensland, gone – to northern NSW; occasionally gone – to or into Papua or Bougainville. His mother's family were local to the area, and with his father being so peripatetic Upwey seems wonkily central. A wonky rural axle.

That early studiousness long gone, Trevor was now 15 and trying mostly to act tough. The gangs in town were made up of apprentice butchers and sparkies and they were tough bastards so he was trying mostly to avoid looking soft. A few months earlier one of them had slashed his hand with a knife.

Helping his mother prepare dishes made him uncomfortable.

She was a good cook and because his father was away for so many weeks of the year they had spent more time over the dinner table than most mothers and sons. They got on. Thin and with prominent cheekbones, her face and figure were more resigned than satisfied. In physique as well as loquaciousness, Trevor took after his father: the barrel chest, the Polish nose. His mother was never talkative at home and even when serving in her parents' bookshop – where customers in a small town were often locals, even "friends" – she kept conversation on the simmer at best. Modesty, attention to detail, a sequence of repeated actions. He knew she was forever susceptible to the charms of his father; mysteriously, it seemed to Trevor, given the long intervals of absence.

Kazimierz wanted borscht for her party because he likes it (he could have had buckets of it if he'd come home more often) and his mother has refused, which has annoyed him. Her birthday was his big day. People to entertain, and impress. 'Borscht,' as she told him, 'is staining, and in bowls for people who are standing around talking? The deep beetroot colour would end up down people's fronts.'

But he likes it! And it's healthy!

And he wanted those roasted chicken pieces, her oven version of paprikash. So she returned to inspecting the small burn on her left wrist from when she checked them. The quicks of her nails quickly stained purple. Her body was a marker of his enthusiasms.

With his father's help, Trevor had arranged several tables on the back lawn, draped now with white tablecloths, and they rigged up a line of lights above head level. No BBQ for this family occasion, no, she was also cooking a long beef roast, trussed and done Sauerbraten-style, plus the chicken paprikash and even a fish-and-prawn stew. All kitchen-hot food. Plus salads, a selection of processed meats, Polish sausages, mustard, horseradish, sauerkraut. Crusty bread.

First to arrive were his grandparents. They were still managing their bookshop despite the supermarket, of all things, selling bestsellers and biogs etc. *Coles!* Trevor liked his grandparents. People amiable from long years of serving customers. *Soon they would retire*, his mother had told him, *and he would no doubt see more of them.* His father was not the dill pickle; he was the cuckoo in the nest.

By now his father had drunk several glasses of wine and a few shots of vodka, his favourite warm-up for show time. As people arrived he topped up with whatever drink seemed close by. He mixed things together that would make most people sick. Until the guests had gone he was happy. With no one left to impress, his persona darkened. Telling his wife she was looking too made-up, that the neighbours laughed behind his back because of his accent, how his own son had become a stranger.

Being forever absent had no purchase in this.

When she had brought out the last box of serviettes, Trevor's mother smiled at him, said thank you and had her first glass of white wine. By now several couples were eating and drinking, the noise level was enjoyable and his father was, as always, circulating and *talking to the ladies* as he liked to announce it. And them.

'I came down from North West especially for my lovely Susan,' he had said, 'she is 40 years young and I have to kick myself to see we still love each other. Yes, we do. I am all the time up in the desert, you know, but when I come home: phwar!'

She'd had to laugh.

'He's a real case,' she'd said, now that everyone was listening, 'as you all know. We're hoping he'll get work down here at head office. It will civilise him at last.'

'About bloody time,' shouted someone.

'Now it's her birthday so we sing *Happy Birthday!*' His father began quietly, then as others joined in he sang louder and louder. He had a high baritone, a strong, trained voice and everyone knew he liked showing it off. Then he sang, alone, his version of *Sto Lat*, the Polish birthday song. The flow of notes ringing clearly in the night air. Across the street neighbours heard him and no doubt made knowing responses.

(*There he goes again. Still, the bugger's got a great voice.*)

'My friend Yuri,' he said to the woman beside him, 'he was good enough to sing in Polish opera, but the Russians wanted him. They wanted me, too, to train in the Russian opera. The Russians ran Poland, so we used to say Poland has the car but Russia has the steering wheel. Until, of course, Polish hero Lech Walesa. I wasn't even 20. Opera, you know, big voices, very Romantic and very sad. Anyway, I have no rhythm.'

He started singing the Prologue from the opera *Pagliacci. Si può? Si può?* Everyone stopped and listened dutifully just as they had stopped and listened the year before and, for some, the year before that. *Oh how the man likes to sing, but why always the same aria?* He extended his left arm, palm open. Playing the full parody. But he was good. Really good. They knew he was good.

Then he stopped and broke into *Happy Birthday* again! And everybody toasted Trevor's all-too-resigned mother. She had an actual gift, where the rhythm was hers and carried as it should. These were her friends, not his.

'Wait,' his father said quietly to Trevor. 'I have a surprise.' And he walked back up to the house. Trevor had almost forgotten, and managed to collect a second helping of the food, when there was a shout from behind him. There was a clown! *As an act, a singing telegram?* No, he could hear the voice. It was his bloody father again.

'Wait, everybody,' the man called out. 'Wait, wait, I'm doing more. Yes, I'll sing the clown! I am Canio the clown. I am like Caruso, see, Caruso the baritone who became a tenor.'

The guests stared at him, startled. For God's sake! Because this was new, Kazimierz mad as a cut snake in a hired clown costume. He launched into Canio's famous aria. Amazingly he strained the rising tessitura and hit through the maudlin climax. Sobbing in big melodramatic gulps as he finished.

Then stared at them, overjoyed with himself. This clown who couldn't abide a party for someone else. His wife forgotten once he got going, except by the women, who were not taken in, who paid her especial attention when he eventually shut up.

If his father preferred the company of adults, and women, and his own voice, he was still affectionate and walked over again to place his arm around Trevor.

'My boy,' he said and to the few people near the table, 'my boy is a good lad, he just needs a job in something that makes lots of money! George, have you a place for him in your business? No, just joking. He's a good boy,' and before Trevor could avoid it – and awkwardly in this situation – his father planted a huge kiss on top of his head. 'My boy!' he repeated.

Then he whispered: 'Make sure everyone has enough food, they must eat, eat, is Polish to eat as much as you can! You're a skinny boy, so you eat too. You must eat more. Your mother starves you.'

It was only later, when his face contorted, that he said there were people there who spat on him, thought him beneath them, because he was a foreigner. A wog.

'I make more money than any of them,' he said. 'I break the rules, I am not a fucking sheep.'

Then he cursed his wife for being too friendly with the man from a few doors down who was always staring at her, and he saw her, bitch, she was making eyes at that stupid public servant man who works behind a desk, a desk boy not even a man, in his white shirts, and anyway he …

Just a few weeks ago he had learnt that a real estate salesman called at the house and she invited the man in. His wife was having an affair, or trying to have an affair, with that man in his uptight black suit. If she was – he wasn't saying she *was*, just it looked a bloody hell lot like it, yes it looked bloody bad, and the neighbours, the dirty-minded neighbours, they must have been thinking terrible things.

And so the shouting ramped up, he told Trevor what a weak excuse of a boy he was, what a feeble boy. 'Don't take your mother's side!' he yelled. 'You look while I'm away,' he insisted, 'you tell me what your mother is doing. You are my eyes and ears.'

The morning after this outburst – and there were many outbursts – his father would be remorseful like every other violent and indulgent drunk: 'I'm sorry, my boy, I drink too much. It's the booze talking, not me. You forgive me, don't you? Here,' (hug, hug) 'you do, go on, you forgive me. Your mother, she is a good wife and mother. I am a bad man.'

~

When Elizabeth bought her house the adverts described her kitchen as *featuring a recent renovation* with *Smeg appliances* and that it was *compact*. Clever, really, modest, too; downbeat; and small, simply out of the question. Her kitchen is tiny.

Standing behind Trevor as he prepares food. She admires the co-ordinated handling of meat and vegetables as he trims and dices, or peels and slices, each phrase rolling from her editor's phrasebook. She is narration, he is verb. Several times now she has worked with food writers but only on the words, in the head space, never in the kitchen. No smells and spatters and elbows. No things falling on the floor. Whatever Trevor does she smells in situ, and sees plated up, the cutting and swearing; she knows him through her senses. Something he cannot know she knows.

Handling fish or chicken, he wears a plastic glove on his left hand. Now with three stitches in his right hand he gloves his right, too. Just squeezing in. A reverse image of the butcher with the chain-mail glove.

He settles a long fillet of rock ling on the plastic cutting-board and, holding the tail end of the fillet with his left hand, slithers the knife flatly underneath to the right and thus separates the white flesh from the weirdly mottled skin, pink and somehow disgusting, which he lifts and drops into the bin. She would never bother, just ask at the market for skinless fillets.

It surprises him, her standing near him while he works. Pleasant, though a problem if he needs to turn suddenly to the sink from the bench. She is expelled when cooking proper begins – too dangerous. In fact it began as her attempt to remind him how small the kitchen is and that she would like some of it.

He imagines the tactile woman behind him, distracting really, for various reasons: her kitchen and equipment, her rules of engagement, her heat almost, in the confined space; and of course her being bare-armed and smiling the innocent charm of genuine interest. It is a curiosity, this: his forearm and wrist and hand skills and her lithe limbs in repose, one assumes, arms warmly folded, and the weight of her leaning on the dishwasher.

An attraction. The honest man knows.

So here they are. Lodger and watcher.

At times Elizabeth feels these roles reversed. Having a stranger living every day and night in your house makes self-consciousness unavoidable, the lack of privacy acute. Even with those you like and whose company you enjoy. Even a relative.

Elizabeth has not been living alone by accident. Quite apart from her annual, intermittent fatigues, or whatever they were, when she lay in bed and imagined delirium. Loneliness is unchosen, a deep, undercurrent state; because aloneness as a relaxed and open-breathing independence, by the hour, by the day, trumps it. Do aloneness and loneliness shift one into the other? All the time.

'There should be something for the lonely,' she says to Trevor, who agrees.

'A saint? Get the Pope onto it. He needs more saints to catch up to his predecessor but one. Yet another pushy man from Poland.'

'Yes, a patron saint of the lonely. In the meantime, the lonely earn their keep every day.'

'There are more people living alone in the Western world,' he says, 'than ever in history. Because of age, widows usually, more divorces, men who can't get over divorces, less family cohesion, more people choosing to be independent.'

'For me there's something extra,' says Elizabeth. 'Just think about this, all these people I see in my life who are *nearly* familiar but none whose faces warm me the way anyone feels about someone close to them.'

Now she is silent. He confesses he enjoys returning home each day.

'I look forward to it', he says.

To talk and not to sell. This is what he's thinking. *And to see her, yes? Does it count as living 'alone', for them, given the relationship, whatever it is, of sharing only the house?*

She tells Trevor he is a pleasure to have around. She's glad she accepted him and in fact … she never thought not to.

This, he thinks, *is a compliment people would rarely put in raw form.*

He places the knife down.

'Are you surprised?' she asks him.

'I'm pleased. No, I mean, um, flattered. But why do you feel like that?'

'Because I get lonely, you silly bugger. I like seeing you arrive home.'

Suddenly her mouth is turning down in the corners as she says it. He feels his heart shift, he wants to hold her. He has not been listening well enough. Not for the first time he wonders what it feels like to see a current lover and not recognise them immediately.

It had always seemed to him a stranger's face made the first exciting impression, which then became deeply familiar, admired, and that love with its profound fondness grew from this familiar. She would have to adjust anew each time. The proverbial gamut: she would rush through exciting, familiar, loved in fast forward every day.

'Anyway,' she says, 'you understand, you've joined the sorry club, too.'

'Ah, the sorry club.'

'I'm just young enough to get fellas without having to sit in the front bar like some toothless old sheila.'

'Oh, Elizabeth, don't exaggerate.'

'Oh,' she mimics, 'is that flattery?'

She is not good at accepting compliments, even neutral ones.

'Test yourself on Tinder.'

'Ha. And would you swipe me?'

'Trevor,' she says before he can answer, 'don't talk about me using Tinder, please. Just because you're wondering about it. By the way, you pass the main criterion but fail the next one.'

'Touché. Sorry. The criterion …?'

'Above 183 centimetres. And below 40 years old.'

'Fuck, what kind of world is that?'

As if he doesn't know. Still. Above 40 you aren't sexy but you are sentient. During quiet time in his room is he moping like a teenager as life passes him by, or is he simply a loner after all? By nature? There are many such faces. And as for swiping?

'I would swipe you,' he says. 'If I wasn't over 40.'

'Thank you. You are a tiny bit gentlemanly.'

He eases back his chair and walks down towards the back door. She says quietly after him:

'I like a man who apologises.'

Whether or not he has heard isn't important. She said it to say it. To remind herself, like a self-administered pat on the back for something done well. A certain amount of self-consciousness is good. Living alone there is no one to reflect you. No one to see you.

He sees other things too, not personal. Trevor knows the location of everything. As in the shop, so too in the house. She is hopeless at this. If she is on her way out, already late, wailing about losing her keys or her bag or her mobile, or the books she had fetched earlier, ready to take with her, or ... Trevor obliges. *Under the front window. On the kitchen counter. On the second shelf near the phone.* Anything, anywhere, lodged in his brain as surely as he is lodged in her house.

~

They drive over to Martina's house for the meal she has promised them. Elizabeth double-parks, suggests Trevor go in while she finds a parking space. With that done, she locks her old car. Those plastic stalks on each door that require the manual click-down of finger prods. She enjoys this old engineering, its particular tactile reward, like the click of light switches.

How she loves her 1965 EH Holden, steely grey and shiny. *To think they are of the same vintage, she and Trevor and her car. ... And Martina at a squeeze. Within ten or so years, anyway.* When she was a child the EH was everywhere, the handsome car that made Holden proud, the Bathurst winner. Now the EH is parked on the street, and she is standing beside it, and he is nearby, inside the home of her best friend, and Elizabeth is content somehow, even as time is moving away from all of them.

If Martina had stated a choice when she had them, she would have let her adult children fly away and ring home on occasion, which is more or less the way things turned out. The umbilical cord lives for nine months, she says, and not for eighty years as some Mediterranean love-them-to-death mothers insist.

Her son lives in sweaty and glary Brisbane; her daughter prefers London to anything remotely Australian. He is silly about money and the beach; she is a fashion blogger. It has an element of loss, coming after the funeral experience.

'It takes all sorts,' she admits to Trevor. For an empathetic person she is caring, not clingy.

Elizabeth laughs as she sits down, given her own position midway between her old hippie mum and her Gen Y daughter. The *fearful symmetry*, as Blake might have said.

'In between,' she says, 'is not an easy place to be. Or it is *too* easy.'

Now they know that loss is his only form of parentage, Trevor listens to these two friends who are parents, and the big thing so central to the books he sells every day – family. As always in conversations, Elizabeth's mobile rings. She hisses to them 'It's the newbie!', meaning the invisible novelist, and leaves the room.

'I have been reading,' Trevor says, looking over to Martina, 'that according to some scientists there are cells from the foetus which pass through the placenta into the brains of their mothers. They call them microchimeric cells. The chimera of their children.'

Only now does he dare look into her eyes.

'It's creepy, isn't it?' he says. 'Yet in a funny way it's almost intimate, if you think about it. The one flesh. It gets creepier: they think the cells of these older children pass through the mother into the younger children through gestation and breastfeeding.'

'Now you have to be joking.'

'So any mother will have cells in her brain that came from her mother, her siblings and her children.'

'This is very strange. Are we not ourselves??'

'Not entirely ...'

'I have to admit I can't stand the idea of this thing they are saying,' she says, suddenly sounding very un-English.

'I bet the neurologists who claim this were so excited they never thought about incestuous misgivings. The smudge of biology in us.'

At which point Elizabeth returns from outside. She stops and pulls a strange face.

'I don't really know what you're talking about, Trevor, but it sounds pretty dire.'

She stands there looking healthy.

He explains, and they watch her face shift as these cells move from her mother into her and back, and then from her to her daughter and back. It's enough to make her put on weight.

'God, that's weird. Talking of mothers, I had another call when I was coming back in,' she says. 'My mother's had a turn or something. She's in Ballarat hospital and wailing for me to see her. I'm sorry, Martina but I have to go, have to save the staff. She will be complaining about everything that's wrong with her and at the same time telling them her history of excellent health.'

They all look at each other as they laugh.

'Trevor, do you mind? Can you make your own way back?'

By now there is a twist of anguish in her voice. She knows, regardless. Her mother has been less steady on her feet. If she is less sharp at times, she is therefore less consistent, confused about things she should not be.

'I'll drive up to see her straight away.'

'It's those bloody cells calling me, Trevor, my internal SIM card. I mean just now, about my mum. Family, protection, care. Tribal stuff. Whatever.

'Perhaps they're all the same thing,' she adds, waving her arms sannyasin-style.

'But, Elizabeth,' says Martina, 'you should eat before you drive that far. It's already been a long day.'

'I'll eat hers,' suggests Trevor.

'You look as if you already have,' Martina smiles. Silence. They are trying to ease Elizabeth's worry, if not very well. Elizabeth is holding her mobile tightly against her chest.

Then Martina nods and hugs her, kisses her briefly. Elizabeth grabs her keys and is gone.

Martina knows her friend – missing a meal is normal. She turns to Trevor. 'Now when Elizabeth is talking to her mother,' she says, 'and holding her hand, she will be thinking about your silly cell theory.'

'It's not mine.'

Martina is still shaking her head at the idea.

Once the meal is over they sit on her balcony looking out across the street. Cars are moving slowly towards the one-way intersection which controls the traffic. A row of vehicles builds up as the lights glow red.

She is tapping the side of a glass of Australian fizz. The bubbles are tiny glistening cells rising up and bursting. Simple cells.

'If I were a neurologist,' he says, 'I'd be looking for ways to boost language learning and playing the violin without years of practice. Smart pills, except I don't like Big Pharma. Elizabeth is right. Being with her mum so often is like the rituals of tribes rather than sects. Empathy and flesh. She says her mum never stops talking. Perhaps she developed the habit so her face-blind daughter always knew who she was. Voice recognition.'

'You are a very strange man, do you know that?'

He smiles.

'You have been good for Elizabeth,' she announces, in her particular Martina way: intimate, somehow bossy.

This sort of comment makes him curious.

'She is happier,' Martina says, 'and she's put on weight. That's good for someone who has, if her GP's correct, orthorexia. Well, as an explanation that's as good as any other. She has been eating.'

'How can you tell?'

'You are too close to see it but I know Elizabeth. She improved the moment you moved in. It was odd really.'

'Is that a backhanded compliment? *Odd?*' But he knows what she means and it pleases him.

'She has been looking,' he hesitates '… healthier. I cook every night. She has stopped worrying and started eating.'

Since Trevor's arrival, she explains, Elizabeth has been unable to lie in bed complaining of viruses and strange inner symptoms. In Martina's opinion the reason she left full-time work was not problems with authors, or bullying, as she dramatised it, but to be unwell whenever she felt like it.

'Have you noticed her hair is thicker, and longer? She's growing it out. She's brushing it instead of clipping it back … ugh, those awful clips. And no more of those silly colours she was hurting herself with.'

'Well … I agree.'

'Even her boobs are growing. Trevor, I'm sure you have noticed *that*. It's where the weight goes on last so that's a good sign. Sadly, it's where the weight is lost quickest, you know? A woman loses two kilos and her boobs flop around in her bra.'

There is no chance of Martina's going anywhere.

Although he says nothing, he has noticed. Elizabeth has leant across him in the kitchen, where body contact or *touching*, as the tabloids have it, is acceptable, and he has felt her breasts against him. Fuller and firmer.

'Yes,' he says, eventually.

Only when he has acknowledged this does Martina look directly at him.

'And you, you have *lost* weight.'

'You've caught us out, Martina. It's all the sex we're having.'

Martina's eyes truly open wide, until he laughs.

'It might be a good thing,' she says. 'But you *have* lost weight, a lot of it. It must feel good when you tuck everything in and do up your pants in the morning. Your belt position. Or when you weigh yourself, which you should do naked, of course.'

He wonders if she talks like this to everyone.

'Elizabeth,' says Martina, 'has a body equal to her profession, trimming a shapeless manuscript into a slimmer thing altogether, for economy rather than excess. But she had been editing herself and gone too far. Having a man to cook meals, more often and more varied than she'd have ever prepared for herself, is relaxing her.'

'I have to eat less,' he says, 'and she has to eat more. Imagine this stretching to infinity – me so thin I can't get up to cook and Elizabeth so fat she can't get out of bed to eat.'

'It's a kind of symbiosis,' she adds, possibly ignoring him. 'For Elizabeth it's the best kind of approach.'

'Yeah? And what's the worst kind?'

'Oh, I don't know if I should say. Anxiety?'

So he admits his three-a-week gym visits, how he isn't merely losing weight so much as losing fat *and* bulking up with the serious stuff. He shuffles around as he says, placing his hands on his arms and chest, that he is getting muscles under his clothes. 'A man knows this,' he says, when his initial attendance at a gym shifts from embarrassing to quietly trying to impress. 'Male, female, the same.' Along with his osteopath visits and fighting the weight machines at the gym, Trevor the muffin is no more.

Even his cheekbones have emerged.

He has continued driving out to the Fairfield boathouse every week to row real boats and do real work. A change from the gym with its Lycra and its awful carpet and alien machines, the egotist radio DJs loudspeakered from every corner, and the admittedly lovelier sweaty people. The river is a living resistance, not the serial mass of cables and steel blocks.

When is her husband returning? he asks and she laughs, saying he's overseas on yet another business trip. Pleasing Trevor, this, no husband to come home and make everything conventional.

Then she stands, upright, head back like a dancer.

'Oh, I should be going,' he says, standing.

She immediately sits down again.

'There's no need to rush home,' she says. 'I'm sure Elizabeth would want me to drive you home. You can stay.'

So he stays.

~

In fact, Mrs Sermon is stacked against the linen-service pillows like a bag stuffed with old clothes in a corner of her house. She is not leaving her hand out to be held. Whatever it was that came over her has left behind a terrible malaise. 'Malaise!' she exclaims. 'Not a stroke, thank God.' It seems she is safe from that one, not a drooping lip and a damp area on her blouse.

What use is astrology if it hasn't warned her off this ward of smelly food and other people? To her annoyance she has even seen some of her old astrological clients, one of whom is looking much healthier than he should. The people that want to live past 90? … are the people who are 89. Life has made a mistake and kept adding years to her life, dammit. It is meant to be *her* life. Except she can no longer decide if she wants more years or not.

Her Boundless Lustre is long gone.

And to be humiliated by her own daughter arriving in the ward and swivelling around staring at all these old ducks in turn, including herself, then turning away again, unable to recognise her own bloody mother until she calls out '*Elizabeth!*' And then – even then – has to wave her arms to be seen. What a weird thing her daughter is with that ridiculous condition.

It must be a punishment for some wrong in a past life. But whose – her daughter's or her own? It is she who suffers the ultimate indignity. Her own daughter, blind to her.

Back to being Mrs Sermon, she is frowning. She feels more than usually exposed, not just to the medical, the forensic, but to the frighteningly empty space she lies in, with no protective towers of newspapers or avenues of plastic bags, boxes, supermarket items, JB hi-fi cables and appliances – her endless, unadulterated and beloved junk.

Can't complain, thinks Elizabeth. *The old ladies do look the same in their hospital garb, crocheted covers and hospital beds, side by side against the pastel wall.*

They are doing what conventional medicine does, her mother is grumbling, 'Tests, tests, more tests.' Every few hours, she can't get enough time for sleep. Then she manages to laugh. *Whatever was wrong with her has gone. Now she is suffering from tests. What will she die of? Testness.* All right, she has *had a turn*, an untestable saying her own mother was fond of using; and in the moment of echoing her mother's idiom for her own condition, annoyingly, she likes it.

If there are no worse signs Elizabeth has been told they will discharge her mother, so long as she doesn't drive or handle machinery. *Fat chance of that.* Like taking older-generation antihistamines. The "drowsy" warning was always a small pleasure for her because in all the years of taking the little pink pills she never once felt drowsy. Then again, the pills hardly ever worked.

So by now Elizabeth is calm and the various scarier imaginings she had while driving up from the city are on hold, at least. There is the first time. Then everything else is more, and worse. Her mother has always had extremely low blood pressure without any corresponding ailments. Her pulse is eerily low. If she has any kind of operation the machines go off signalling she is nearly dead. Now, who knows, she may simply have let herself become dehydrated. Unable to find the tap amidst the junk.

Elizabeth worries: if she is to stay the night she will have to sleep in her mother's bed because by now there is not a square metre of space anywhere else. Full of rubbish. She has always driven back to the city at night. Free of the suffocations come of the endless garbage in her mother's house and upwards of an hour's drive from home, she breathes her own fresh air and returns to the sanity of open spaces the way a station-owner stands outdoors without a fence in sight.

Her mother sits forward and glares at her.

'It seems I must expect you to look after me, Elizabeth. Who else do I have? I am all alone. I need you to be more careful, to call me more often' (so she can talk forever, in other words) 'and here's the proof: you should have been here this morning. But no. Doing nothing as usual in the city. Haven't even managed to keep a husband and now God knows what you do. Yvonne never rings me regardless of you saying she will, or that she has.'

'Mum, you …'

'I'm all alone.'

'So am I!'

'That's your own silly fault.'

So this is her mother's best appeal for compassion. They know you must provide for them. Just do it.

Every dutiful daughter knows the bind her mother places her in, that society places her in, and how tightly it seizes you by the conscience, that part of the anatomy even more sensitive than the throat. Struggle is pointless. Escape is temporary.

Therefore Elizabeth does not stay over at her mother's. Instead she drives the relaxing eventual 120 or so kilometres back to Melbourne, drinks three armfuls of blood-red wine and is in bed asleep even before Trevor arrives home from Martina's. Whenever he does.

'Her own silly fault.' Her mother. How these sharp words bang in her head all night. At moments, waking from this shunt of sensations, she even wonders if Trevor has returned, or not, this quite unexpected worry, then nervousness, as she listens and eventually hears a faint snoring from downstairs. Reassured she is not alone, admitting it feels good, even right, that he is downstairs. *Relieved he isn't still at …*

The only worry she has been trying not to consider is whether her dream image of the neighbour meant anything. A few days ago she felt she'd seen him in the meat section of Queen Victoria Market and he – if he it was – kept looking up the aisle towards her. He seemed bothered. His face had a smudged, sort of knocked-about look like some of the men begging on Errol St. Then a different guilt came with her own words returning, that the man needed talking to again. *Talking to, not ...* Trevor doesn't pretend to be an angel, but would he really do this? It worries and then, admittedly, surprises her. *He said he knew people – a retired cop or something?*

Next morning she strides around Royal Park by herself, unbothered by the light rain. There was no sign of Trevor when she left home. He doesn't volunteer as often now, after saying he would. Cold weather, rain, warm bed. It bothers her, the image of the neighbour's bruised face, her shitty neighbour, and the illicit thrill in her that Trevor confronted him.

She is trying not to think, just be a breathing and moving bubble of one woman and one dog, except Gordon keeps breaking off to rush among dogs all free of the leash and back in touch with their inner lunatics. When he was a pup Gordon was avid for the variety of life, as long as it was chewable: mainly hoses. Then into the backyard to lift a leg and ease his thoughts out onto the grass. He knows how to make the most of his public walks. He's rushing rushing. At anything at all, whereas at home only barking at the neighbour helps.

She has opportunities to join the other walkers as they move around the circuit, alone like her or in groups, on this early-morning series of repeated passing and approaching and encounter. One group is always out there, the man whose exercise is a variety of verbs: he talks and gesticulates loudly and wildly, while laughing to the others in the group, so keen to maintain eye contact with them that he walks sideways, turning away only and always to say a big

Hello, good morning and how are you? to anyone walking towards him. The same again on each re-encounter a lap later. His arms are tattooed and he sounds educated but his manner is needy.

Or the tall, middle-aged women with a large poodle each, big intelligent dogs and classy ladies who never say hello or good morning to anyone. No second life there. The girl with the bouncing chest, always a worry; the aged man who for all his forward years, his stoop and garish trainers charges around the walking track faster than Elizabeth. All the dogs have a sheen of rain on their coats, shiny for the longhairs, speckled for the shorthairs. Poodles look as if sprinkled with flour.

The slim woman who lives several houses away from her is striding around the track with a jolly expression on her face and swinging her jolly arms like an old-fashioned toy soldier or the Little Drummer Girl. Her floury poodle – everyone has a poodle out here – runs ahead and slows and runs ahead again, keeping an average lead of about 10 metres. The woman looks like a caricature, the dog like – a dog.

Oh, how good this walking in the morning is for everyone with its goody-two-shoes look and feel, which is why she has asked Trevor if he'd accompany her and why he probably doesn't. Up to him. It's a curious feeling knocking gently on his door on the sunnier mornings, which is his condition for a yes, maybe.

Though not today. She isn't sure what time he got in. She keeps thinking about it when she really shouldn't.

Although she was sceptical about late careers, Elizabeth is curious to see Trevor's newest paintings. *How long has it been?* She wants to be more of a stickybeak. What he does concerns her. Painting in here all night, possibly punching the neighbour, pursued by a dead father. *What a strange man he is!*

The hinges sound guilty as she drags opens his studio door. *It isn't his diary she's going through, for God's sake.* Her local lorikeets are screeching above her like art critics full of opening-night champagne.

Two large boards propped against the wall but from the range of spatter and spillage on the floor she knows he has been painting them flat down Jackson Pollock-style, and the un-spattered areas are exactly the size of his boards. One board seems to be a collage with the point of view from below: a fragment of wheel of some kind, a screen, broken walls, branches? Rows of shadowy spikes rising towards a limited area of what might be sky except it's purplish and looks like a haematoma or an illness.

Garish. Disturbing. Hard to look away from, though. All that rubble and gash of edges. The energy of bold brushstrokes. Inside this sort of blustery cross-hatching are several small windows or boxes of busy street scenes, ploughed paddocks, untidy house interiors worryingly like her own lounge room of papers and scattered books.

Flattened images from newspapers and magazines. Posters she has seen in his shop window, here, plastered onto the frame. The collages she's seen before. Last time.

The second board is the reverse, an aerial view: contained in boxes or windows, occupying as much surface as chaos was in the first, are the top floors of skyscrapers with fans and masts and air-conditioning units, even rooftop environmental gardens. Cars in ant formation in streets far below. Shopfronts, people, graffiti. Streaks and spikes imbedded in the surface of the board as if it were a screen and very like the spike shapes in the other painting. In the thin spaces between boxed images are the sloppier stuffs of soil and riverbanks and sluicing bodies of water seen from above, and roads, and shorelines. Tranquil. Hell. Heaven. Fallen. Risen.

This interpretation doesn't satisfy her. Are they any *good*?

Several more. Each surface is a flat colour overlaid with one or two colours in a kind of coupling presence. They are to varying degrees viscerally flattened, scraped, ridged, scumbled and – in hairlines of nervy intensity – scratched. There is no representation. All the texture is colour in shapes of application and or rearranging. The paint is thick and serrated, almost dropping back to flat and relaxed. He told her he was painting Rough Rothko. Barbwire Rothko.

She is astonished to see so much new work. They are more striking than the paint-stricken floor. The ultimate test, which many artists fail. She senses in them an unexpected energy. The paintings she saw weeks ago now seem like forerunners. If there were questions in her mind, these are impressive answers.

One last painting is still sketchy and trowelled over with thick paint in the centre. A more conventional work, a squashed and halved image of a face. Whiskery. *Is this the man claiming to be his father?* With her condition it would hardly matter if she had seen him before. Nor can she interpret, except to think of a trickster.

His face is like a reservoir of colour.

It returns while she is back working in her study. The imagery, the paint. *For an unknown artist entering his 50s to be painting in 2-D. Too conventional?* Though who is she to say, or not say this? There is something to do with mortality in them. Ageing. The gap between attempt and achievement … one of pain and possibly dread. 'To feel it in your organs,' he'd said, 'the proverbial pit of the stomach.' If the mind can stay supple long after the body has slowed and stiffened. Then again, she has read that older martial-arts masters bring their chi into play and can for short periods leap and strike like cats.
And climb walls. Sure.
All the same, his paintings have made her remember things.

Yvonne arrives a day later and immediately leaves to see friends at her favourite bar in town. Of course she does. Even if she is only staying for a weekend or so. But not before meeting Trevor.

Elizabeth has called him up from his room to meet Yvonne. 'What time did you get back the other night?' she asks him. He looks surprised and shrugs.

He shakes Yvonne's hand and they smile at each other, she at him with a rather sly expression, he thinks. A vernacular sly, which knows the silence between generations.

'What's this Trevor guy like?' she had asked her mother.

Elizabeth knew to be vague but unworried (and was aware she was hiding her feelings) so she said, 'He's fine, he's no bother, nothing to be concerned about.' She said he cooks and does the dishes, too; the first being unusual, the second – if following the first within the same twenty-four hours – rare.

'It's *fucking* rare!' she added, and laughed at this rarity.

'So you like him then,' asked Yvonne. Or stated.

And now here Trevor is. She thinks he looks OK at first viewing. She thinks her mother is pretty cool and, of course, *she's* cool. It'd be disappointing to have some guy here who was a dag, totally embarrassing.

That he is, at his age, living and paying rent in the house of a woman who is hardly younger than him is the oddest thing. Or just younger or maybe not, hard to tell without asking. To Yvonne they are both *old*. Though with Elizabeth's hair maintained as a respectable light blonde, no grey hair. None in his, anyway. No hair at all.

It can be cool, thinks Yvonne, *to be so off the norm*. He's big. And reasonable-looking, in an older way.

A collection of tradies has gathered at the modest house three numbers up from Elizabeth's. It is being renovated by young men who dress like older working-class figures. Except two of them wear hipster beards and hairdos, and one even drives a European, meaning very German, car. At lunchtime if it's fine they unfold collapsible chairs and sit under a tree on the median strip eating their packed lunches and speaking quietly. None of them smokes, none raises his voice and they speak in polite, middle-class ways.

Trevor has been talking with them. Just being curious.

Over breakfast the following day, Yvonne tells Trevor about the tradie she used to drink with. An electrician.

'Makes a change,' he says. 'I keep hearing about young women who are hitched to a bloke in IT. I don't get it – sexy, slim women in their prime living with overweight nerds.'

'I happen to like tradies,' she says. 'They're down-to-earth, you know, good at physical things.'

She is teasing Trevor. *Why not amuse herself while he's there in the house?* She quite likes him, the very little she's seen.

'Tradies, or desk types, or complete crooks, we're all the same,' he says, 'we work during the day, eat, drink, fart, and when we sleep at night our skin flakes off around us and settles on the bedding or we inhale it. Then we wake up and get moving and do it all over again.'

'Funny to think,' Yvonne laughs, 'that you're downstairs sleeping in my old skin.'

'I vacuumed,' says her mother.

Obviously her mother feels relaxed with him. Enough to have said so every time Yvonne has spoken to her. It was important that they talk about it, after all. Apparently Trevor has even taken her side a few times, on the sidelines of these phone conversations, though it occurs to her that might be for other reasons.

'Not all tradies are up to my standard,' she admits.

Her mother hoots at this.

'Do you mean,' asks Trevor, 'in their professional standards? Or their manliness?'

'For being dickheads, you dickhead.'

She laughs at her nerve. So does he, which makes them both laugh.

'I met this guy at a bar and he was pretty hot and we hooked up straight off. He came around the next day in his SUV. I was all for him and then I saw the sign he'd stuck in big white letters on his back tinted window. It said MissiBitches.'

'That man is a bit confused.'

'Yeah. But the really uncool thing about them is they're no different from the up-themselves boys who live in the city and take selfies all the time.'

'Right. You see me nodding.'

'They used to be tough, or that's what I thought. Hard workers, you know, muscles, tattoos – but now even private-school boys are into ink. And if something goes wrong? Woo woo! They're as wussy as hipsters.'

'How did I miss all this? Who would have guessed?'

'Are you serious?' But she laughs.

'I'm someone who worked around,' Trevor says. 'Doesn't matter what they do, if otherwise healthy people can't stand on their own two feet I have little time for them, tattooed, bearded, green-haired or drawling from the back of the throat. Or not.'

'You make people sound weak.'

'No. I mean self-centred. Most people are weak but they push back enough to get through stuff. I mean entitlement. That's what makes the rest of us want to slap them.'

'What?'

'Yeah, embarrassed parental slap. Don't you? Ask your mother!'

Jesus, he thinks, *did I say that?*

'Mum knows all about tradies,' says Yvonne. 'My absent father for a start.'

'Yes. And your grandfather. Women in your family have a thing about tradies.'

'What? You knew?'

Afterwards, Elizabeth tells him he would have enjoyed having kids. The sudden shift in his expression says, *Do not repeat this.*

~

Trevor decides to drive the small distance to the shop to collect a book on first aid he recalls being on a lower shelf near the desk. Just in case. A random pain in his leg has been pinching overnight. The night before was the cause: he drank too much, slept dead under the doona. Trevor tried to make himself sleep with his leg up, or down, or on the left his side or on his back. But his self-alerting tricks were as drunk as the rest of him. He had returned to the pub Lester kept in business. There were things to laugh about, including the father idiocy. The man was there, drinking alone as usual and filling in the sudoku.

'It's more like my kind of work,' Lester said. 'I mean when I had work. As for your father, well, fuck me, I remember you saying he'd buggered off, how no one quite believed he was dead. And the law has to say yes or no, eh, and did! So it was dead dad. It's pseudocide then, him coming back. Did he – I mean does he – owe people?'

'I bet he does. You can't tell with him. It's bloody jarring seeing him at all as my father. Anyway, debts or the like, he hasn't said. He's hardly a reliable witness. I can't ask him until he comes back, if he comes back.'

'How about his tax?'

'Not sure, probate would get that, wouldn't it? Lester, he's as cagey as he ever bloody was. I could only go on what other people said when I was young. He was strange, even I knew that. Psychologically he owes *me*, and emotionally I mean. My mother was left in nowhere-land. Depressed and left suspended there, not knowing a thing. He was God knows where, laughing and carrying on. When I was older she told me every time he went on these trips up north he gave the impression he mightn't come back. To do that to someone. He was a complete shit.'

'You know he could be jailed for this.'

Whether Lester is trying to or not, he looks as if he's scheming. Once a detective, and a superannuated one at that, he weighs up the proceeds of a crime in a way ordinary citizens might not. Even if an acquaintance is party to the case, and not a beneficiary of the scheme. In Lester's past were many schemes, and schemes to him meant outside the bright light of fair play. Stare down the crooks for too long and they will stare back out from your eyes.

'You're a strange man yourself, Trevor.'

'You can talk.'

Then far too much to drink. Back home he hardly said more than hello to a wide-eyed Elizabeth before stumping downstairs. Little point acting otherwise, and no acting at all inside a hangover in the morning.

It is all very well for the detective and his sudoku, no one else is involved.

At the last intersection he waits for a red light and feels pained then pathetic. *How difficult would it have been to walk, using his stick and taking his time? Does gym-work sometimes exacerbate internal injuries?*

Then from these shallows he feels a spike of anger. There's no chance of parking in the alley beside his shop because of more cobble-lifting and black-dirt digging up by City Water. The alley and pavement are wet with mud and slop. Again! And they have taped off the entrance. This makes it the third time in a month. Are they absurdly incompetent, or are hydraulics always a problem; as Freud suggested, prone to recurrence? Like his leg pain.

Haven't they homes to go to, AFL teams to get pie-eyed over? Something strange about this group of men, too, in navy blue overalls and orange visibility stripes, the way they ignore him at first, then stare in unison at this big man in his little car stationary in the left lane. Their chin-lift smiling as he drives off.

He has to limp with his stick 100 metres from the nearest parking area back to the shop and enter through the front door.

'G'day, mate,' one of the workers says. 'Are ya gettin' any?'

'Jesus, it's Sunday, mate,' he answers.

Trevor moves straight through to the rear room to make some tea and as he pours water into the jug he sees the hole. A rectangular *hole* with a rough chalk-line scratched around it.

Or half a hole. Three bricks wide, sawn one course of bricks deep into his common wall with the jeweller. Someone has cut and gouged the mortar and simply removed the loosened bricks. Dust and red brick fragments are scattered over the floor, there are even footprints in them.

But only one course! The second course, on the jeweller's side of the wall, is intact. With as much time again they'd have been all the way into the jeweller's, the gap just big enough to crawl through. They must have been disturbed, or spooked by something.

Gentle Jesus! They really were trying to use his shop as access. Allen will be spitting keys. Or swallowing them. When he implied precisely this, Trevor assumed the man was being pompous. What about his claim of a sensing apparatus, with warning systems jangling or whooping as uniformed men sit staring left and right at CCTV screens, or at ganglionic banks of lights like nerve endings from all over the city? Lights suddenly flashing like diamonds. It is so top-secret not even the security firm can see it.

When Trevor goes into the back room he sees his side door is broken but holding in place, just. When he pulls it open the door sags inwards like a drunk, the wood splaying and splintered, the metal locks intact but hanging uselessly in the open space. He pushes it back to a closed position. *The water workers never saw it as they prised apart the cobbled laneway?*

He returns to the rectangular hole in the party wall. Bending closer, he sees a chisel-sized hole through to the other side. There is a small draught of jewellery air coming through. Mission impossible it's not, just two ageing courses thick, a bit of noise overnight where no one lives, no one to get annoyed at the grinding or tearing or whatever sound a drill or cutting machine makes revving into solid brick. It would have been gravelly music.

A man could wriggle though on his belly. Unless he was fat.

It is almost funny. The prat from next door with his combinations and secrets, the deadbolted door to his panic room. Except someone has gone straight through the wall behind it, the doors still locked. Or nearly.

Trevor rings the police. This time they sound interested.

'Don't touch anything,' they say. Sure. They're on their way. Well, given he's inside his shop does that mean, *Don't move?* His entrance through the front door has kept the main area of the back room clear. The side-door area clear, ditto, but the wall …? No, he even bent down to peer through the small opening. His footprints will be in the mix. Surely the crooks will have thrown away their shoes after the job (size-10 Burglar-series Nikes).

They must have known Trevor wouldn't be there on a Sunday, and after two days with the shop closed. He waits. The dark hole looks at him like a malevolent and damaged eye.

Wait till he tells Lester. A bit of light relief for the man.

Let the law ring the jeweller and announce the first premise of burglary – the point of access, and, in this case the same, point of exit. He listens to the City Water men thudding and cutting open the innocent vault of the alley. *Damn. They may have erased evidence. It's probably too late to tell them to stop work. Would they even listen?* Still, he thinks he should, so he leaves through the front door to explain the situation to them. Then he sees what he has overlooked.

By breaking through the side door the crooks have gouged their way through the Galilee Basin. The mural shines in defiance, the door the only clue.

Slow cops … if they even bother to come, given they didn't last time, though suburban jewels are known to be worth more than great books. Generally considered. He gets up and inspects the books by his front, not bashed-in door display, noting the new title by a local author: *Waiting*. Yes, quite. He waits.

It occurs to him that Allen the jeweller will probably try on a new security trick no normal person would think of suggesting and no law could impose on anyone. Trevor hopes. Something odd yet logical if you think about it: Allen the jeweller will insist Trevor the bookseller replace his broken wooden side door with deadbolts and monster bars because nothing less is secure enough to provide protection – not for the books but for *his* bloody jewels.

Imagining the hole staring at him makes him think. *A man with a wall-eye. The sooner this bloody hole is bricked in, the better.* And think next of Elizabeth's eyes and yes/no laser operation. And of William Blake, who saw more clearly than most:

> *This life's dim windows of the soul*
> *Distorts the heavens from pole to pole*
> *And leads you to believe a lie*
> *When you see with, not through, the eye.*

Though it is well understood that at times the poet and painter Blake also saw what no one except William Blake saw. He wrote it and painted it. They thought he was mad. He probably was. But he was right. He was a visionary.

Two men enter the shop. Trevor knows they are detectives because they are dressed like detectives. Before they ask him anything significant they inspect the wall and its strange brick-breakage.

'We have an opening here,' says one of them.

'No we don't,' says the other. 'We only have half an opening.'

(They must get incredibly bored on the job.)

The second one, the half-opening one, is shorter than the other but behaves as the senior. He is heavier and looks as if many years of sizing up crims and dimwits have sent him to sleep. Or is it post-traumatic stress disorder, something Trevor used to see much of? Police who have shot or been shot at. Bodies seen in all states, sometimes more blood than body. Children, women, heartless actions.

This is just a hole in the wall. They can have a laugh.

The older detective explains to Trevor, and the other detective, how this crim used a tool of some sort, probably something small and quiet. He says, 'See these bricks, our fucking crim has been up all night grinding out the mortar like a confused termite. Yes, it might have been a hand tool with very sharp gouging edge or even, crims being so fucking lazy, something electric. Therefore' – he walks over to the nearby power point and inspects it – 'this here, just in case the rechargeable battery pack had run out. Or it wasn't that kind of tool, it was old-fashioned AC, not DC. Then he definitely tapped into your bloody power supply, mate. Don't think it'll whack your bill very much.'

'You probably haven't heard,' he goes on, 'of the "Drywall Burglar" in the US. He used a fucking knife or something crude – a tungsten screwdriver, I'd guess – to scrape through the wall into an apartment which he then proceeded to rob and pilfer.'

He says *pilfer* with exaggerated p's and f's and *-er* as 'aah'.

'Not content with apartment No. bloody 1, he scraped through the wall into the adjacent apartment. And robbed that one too. And kept going. They were up for sale but only being inspected during the day and this crook, being a crook, of course only worked night shifts. Dunno how he covered his tracks but he did and then like one of those ear-wig stories – of the bloody thing poked in someone's ear and then eating it's way across the brain until it comes out the opposite ear – this guy went through ten apartments in a row. A whole fucking row of apartments, you gotta hand it to him.'

He stands back to eyeball Trevor, and his workmate.

'Fucking crazy, eh? True but.'

His accent changes into something unsuccessful.

'Yeah, the Drywall Burglar they called him. Not a lotta people know that.'

Jesus, thinks Trevor, *the guy is doing a Michael Caine impression.*

'Then there was the Hatton Garden Mob, you know, the old guys in London. They bought a diamond drill on the bloody internet and cut through a metre of concrete into a London bank vault. Confused a great many people, they did. But they got caught. Funny buggers, thieves. The public like 'em. They become heroes by the time they're old and grey. Or are already, that mob.'

After they have gone Trevor walks to the non-fiction bookshelves and pulls out *A Burglar's Guide to the City* by the American author Geoff Manaugh. Yes, the Drywall Burglar is in it. Along with amusing accounts of crooks and safe-cracking, and every kind of burglary, all within one set of covers. The anarchic pleasures of theft for safe readers who imagine being safe-crackers. His shop is a pleasure zone of vicarious experience and not for the first time Trevor wonders what proportion of vivid human experience *is* vicarious – that is, imagined not lived. Ronnie Biggs and the Great Train Robbery. As the detective said, the public have a soft spot for thieves.

For fun, he rings Elizabeth and tells her, firstly, about the jeweller's likely lament and then of the Michael Caine impressionist. She laughs just like the workmen had, she's all squawking and excitement as he hears her pass on the information to Yvonne. Whatever happened to people feeling scared or concerned? Then concerned she becomes, and apologetic, as if reading his mind after all and wanting now to console him. Then just as suddenly laughs again from what is clearly the real her, then calms down. *What a woman!* He says if she and Yvonne want to come and see the damage for themselves, the police may not be happy with that until …

'I'm driving,' she says.

'Oh.'

'And the EH somehow missed out on Bluetooth back in the '60s.'

He hears Yvonne giggling.

As he waits he realises this is what his life is: there's a hole cut through one side of it and things keep blowing out the other.

Wives, friends, safe-breakers. Trepanned. Not a migraine. Not, as he sits there in the shop, feeling it right to left, as he looks in on it, like someone entering the shop from the front. Even the way the broken fence looked like an open gate.

It makes his head hurt just to think it.

Even the surly bugger who pushed him over on Friday approached from the right side. Perhaps it's something to do with right-brain activity, not words, just where the bloody doors are. He thinks of Elizabeth on the right, her daughter on the left, sitting on that pleated bench-seat in the EH.

In his early 20s, when house-sharing with the alarmingly dysfunctional psychologists, Trevor had taken a Myers-Briggs personality test. The psychos, as he called them, did not take Mrs M and Mrs B seriously. They said the M-Bs were a joke to take 900,000 or so words of Swiss psychoanalyst Carl Jung and reduce them to this simplistic and changeable test. It was a T20 match in duration but Test cricket in its likely scores.

Trevor had emerged from the test as the Introverted Sensing Feeling Judging type, and it concluded he must be ...? Was he really Judging? Trevor's sensory self-absorption had gaps either side of its hyphen: he took in the world so he could stand in the centre of it.

But he was an outsider, surely.

Outside the IGA the woman is sprawled with her back against the wall, legs in front of her like a rag doll. Her face is dusty, uneven. Trevor asks how she is, if she's all right. Empty questions. When he hands her $10 she starts crying. Like last time. It looks like an act but it's spontaneous. Sudden.

Around the aisles he goes, distracted. On his way out the woman looks up and asks him for money again.

Elizabeth and Yvonne are home when he returns. They have already forgotten about his burglary drama, in favour of preparing dinner. Or Elizabeth is preparing dinner – taking advantage of Trevor's absence to reclaim her kitchen – and Yvonne is standing nearby, reading something on her mobile.

'The medium-sized pan,' says her mother.

'Yeah, yeah.'

'I mean now.'

Her daughter makes exasperated noises, glares at her and places her phone on the bench.

'Not there!'

'For fuck's sake, Mum.'

'And don't get all sweary and petulant just because you're …'

'Hello girls,' says Trevor, all cheek and inappropriate cheer. Much as he thinks it, he does not say *Domestic Goddess and Kitchen Princess*.

Soon enough he's updating them. Yvonne, who at first stood listening, almost unknowingly begins to help her mother. How a couple of detectives arrived and took details and photos and prints from both doorway and wall. Funny buggers. They were thorough, precise, even if the gab surprised him. Trevor shut the side door and eventually relocated the bolts. The lock would have to wait. No one was after his bloody books.

Apparently Allen was still on his way back from a weekend in the locust isle of Tasmania. Asking himself: *How, how, how?* Trevor does the funny faces, the pert mouth and the campy hand-wringing.

'Trevor, you are enjoying this too much,' says Elizabeth.

'I'll say,' adds her daughter.

'Your shop life is Dickensian, Trevor. Either that or Freud is sleeping on one of your shelves.'

'The jeweller's a dickhead. Did I mention he has vertical, gelled hair? He's my age.'

'Urrgh, uncool,' says Yvonne, then smiles at Trevor. 'I'm glad you don't do anything like that. All you do is have a shop full of weirdos and out-of-it blokes and creepy fathers. That's cool.'

Trevor can't help himself, he feels flattered. In a backhanded kind of way.

Elizabeth looks up from the stove.

'They should have mugged him and stripped his ear. Is he a big bloke?'

'Nah, he's a prat.'

'I've been thinking,' says Yvonne, 'about ways of marketing your book business. You've got to do it online.'

'I already do. I have a website.'

'Well, that's a start. Do you have summaries and stuff other people have said about the book on the back cover?'

He heads off downstairs and returns with his laptop. Yvonne nods through the website material with her Gen Y confidence there to suggest it's *OK, it's a website, it's ordinary and yeah, nah* – doubting it all.

She sits down and begins checking through the site. He can hear her breathing shift. It fits with his theory about reading and breathing – how reading alters the diaphragm between suspense and pathos and even just enjoyable narrative. *Is it emotional, is it the tension?* She looks up at him. Her eyes are brown like her mother's, something he'd not noticed. Never been so close to her before.

'You're frowning,' he says.

'Yeah, look, this is all good but you need something more. Some marketing would help. A website is really only cool if you have traffic. It's no good by itself. *Who even knows it's up?* Coolness is customers lining up like at the Auction Rooms café in Errol St. You need a hook to bring new customers *in* to the website. Make it work on social media. Think of digital devices, that sort of thing. Think of them as online people who think it's cool looking for books they know about and especially trendy new books they haven't heard of yet. You have to attract them.'

'I seem to be attracting every mad bugger in the district. None of them buy books.'

'Ha ha. Readers are cool. Make them want the stuff because it's cool. Are you on Facebook?'

'Me?'

'No, dummy, your website. Don't be so frigging old.'

It makes him laugh. He can hear Elizabeth sighing from her study.

'Yvonne, don't be so rude.'

Her daughter ignores her completely. Yvonne stands and Trevor sits down, scrolling through some of his more likely reviews to show her. They are, he says, somewhat Trevorised versions of book blurbs, textual teases he thinks up during quiet stretches in the shop. As if to excuse his brain being naïvely in the state he'd once desired, of days passing as regularly yet as differently as weather.

The way darkness and light are portrayed in this noirish novel by Stephen Allers will make you look twice at your friends. The victims pile up and detective Don Talisker is hard pressed to find the connections until a dramatic detail exposes everything. The prose in Midnight by Menace *is a revelation of here-ness and has the pace of Usain Bolt.*

All he can say is that blurbs are mysteries of hyperbole and bad taste. They are a minor literary form all their own, worth much to the publisher and the reader but worth nothing at all beyond that. 'Yeah, well,' she says. Then he shows her a counter-version which is not viewable on the main site:

While Seating Arrangements *hasn't been written with any insight into the reading experience, the style itself is entertainingly beyond rescue – vertiginous without solid ground and flippant about humourless monsters. The family should sue her till the blood runs.*

And:

This book on tattooing and its modern resurgence is well titled
Extreme Tattoos *because it has been written by an author who
either smiles too much or who has had a smile tattooed over his
mouth. Either way, it's a pain.*

Yvonne laughs faintly even if she only half gets the parody of
style. They seem to be written by an evil wordbot, she says. Even
as he explains the parody, of hackneyed phrases and grab bags of
clichés, he knows he is being stupid. The parodies are not viewable.
By now Elizabeth is standing behind him, reading them. Trevor sits
back to look at her.

'Those blurbs are …' she begins, then spreads her hands like a
preacher.

'The public can't see them. They can't read them.'

'Don't ever show them.'

'I'd thought about movies,' he tells Yvonne. 'They might sell.
DVDs. For instance, *Holy Motors* by Leos Carax, with the actor
Denis Lavant being driven round Paris in a stretch limo which
is his change room. He emerges from it in different clothes and
appearances and performs as ten utterly different personae. From
dawn until late at night. All these crazed characters. He's a lover in
one; a lunatic, flower-munching weirdo in a cemetery in another;
a … A novel couldn't do that.'

They look at him to see if he's finished.

'Yeah, sure,' says Yvonne, 'sounds great but … in a bookshop?'

'Like I said, crazy characters come into my bookshop.'

'Trevor,' she says, with a patronising grin to Elizabeth. 'Maybe
books *about* movies? Do you show online ratings for books?'

He explains the review app he was trying to develop, how he
thought it should work and how the design company his good but

erstwhile wife Diana shared the idea with faffed about, criticised it, then stole it and developed it under their own name. How the ex never chased them up about it.

'What a bitch,' says Yvonne.

He is surprised.

'Oh, shouldn't I have said that? But, Jesus, you mean she let them steal your work? So, make another one.'

He is even more flattered. Her directness. In his favour.

'Anyway,' she says, 'you need something.'

Several days later Yvonne texts him a link to a website about websites. She says it specialises in selling online. For his bookshop. 'And Trevor,' she adds, like a patronising little git, 'you should be using a website to attract interest in your *paintings*. Galleries are so last-century. You can sell internationally online. She knows the drill: lure them in.

Jesus, he thinks.

~

Allen is inconsolable. The break-in attempt came so close. It is making him ugly. He is animated enough to blame those fucking itinerants and fucking lame dogs who hang around the streets begging, and he blames Trevor for existing as a hollow shop with two unsecured walls next to his beloved diamonds so close to lost forever; he even blames the poor old Melbourne weather for being a misery. Yes, with Melbourne's skies being so cold and awful he decided to leave the shop briefly and visit Tasmania, as if Tasmania were a better sibling of Melbourne when it comes to fine weather.

No, none of this makes sense to Trevor either.

Insurance?

Trevor knows and Allen must know that men who plan robberies, who have the specialised equipment, and who succeed are not the same loose men who make abjection their business model outside the IGA. Don't blame these guys who have, at best, only one knowledge of the kind required – they might have observed the shop being closed on said days.

'Were there no motion sensors *inside* the locked vault?' In the teasing vault of his thoughts Trevor considers this. Coming from the man who criticised him for lacking security.

Before leaving, he inspects the new side door and approves the carpenter's work. The bloke has been there all afternoon, said almost nothing. Eye contact, smiles, straight face. Silent work being good work. Now the door to the lane is solid timber, no panels, hung on four recessed hinges, secured by two deadlocks – one above the centre line, the other below it.

On the other side, of his brain, he thinks again. The brickie has inserted the few extra layers of bricks onto fresh wet mortar and, until it sets, the wall feels weirdly wrong. As if a body were bricked up behind a wall. Crime performed slap-bang in the middle of the detective books.

He should get out more.

Trevor locks the front door of the shop. This is considered secure enough and is visible from the street. That is the risk he will take. Just as he turns away from the door the man formerly known as his father is there, calling to him from across the tram tracks, arms wide.

He and his father look across the glary street at each other.

How ridiculous. Trevor's discomfort is equalled only by his father's insouciance. The white hair and bristles of white beard, and his old-man's large ears.

The prosopagnosia Elizabeth is afflicted with is momentarily Trevor's.

His own dad, Kazimierz Novak; or simply Ken for those simple Aussies. In the years after his father had gone missing, Trevor checked the meaning of this name.

'Well, you're back again. Again,' says Trevor. 'Thirty years, and now – the intervals are getting shorter. Are you all right?'

'The what? No, I'm over 70 years old and I want to see my son and see what he does in the world. And he makes these comments.' *The man might as well be addressing an audience.* 'I want to hear the sound of your voice! I'm here, you don't have to worry.'

'Worry?' Trevor is more confounded and upset than worried. His big father, the overbearing father of his childhood. Now so small.

'I am strong still,' says his father. 'Why are you looking at me like that?'

'I haven't seen you since I was 15. You've ... changed completely. You could be anyone. You implied you were dying.'

'No. I call you "my boy" and "Trevvy" and I know everything. No one else would know that, and the money, yes, who knew about the money because I bet, eh, I bet you didn't tell anyone.'

'Where *were* you for thirty years? And why didn't you contact Mum?'

'Ah, yes. Not good. Here I am to explain. I travel everywhere like always. I told her what had happened. Like I said to you, I was in trouble with bad men over money.'

'What do you mean, you told her? That you planned to disappear?'

'It was best you not really know where I was, know nothing, then you couldn't accidentally say it to anyone. I had to disappear. A lot. Completely. I went back home. Better than when I left, my boy. There was a Polish Pope. There was Lech Walesa, Polish hero.'

Poland!

'Hey, my boy, it's so good to see you after all this time. I thought I live with you for a while! My own son.'

'You can't stay with me. After thirty-five bloody years you can't just ... Anyway, I don't have a home. I am renting. I have a landlady.'

'You have a *landlady*? Eh? You are renting a room like a student?'

'I have a wife. We're separated. You should know all about that, you had a wife you didn't live with. Remember?'

'I have grandchildren!'

'No, you don't.'

'Hopeless boy. You can't even do that properly.' The man looks genuinely distressed. Then revives.

'But you do have a wife. I go and stay with her!'

'Fuck,' Trevor groans. 'You really are nuts.'

There is a fuse shorting out in his ancestral head. He wants to turn back inside and sit behind his desk. He wants to go up in smoke. Ken sways in front of him.

'Hey, don't call me names any more. I know I've been a strange man, yes, yes, all that. Still, no need. Why can't I stay with you? Or ... my daughter-in-law?'

'Dad!' (Even after thirty-odd years Trevor is enough of a son to say the word.) 'Your daughter-in-law has never met you ... *I* hardly know you, Mum died thinking you were dead. What sort of man are you?'

'I'm a new man! Novak, you know what it means. I've returned from the dead. I am like Jesus!'

'No, you're still dead.'

What else to do but laugh and hit the man ...?

'It's not funny.' The old man is suddenly angry. 'No! Laughing at me because of your stupid government is full of shit.'

If people mood-shift like this, they are nutters or thespians. Or his father, who is both. Trevor stares at the bookshelves. *Where to locate this inept memoir, a book even the shining woman customer who urged him to go vegan wouldn't want to read?* It is compressing his nerves.

'Do you know what Kazimierz means?' he says. ' "Destroyer of peace". I've been Googling a lot recently.'

He might say more but his father is silent, looking out the window into the street. Caught in hiatus or, possibly, indifference. He sits in the chair beside the counter, palming his hair back with both hands like the old Brylcreem ads from his youth, and then smiles.

'Destroyer of peace? I never knew that. Ha.'

'Sinner, more like. Aren't you a Catholic?'

'Catholic? Ha ha. We must have a drink to celebrate me coming back,' he says, suddenly standing. 'Remember, it's good to be kind to your father.' He pulls a face. 'It's Polish. We have a drink. Where do you go?'

And he opens his arms, again, renewed. Trevor feels, as he always did with his father, bereft of options.

So, reluctantly, the Town Hall Hotel it is, nearly full at the end of the day. They drink for a desultory half hour while his father talks about the brilliant Polish Pope, about the fucking Soviets and the shitty Russian mafia and, abruptly happy again, sexy Polish women. If he talks he's happy, he cannot seem to listen. He is getting drunk very quickly, the old man.

'Listen to me,' he says, pushing back his chair and standing up. The alcohol is turning his face red underneath the white whiskers. This is the main street and people are walking past. He is becoming excessive.

'Listen!' he says again, loudly, ordering everyone in sight. 'This is what I nearly was, yes, opera singer.'

He starts off in a high baritone, the Prologue from *Pagliacci*. People stop. *Si può? Si può?* He stands and extends his left arm like a parody of opera singers, except he is serious. He knows the effect his voice has. It is stunning, out of nowhere from a stranger, an old man, this big voice ringing out against the buildings.

People immediately lift their mobiles, take pics and video of him singing. He will go viral!

No one has heard anything like it except Trevor, who is suddenly a 15-year-old boy again. It falls on Trevor like sudden dread. Recognition betrays him with goose bumps up his back. His father stops.

'My friend Yuri Mazurok,' he announces now that everyone is listening, 'yes, Yuri he was good enough to sing for Polish opera, but the Russians wanted him. But me, I wasn't even 20 years old, the Russians they wanted me too. They said. "Come and train in Bolshoi!" The Russians everywhere in Poland, so we used to say Poland has the car but Russia has the steering wheel. Then Polish hero Lech Walesa. Ah, yes. But I have no rhythm.'

Trevor has heard it *all* before. Depressingly, exactly the same words, the unchanged anecdote; and depressingly, too, because the only deep pride he feels for his father – and this is, beyond any doubt, his father – is for his voice.

His father bellows the rest of the Prologue. It is ridiculous that anyone would do this, anyone, totally without self-consciousness. Yet here he is, an old man, mouth wide open, building the drama, his voice rising and hitting the high A almost perfectly. Of course, as he holds the note he cracks. But he cuts it short, to disguise it, like a pro.

Everyone is yelling and applauding. Even the gaunt guys wanting money are shouting. Everyone keeps on shouting and he stands with his arms wide, accepting the bravos and the filming. A man might well return to life for this.

'See,' he says to Trevor afterwards. 'Is my same voice. The same.'

It is devastating. The years in between, the same, brilliant show-off.

'Just how many *times* in your life,' asks Trevor, 'have you done that – he mimics – "My friend Yuri, listen-to-me I-was-nearly-an-opera-singer"?'

But the old man has turned away.

'I could sing the clown, too,' he boasts to the crowd, 'the tenor part, yes, my voice is nearly that high. I could, I could, when I was young. The great Leonard Warren could sing a high C. Not bad for baritone, eh? Yes, a high C.'

He begins the opening phrase of the famous *Vesti la giubba*: '*Recitar ...*' but stops and bows.

'Hey,' he whispers to Trevor as he sits down. 'I forget to say, I'm not Novak any more. Had to change my name for, you know, so I'm Ken Warne. Don't tell anyone Novak.'

But he pronounces it Wone. Trevor laughs, almost knocking over his drink.

'You sound like that dopey Sydney Harbour artist.'

'No, not any artist. After the cricket player. What could be more Aussie than that? And he likes the girls.'

Trevor looks for signs of distress or sadness in the tanned face. If there are any he can't see them, the man must have been incorrigible all his life, the kind who shouldn't marry and have kids. And always does. How apt: this father, the new man, or new face, and the bowler of flippers and wrong-uns.

With alcohol loosening his ageing system, the old man admits he amassed windfalls of money from his geological business. All the money accruing interest in the banks, bonds, term deposits rolling over every year like silent birthdays. 'The interest rates were crazy back then. In 1989 it was 17 per cent! For nothing!'

Of course he got into trouble, financial and with women, the Warne in the man; and with business partners, ventures sidelined, investments lost, mining claims mysteriously changing hands. All predictable. He is melodramatic yet vague in telling it. Hard to discern which was the worse offence, the women or the wealth. It wasn't criminal but the threats he received were.

Yes, he says more than once, the Pilbara was run by cowboys. Wearing suits and ties in air-conditioned offices, but cowboys. Don't follow the rules, make new ones. So he did a runner. Poland for twenty years, almost forgot his English which was never fluent because he learnt it from his mother, who had taught herself. When he returned he had worked in Queensland: 'Nice tan, eh.' Doing the job, drinking all hours after work. Polish men can do this. 'Cast-iron constitution', his favourite English expression.

And here is his son behind a counter selling books. *My God.*

Telling this, he is eyeing off one of the women at a nearby table. Nothing a 70-year-old can't try. Or 80. He calls out and winks at her. His right eyebrow reaches for high A. In a few minutes he will be singing *Don Giovanni*. She looks embarrassed but laughs among her friends and simply turns away.

'Hey!' says Trevor, he almost hisses it. 'Stop ogling. The world has changed a lot since you boasted of being a ladies' man.'

'Not boasting, I *was* a ladies' man. Everybody said. More than *you* ever were, ha! That talent you never got.'

'You haven't seen my wife.'

'I want to see your wife!'

'She's gorgeous.'

'Ha, now who's boasting?'

And he is, he is, pointlessly. He feels terrible. But it's worth it, his father has gone quiet. Briefly.

'Money, my boy, that's the thing. Now this shop of yours. You can't make a profit selling silly books. Amazon, yes? I know, I looked that up. If it was me, yes, I could sell anything.'

'You think you could sell books?'

'Yes. No – we sell the shop. Buy a house for me. You live there, too, if you like. Father and son! The money, some I have to give back to a businessman first but … Go back to your old job. Better paid, much easier. Be invisible the way you like.'

How much more invasive can the man be? Ordering him. What he won't have realised is that Trevor's shop is only leased. The rest of the money is invested. The shop was never up for outright sale, the all-new book stock cost a fortune.

Every one of the books bar those with swearwords blotted out. His father is trying to force his way out of the blotted word for "father". *Dzzzt.* He is the worst swearword of all.

~

Diana inspects the woman in the doorway. Their height difference is obvious. And weight. Having only just knocked, waited, said hello and introduced herself doesn't stop Diana saying what she says.

'So, Trevor likes his women tall and slim now.' She doesn't add older and plainer.

It nearly makes Elizabeth snort.

'I'm not his woman – and nor are you any more. I hope Trevor never said we were anything else. He has an ensuite room, he is a *lodger.* If you want to see him, he's not home.'

Hears herself utter "home" with a possessive Trevor-shaped bump in it.

What she would like to do, Diana explains, is inspect his paintings. She has always admired him as an artist, regardless of his – apostasy. She says this, "apostasy", to Elizabeth because he used to say it of himself.

Elizabeth is stalling.

'He said it was OK,' Diana says. 'He wants me to look at them. He knows I'm his biggest fan. I'm really curious. Now everyone says they are *passionate about* … this or that. Something he hates by the way, that saying. He is, though, again, at last. Passionate, I mean. My God, it has taken him long enough.'

So they walk through the house, Diana stickybeaking at everything. She says of course Trevor can be ingratiating, even when he's being selfish. Yes, he'll take over her house unless she's careful. 'He's a homebody and, frankly, a bit of a bore,' she says. And he's getting fat.

'Fat? Not any more, he isn't.'

'Unlikely!' Diana laughs in disbelief. They have stopped near the back door. Elizabeth looks at Diana, the rather fulsome but bitchy woman who is still his wife.

'You clearly don't know he's become a gym junkie.'

'What? He has always laughed at gyms.'

'Except it's working. He is slimmer, and he's stronger, fitter. You'd be surprised.'

Somehow, despite not wishing to, Elizabeth is thinking how this woman gives off a sense of easily assumed judgement. She has none of the melancholy that surfaces in Trevor. Whereas Diana is still doubting. *Who is this woman and what's going on between them?*

Despite her good clothes and high heels, an essential for her height, and her business-designer suit, Diana drags the paintings out from the wall and faces them into the shed.

'Wow,' she says. 'Fucking wow!'

Hardly art-critic-speak. Perhaps it should be. She stares at them close up and then from across the open floor space. She looks over the older pieces at first, looking for what she recognises, then takes her time to inspect each of the other as she realises what they represent.

'Restless bugger,' she sighs, 'even in what – five or six months? – he's gone through these different stages? See the way his composition has changed from this one to this one, and then here. And the way he's handling paint. The surfaces. In the earlier ones he painted everything from scratch.

'Here,' she points to several big canvases, glowing and darkening in house-painting brushstrokes. 'He's changed from '30s collaging to photomontage, a bit like Daniel Pitin. The Czech artist? Media images painted over so some it shows, all shaky and nightmarish, but the rest is distorted and parodied by him painting over them. I like them! The doom of it! It's cool.

'The modernist styles keep coming back,' she says. 'In writing, too.'

While saying this, Diana has stepped around the various paint tins and rags towards the back wall. There are three more works that have been turned away, facing the wall. Diana turns all three round.

When the cry comes from her it shocks Elizabeth who is expecting more words and comments. It is the same cry Martina made all those years ago at the café in Fremantle when she heard the flamenco singer call out on the CD. A release of emotion. Diana has both hands to her face.

Then, with one hand over her mouth, the cry mouth, she reaches out and touches the red paint, its wild drama, rubs it and sees the faint colour on her fingertips. Now she is silent. Stands there, staring, for a minute, more than a minute.

'Has Trevor said anything,' she says finally, 'about us losing a baby?'

'Oh.' (This is so unexpected.) 'He …'

'This is new, the paint's wet. He's painted it: the blood, all the blood – a kind of radical Rothko. Only now' – a small sound escapes her – 'he is painting it.'

There is nothing Elizabeth can say. Diana's voice is quiet, deliberate.

'I know it's subjective – another term he hates, but I know it. Like those earlier paintings, like the Weimar artists, women too, you know, not the men; and, unusually, Dada women. But there's so much feeling in the new work. My God, this is really going somewhere.'

Elizabeth now knows the bond still there between them, and would almost be jealous except now she, too, is feeling Trevor's artistry coming through. Its intimacy tangible, and red.

'Then why *did* he stop painting? What actually happened?'

Hesitating, Diana nods and then folds her arms. As if covering herself for having been so open.

'He used to see himself as a wayward out-of-town boy who moved down to the city. He said his father always told him when he was a boy that arty things were shit, they were pointless. Only facts mattered.'

'The philistine father. God help us.'

'And making money. You can count it. Trevor was in a car crash with some friends, ex-uni students. He has to have told you about his limp?'

'Well, yes, a bit. He seems pretty reluctant.'

Standing out in the studio among the blood paintings and the directness of Diana is making her disoriented. Yet Diana seems unwilling to leave.

'They were drinking all afternoon,' says Diana, 'and they drove off in two cars taking forestry roads to the local weir, one of those places to have a barbecue and snags-and-beer dinner. But they never got there. They were probably pissed when they crashed, that's what they were like. Trevor was a bit of a ringleader like that. Unfortunately. That's why the accident got to him so much. His fault.'

'I know,' says Elizabeth, 'he mentioned an accident. Not in any detail. More that he hurt his leg and how it still causes him grief. His leg, I mean.'

'The accident was terrible. He went off a corner and smashed his car up, and damaged his right leg pretty badly. But that's only the half of it. A mate of his, driving flat out behind him on this shitty gravel road, was blinded by the dust from Trevor's car and crashed right into them, then into a fence. The two of them. Bang bang. It'd be traumatic enough dragging yourself out of your car, but then to have another car crash into you and end upside down on a fence? His mate was far more badly injured than Trevor. Trevor never forgave himself. Nor did his friend, according to Trevor.'

'He never said anything about that.'

'I think, well, I'm not sure he's right about his friend. I was there, I mean we were together at the time, and the accident was only part of what happened when ...'

Eventually Diana continues.

'They were in the middle of nowhere on gravel roads somewhere out of Upwey. Not sure where, it was twenty years ago. No one around. Their cars wrecked, one of them was upside down. He said he kept seeing its wheels.'

The two women stare at each other, so removed from the events they are shaken by. The young men, their screaming. Diana explains: they had to wait for a car to arrive to drive off for an ambulance. No mobile phones back then. Trevor said he stayed slumped in the car, his leg bleeding and hurting; the other guy they thought would die.

'My God. What happened?'

'Eventually some bloke turned up. A farmer.'

'It was the crash that made him stop painting?'

'All that. Two operations, a slow recovery, lying in hospital for weeks doubting himself, feeling he had made it before he knew who he really was as an artist. Also – I was pregnant. But – then I lost the baby.'

She shakes her head, simply runs out of words.

At which point Elizabeth almost gasps. She sees him watching TV and wiping away tears. How he sometimes stands in the one place for so long.

'Anyway,' says Diana, 'you weren't to know. You just said you don't talk much.'

'No, we do.' She stares at her wrecked lawn. 'We're sort of mates, but he doesn't go on about himself. Unlike most men.'

Diana's expression is suddenly cool.

'Oh, he can. Don't worry about that.'

When Elizabeth is this concerned she makes small fists under her chin and leans forward. A more direct response than Diana expects. Elizabeth is thinking only about him.

'No wonder, then ...'

'Well, no wonder what?' Diana says. 'Compared to a pile of wreckage, and this guy nearly dying, and then losing our baby – his paintings. That's what he said. He said whatever talent he had wasn't real or *he* wasn't. That he felt like an impostor. It's a syndrome. He felt like *that*.'

'I wondered if his father ...'

'Oh, his fucking father. It's a great big old-fashioned guilt, of course. His father has to be a problem, too, all a bit Freudian from my professional viewpoint. A lot of grief but also a lot of guilt and blame. It's a kind of self-harm.'

'Has he told you his father turned up recently, living and breathing?'

'He told me. Which means decades of having lost his father are ...?'

The two of them stare at the various paintings, the assorted images refusing easy answers, and the Rothko surfaces now so suggestive of blood, and birth, the collages of a lost world. Apocalypse. Elizabeth dazed, Diana suddenly restive.

'Look at these. Anyone can see Trevor has loads of talent. I read what people said about him back then. Maybe his success was too easy. He just couldn't keep hold of it: he lost the meaning of actually *being* an artist. I was grieving, he had to find work. But fancy getting a government job after all that! He made the wrong decision.'

'What sort of job did he have?'

'Huh, he never tells anyone. Maybe I shouldn't either.'

'He's living in my house. And after what you've been saying?'

'Well, you won't believe it. The police force.'

'He was a *cop?!*'

'Not quite, he had a desk job, sort of, in the psychology unit. He talked a lot of bullshit and he got the job. He'd done a double degree, Art and Psychology, like me, that's how we met. Using role-play and discussion groups to make cops stop and think about racial prejudice, domestic violence etc. Reading groups, ha, imagine it. He was part of a team to keep plods human. But he mixed with them socially too, sometimes. They're a hard lot, cops. And he's a strange man, Trevor. Very undecided. Obviously.'

'A lot of us are.'

'That mate of his who was injured, he died a year or two ago. In a car crash. Would you believe it!' She shrugs. 'I think that's why Trevor started painting again, he was free, and I bet he never told you that. That and getting the inheritance so he could leave work. He was painting at home in the apartment to begin with, no room to swing a cat, but now – he's with you. He's the happiest he's been for years.

'I'm going to make him approach some galleries,' she adds, 'otherwise he'll put off doing it himself until he's old and decrepit and hungry for a bit of recognition before he carks it.'

Elizabeth is about to say, but doesn't.

'I will,' Diana continues. 'I'll nag the shit out of him. I can nag, I tell you. This is about him, not me. I will pay for it if he can't. Oh, by the way,' she adds, 'don't tell him I'm thinking along these lines – he'll just clam up and do nothing, just out of ... Could you do that?'

Elizabeth cannot promise anything.

'Aren't you selling the apartment?' she says instead. 'He'll have plenty of money.'

Diana's head jerks slightly.

'Did he say so?'

She looks down towards her bag, shuffles things around and removes her phone.

'Oh, that reminds me. Tell Trevor his bloody father fronted up at the apartment the other night. That's if it is his father, because how would *I* know? He played all sweet and charming, trying to be witty, trying to flatter me. The old perve said I had a nice voice and a nice – figure. Can you believe it? He wanted to know if the apartment was in Trevor's name. When he left he tried to give me a kiss and a cuddle. I had to push him off! "His lovely daughter-in-law", he said, meaning I owed him a grope. He's a shocker.'

~

Elizabeth's mother is getting worse, a relapse into whatever it was. Another wobbly fall, possibly infection, pain and painkillers, hospital, her immune system not up to much any more. More worryingly, a slow, too slow, return from confusion. In the Respite Care unit she occasionally forgets names, the staff are saying, at her worst she's had speech lapses that were not digressions. It sounded more like the unlearning of a mind facing nowhere – they didn't say – with her syntax garbled, words unrecognisable. Elizabeth will have no excuse this time, she must return to Ballarat and stay there for as long as it takes to transition her mother into home life again. That or a nursing home. At least she has forgotten Dr Nitschke.

'The ultimate catch-22,' Trevor says. 'When you discuss euthanasia you probably don't need it; when you need it you probably can't remember.'

He is drying the dishes. Wiping the *tabula rasa*.

She says Respite is full of people who complain of being sick, and if they're not sick they complain about when they were. Which sounds more like her old self.

Elizabeth is talking from inside her study.

Then she tells Trevor she will have to stay in Ballarat for some time, so what to do about him? Under the circumstances, perhaps he should, perhaps, she's really sorry … consider finding another place. Trevor living alone in her house for however long – months, maybe – would be a bit odd, wouldn't it, her lodger? *What can she do?*

He is devastated.

'You can let me stay.

'No notice, no fault?' Not that he wants to criticise. Quite the reverse, he wants to stay. Is he only a lodger and not adjudged a tenant? A *friend*?

'My paintings. Fuck. I've only just got it all moving again. Jesus, you can't kick me out like this, make me *go*. I might never find anywhere like this ...'

'Now don't lay a guilt trip on me, Trevor, it's hard enough already. I don't want to do it but what choice have I got?'

His reaction is proving her the betrayer she knows she is. It hurts her more than she thought it would, she doesn't want to. Her thinking is stuck. She squints into her computer screen as if in pain.

'If I leave,' he says, 'the house will be empty. Lights off, leaves on the porch. Burglars look for that – places that are vacant. Who knows what that fucking neighbour of yours might do? If you're not here he'll dump all of his rubbish in your backyard, probably burn it on your lawn. Hold barbies here with his scungy mates. You wanted him warned off, and he'll be angry. He *is* angry.'

She emerges from the study and he sees her face.

'Trevor. You're trying to scare me.'

'You think I'm being unrealistic? You know the guy. I'll put out the rubbish *and* bring it in again, empty the mailbox. I could even learn to rake the verge and gossip to the neighbours ...'

'I hadn't thought of The Creep next door. (But she remembers him at the market.) Mum's going downhill. It would have to happen just when I'm head first into *Collectors*.'

'You can work in Ballarat. What difference does it make where you are? You could even go and see the woman. Didn't you say she lives up there?'

She drops into a lounge chair. He's right, she cannot go through with it. Obvious reasons – now they're obvious. And. Not wanting him to disappear.

'You never told me if they caught anyone about your shop,' she says.

He tells her they haven't solved anything, and probably won't, how actual policing suffers from rotten storylines and absent characters, i.e. the crooks. It's not like fifty-minute TV shows. People get attached to crime stories, for the cathartic endings, but it doesn't happen that way.

'So,' she sighs, 'the break-in was just another event that begins here and then slips through to the other side.'

'Except in this case they didn't get through.'

She can hear the city scraping along outside. On the other side of the wall.

~

Trevor has his back to the door, listening to a customer talk about his cats and his dog and how his missus loves those Irvine Welsh books full of foul-mouthed rants and violence. She finds them exciting. *Ha ha.* Then the old fella turns for home, carrying a copy of the novel *Trainspotting 2* is based on, which is called *Porno*.

The closest the new shop has come to being the old shop.

Trevor realises there's someone behind him. It's the Frank Miller (*Where's my fucken DVD?*) bloke. He can smell the awful deodorant. It makes him step back. The man looks better fed, better dressed, meaning that instead of his clothes having been dragged at random from the bags at St Vinnies, they almost suit each other – and they fit.

Trevor is angry. *Is there a mental or karmic app drawing the crazies through the front door? A warp app?*

He jabs his finger at him.

'Nah, nah,' says the man. 'It's not what you're thinkin'...'

'Get out of the shop,' says Trevor.

This time he's prepared for the worst. Assuming, that is, endless sessions at the gym have made him stronger, even if the dash of vanity is slow. At first the man can't see the anger in his eyes. The garish tattoos on the man's neck and throat seem to flare like bravery.

It must be the adrenaline thumping fast in Trevor: the guy hesitates. When he clears his throat, a few decades of smoker's cough leap ahead of him as sound effect. To Trevor it sounds like aggro.

'Keep off!' shouts the man, and jerks up his fists, seeing it now.

For years Trevor worked with hard men. All that futile role-playing to diminish their aggression. How they set that deadly stare on a man. As *he* stares now, and all the skinny length of the bloke tilts away until he almost falls over.

'Fark!' the guy whines. 'Jesus, lay off.'

He fends off the blows he's imagining.

'I'll show you something, you stupid prick,' growls Trevor. 'My fucking bills. The MRI on my leg and knee, the osteopath, my sub at the gym. You owe me thousands.'

The man tries to scramble off but Trevor blocks the doorway. Trevor may have shed a few kilos in his time at the gym but he can still be a wide man if he needs to be.

'Fucken hell, mate, I never come in here to fight. In fact it's fucken hard but I – was goin' to – say sorry for knocken ya about. I mean ya went down pretty easy, I wasn't tryen. Ya *were* bein' a cunt, I'm not takin' that back but I shoulda just left.'

'What? You expect me to believe that? And I'm *not* a cunt. … I might be a smart arse.'

'Same fucken thing. I gotta do this so there ya go. The Salvo bloke told me I had to come in and apologise.'

'The Salvos.'

Trevor stands there. This time, silence is the intimidator. He is aware of the man's reptilian legs. That overpowering use of spray deodorant. The man has probably been rehearsing his speech for as long as Ken Warne spent on his.

The man looks as if he means it, even if he doesn't.

'You admit you came in and assaulted me. I ended on the floor.'

'Nah, you tripped.'

'Is this still part of your apology or have you forgotten how an apology works?'

'Mate, you think someone like me can't be serious, don't ya.' He tries to move away. 'You're not used to people like me bein' serious. The Salvos said it was important. For me, mate, for me. Not you.'

'For *you*. I've heard everything now. Then admit it.'

'I said it once! I didden come in here ta start a bloody friendship! I come in because he said I should do the right thing. And all I get is a shirtfronten.'

'You have to pay a price for doing the right thing. It's a privilege.'

'What a load of shit.'

Some silences are stranger than others. Trevor cannot resist stereotyping the guy, nor is the guy any more admiring of him. The guy thinks the bookseller is someone who sits in his safe world, in a permanent state of the warm and fuzzies, making money out of people who read friggin' books and never watch the footy. Women, of course, who blokes like the bookseller suck up to all the time.

The bookseller looks his "apologiser" in the eye.

'What's your name?'

'None of your business. ... Dwayne.'

'Dwayne!'

'Yeah, fucken Dwayne, what's wrong with you?'

'Right, OK.' Trevor is shaking his head. 'I'll take your word for it.'

'That's mighty bloody big of ya. I've been called every fucken name under the sun, by evil fuckers using evil fucken insults you wouldn't fucken believe.'

Trevor looks at him in his floral shirt and, despite the weather, the garish synthetic jacket. *The Salvos have no taste.*

'Anyway, what's *your* name?' asks the bloke.

'None of your business.'

'Yeah, that's what *I* said, so what is it?'

'Trevor.'

'Trevor! Ha ha ha. That's no fucken better than mine.'

The two men could almost be drinking mates. Whether or not he can define the term "irony", Dwayne is more accustomed to the reversals and absurdity of life than the so-called ironist who reads and sells books for a living. Trevor looks at the tatt on the guy's wrist, three barbs on a strand of wire.

'As long as you're here,' he says, 'do you want that DVD?'

'Jesus Christ. Ya mean ya got it?'

'Yeah.'

'Nah, fuck it. Sell it to someone else.'

And with that the man shuffles out. He won't be back.

It takes a few minutes for the irony to arrive in Trevor's mind. Because the guy knocked him down he began his gym routines and made the effort to get fit, which means he's bulked up enough to intimidate the man who, thanks to the Salvos feeding him, is healthy enough to be pushed around.

A strange nothingness comes into him, occupies him. He feels affectless, thoughtless. There but not there.

Only after however long it is – fifteen minutes, forty? – does he begin to relax. His life is a churn. Even this silly bastard and the fuss over a DVD Trevor never in fact bothered to order. Which was meant to be his punch line.

Why, when he should have been feeling like shit, is he beginning to feel so good? On top of that, the guy has made three visits. He counts as a regular customer.

Trevor looks at himself in the bathroom mirror. Elizabeth was thrilled when he confronted the guy over the back fence. From the left-over adrenaline in him, he feels the urge to scare him off again. Naked, his muscles are defined where the padding had been smooth. He has quite a lot of body hair for a man with a shaved head.

He lifts his shoulders and makes two fists at his side. His police days had edges he has not admitted, and will not admit, to Elizabeth.

She has let him stay.

That night he dreams of the studio with white sheets hung over it, from roof gable to ground level. Covered on all sides as well as front and back with white sheets that have some kind of faded pattern on them, creased from hanging against the frame. Even if they don't quite resemble it they remind him of the mausoleum of Sir Richard Burton and his wife, Isabel, the marble tent where they reside in the London Borough of Richmond upon Thames. Richard, the old devil.

Over the next few days his father calls repeatedly on his mobile. He makes it painfully clear he wants to sell the shop. 'How unique,' Trevor points out, 'a dead man claiming back my inheritance.' Count Dracula. Had he left big debts when he disappeared? He's changed his name – obviously somebody is still after him and it isn't over probate. His father like the man behind the back fence. Remember I have friends, he wants to say.

A little bastard of a voice keeps telling Trevor he is compromised. The business. *Couldn't have afforded it without the money.* Still, he had super to use. *Money still in the bank.* His much younger father had been naughty-minded and fun. *Sometimes.* The wilder times they'd had, the long fishing trips in the country. Trevor, mind and muscle-bored in the gym amongst the lifting machines, hears these nagging demands heavier than weights – he can't lift them. *If his father had returned a year ago?* He may not have deserved it but the money might, legally, have been his. *Or not.*

It's churning in him. Do the right thing, borrow, or sell out, split the money with the old crook? No, do *not. Fuck the old man.* Selling a business with a lease is chaos. Demand Diana sell their apartment now, free up his 50:50 or buy him out? *Buying him out is better. Keep the shop.* Amicable until the money discussion. Some say that about divorce. But inheritance – stranger things possess people. A cosmic demand for themselves. *The old man is a bullying bastard.*

How to kill this parrot-like voice when there is no neck to wring?

Next day his father shoves his way into the shop. No niceties now, no more *My boy* and *Trevvy* and *your-dear-old-dad* stuff, no wonderful baritone, just 'Get off your arse, I need the money.' He must be slipping, because for once he doesn't say *my* money. This time Trevor, with customers inside, shuts the till, pulls the old man out onto the pavement and gives it to him straight: yes, his father might be in trouble – only *might* – but lives won't be thrown under the bus again, *his* life now that his mother is dead. *The whole thing was probably what killed her.*

The old man tells Trevor he'll get half the apartment when he gets divorced so he should hurry up and do it.

The son, the father. The gall.

'Ken,' he says. 'You're finished. Run before the bad guys get you.'

'Don't call me Ken. I'm your father, call me *Tatus* or Dad! What would you know about bad guys?'

'The last time I called you Dad you *were* a dad and I was *15.*'

The old man is white whiskers again, white hair, red face, like an old alcoholic, standing in grubby trousers, asking for spare change.

'Look,' says Trevor (the idea has just come to him), 'some guy has been ringing me, asking about my father. Does that sound like you? So they know!'

Ken is taken by surprise. And that his son has refused him. A look of hatred returns to his face, a face pinched in with its eyes clenched small. Then his bully's face – which Trevor saw in that of a man thirty years younger – looks scared. Inside it there is no one Trevor wants to know.

'You are a crazy boy,' he spits, 'you are schizophrenic, turning on your father like a snake. You betray me. My fucking son, who won't call me *Tatus*, my son won't even call me bloody fucking *Dad!* Now talking about me to people who you don't know.'

He regresses. And he bloody well regrets.

'Why didn't you tell Mum you were alive?'

'You know nothing! I wrote to her. Twice I wrote to her.'

They are standing on the pavement, people are walking past as traffic mounts up before the lights, tram cables stretch above them like the lines in Lester's weird paintings.

'What do you mean?'

'Ha, she didn't tell you then, and why is that? Because she wanted the money for herself, eh? When she started to make them certify me dead. That was after my second letter. She died, and so she was guilty woman and it made her sick.'

He turns away, swearing in Polish. Trevor assumes it's swearing: normal speech doesn't sound like that, even Polish, where the land-locked vowels are squashed between consonants.

Trevor shouts at him:

'You ruined her life. If you had been a real man ...'

But the unreal old man is stalking towards Errol St. Something makes him stop and turn around to stare. The huge STOP ADANI mural on the side of the alley wall. He raises both hands above his head like an opera singer nearing death.

'She knew,' he shouts back. 'She didn't tell you! You never earn the money for the shop, just wasting my money.'

People are watching them. Yelling insults at old men in the street will not sell books. He is shaken in a way he's never felt before. As soon as the adrenaline subsides he falls into ghastly hangover, depressing and dispiriting, and with it sickening guilt.

Lester hasn't been answering his mobile. Typical of a man, of a loner. It means a visit to Lester's usual. The man will appreciate the two break-in stories by the *dim crims*, as Trevor now refers to them, in Chinese tea-house style. And Dwayne. The apologetic angel from the Salvos. And especially, as Lester calls him, his dead dad.

Lester will be reassuring. Over the next few days Trevor walks across to the man's house, fairly sure the terrace is the one he visited. There's no doorbell so he clatters the iron knocker. Then again. Pigeons flutter up and land again on the upper balcony. He waits for a minute then raps the old metal knocker again.

Still nothing on the mobile number.

At Lester's usual haunt, Trevor asks the bar staff if they've seen the man who sits by the window alone, doing the sudoku in *The Age*. No. At any time over the last few weeks? No. It's a shock, a sudden emptiness. It begins to look as if this man who left the force, left his meaning, left his salary for his super, and was himself left with all the scars inside and out, has left again.

His father had stayed quite sober for one more week and took young Trevor into town, then for a long drive along the coast. No school when your *tatus* is home, he declared, as he always declared. Trevor remembered his primary-school days like this: driving, camping on-site in caravans, meandering like tourists for a week of unworried days along the coast.

While Polish might be landlocked, his father always enjoyed coastal fishing and the two of them sat on jetties and flung their lines out over the water, hoping the prawns baiting these tiny hooks would bring something to bite. Or even better, as a special treat, they returned to remembered bridges where lower platforms just above the water were dark and bright with dried fish guts which had been trodden down into crust formations for decades, where fishers had in the past hooked up tailor, those clean silver fish almost too easy to catch as schools rushed against the pylons to escape the aggressive salmon at the river mouth.

To reach some of these fishing spots his father drove into logging coupes and hooned along forestry tracks, throwing the car into lunging slides around the corners and braking hard, drifting sideways, churning gravel, sometimes spinning the car in handbrake turns of 180 degrees, all for the sheer hell of it, he said, *the sheer hell of it* – good Aussie saying, he said – loving every second. His father wasn't especially skilled at this wild driving but he was frighteningly fearless and laughed as the car swayed and lurched in the dust.

This was the father Trevor adored, who returned from his work trips and broke the rules just for him, to have simple pleasures with his son. Outrageous pleasures at times. Sometimes on their fishing adventures he let the boy drive, let him drink beer. Often they pitched a tent by a river and after fishing, then cooking on an open fire, they sang songs. Until the mosquitoes tried to kill them. 'They don't like your singing, my boy,' laughed his father, 'but even mosquitoes like mine.'

They were mates, if only for these special days, mates without his mother or family obligations, and without the unpredictable father who was a show-off, a bombast, the angry, pinched-faced thrower of tantrums and paranoia.

And yet his father was endowed with something less reassuring than even this. To the people he met in public he was all smiles and charm. No opportunity was overlooked. Down at Lakes Entrance on one trip they stayed in a motel within walking distance of the boat jetty and the water, those briefly unmoving levels of lit cloud on the horizon and their reflection in the gentle movement of water and light in the inlet. A kind of bliss.

His father had been sweet-talking the woman at the motel reception, telling her she was as charming as the lovely scene outside, that she reminded him of a famous German actress, *What was her name?* A beautiful middle-aged couple dance in a house in Prague during World War II. They are backlit, the film is in black and white, the floor-boards have a slight shine as the couple dance in silence. They know the Germans are encroaching on them, their lives will change, or be lost, but they have just, after years of delay, admitted their love for each other. They dance as slowly as they can, with grace and elegance, they dance celebration and defeat, one into the other …

And another movie, the man and the woman, down by the lake – and they still smoked in movies then! Yes, they smoked and talked in low voices, but soon they were kissing. 'Ah,' he said, 'the music was so beautiful, the light was ravishing, they were only kissing but it was as if they were alone in the world and soon they would be making love' … and Trevor knew, knew as his father was telling this story or some other that was complete invention, that his eyes were glistening.

Yes, his father said to the woman at the motel, she reminded him of this actress by the river, if only he could remember her name.

They were lucky no one overheard him. The woman was enamoured, no man had ever spoken to her like this. He was spinning magic. By the time they had returned to their room his father was grumbling about the poor reception on the TV set and complaining that the food in small towns was always crap.

~

Elizabeth has been going through the dizzying tranches of her mother's junk, dividing the personal from the plastic, the value from the trash. It is disgusting. Her mother is catholic right enough – nothing remotely to do with the Pope, but in her taste. Mouldy clothing, fine silver, a kitschy painting, a small Wedgwood teapot crusted underneath Ballarat Show bags and oozing packets of God knows what.

Among the old photographs are too many of her mother from the Orange days, among the vividly similar sannyasin, and several of a young girl who – unbelievably – must be herself. She looks like a boy. Her long body is so narrow, with such slim, androgynous limbs. Then others where her limbs are strong, defined, her gymnast days when she was a teenager but still looked like a child, sexless and narrow-hipped, flat-chested, but oh what balance!

She is keeping these.

Days and more days, scraping off and down and out from unexpected places her mother's rotting food and rubbish and all such mush – or mush now – and packing up solid things (they surprise her, these things, by being that: solid, and themselves) cleared from amongst the surrounding waste. Record players, radios, small boxes of jewellery, food blenders, toasters – *Why so many toasters? It's not as if she's forever getting married!* – vacuum cleaners and spare parts for anything and everything.

They are made solid by extraction, like a complete molar removed from the jaw and the complete shape of cap and body and roots, when inspected, found to be stained, bony, shiny, and somehow both familiar and completely alien. Like a found-object sculpture. Duchamp was right about found-objects.

A week later Elizabeth rings her over-exercised lodger-tenant again. Is everything OK with the awful neighbour? His vexatious father? Or should that be the other way about? Trevor explains the last few days of standoff, the walkout.

'I'm really sorry,' she says. 'What a pain. He should have taken up with the Russians like he said. Singing for his bowl of borscht. For the oligarchs. If any of that was true.'

'At least your mum's just eccentric. Or is she losing it?'

'Oh, talk, talk, talk, and what a wonderful person she was. But she can't remember the name of her street. She called me Osho. She thinks I'm her old dead guru in India. She thinks her father is still alive. On and off she makes sense. Then she says really strange things. She's back to wanting God again.'

'Old Catholics. What was it the Jesuits said? *Give me the boy until he is 7 and I will give you the man.* Or woman. Your mum's over material things. She's hoarding her chances for an afterlife now.'

'She asked me about a throw for her bed, then described how it was folded over the rack in the spare-room wardrobe. You can't get into the *room*, let alone open the wardrobes. She's flipped. In her mind the house is like Tidy Town. Unlike her actual mind. If you can imagine it.'

'I can't unsee what I saw.'

'So I've been throwing everything out. Anything that stinks goes first. There's stuff stacked up like another house inside her house. If I'm quick I can chuck most of it into a skip. No need to tell her. She lapses then she recovers to a lower level each time. She's forgetting more and more.'

'That memory redaction thing I mentioned,' he says.

'It's a bit frightening, Trevor. Even if she seems fine she eats, drinks, walks around with eyes front. It's full care she needs, and … Oh God. I mean, once it's started it only gets worse. The cranky old mum I knew is disappearing. And it costs now, those bloody accommodation deposits. Or RADs as they call them. Have to sell her house to do that. They make you pay until you bleed, just to get a room with a toilet and a TV.'

'Yeah, and then you die.'

'She'll kick on for years.'

'You could find an aged-care residence down here. Old people going starey-eyed and gurgling at the lunch table. You could visit her regularly *and* keep your own house.'

'You've been thinking this through.'

'I can stay on. You'll keep my tax-free rent and my lively company.'

'I suppose aged care is much the same anywhere.'

'Of course it is.'

'It'll be a challenge for her. No need to turn *my* life upside down.'

'It will anyway. You'll work it out. You're good at everything, you are.'

'Oh, you're pissed. But it's nice to talk,' says Elizabeth. 'Nice hearing your voice, you know, just your voice.'

'That way you know it's me? You don't have to check my gammy leg.'

'Trevor.'

'You too,' he says, aware her voice is lower, quieter. 'I've been a bit down and out here. I hate to admit it but – you don't mind, do you, me saying, um, I'm sort of missing you?'

She is silent for a few seconds. She clears her throat like an old Lake Wendouree duck. Then coughs again. What he won't say is how his heart relocated when the phone rang. He couldn't.

'Me too.'

She is not going to say anything more. Doesn't want to add to his words going as deep as they have. Doesn't want to speak in case the feelings of either of them slump. *And what will she do then? Remember to breathe in.*

She realises that, whereas she knows herself as an inner voice and being, other people not only look the same to her but, in her perception of them, they are overwhelmingly physical beings. Is it just her, related to her neurological deficit? And now, limited by this phone call, Trevor's voice *is him;* more accessible as him than when he's standing in front of her.

'When not visiting Mum,' she tells him, or trashing her trash, 'I've been re-editing Newman's ever increasing manuscript and removing her ever increasing use of *and*s. She seems to spawn *and*s, she has androgyny, and I'm going through and … killing them off. And I'm sick of it. It sort of blinds you mentally. After a while you stop seeing more important things, good and bad.

'You're saying "and" all the time.'

'Then I'm going nuts – I'm cutting them out of her manuscript and they're coming back in my head.

'That's your guilty-conscience recurrence.'

Trevor's turn to be normal.

'Didn't Freud say narrative is formed of … *and then* … moments?'

'Did he? You're full of surprises. The thing about Newman is that some of her off moments are better than her overall work. She's a contradiction. Actually I mean that literally – a *contra-* diction.

A kind of very stylish noise. Even sort of great. Her power comes through piercingly, with less rather than more. Perhaps it's me, my editor's red pen. I don't like her style as much as she does. As her editor I have to merge with her.'

'You merge with her greatness and not with her ...?'

'I merge. Writers sometimes deliver kilos of manuscript without any convincing line through it. Like some talented public speakers great at a prolonged outburst, weak at the decisive statement. Yes, she might become a great writer ...'

'If she loses the bits you've suggested?'

This kind of sense flies through him like (only) a flesh wound, as they used to say. If he wrote a novel he'd want to keep posing the same doubts in different masks, turn over and over recurring terms and phrases, alternate appearances with disappearances then ending on questions never answered. The nots. His paintings are nots. They answer nothing of the pushed-about shapes of his questions. Can you ask anything of a surface? Can you ask *on* a surface questions without surfaces?

Not that he says this, he knows it's silly and possibly drunken ...

He has his right leg stretched out and raised on one of her chairs. Strong man or not, aiding the circulation. She is confined and upright in her mother's kitchen, which is almost bearable after the foul bags of rot have been removed.

'I know,' she says, 'that writing has a personality, a being. What makes it mysterious is ... this being recurs in the reader. A sensibility that sits right with me yet isn't me. The characters think and talk in me ... without me thinking "No, they don't."'

'You make it sound like some internal parasite.'

'Fuck off, you.'

Their voices are very quiet and she realises they are confiding, almost like lovers. Or people who are quietly boozy.

'So ... Shia's writing *isn't* like that?'

'Look, she's very good, no question. People will love it. The manuscript is finally finished, I think. They will want to sell translation rights in Europe.'

'That's great.'

'If. ...'

Perhaps it's the mobile-phone disconnect effect, the distancing, acting on her like a good Catholic in the confessional. She is admitting things. She seems to awaken from it.

'Trevor, I've made an appointment to have laser surgery on my eyes and I wonder if you could drive me there – it's in East Melbourne – then pick me up an hour or so later. I'll need to stay home overnight because I have to go back and have them checked the next day. I can always get a taxi but ...'

'Of course I will.' In fact he is flattered, even if it is a very ordinary favour.

'... I'd prefer you took me. Thank you.'

'As long as I can drive the EH. By the way, how's Gordon taking to Ballarat?'

'You'll have to ask him when I come down.'

'By the way,' she echoes, 'can you go to the calendar? I put a yellow sticky on it with Newman's address. You can probably see it in your mind.'

Despite his memory of it there is no sticky on the calendar.

'Are you going to visit her? Will she like that?'

'Probably not. That's why I'm not ringing first. Given she lives up here, given she might meet me face to face. Depends how many people are to know who she is. Maybe she has cabin fever, I bloody well have. Can't stand my bloody mother every day and when it's not her, it's her fungal bloody house. Yuk. I know the number was 65 because it's the year of the EH. But the street. ... Was it something starting with F?'

'Um. Forster? No, Foster.'

'Foster, that's it. 65 Foster. Thanks Trevor, you're good for something after all! I think I know Foster. Am I too old to be excited?'

'You looked around the F's. Ferrante. Remember I said that the first time you came into the bookshop? There's something in this anonymity.'

Yes, she intends to see if Shia is in the flesh as clever as her offcuts or just her basic text. *Surely she is superior to her sometimes charmless emails?*

As soon as he places his mobile on the table Trevor feels happy and, at the same time, a bit hollow. *Oh yes*, he thinks. *He's not being the person he is either.*

Only he knows that in the studio all his paintings have been scrubbed back to nothing like the paintings and sketches of Frank Auerbach. Nothing is ever finished, it starts and starts again and in between it is scraped off …. Then he has painted the canvases white. They are as blank as the old couple under the shadowy branches in the park. Their negative. Every face or representation has gone. What he knows is not always why he knows. Only one painting is left untouched, his bloody red one, the paste of his new agency. If that's what it is.

Something has become clearer to him. For the first year of disappearance his mother had been full of grief. Then she wasn't. It was never like her lost child. Her mood became resigned and, looking back now, perhaps it had hardened. If she *hadn't* known she would surely have remained upset; her hardening must have been her knowing, at last, that he was alive. The bastard had felt nothing for them. No thought of her feelings, *nor his son's.* And still none.

Had he, in the second letter, intimated to her that he would return for his money? He may have been telling the truth, that she wanted him certified dead so he couldn't access it. So she instigated the official process. He lost his own trick.

Trevor looks into the stillness, the silence.

Then he looks at the back fence, stops and laughs.

He had thought Elizabeth might, well, just might have left Gordon behind. How the hell can Gordon rush about in the floorless, rubbish-strewn house? Nowhere for him to sit, let alone live. And in any-weather Ballarat, his routines broken and homesick for his usual sniff-and-runs and poohing all over Royal Park?

He remembers Elizabeth correcting him on human-dog love. That animals *allow* humans to love them back. He … is nearly 50, has no home, no wife, no family, his father is not a father or a con man but a father *and* a con man – and off his head about the inheritance.

He will begin again. He wants new paintings to go on these blank white surfaces, and thinks he can, then worries he can't. It's never as simple as the idea turned into paint, a process without *process*, as the public thinks it is. Nike it's not. But so many people want art to be romantic gestures and a clutch of the bowels, a dazzle born of insanity (first), suffering (second) or heroin, or beautiful lovers or genius from the fucking stars. Oh, art! Our body is made of stardust!

No, it's not.

As soon as the door opens Elizabeth sees Caveman, not Cave-woman. He is pale, unshaven and has long hair, which he might have considered washing more often.

Knowing how oblique this visit is and out of nervousness she gabbles her hello and, yes, she knows she never emailed, never rang, but she would like to talk with Shia. They have been emailing for several weeks and hey, her own mother's a Ballarat local –*How about that, eh!* – but in hospital right now so here she is, yes well, too good an opportunity to miss? (Rising inflection.) 'Is Shia at home?'

No, she thinks, *don't tell me this is Shia.*

Elizabeth's thoughts race ahead of her tongue. A writer who types his thoughts and lies about his gender would have a better reason than most to guard his anonymity.

That's why he won't use the phone. And then, caught out: *Shia is also a boy's name.*

Behind him she sees the house is a mess. Why had she imagined Shia would be neat, in all probability obsessive about order, as close to OCD as – or even closer than – any highly intense novelist whose writing races but always on tight rails, not a word loose, just many, many of them. This place looks more like her mother's.

'I have a problem,' he says, in a high-pitched voice, and rather loudly for someone a metre away. They might be on opposite sides of the street.

'With names,' he says. 'You are ...? Who shall I say ...?'

'Oh,' she realises, embarrassed. 'Sorry. Elizabeth. It's OK, I have a problem with faces.'

'Elizabeth,' he grunts. 'With faces, well, that's new. Is she expecting you?'

Only now does she stop seeing what she expects. This is all wrong. His face is not going to help. It never occurred to her. *Fuck, fuck, fuck.* Her back seizes.

'I think I've made a mistake,' she says. *The voice is wrong.*

The man's face is as bland as a white carp. Her question makes strange movements on it.

'Yes, do you want to know my name?'

'Your name? Don't tell me you're using a pseudonym. I just need to ...'

'Why not,' he scowls, 'come inside first?'

In the pocket of her jacket she fiddles with her mobile. *Does he look anything like the out-of-date portrait she'd been shown? If it was genuine. A brother or ...? He must be about 40, which is too old. If any of the details are true. If ...*

'Nice car,' he says. 'Is that yours? An EH Holden. *Circa* 1965. Is it a 149 or a 179? I think I can see the …'

He likes her car? Then, as he turns to go inside, she hesitates.

'Does Shia live here?'

If there is a feral trickster writer then this man is its drab exemplar. He speaks well enough, his enunciation. His voice, though, in her voice detector, suggests nervousness, which is not a good thing. Her mobile plays a waltz.

'I've found the yellow sticky,' says Trevor. 'The address is 65 Foster Road, not Street.'

She walks straight back to the car. The man is behind her immediately. She keeps moving as she explains over her shoulder.

'Have to go, my mother's just called. She's had a fall. I have to go.'

'You're bullshitting me,' the man says, suddenly voluble. 'I know your sort, you bitch.'

She runs to her car and he turns his back, slump-shouldered, but stays in the exact spot. Even as she drives off she can see him standing there as if his batteries have been removed.

As soon she opens her own front door Gordon bundles across the room and leaps up at Trevor, who stands back from the table to give him a big hug and say nice things to him. She had thought her dog was rushing to be nose first into his home smells, not back with Trevor. *Unfaithful bloody animals.*

Driving home she had broken the mobile rule and rung Trevor to express as much as explain. It was the wrong house, obviously. It has shaken her up. When she gets home she wants a strong cup of coffee and big shot of whisky like the night he hurt his leg. It's her turn for his remedy.

She drops her bag and walks over. When he opens his arms she moves in without hesitation, huddles against his chest like a child as he hugs her, then just before he has released her she lifts her arms up around his neck so he can move in closer, enfolding her.

She rests her face on his arm, smells his neck and hugs him as hard as she can. At which point he thinks she'll let go; at which point *she* thinks she'll let go. But they remain like this. She can feel his big body against hers, the hardness of his back in her arms.

Stepping back she is all smiles but turns immediately towards her room, picking up her bag on the way. She will not show her tears. They haven't said a word. Now Gordon waggles up against him, his tail beating the chair leg. They have all missed each other. *How good it feels. Better than good.* And why Elizabeth insisted on driving back in the dark, something she prefers not to do.

When nearing home, she says, driving through heavy traffic, and perhaps because her adrenaline had at last slowed down, she became overwhelmed by a terrible shame, a plunging rift, not just over the creepy awfulness of the man – a creep who thought he had a woman on a plate for that brief moment, an opportunity she is sure he was going to take. But over her own stupidity. She felt as if she were underwater. It was not a tangible feeling, it was a smothering one.

Shaking her head helps in the telling. Trying to break the surface.

'I invited my way in,' she says. 'I just assumed.'

'A normal man would have explained the mistake,' he consoles her. 'He was yet another creep. Anyway, you're right, it's normal to be scared.'

'I won't tell Shia, she'll write something. I do *not* want to read some kind of entrapment of a woman, I mean she is a bit like that. I think she's drawn to sects in a spooky kind of way. I've asked her if anything like that was in her background. No answer. Who knows? Anyway, what is it about that bloody town? Paedophile priests, one with a gun on his hip, an alt-right group that fights against a mosque, domestic violence behind doors and high-class Melbourne foodie cuisine in the restaurants.'

'You have a knack for this sort of thing,' he grins.

Not that Elizabeth looks in any way comforted. She sighs and slumps.

Trevor urges her to have a shower. He'll make her that coffee. Pour her that gin and tonic she never had. He'll sit with her if she would like him to.

Later, after sitting together on the lounge, after drinking her drinks – and he his, because he had poured himself the same medicine – she asks if he would do something for her, exactly as she says and no more, and he agrees. He collects his doona from downstairs and sleeps fully clothed on top of the bed beside her. His shoes on the floor.

The following day, while the shop sign says CLOSED, not BACK IN 5 MINUTES, he takes up position behind the wheel of the old grey Holden. He has always wanted to drive one of these famous cars. The Bathurst races, cornering with the front inside tyre completely off the ground. Or both inside tyres. *What a thrill!* Enough to forget, almost, why he's sitting there. He turns the key.

She can hardly interrupt him, his grin as it starts is like nothing she has seen anywhere near him. The little boy is here and can't be shifted.

'Um, I do have to be there early, Trevor. Forms to sign and all that. Have to allow time.'

He shoves the accelerator and hears the old six under the bonnet noisily sucking in air. Those carbies, the Strombergs on the famous red engine he has already seen under the bonnet, mean something she might not realise. Column shifts are archaic but he has used them before, and the mechanical clutch, brakes and steering, none of them power-assisted.

Once he gets a break in the traffic he floors the thing and the old EH surges, air gasping down the throats of the carbies. They hurtle from the lights grinning like bogan kids before "bogan" was a term.

'Bloody hell!' laughs Elizabeth. 'What's that noise at the front?'

Then the car is speeding where it shouldn't, downhill on Flemington Rd towards Victoria Street. If the engine isn't silent, he is – chastened at having to stomp repeatedly on the brakes, those hard and nearly useless drum brakes, or back-end the car in front. Stopping was less of a virtue back in the '60s.

'I have never,' she says, 'ever felt her go like that.'

Then she remembers Diana's visit, the country boy and his car, the drink-driving. The crash.

Stationary at the lights, and safe, he tells her she has the higher-capacity engine, the 179, plus high-performance tuning and carburettors that open only by flooring the accelerator. Well, she's not going to play the girl and admit she never knew this, like hell she would. On the way back to Ballarat she will try it for herself.

For now, she just says, 'I think you should slow down.'

When the staff check Elizabeth's blood pressure before the op, which has been elevated by Trevor's driving, they see no significance in how pleased she is to hear it's 121/79. They lead her to the chair. There are shiny surfaces, the same eye expert featured in the glossy advertisements, his young assistants: it's like a TV series. Now she has only to relax, think nothing, worry about nothing and try not to see replays of Trevor's bloody DVD again and again. The clear tissue of the cornea as the blade in the dinky little guillotine slices it, and steel tools like tiny Korean chopsticks peel it back, smear it with water to hold it, the laser beam drawing hieroglyphics on the eye's surface – and this eye is not his but hers. They are now of the same eye-flesh.

What a shame it won't fix her prosopagnosia. A surface operation only, her literal sight. No wily operator can move along her neurological pathways, except perhaps Trevor in his lyrical and slowly-seeing way towards her, gently, intimately, to be recognised. Like a piece of writing.

Like a studio full of blank canvases.

While he waits outside, Trevor keeps thinking about Dwayne the so-called apologiser. In contrast to the Foster St. Creep, who might have done anything, or The Creep over the back fence, who bullies a single woman, Dwayne seemed happily benign. *Just a bit violent. Accidentally.* So it's not all depressing and tragic, it's just weird. Differences of class, differences of social fate, differences of character. In no class is a woman entirely safe. Rich men *never* hurt women, do they, nor anyone else. *Sure, try selling that to someone.*

If only he knew. Perhaps he should write a book about what he doesn't know and doesn't understand and therefore has no answers for. It would take the rest of his life, and no one would read that either. All he knows about life is that it's not what people think it is.

It has to be said that when Trevor offers his arm she slips hers through his without hesitation. She looks like a long-legged fly. Each eye has a plastic shield with small holes in it for aeration. Her oversized dark glasses, beachwear, just fit over the silly shields. She feels his arm, his careful smaller paces beside her as they walk to the lift, stand as it descends, then move through the car park to her Holden. He feels her right breast firmly against his arm. Her quietness. Without a word they both feel married again.

The surgeon has told her she cannot drive herself back to Ballarat the next day. Instead they must check her eyes. She will have to wear the plastic eye-shields overnight though they're not essential after that. Dark glasses, they insist, wear dark glasses at all times when out of doors. And rest. Allow time for the tissue and the eye to adjust. Healing begins from day one. Somehow she is not surprised. It will be midday before she is free.

'I have a surprise for you,' announces Trevor. 'Tomorrow, after they let you go (he can't resist this one), I'm going to hire a boat and row you up and down the river. A sort of poor man's punt. No lovely Cam, flat as an aristocrat, just the shifty old Yarra.'

That night, every few hours, he squeezes the drops onto her blinking eye, makes her stop still long enough between laughs for them to land on her cornea, eye drops like little delicacies of light.

In the morning she grabs the nearest book and opens it, eases her eye-covers aside. She can read perfectly! It was her only worry – that her close eyesight might be lessened in trying for the overall improvement. Just then Trevor knocks on her door. Yes, she can focus on the door. That too. He asks her to come outside – test her long-range eyesight. Her eyes won't be affected by the mild morning light. She pulls on jeans and T-shirt. He leads her down into the garden and she completely removes both her dark glasses along with the eye-cap protection.

'My God!'

She can see. *What?* She sees the back fence – completely repaired. It is evenly and handsomely filled in with new pickets. And has been painted white.

'Trevor! You …?'

'No, not me,' he replies. 'I came out this morning and it was – there. I haven't been painting, I've been going crazy at the gym, and I have been eating out, making up for cooking dinner every night.'

'You know you don't have to do that.'

They both stare at the fence.

After the eye surgeon has approved his own handiwork and assured her all is well, Trevor drives them out along Hoddle St. and through Clifton Hill, home of neat cafés and a gay community as big as Tasmania, before executing a U-turn, struggling with the EH's paddock-wide turning circle and its tractor steering, then heading left into the Fairfield boathouse car park.

This time she lets him support her as she steps from riverbank to rowing boat and onto the seat in the stern.

As he uses one oar to shove the craft away from the bank, he tells her they are hand-built rowing skiffs, made in Portsmouth from clinkers of real wood, or so the boathouse claims in its advertising. They are not tinnies – no, that means aluminium – nor are they remoulded from piles of molten outdoor furniture.

She is impressed, by his enthusiasm if not his gab.

As he rows she becomes aware of the co-ordination and power of his stroke. Rowing made to look easy: the graceful plunge of both oars into the water and his drawing back on them to lift the boat forwards. Then he lifts them free of the water and as he leans forward the oars reach back, water trailing from their tips. And then plunge and lift, plunge and lift, plunge and lift. The rower always facing the stern.

Because it is Saturday there are many inexperienced rowers out on the river. Skiffs are jerking and zigzagging more like water-beetles than waterbirds.

Trevor continues rowing with the current, turning to check on the others, then eventually reaches clear water and ships the oars.

'Move over to the side,' he says, 'but do it slowly.'

'Eh?'

He gestures to her and as she shifts to her right he moves in a balancing crouch across her on the left, then turns and lies flat on the slatting, his head on the rear seat. She slides down with him. They lie side by side in this quiet rowing boat and the leisurely current carries them forward.

She giggles, impressed and feeling like a teenager.

Above them they can hear magpies sing and mimic, and see herons sitting on high branches. Even a white crane sweeps overhead. At this time of the day and year there are no other boats moving this far downstream, the few people hiring look like tourists and are still whisking their vessels around within 100 metres of the boathouse. They are alone.

There is no closer sound than the kiss of water along the hull, either side of them, underneath, enclosing them. Silence, birdsong, water against the hull, peacefulness. Her dark glasses make everything strange, but the scene is strange. The timelessness of water spreads beneath her, and equally timeless, it seems, are the closer and more distant sounds, the birdcalls, the man lying parallel beside her, their arms and legs touching, as if lying in bed. Nothing said at all.

'I have learnt something important,' he says eventually, as they glide past the bank. She can see overhanging branches only 10 metres away, their green foliage reaching out and overshadowing the understorey like all those river paintings.

'About ...?'

'My father. Him being such a vexatious prick. It's been really bloody painful. Then the money thing and my sense of obligation and guilt. But. Obviously I thought he was dead. But that *if* he ever returned it would fill a psychological gap or loss. That isn't what happened. I think it has freed me. Because now I can *reject* him. You can't reject a ghost any more than you can bury one. It makes a ghost of *you* if you try. It haunts you. As a child I was half in thrall and half appalled by him. It's been coming back to me a lot. At last I'm able to throw him out. And I have.'

'Trevor,' she says, as her new eyes fill with tears. She holds his arm as they glide along in this very ordinary boat.

After a while he returns to the central seat and begins rowing them back. The oars drip and plunge, as their leather cladding squeezes and releases from the rowlocks in the same back-and-forth motion, again and again and again.

When they return he drops her off at the end of the street and drives on to the IGA for shopping. While waiting at the lights he idly looks over at his shop. Someone has blacked out the words STOP ADANI on his mural. Like the swearwords on the garage-sale books. A job for tonight.

Inside it is silent. She calls him. She stands in her bathroom, facing the mirror. He moves in behind her, which she sees afresh with the clear focus of her face, and behind, slightly to one side and over her shoulder, his face, clearly. He places his hands gently on her shoulders.

'I think I can see where I'm going,' she says as she smiles at his face in reflection. Her loose straps are under his fingers, her shoulders are bare.

~

Returning from a walk in her exaggerated sunnies, Elizabeth sees a white-whiskered man standing inside the front yard of her house. *In the yard.* Immediately she knows that this must be the lost-and-found father. Somehow he has discovered her address dug it up, perhaps, given his past as a geologist.

When she approaches he steps onto the pavement, grins a big welcome and makes a silly bow. He reaches for Elizabeth's hand, playing the part of the Polish count he is surely used to performing.

Except she can read the old fool a mile off and moves both hands behind her back, which makes him frown. She stands front-on, as if hiding a gift from a child.

'What are you doing on my property?' she says.

'Oh, yes. I have come to see you, Miss Landlady,' he says, all smiles and with a waggle of his head.

'*Miss Landlady?* My God,' she says. 'There's no one of that description here.'

'Yes, yes, this is the address. My son gave it to me.'

'No, he would *not* have given you this address.'

'Ah, I can see why my son is staying here now, with you. You are a beautiful woman. He is my son and I love him, of course, but perhaps you are wasting your time on him. What I suggest is …'

'You have no idea,' she laughs, 'no idea at all, have you?'

She can hardly stop laughing. He is immediately annoyed.

'Somehow you have emerged, unchanged,' she says, 'from a lot longer than thirty years ago. You really are like Rip Van Winkle – it's hard to believe.'

And then more seriously:

'Things *have changed*. You even tried to grope Diana. How could you?'

'Grope?! She's my daughter-in-law. I just give her a hug. Every woman,' he boasts, 'likes a man who knows what he is. And what a woman is, yes?'

'You're way out of order. *Miss Landlady. Daughter-in-law!*'

She finds herself saying words she couldn't have anticipated.

'You think Trevor is a child you can manipulate. You don't know anything. You don't know what he's like at all. You probably never did, you abandoned him when he was a child. Don't expect any money, you old creep. He is much stronger and much smarter than you. On top of that, he's a good man.'

'Huh!' says the old stager, in an unexpectedly high voice. 'What use is a good man?'

She has a terrible urge to say *Fuck off and die*. As he starts talking again, she watches him and sees every bristling whisker on his face as if magnified. She can see everything with clarity now. There are features he and Trevor share – the nose perhaps – but they are unlike in every other way. She turns and goes inside.

Acknowledgements

I want to thank Transit Lounge and Barry Scott for accepting *The Returns* for publication, with a special thanks going to Ken Haley for his meticulous and good-humoured copy editing of the manuscript. My gratitude also goes to Ed Wright for his thoughtful reading of two early drafts and for the suggestions which led to essential streamlining of the later ones. I suspect the book's air-speed has been much improved.

Praise for Philip Salom's fiction

Waiting
(Puncher and Wattmann, 2016)

Shortlisted for 2017 Miles Franklin Literary Award
Shortlisted for 2017 Victorian Premier's Literary Awards
Shortlisted for 2017 Prime Minister's Literary Awards

'Brilliant and unsettling ... There is a calm to Salom's prose that speaks of unobtrusive craft and compassion, as when we read how "the lonely meet sometimes, compatibility is indeed a strange thing". This is an accomplished and absorbing novel.'

Peter Pierce, *The Australian*

'Towards the end of the book, things change gear, as the strands come together: the two couples, the house, the long-awaited Adelaide denouement, fears, hopes and loves acquiring a kind of critical mass that dictates change, however modest. The book becomes heavier and heavier and then as light as air, and all the poetry is still there, waiting for you.'

Peter Kenneally, *The Age*

'*Waiting* is a richly rewarding story, with characterisation and plot that made me see the world differently. Salom has an astute poetic sensibility that makes his sharp observations politically deft and often very amusing, but it's his empathetic portrayal of misfits that stole my heart.'

Lisa Hill, *ANZ LitLovers*

'*Waiting* is a tour de force of sustained and affectionate wit. It constantly dares the reader to undervalue its characters. It does not romanticise poverty but nor does it impoverish romance. It suggests that there is no such thing as the end of the line.'

Michael McGirr, *Australian Book Review*

'This was a beautifully executed novel and I was sad to have finished it.'

The Saturday Paper

'*Waiting* is a laugh-out-loud, poignant novel about the struggle of individual mortals to relate to themselves and each other in a brutally capitalist, godless world. This novel explores the very real differences between people even as it reveals the universals that unite them. Our culture needs writers of this calibre to challenge not only how we see ourselves and Others, but how we use language to enable or blinker that seeing.'

Helen Gildfind, *Text*

Toccata and Rain
(Fremantle Press, 2004)

Shortlisted for the ALS Gold Medal
Shortlisted for the WA Premiers Prize for Fiction

'The phantasmagoria of disintegrated personality are one of the
perennials of literature and cinema. Reading this book, you are
put in mind not only of films such as David Lynch's *Lost Highway*
and *Mulholland Drive* or Bergman's *Persona* or Hitchcock's *Vertigo*,
but all the bizarre and fascinating characters who have populated
European writing since the 19th century: Heathcliff and Kathy,
Miss Havisham and Bradley Headstone, half the people in
Dostoevsky.'

The Age

Playback
(Fremantle Press, 2003)

Winner of the WA Premier's Prize for Fiction

'Salom's rich, suggestive prose ... has an arresting, dreamlike
quality which ultimately finds truth in abstraction, the landscape,
eroticism and ... reminiscence of the common man.'

The West Australian

Philip Salom lives in North Melbourne, Australia. In 2017 his novel *Waiting* was shortlisted for the Miles Franklin Award, the Prime Minister's Award and the Victorian Premiers Prize. His novel *Toccata and Rain* was shortlisted for the ALS Gold Medal and the WA Premiers Prize for Fiction, and *Playback* won the WA Premiers Prize for Fiction. His poetry books have twice won: the Commonwealth Poetry Book Prize in London and the Western Australia Premiers Prize for Poetry. In 2003 he won the Christopher Brennan Award, Australia's lifetime award for poets, acknowledging 'poetry of sustained quality and distinction'. His fourteenth collection *Alterworld* is a trilogy of *Sky Poems*, *The Well Mouth* and *Alterworld* – three imagined worlds.